Praise of the Novels of Barbara O'Neal

The Lost Recipe for Happiness

"*The Lost Recipe for Happiness* is a delectable banquet for the reader.... This book is as delicious as the recipes interspersed throughout an unforgettable story."

—SUSAN WIGGS, *New York Times* bestselling author

"*The Lost Recipe for Happiness* is utterly magical and fantastically sensual. It's as dark and deep and sweet as chocolate. I want to live in this book.... A total triumph."

—SARAH ADDISON ALLEN, *New York Times* bestselling author

"Beautiful writing, good storytelling and an endearing heroine set against the backdrop of Aspen, Colorado, are highlights of O'Neal's novel. A tale that intertwines food, friendship, passion and love in such a delectable mix is one to truly savor until the very last page."

—*Romantic Times*

"Will appeal to women's fiction fans and foodies, who will enjoy the intriguing recipes...laced through the book."

—*St. Petersburg Times*

The Secret of Everything

"O'Neal has created a powerful and intriguing story rich in detailed and vivid descriptions of the Southwest."   —*Booklist*

"Readers will identify with this story and the multilayered characters.... And with some of the tantalizing recipes for dishes served at the 100 Breakfasts Café included, O'Neal provides a feast not only for the imagination but the taste buds as well."   —*Romantic Times*

"Barbara O'Neal has masterfully woven local culture, the beauty of nature, her love of food and restaurants, and a little romance into this magnificent novel."   —Fresh Fiction

BY BARBARA O'NEAL

The Lost Recipe for Happiness

The Secret of Everything

How to Bake a Perfect Life

How to Bake a
Perfect Life

How to Bake a Perfect Life

A Novel

BARBARA O'NEAL

Bantam Books
New York

2011 Bantam Books Trade Paperback Original

Published in the United States by Bantam Books,
an imprint of The Random House Publishing Group,
a division of Random House, Inc., New York.

BANTAM BOOKS is a registered trademark of Random House, Inc.,
and the colophon is a trademark of Random House, Inc.

ISBN 978-1-61129-158-2

Printed in the United States of America

For my mother, Rosalie Hair,
who is nothing like any of the mothers in this book.
Well, except for maybe that earring thing.

ACKNOWLEDGMENTS

As always, a zillion people helped with this book. Many, many thanks to my sister Cathy Stroo, who helps me with medical knowledge on nearly every book, and this time helped me understand the struggles of burn patients. For help with the process of how wounded soldiers are moved through the hospital system, I'm extremely grateful to MaryAnn Phillips, who heads up the volunteer organization Soldiers' Angels (www .soldiersangels.org), a valuable and devoted group who serve soldiers and their families at one of the worst times in a soldier's life. All mistakes or missteps are entirely my own. Thanks also to Terence. *Muchas gracias,* my friend.

My grandmother Madoline O'Neal Putman, and the late great Merlin Murphy O'Hare kept me company all through the writing of this book. Miss you both lots and lots.

And, as ever, thanks to Christopher Robin, who tastes everything even if he is sure he won't like it.

Starter

Sourdough starter—or mother dough, as it is known—is made from wild yeast that lives invisibly in the air. Each sponge is different, according to the location where it is born, the weather, the time of its inception, and the ingredients used to create it. A mother dough can live for generations if properly tended and will shift and grow and transform with time, ingredients, and the habits of the tender.

The Boudin mother dough used to create the famously sour San Francisco bread was already fifty years old when it was saved from the great San Francisco earthquake of 1906 by Louise Boudin, who carried the mother dough to Golden Gate Park in a wooden bucket. There it was packed in ice and used to make bread daily until a new bakery could be built at its current location. The mother dough, now more than 150 years old, is stored in a vault, "like a wild beast," and bread is made from it every day.

ONE

When the phone call that we have been dreading comes, my daughter and I are gathered around the center island of my bakery kitchen. Sofia is leafing through a magazine, the slippery pages floating down languidly, one after the next.

I am experimenting with a new sourdough starter in an attempt to reproduce a black bread I tasted at a bakery in Denver a couple of weeks ago. This is not my own, treasured starter, handed down from my grandmother Adelaide's line and known to be more than a hundred years old. That "mother dough," as it is called, has won my breads some fame, and I guard it jealously.

This new starter has been brewing for nearly ten days. I began with boiled potatoes mashed in their water then set aside in a warm spot. Once the starter began to brew and grow, I fed it daily with rye flour, a little whole wheat and malt sugar, and let it ferment.

On this languid May afternoon, I hold the jar up to examine it. The sponge is alive and sturdy, bubbling with cultures. A thick layer of dark brown hooch, the liquid alcohol generated by the dough, stands on top. When I pull loose wrap off the top of the bottle and stick my nose in, it is agreeably, deeply sour.

I shake the starter, stick my pinkie finger in, taste it. "Mmm. Perfect."

Sofia doesn't get as worked up over bread as I do, though she is a passable baker. She smiles, and her hand moves over her belly in a slow, warm way. Welcoming. It's her left hand, the one with the wedding set—diamond engagement ring, gold band. The baby is due in less than eight weeks. Her husband is in Afghanistan.

We have not heard from him in four days.

I remember when her small body was curled up beneath my ribs, when I thought I was going to give her away, when the feeling of her moving inside of me was both a terror and a wonder. If only I could keep her that safe now.

The bakery is closed for the day. Late-afternoon sunshine slants in through the windows and boomerangs off the stainless steel so intensely that I have to keep moving around the big center island to keep it out of my eyes. The kneading machines are still as I stir together starter and molasses, water and oil and flour, until it's a thick mass I can turn out onto the table with a heavy splat. Plunging my hands into the dark sticky blob, I scatter the barest possible amounts of rye flour over it, kneading it in a bit at a time. The rhythm is steady, smooth. It has given me enviable muscles in my arms.

"What do you want for your birthday?" Sofia asks, flipping a page.

"It's ages away!"

"Only a couple of months."

"Well, I guess as long as there are no black balloons, I'm good." Last year, my enormous family—at least, those members who are still speaking to me—felt bound to present me with graveyard cakes and make jokes about crow's feet, which, thanks to my grandmother Adelaide's cheekbones, I do not have.

"A person has to suffer through only one fortieth birthday in a lifetime." Sofia turns another page. "How about this?" She holds up an ad for a lavish sapphire necklace. "Good for your eyes."

"Tiffany. Perfect." At the moment, I'm so broke that a bubblegum ring would be expensive, though of course Sofia doesn't know that the bakery is in trouble. "You can buy it for me when you're rich and famous."

"When I am that superstar kindergarten teacher?"

"Right."

"Deal."

I push the heel of my palm into the dough and it squeezes upward, cool and clammy. An earthy bouquet rises from it, and I'm anticipating how the caramelizing molasses will smell as it bakes.

A miller darts between us, flapping dusty wings in sudden terror. Sofia waves it away, frowning. "I hope we're not going to have a crazy miller season this year."

I think of a Jethro Tull song, and for a minute I'm lost in another part of my life, another summer. Shaking it off, I fold the dough. "It's been a wet year."

"Ugh. I hate them." She shudders to give emphasis. Then she closes her magazine and squares her shoulders. "Mom, there's something I've been meaning to talk to you about."

Finally. "I'm listening."

She spills it, fast. "I told you Oscar's ex-wife was arrested in El Paso and Katie has been living with her best friend's family, but Oscar really wants her to come and live with me. Us. She's got some problems, I won't lie, but she just needs somebody to be there for her." Sofia has eyes like a plastic Kewpie doll, all blink and blueness with a fringe of blackest lashes. "She can sleep upstairs, in the back room. Close to me. She lived with us before Oscar went to Afghanistan. It was fine."

"Hmmm. I seem to remember it differently."

"Okay, it wasn't fine. Exactly." Sofia bows her head. Light arcs over her glossy dark hair. "She was pretty angry then."

"And she's happy now?" I scatter flour over the dough and table, where it is beginning to stick. "Because her mother is in jail and her father is at war?"

"No. I mean—"

The phone rings. I glance at it, then back to my daughter. Obviously there is no possible way I can say no. The child has nowhere to go, but—

To give myself a little time, I tug my hands out of the dough, wipe them off with one of the thin white cotton towels I love for covering the loaves when they rise. "How old is she?"

A second ring.

"Thirteen. Going into eighth grade."

"Middle school." Not the most delightful age for girls. Even Sofia was a pain at that age—all huffy sighs and hair-flinging drama. And tears. Tears over everything.

The phone rings again, and I hold up a finger to Sofia. "Hold that thought. Hello?"

"Good afternoon, ma'am," says a deep, formal voice on the other end. "May I please speak with Mrs. Oscar Wilson?"

Every atom in my body freezes for the space of two seconds. Here it is, the moment I've been half dreading since Sofia came home four years ago, her eyes shining. *Mama, he's the most wonderful man! He wants to marry me.*

A soldier. An infantryman who'd already done two tours of Iraq during the bloodiest days of the war and would likely do more. Oscar is older than Sofia by more than a decade, divorced, and father to this brand-new adolescent who has a very troubled mother.

Not a soldier, baby, I kept thinking.

And yet as soon as I met Oscar Wilson, with his beautiful face and kind eyes and gentle manners, I knew exactly why she loved him. It was plain he worshipped her in return.

But here is the phone call.

"Yes," I say with more confidence than I feel. "Just a minute please." I put the mouthpiece against my stomach, turn to my daughter. "Remember, they come to the door if he's dead."

Sofia stares at me for a long, long second. Fear bleeds the color from her lips. But she has the courage of a battalion of soldiers. Taking a breath, she squares her shoulders and reaches for the phone. Her left hand covers her belly, as if to spare the baby. "This is Mrs. Wilson."

She listens, her face impassive, and then begins to fire questions, writing down the answers in a notebook lying open on the counter. "How long has he been there? Who is my contact?" And then, "Thank you. I'll call with my arrangements."

As she hangs up the phone, her hand is trembling. Unspilled tears make her lashes starry. She stands there one long moment, then blinks hard and looks at me. "I have to go to Germany. Oscar is . . . he was . . ." She clears her throat, waits until the emotion subsides. "His truck hit an IED four days ago. He's badly injured. Burned."

I think that I will always remember how blue her eyes look in the brilliant sunshine of the kitchen. Years and years from now, this is what I will recall of this day—my daughter staring at me with both terror and hope, and my absolute powerlessness to make this better.

"I have to go to him," she says.

"Of course."

I think, *How badly burned?*

She turns, looks around as if there will be a list she can consult. She's like my mother in that way, wanting everything to be orderly. "I guess I should pack."

"Let me scrape this into a bowl and I'll help you."

As if her legs are made of dough, she sinks suddenly into the chair. "How long do you think I'll be there? What about the baby?"

"One step at a time, Sofia. I'm sure you'll have those answers before long. Just think about getting there, see what . . . how . . . what you need to find out."

"Right." She nods. Touches her chest. "Mom. What about Katie? She can't stay where she is."

A thirteen-year-old whose mother is in jail, whose father is wounded, and whose stepmother is pregnant with a new baby and flying off to Germany, leaving her with a woman she doesn't know. "She's never even met me. Won't she be scared?"

"Maybe for a while, but I can't let her go to a foster home. She can come just for the summer. Grandma will help you, I'm sure, and Uncle Ryan and—"

I hold a hand up. There is only one answer. "Of course, baby. Let's get those arrangements made now, too, so you don't have to worry about her."

She leaps up and hugs me, her mound of belly bumping my hip. It is only as I put my arms around her that I feel the powerful trembling in her shoulders. I squeeze my eyes shut and rub her back, wishing I could tell her that everything is going to be okay. "Do your best, Sofia. That's all the world can ask."

Her arms tighten around my neck, like iron. Against my shoulder, I feel her hot tears soaking into my blouse. "Thank you."

TWO

Together, Sofia and I arrange for Katie to come to Colorado Springs, then we gather Sofia's things and I drive her down to Fort Carson. There she is met by the women—wives of other men in Oscar's unit—who will kindly shepherd her through the flight and to her wounded husband's side. Her spine is straight, her face pale as they gather her in to their circle—three women, smartly dressed. Women, I think, stepping back, that I have seen on the local news all of my life, raising money for causes, standing by their men, sitting in the front row of the chapels where empty boots and photographs are lined up for memorial services. It's a large base. A lot of memorials the past few years.

"Take care of her," I say, and, to my horror, tears well up in my eyes.

One of the women sees them and gives me a hug. "We will, I promise. She'll call you as soon as she can."

I want to be as sturdy as my daughter, so I turn and head to my car. Sofia's voice calls out, "Mom!"

When I turn, she kisses her fingers and flings it toward me. "I love you!"

I return the kiss and head home, trying to focus on all the things I need to do to get the house ready for Katie's arrival tomorrow. The room needs to be aired, the bed made—if I wash the sheets tonight, I can hang them out to dry first thing in the morning. It's such a homey, welcoming smell.

But when I pull up in front of the old house that contains my bakery and the two-story apartment above, there is a lake in the front yard.

Not a puddle. Not a sprinkler left on. This is a pool of water that engulfs the lawn, covers the sidewalk, and pours over the ancient concrete curb into the gutter. "What the hell?"

My phone is out of my pocket and in my hand before I've fully formed a question. I dial my mentor. A deep, heavily Italian–Brooklyn-accented voice answers. "Ramona," Cat says. "Is Sofia gone?"

"She is, but that's not why I'm calling. I have a swimming pool in my front yard. Something broke, obviously. Who do I call?"

"Let me get right back to you."

I hang up and stand in the gloaming with my hands on my hips and a strangling mix of terror and grief in my throat. There is absolutely not a dime left for another old-house disaster.

Swearing under my breath, I walk around the edges of the pond to get to the walk at the side of the house. How will I even be able to open the store in the morning?

Cat calls right back. "My guy Henry is coming over to see what's happened. I've got a little issue here at the restaurant, but I'll be there in an hour or so."

"The phone call is enough, Cat." I've been trying to establish some boundaries with him. "I can manage from here."

"I'm not questioning your ability to manage, *tesòro mìo*. You've had a bad day. Won't be so bad to have a friend to lean on."

I have a headache behind my left eye and no energy to argue. "I'll be here."

· · ·

Henry arrives in fifteen minutes and pronounces the problem a broken water pipe from the street to the house. I've had trouble with these old pipes in the past—they're clay and the tree roots infiltrate them every spring—but I've never had an actual break.

Naturally it's going to cost several thousand dollars to fix, and of course there is no choice but to say yes. It will eat up every last bit of the credit remaining on my last card, and as I'm standing there in the dark, alone, it seems to me that maybe this bakery dream of mine might be dead. I started with a solid plan, a business and marketing degree, and plenty of cash flow, but the economy and the credit crunch are crippling me.

"Can you get the water out of there tonight?" I ask the plumber.

He shakes his head. "Sorry. But we'll get you fixed up in no time. I know it looks bad, but it's really just a matter of digging up the bad pipe and replacing it with new. It'll be good as new by tomorrow afternoon."

"All right. Thanks."

As he heads for his truck, a blue SUV pulls up and a tall lean man gets out. The streetlight shines on his mostly silver hair. He stops to shake Henry's hand, claps him on the back. They exchange a few words in the language of men.

Cat Spinuzzi is close to seventy, though he lies and says he's sixty, and he's vigorous enough to get away with it. He'd never go running like a lot of men in town, but he stays fit with hard rounds of racquetball every week and daily reps of sit-ups and push-ups. As he comes forward, I can smell his cologne, as spicy as a Moroccan market, wafting ahead of him. "He says it's not a big deal. You'll be open again in a couple of days, no problem."

I nod. Two days of lost receipts, plus this no-doubt-enormous bill, is going to take me precariously close to the edge.

"Let's talk," he says, nudging me toward the side yard. "Make me an espresso, Ramona. Do you have any of those little croissants I like so much?"

"You know I do. Come on."

We go up the stairs to the apartment kitchen, and he settles at the table. He's wearing jeans and a crisp dark-blue shirt with a linen-and-silk blazer and the Italian shoes he pays too much money for. In the harsh overhead light, age shows at the corners of his eyes.

I put a plate of *pain au chocolat* before him, along with a blue-and-white china dish inherited from my grandmother and a snowy napkin. He likes these details, old-world and elegant. "Beautiful," he murmurs.

The espresso is made on the stove, over the flame in a sturdy small pot, not in a machine. The pot belonged to my grandmother, and although it took a bit of mastery, I learned for Cat's sake. As I wait for it to boil, I'm thinking in the back of my mind what to do, how to manage this new crisis, but Sofia crowds everything out. Is she in the air yet? How long will it take to get to Germany, until I know more about Oscar?

My primary fear is that they are calling her over to say goodbye to her husband. They usually ship soldiers through Germany very fast these days.

I rub the tight spot in the middle of my chest, turn the flame down beneath the pot. When it is finished, I pour it into cups and sit down with him.

After a moment I say, "It might be time to let the bakery go."

"No, no. It's a solid business model, Ramona. This problem with the pipes, it's nothing."

I look at the dark, dark coffee, shake my head. The economy has not been as terrible here as elsewhere, but it's been bad enough, undercutting and undercutting and undercutting my business, not to mention the value of the house. And no one is giving small-business loans these days. Without an influx of cash, the business will fail.

"I need you, as my mentor, to just listen to me for a minute. Can you do that?"

"You know I can."

"If I quit now, I won't lose the house—and you know my family would never forgive me if that happened. We practically grew up here."

"Your family," he says with a shake of his head. "What have they done for you that you have to worry about what they think?"

"I would never forgive *myself*, Cat. It was my grandmother's house. She left it to me in good faith."

"You won't lose the house. You're gonna be all right."

There must be answers, but I'm strung out from disaster and can't see them right now. "I hope you're right." I take a sip of coffee, think about the long list of things that I have to get done. "Anyway, I have a lot to do, so thanks for coming, but I have to get busy."

He carefully finishes the *pain au chocolat,* brushes his hands, and regards me silently for a moment. Once, the story goes, he was in love with my mother, but my father swept her off her feet and she married him instead. Cat opened a restaurant to compete with my father. For decades now they have jockeyed for top honors in the city. When I look at my father, sturdy and square and blessed with Paul Newman blue eyes, I see that he must have been handsome once, but I fail to know how he could have outshone Cat.

They are mortal enemies, which made it satisfying to turn to Cat as a mentor when I left the family business. What shames me is that I somehow allowed him into my bed for a time, and although I broke it off more than a year ago, he has not lost hope.

I can see in his eyes that he's going to make the offer tonight. In a way, it would be a relief. To let go, let someone hug me, let someone else hold up the tent for a little while.

But I put up a weary hand. "You need to go."

"All right." He stands. "Remember, you do have a friend, Ramona. Can you do that for me?"

"I appreciate it," I say. "Truly. Thank you for your help. I'm just worried sick about Sofia and Oscar."

"Give it to the Blessed Mother. Sometimes there is nothing else to do."

He is as Italian and Catholic as I am Irish and Catholic, though his faith is a big sweeping thing and mine is faint and faraway. "I'll try."

When he's gone, I wander down the back stairs to the back-yard that was my grandmother's refuge. The lilacs are in bloom. Ancient bushes, some six or eight feet tall, line the old wooden fence, and the scent hangs in the air like syrup, sweet and thick. I swim through it to a bench beneath a tree. My cat, Milo, a long-legged Siamese, sidles out from a bush and winds around my feet. "Hey, you." He mews, leaps up beside me, and lets his paws drip over the side of the bench.

I feel acutely the absence of Sofia. To get her safely off, to make her feel brave, I have kept the terrible news of the day at arm's length, but now it floods through me, dark and immovable. Her life is forever changed, and I suspect her road will be very hard.

Bending my head, I let my tears fall. Here in this safe place, in my grandmother's garden, I can weep freely. It often feels that my grandmother Adelaide, is with me here in the enclave she created. Sometimes I imagine I can hear her softly humming a nameless tune.

Lilacs were her favorite flower, and tonight in the warm evening, they offer respite. Taking a basket and a sturdy pair of shears from the shed, I cut great armfuls of blossoms. It's impossible not to feel my grandmother tagging along as I do it. This was her house. This was her ritual, cutting lilacs that trailed dew and purple petals. The warm day has released their fragrance, a scent so powerful it almost seems to tint the air. I'm helpless against the dark and light blossoms, the dazzlement of their short season, the droplets of stained water that fall on my wrists.

I carry some upstairs; others I put in gigantic vases along the porch railing, where anyone who sits at the scattering of café tables can admire them while eating a croissant and drinking a coffee. I put a vaseful in Katie's room and then one in my own bedroom, where I fall on the bed, just for a moment. As if the flowers hold some magic presence, I fall asleep, the scent caressing me like a hand, as if my grandmother is smoothing my hair away from my forehead.

RAMONA'S BOOK OF BREADS

EASY PAIN AU CHOCOLAT

This is a recipe my aunt Poppy's best friend, Nancy, loves like crazy. She makes it the long way, which I do like, but it's also fun to make the fast version sometimes, too.

2 sheets frozen puff pastry, thawed
1 large egg, beaten with 1 tsp water
12 oz. bittersweet chocolate (chips work fine)
sugar for dusting

Prepare a baking sheet by lining it with parchment or oiling it lightly. Cut each sheet of pastry into 12 squares and brush each with egg glaze. Then sprinkle ½ oz. of chocolate (a few chips) on each square and roll up tightly around the chocolate. Place on the baking sheet, seam down. Cover with plastic and refrigerate for 4 hours or overnight. Refrigerate remaining egg glaze.

Remove pastries from fridge; preheat oven to 400 degrees. Brush the tops of the pastries with remaining egg glaze, and then dust lightly with sugar and bake for about 15 minutes. Better to cool them at least a bit, or the butter taste is a little overwhelming.

THREE

Sofia's Journal

MAY 19, 20—

I'm writing this on the plane. I don't know whether to call it the 19th or the 20th. It's dark outside, but what time will I use? Middle-of-the-Atlantic time?

Everyone around me is asleep, and I've tried, but every time I'm just about to slide under, I think of Oscar, and my heart starts slamming into my ribs so hard that I feel like it might burst. I keep telling myself, over and over, at least he didn't die, *but there's another little voice that comes after it that says,* yet.

I'm not even going to entertain that thought. What he needs from me right now is strength, courage, honor, positive energy. He needs me to be the face of faith, a hand to hold in the darkness. He needs something to hold on to—his wife, his kids, one on the way, one already here.

Katie. Every time I think about her in that hellhole I want to throw up. I didn't tell my mother what really went on, but I don't even know how the kid survived—and part of that is my fault directly. I could see that there was something wrong with Lacey. Like more than the PTSD she was diagnosed with. War was hard on her, I get that, though it seemed like more than that. But how can a new wife say that about her husband's first wife and expect anyone to listen? I couldn't think of a way, but there were things that bothered me. The dirt under her nails. The odd way her breath smelled. The plain fact that she was way, way too skinny, but how could I even say that? Skinny has never been my issue, which Oscar says he likes, and I honestly think he means it. He likes my curves.

Then she was arrested for meth and it all added up. I worried even then that meth addicts don't get over it. They just don't. One of my girlfriends works in the emergency room at Penrose, and she says meth short-circuits something.

Anyway. Poor Katie. I feel so bad for her.

Ugh. We've been flying for five hours already and won't land for another four. My mother made me my favorite sandwiches, cucumber and hummus on her excellent sourdough, and it is heartening to eat bread she made. I have a whole loaf in my bag, which the security people thought was very funny, but you know, being pregnant on a nine-hour flight is really not a big happy joy. My legs are all jumpy and I think it irritates the guy next to me that I keep tapping them, but I can't help it. My back is killing me from sitting, and every hour I walk up and down the aisles to keep my ankles from swelling. I have to pee so often it's embarrassing. One old lady with hands like cool silk reached for me as I waited in line for the restroom. "How are you doing on this long trip, Mother? Is there anything I can do for you?" It brought tears to my eyes.

How oh how oh how, am I going to do this?

FOUR

Ramona

Katie is due to arrive at ten-thirty this morning. There is no baking to keep me busy, since customers will not be able to make it to the front door. Henry's crew arrives at eight on the dot—prompted, no doubt, by Cat's influence—and once I see that they seem to be able to do their work just fine without my constant, hovering supervision from the porch, I head into the bakery to start some bread. It's the only thing that can soothe me this morning.

My brother Ryan sends a text at ten forty-five.

The Eagle has landed. Be there in 20.

I stop to run upstairs, change my blouse, and put a little lipstick on. As I lean in to the mirror to make sure there is no color bleeding into the lip line, I'm startled to see my grandmother's eyes staring back at me. All these years I thought I looked like my mother, but lately it is my grandmother's face that keeps surprising me in the reflection.

I'm nervous. It's been a long time since I've mothered a child. Will I remember how?

Downstairs, the bell over the front door rings. I rush down to the bakery, coming around the corner just as Katie comes through the door, eyes too big for her face. She is very thin. Every inch of her thirteen-year-old body screams resistance—elbows crossed, hair in her face, shoulders hunched over to protect her torso. She looks as if she's been crying, or perhaps only sleeping hard: eyes swollen, red-rimmed. I come forward with a smile I hope will reassure her. The old wooden floor squeaks under my feet. The girl looks alarmed.

"Don't worry. It's old but sound." I catch my hands together to keep from reaching out. This one is a cat, and a cat needs coaxing. "I'm Ramona Gallagher. You must be Katie."

"I thought Sofia's mom was going to take care of me."

"Right. That's me."

She scowls.

"I was pretty young when she was born."

A nod. Her hair is a crazy tangle of curls, a naturally streaky mass of brown with copper and gold woven through. It's too long, unkempt. My mother always says you can tell a child who is well cared for by looking at her hair and skin. Katie's olive skin is dry, and she isn't pretty, not yet. When she grows into the too-long limbs, she will have the grace of a swallow. Her eyes are the same light green as her father's, and it gives me a pang, thinking of him injured, far away.

Katie has a book in her hand, a backpack slung over her shoulders, and hostility in her gaze. "I don't want to live here," she announces. "My mom will be getting out of jail pretty soon and then she can come get me. I don't need anybody else to be my mom."

Pierced by her loyalty, I nod. "Fair enough. You don't have to stay forever. It's just that Sofia wanted to be sure you were safe before she left for Germany."

Her eyes fall. Germany. Her father. I'll wait for her to bring it up. "You can call me Ramona."

"My dad doesn't like me to call grown-ups by their first names."

"Mmm. But I'm a relative. Stepgrandmother, right? So do you still have to call me Ms. Gallagher?"

She shrugs, and I let it go for now. "Do you have any luggage, sweetie?"

"I've got it right here." My brother Ryan brings in a thin, hard-sided suitcase of a style that hasn't been made since the sixties. Katie gives him a look under her eyelashes—his black hair and blue eyes give him a reckless aura—and he puts the suitcase on his shoulder, holds out a hand for the backpack. "Want me to carry that up, too?"

Katie tucks her thumbs under the straps. "That's okay. I'm fine."

"No problem." He points at me. "Tell Ramona about the dog."

Katie still hangs at the door, as if she will run away the minute we turn our backs.

"Dog?"

"They made me leave my dog. In El Paso. At the airport." Tears well up in her eyes. "He didn't have the right carrier and they've got him in some container place, but I need to get him here. He doesn't have anybody else but me, and he's gonna be so, so scared."

"Oh! *Your* dog. I didn't know you had a dog."

She lifts her shoulders. "I haven't had him very long. I found him by the railroad tracks. His name is Merlin."

I struggle to keep my expression neutral. My cat will not be pleased. And a dog that's been living as a vagabond might have all kinds of issues, not the least being he might consider cats a good protein source. "How long ago did you find him?"

In a voice that's too loud, she says, "The day my mom went to jail. He stayed with me all night, and otherwise I would have been alone. And I'm not leaving him."

I tell myself that the child has lost her mother to meth and her father to three tours of duty and she needs something. But I don't have to be thrilled about it. "Tell you what," I say. "Let's call the airport and ask them what we need to do. I'm sure they can put him on another plane right away."

"Really?" Her eyes overflow, and the sight goes straight through my solar plexus. I have been this child, this lost and lonely girl. The person in my corner was my aunt Poppy, and I can try to be that person for Katie.

"I promise I'll make sure he doesn't get in any trouble," Katie says.

"I believe you." I gesture toward her. "You must be starving."

"Yeah."

"Let's head upstairs, then, and I'll fix you some lunch." I point to the glass case, which holds a few loaves from yesterday. "How about some samples of bread?"

"Okay. I'm *really* hungry," she admits. "They only had stuff to buy on the plane."

And nobody thought to give you any cash. "Luckily, some bread just came out of the oven. Pumpernickel. Have you ever had it?"

Katie winces. "Isn't it all, like, black and stuff?"

"It is. Let's find something else."

"Wait." Her chin juts out and she sends me a fierce look. "Is my dad going to die? Please tell me the truth. I can't stand it when people lie."

"Okay." I pause, considering. "Honestly, I don't know, Katie. I don't think so, but he's badly burned, so it will be a little while before we know for sure."

"How bad?"

"I don't know that, either. We'll know more when Sofia calls. She won't get to the hospital until tomorrow."

"Is his face burned?" Her voice cracks.

"We can ask."

"Okay." Her arms ease, and she puts a hand on her belly. "I guess I can eat now, okay?"

"Yes." I wave my arm toward the bakery cases. "Pick some bread and I'll make you a grilled cheese sandwich, how's that?"

"Good," Katie says. "Thanks." She dashes a hand beneath each eye, wiping at tears that have leaked out, and peers at the loaves. "Wow. What are all of these?"

Some tension drains from my shoulders. Bread I know. Bread I love. Bread can hold this young girl in its cozy grip for a moment of peace. "Usually there would be more, but we had a problem outside." I point, naming the loaves. "Sourdough wheat. The previously dismissed pumpernickel. Oatmeal and sunflower seed. And white." It's fresh, maybe still warm, and as fluffy as a cloud. I add a little semolina flour for texture and flavor. "Are you a white-bread kind of person?"

"I guess."

I pull the loaf, light and airy, out of the case. "There's a reason it has always been so popular." Yes, I think. White bread will mist over her troubles, obscure some of that terror.

My brother clomps down the stairs in his heavy boots. "All set." He lifts his chin to the front yard. "What the hell happened out there?"

"Broken water pipe."

He shakes his head. "You ever do anything the easy way?"

I shrug. It's a sore point today. My family all tried to talk me out of using the house as a bakery, but I believed in the location and the model—a *boulangerie* nestled into the mixed residential and business district on the quaint Westside. I thought I understood how much work an old building might be.

I underestimated it by about 500 percent.

He points behind me. "Don't look now, but you've got help."

I turn around in time to see my mother. My first urge is to

hide Katie behind me. "Mom! I didn't realize you were coming this morning."

Lily is a small, trim woman with blond hair she keeps clipped short, once every three weeks, like a man. She's wearing a tidy knit pantsuit, black with purple piping. "Good morning!" she says. "I thought you might need some help. And besides, I had to bring doughnuts, didn't I?"

"Mom," I say, gesturing to the shelves of bread around us, "you have noticed that this is a bakery?"

"No, you're the one who says it's a *boulangerie,* which is breads, not pastries. You don't have crullers, do you?" She shoves the box from Dunkin' Donuts into my hand and bends toward Katie as if she is six instead of thirteen. "Hello!" Her voice is a little too...bright. "You must be Katie."

The girl nods, clutching her book close to her chest. "I like doughnuts."

"See?" Lily waves her hand. "C'mon. Let's all have some." She marches toward the door that leads up the stairs to my home kitchen. "You coming, Ryan?"

"Uh...no." My brother wiggles his nose. "Gotta get back to work."

Katie plants her feet. "What about my dog?"

"You have a dog?" Lily asks.

"She does," I say. "And maybe, Mom, that would be something you could do. The dog is stuck at the El Paso airport. He had the wrong carrier, and Katie, I'm guessing"—I look at her for confirmation—"didn't have the money to get the whole thing sorted out."

"Baby, don't you have a cell phone?"

Katie all but rolls her eyes. "I don't even have lunch money."

I smile. She can hold her own with my mother. "Let's call the airport right now. See what we can find out. Upstairs. With food." I open the box. "Have a doughnut to tide you over."

She takes two, and by the time we get upstairs, the first is gone.

My mother is in charge of looking up numbers while I take the bread to slice and butter for a grilled cheese sandwich. The loaf is fragrant with baking. "Smell that." I hold it out to Katie.

She bends forward and sniffs politely. "Uh-huh." She narrows her eyes when I start to slice a chunk of white cheddar for the sandwich. "Do you have any normal cheese?"

"It's just cheddar."

Lily looks over the top of her rectangular purple glasses. "She means American, Ramona. All children like American cheese." To Katie she says, "Yellow slices, right?"

"Yeah. Like in those little wrappers sometimes."

I'm pretty sure there is no American cheese in my fridge. I'm a cheese freak, but not for that. "Sorry, honey. I don't have any. Do you want to try this?"

Her left foot swings. She is very, very thin. I can see the exact shape of her wrist bones. "Can I just eat more doughnuts?"

"No. You need some real food."

"Peanut butter and jelly?"

"That I can do."

"Not the crunchy kind, though, is it?"

"No." I smile in spite of myself. "It's smooth."

"Good." Katie sits gingerly at the table, her backpack slung around her shoulders, the paperback still clutched in her hands.

"Do you want to put your stuff away first? Maybe wash your face and hands?"

"I'd like to go to the bathroom."

"Oh, of course! I'm sorry. C'mon."

The bakery occupies the entire lower level of the Victorian, but I live on the upper two floors, big spacious rooms with long, double-hung windows that let in buckets of light. Some of the rooms are a bit shabby these days, since all the money is going into the bakery, but the floors are hardwood covered with my grandmother's rugs, and there is the grace of knee-high base-boards, intricately carved. The kitchen, which I updated at the same time as I did the bakery, faces east and the side yard. The living room is in front, facing south and the street, which is lined with elm trees that break and bring down the power lines whenever there is a heavy snow.

My bedroom is on this floor, too, along with the gigantic bathroom with its claw-footed tub. Both rooms look to the mountains, burly and blue and very close by.

"You're up here." I lead Katie to the third level, under the eaves. It can be hot in the summertime, but Katie's bedroom has windows all along the north wall and a small screened-in balcony that overlooks the backyard. It will be a good place for the dog to sleep, I think now.

"This is my room?" Katie says.

"There's no television because there's no cable up here, but if there's something else you can think of, say so. The bathroom is tiny, but it has a nice view and a good shower. If you want a bath, you can use the one downstairs—it has a great tub. Sofia and I really like it."

Katie looks winded.

"Sorry, I'm talking you to death. Why don't you take a few minutes, get settled, and come down whenever you want?"

Her expression is one of loss. Patting her shoulder, I say, "Take your time, sweetie."

FIVE

Katie

Katie sinks down on the bed, and it's so super-super-soft that it almost calls her name. She falls backward onto it. The covers poof up around her arms like clouds, and through the window comes a breeze that tickles over the top of her head. The wallpaper is old, with tiny orange flowers on it, making her think of a book she found at the library where a girl traveled back in time through a closet. On a stand in the corner is a huge blue vase with purple flowers. Katie can smell them from the bed.

After a second, she gets up and looks out the window, where she can see the tops of trees and a tiny bird sitting on a branch, whistling, and, way far away on the ground, a stream. Purple flowers are on bushes all over the place.

Not what she was expecting. None of it.

Out of her backpack she takes a notebook. There are two girls on the front of it, with bandannas in their hair and high heels on their feet. Madison gave it to her at the airport. "Write to me every day," she said. "And when you can get to a computer, email me. When we go to the library on Fridays, I'll email you back." Madison's computer broke a while ago, and they hadn't gotten a new one yet. Maybe when her dad was deployed again, her mom had said. Her mom was the one who'd told them they could write letters, too. Like in the mail, with an envelope. Mrs. Petrosky had given Katie envelopes and stamps, with their address written right on the box of envelopes.

Katie tried not to cry, and so did Madison, but they were best friends. They'd been through a lot together—they both had parents who were soldiers and they had lived in three of the same places at the same time, and they'd known each other since they were six.

Now, in her new bedroom, Katie opens the notebook and writes:

May 20, 20—

Hey, Madison,

This is the first letter. I'm here. It's pretty. Sofia's mom is nice, but we knew she probably would be, right, because Sofia is so nice. Merlin is still stuck at the airport, but it seems like these people are going to get him home. Right now I'm SUPER hungry, and I'm going to get some lunch. But I feel better writing to you even if you can't read it yet. It's like when you went to camp last summer, right?

More L8er, Katie

SIX

Ramona

When I get back downstairs, my mother is making coffee. "Do you want some, too?" she asks. Like it's her kitchen.

I nod.

"Have you heard anything from Sofia?"

"Not yet. She has to get to the hospital, get herself settled, all that. We probably won't hear for another day or two."

Lily measures coffee into a paper filter. "Poor baby. Who knows what she'll find. I'm so worried about her. I mean— burns, dear God." She shakes her head. "I've got the prayer team on it."

I'm worried, too, but it always feels like my mother is making things into some big drama. Even if this might qualify, I don't want to start hand-wringing. "She's strong. She knew what she was getting into when she married a career soldier."

"Well, it's one thing to know intellectually. Another to have to deal with it emotionally. And she's pregnant." Lily clicks her tongue. "Such a handsome man, too. Is his face burned?"

Would it be better if he was ugly? "I don't know anything, Mom. Nothing."

She finishes the prep on the coffeemaker, presses the button.

Carefully not looking at me, she says, "Katie makes me think of you that summer you went to Poppy's farm in Sedalia."

All I can manage is a nod. That was a painful time for me. Us. I was fifteen and pregnant, exiled to my aunt's house for the summer. The memory edges along my ribs, joins with the present day. I think of Sofia's pale face as she blew me a kiss from the circle of soldiers' wives.

"What was that young man's name?" Lily asks.

I frown, drawn from my thoughts into what feels like a non sequitur. "Who are you talking about?"

"That summer you spent with Poppy," she says, again avoiding the obvious way to refer to it. "There was a young man who worked at the record store. You were just smitten." She laughs. "And it was so strange—he was kind of funny-looking, wasn't he?"

"Jonah," I say, buttering bread. "I wasn't smitten. He was my friend." I frown, looking at her. "And, as I remember, he was beautiful."

"You had the worst crush ever," my mother snorts. "And, no, he was pretty funny-looking."

There are footsteps in the hallway, and I make a chopping motion across my throat. As Katie comes around the corner, I pick up the handset of the phone and give it to my mother. "Why don't you see what you can figure out about the dog?"

"I can do that." She sits down at the table and flips open the little notebook she carries in her purse. Every single one of us has tried to get her to switch to a BlackBerry, but she thinks they're rude. "Katie, come sit here with me and let's see what we can find out, shall we?"

"You can probably look things up on the computer faster," Katie says, pointing to the desktop in a nook in the kitchen, breathing softly beneath the gurgling coffee. "Or doesn't it work?"

I wink at Katie. "*It* works fine."

"So does information," Lily says. "What airline did you fly on, sweetie?"

So it begins. Katie's life in my house. My life with Katie in it.

In the middle of the night, the phone rings and I scramble in the dark to answer it, knowing who it will be. "Hello?"

"Mom?" Sofia's voice on the other end of the line is thin. "Did I wake you up? Of course I did. I'm sorry. I just needed to talk to you."

"It's fine, baby. I'm here." I click on the lamp, push hair out of my eyes, and squint at the clock—2:36 a.m. "Have you seen Oscar?"

"Yes." The word is squeezed flat.

I wait, my lungs thick with a mucus of worry. In the background, I can hear a television or something. "Take your time."

"It's bad. Second- and third-degree burns over sixty percent of his body. And he"—she takes a quick gasping breath—"lost most of his right leg, part of his right hand."

"Oh, honey. I'm so sorry."

"He's in a coma, which they say is a blessing."

"Is there anyone there with you? Do you have a place to stay?"

"Yes, it's all very well organized. There's a house nearby that's run by a private organization, and I have a driver assigned to me." She strives for good cheer, but I can hear the terror in her voice. "The Soldiers' Angels gave us a quilt that's just beautiful, and they have this little backpack they give to soldiers because they might not have their stuff with them, you know?"

"That sounds great." I would have spared her this. *Don't love a soldier,* I would have said, *or a policeman, or a smoke jumper.* In this moment, though, I want only to offer her something to buoy her. "He's lucky to have you there, sweetie."

"They aren't going to move him for a few days." Her breath hitches. "I don't think they expect him to live, Mom."

I say the only thing I can. "They don't know everything. You have to have faith."

"You're right." Her voice takes on some color. "I will." She clears her throat, dons her armor again. "Did Katie get there safely?"

"She did. She is sound asleep in the orange bedroom. Her dog, however, is not here yet."

"A dog?"

"She found him on the train tracks the night her mother was arrested. He sounds like a total vagabond. If he were a man, he would be your stepfather—amoral and utterly charming."

Sofia laughs, that helpless reaction-style giggle. "Oh, Mom! Thank you so much for all of this." Suddenly there are tears twining through the laughter, and—finally—she lets down her guard and sobs, the sound shattering over the tiny nerves on the bridge of my nose. "I'm so scared. Tell me I can do this."

"You're stronger than you know, Sofia. You can do anything. And I'm always right here."

"Thank you." She takes in a big breath. "Kiss Katie for me. Tell her I'll call her tomorrow. But, Mom, don't tell her too much about Oscar, all right? Downplay it."

"That's a mistake."

"Just do it my way, will you?"

"No, sorry." *I can't stand it when people lie,* Katie had said. "I promised her I'd tell her the truth."

"Then don't say anything."

"You're going to have to trust me to do what's right."

"Mom!"

"Sorry. I won't lie to her. Call her tomorrow—our tomorrow here—all right? And, in the meantime, you need to get some sleep."

A pause. "You're right. Okay. I'll call tomorrow."

When I hang up, a middle-of-the-night stillness muffles all sound. I lie on my back, phone warm in my hand, and think about her in a hospital halfway around the world, alone with this. I want the details of the place—are the hallways white or green? Modern or old? What kind of chairs are in the waiting rooms? When she was in college, I had her snap photos of apartments I had not seen so that I could easily visualize her moving around her environment.

She'll have pulled her hair into a sensible ponytail, and her makeup will have worn off by now, and she'll be wearing tennis shoes, very white, with jeans. To accommodate her belly, she's been wearing batik peasant blouses, colored like tapestries, which makes her look like a medieval woman. I imagine her settling a hand on her belly, putting her forehead against the wall, letting go for a minute.

Then I know what she next will do: She will straighten, square those narrow shoulders, and march back to Oscar's bedside.

Oscar. Burned; an amputee. I think of his beautiful hands, his curly hair.

Their lives will never be the same, in ways she can't even envision now. My chest feels hollow with grief, with knowing all that she has lost.

Next to me, Milo starts to purr, very quietly. His body is bumped up against mine, and a paw reaches through the darkness to land on my forearm, a tap. Idly, I run my hand over his forehead, down his back, scratching the place beneath his ears that he loves so much. His fur is as silky as mink. A comfort.

Milo is a rescue, an elegant blue-eyed Siamese who showed up on my porch, wet and skinny and starving, only three or four months old. Even then he was one of the most beautiful cats I'd ever seen, with a soft squeak of a meow instead of an obnoxious yowl. He's aloof and skittish and not terribly friendly with anyone but me. I wonder how he's going to take the arrival of the dog, who will be here in the morning.

Probably not well.

"I'm sorry we have to bring a dog in, baby," I say conversationally. "If it were just me, you know I'd never do that to you, but this little girl needs somebody in her corner, and dogs are good at that kind of thing." Milo nuzzles into my palm, asking for a face rub, and when I do it, he licks my palm delicately, as if I am his kitten.

It had taken my mother nearly three hours to get the dog's transportation straightened out. Merlin had no vaccination records. Without them, he would not be allowed to fly. A vet agreed to come to the airport to administer the shots, and an airport employee would give the dog food and water overnight.

In the morning, he will fly in a new soft-sided $200 kennel to Colorado Springs, where my brother will again be pressed into service, since he is the dog person of the family. My credit card was screaming by the end of the arrangements, but what alternative was there?

I took Katie on a walk of the neighborhood earlier tonight, showing her where things are—7-Eleven and the post office and the tourist strip on West Colorado Avenue, cluttered with boutiques and galleries and bars, and the hilly backstreets populated with Victorians and bungalows with grassy yards. "It's pretty here," she said in some wonder. "I don't remember Colorado Springs looking like this."

"Did you live here?"

"Yeah, I was little. We were at Fort Carson, I think. I don't remember it all that well."

When we got home, she asked to get on the Internet, and I set her up at the kitchen nook with her own ID. She chose a picture of a dog as her icon. She already had an email address, of course—that much is easy these days—and wanted to email her best friend about Merlin. I asked if she had emailed her dad. She shook her head, not looking at me. I didn't push.

Now I can no longer bear to lie here and think of the expenses I can't afford, the disaster that has befallen my daughter, or the challenges of a girl who is as tense and aloof and as skittish as my cat. Gently nudging Milo aside, I tug on some yoga pants and a sweater and tie my long hair away from my face with a scrunchie. Milo tucks his long black tail around himself like a fluffy scarf and returns to sleep.

I patter down the back stairs to the bakery kitchen. Moonlight comes in through the windows and glances off the stainless-steel island, and I think of Sofia sitting there less than two days ago.

The overhead fluorescent lights will be too harsh just now. I turn on the small lights—over the range, over the sink, above the counter. Nearby is the bank of side-by-side fridges.

Stored in the fridges are my sourdough starters, of course. The bakery is built on them. At the moment there are three different sponges made with various ingredients—potato starter and rye; a buttermilk-and-wheat-flour starter I've been experimenting with; a heavy dark barley mash, which makes a bread so rich and tangy that it impressed an anonymous travel writer enough to write it up in *New York* magazine. That article led to other stealthy tasters and even better coverage.

And an even deeper rift with my family. They expected me to fail, and I have not. Yet.

On the counter is the fourth jar, which I have left out overnight. This is the luminary of my starters, mother dough from my grandmother, which has been in the family for more than a hundred years, ever since Bridget Magill, my grandmother's grandmother, carried it with her from Ireland, to Buffalo, then to the mining camps in Cripple Creek.

In the silence of the middle of the night, I turn on the classical radio station, very quietly. The sound will not travel as high as Katie's bedroom, but there is no reason to take chances. The poor girl has such circles under her eyes that she looks haunted. It's hard to imagine what her life has been like these last couple of years.

From a hook by the door, I take a fresh apron, the white cotton worn soft from many washings, and tie the long strings around my body once, then again in the front. On the radio is Mozart's Piano Concerto in C Major, which many consider to be his most elegant piece of work. Humming along under my breath, I take a big aluminum bowl from beneath the counter and carry it to the plastic bins along the wall where we store dry goods—flours, of course, white and rye, whole-grain wheat, and oats; also sugars of various types, brown and white and raw. Stacks of scoops and measuring cups line the shelves above.

The chemistry of bread is not as exact as you might imagine. Everything influences the mix of dry ingredients to wet, particularly with the artisan loaves I am baking tonight. I use the small shovel in the bin to fill my bowl with white flour and take it back to the center island, then gather the rest of my ingredients and tools—some sugar and loose yeast to help the mother dough along, a scraper and plastic wrap, measuring cups and spoons.

As I begin to measure dry ingredients into a fresh bowl, my mind drifts back to Katie. Tomorrow the dog will arrive. Before he gets here, maybe there will be time to get her a haircut, maybe some new clothes. Everything in her suitcase was quite plainly purchased secondhand, and much of it is stained or ragged or too small. Her panties, in particular, pain me. Every single pair has holes. I washed everything and neatly folded it all, then stacked it on a chair just inside her bedroom door. The child slept on, oblivious, her body so thin she barely lifted the covers.

As I measure flour, I imagine her after her mother's arrest: waking up in an abandoned house, putting on those tattered panties, and trying to comb her crazy hair. I have to lean my hands on the cold steel counter, take a long breath against the blistering heat it rouses in me.

How could she have slipped through so *many* cracks? Oscar

was at war, obviously, and Sofia lived here, but didn't they talk to her? And what about her teachers? Parents of her friends? Didn't somebody notice?

Obviously not—Katie had been living with her mother in a house with no running water and no appliances for a couple of months, maybe more. Katie was clearly adept and clever, so she made people believe what they wanted to believe.

Still. Those collarbones.

As if to nudge my darkening mood aside, a minuet twirls out of the radio. I stir the liquid ingredients together, set them aside for a few minutes to greet one another, and transfer the sourdough sponge into a clean jar that is carefully labeled. It goes back in the fridge, in a special small box I have outfitted with a lock to which only I have the key. My aunt Poppy tends a line of the sponge, as well, but each of ours has a different quality, as you might imagine. Poppy has been happier than I, so hers is sweeter.

All of our sourdough starters are born from the same carefully tended mother dough our ancestor carried from Ireland in 1845. How she kept it alive through the famine times is a mystery we don't examine too closely.

What we do know is that Bridget Magill carried her sponge to a big house in Buffalo, where she was a cook in a banker's house, and made the finest bread anyone had ever tasted. More than one matron in the fashionable district tried to steal Bridget away, but she steadfastly cooked for the Mitchell family until her thirty-fifth year. By all accounts the lively, plump old maid then charmed a westward-thinking miner by the name of William O'Hare, who married her and brought her to the gold rush in the Colorado mountains, where she cooked just as happily for miners until she died.

Bridget's good nature made a bread that was sweet as heaven. She also kept her loaves cold for a long stretch, letting them ripen, resulting in a bread that melted on your tongue like sugar.

I am not as prone to good cheer as my ancestress, and tonight my mood sends the yeasts bubbling riotously in the bowl, filling the air with that fecund and piercing scent. It carries with it a promise of rain, and I turn it out on the layer of fine white flour I've scattered across the surface of the counter.

Finally I can begin to knead, and everything slips away, as if I am meditating, as if I am praying.

Only names waft through my mind: *Sofia. Katie. Oscar.*

RAMONA'S BOOK OF BREADS

EASY SOURDOUGH STARTER

Technically, the best sourdough starters are made without commercial yeast, but it's easier to understand the properties of a sponge if you make an easy one to begin with. This one is simple and reliable.

2 cups potato water (water in which potatoes have been boiled until
  soft), lukewarm
½ cup rye flour
½ cup whole-wheat flour
1 cup unbleached white flour
2 tsp dry yeast

In a 2-quart jar, mix the water, flours, and yeast until smooth. Cover loosely with cheesecloth and let stand in a warm spot, stirring every 24 hours, until bubbly and agreeably sour, usually 4–10 days. Taste it every day to know how it is progressing.

When it is ready, store loosely covered in the fridge, refreshing it once a week by throwing away half the starter and adding 1 cup water, 1 cup white flour. Can be used in bread recipes, biscuits, pancakes, even corn bread.

SEVEN

Katie

Katie jerks awake from a heavy, dreamless sleep and sits straight up, blinking, trying to gather information as fast as possible. Where is she? Is she late for school? Is there any trouble?

A bank of windows.

Lemonade light splashing on slanted walls.

And, finally, the living scent of bread baking, a smell that fills her head so much that it makes her feel tilted sideways.

No, she doesn't have to worry about school. She's not even in Texas. She is in Colorado, in Sofia's mother's house.

With a sigh of relief, she falls back on the soft, soft bed and scrunches the extra pillows around her like a nest. Her legs and arms feel buzzy from sleeping so hard, easing some of the aches she feels all the time lately. Growing pains, Madison's mother said.

It is still super-early. The smell of the bread fills the whole room, and her stomach growls. She tries to imagine the empty space of her belly filled with cotton, muffling the sound, easing the pangs.

But it comes to her that she doesn't have to do that anymore. She's living over a bakery! A *bakery*. With a woman who seems to want to be sure Katie has plenty of that bread in her stomach.

Tucking a hand under her cheek, she shifts lazily. But like a blue jay suddenly sensing danger, she hears a blast of warning in her mind—*don't get too comfortable!*—and she knows she has to listen. She will have to be very, very careful here.

The room is like something in a fairy tale. The bed is the best she can remember in forever, maybe even better than the bed she had in Germany, when her parents were still together and they had an apartment where Mom and Dad took turns cooking. That was when her mom was happy still, before she went to Iraq and became somebody else.

When both of her parents were deployed to Iraq, Katie had to go live with her grandma, who smelled like cabbage and went to church all the time and obviously didn't like Katie's mom very much and said mean things about her. It made Katie cry one time, and her grandma stopped after that, but Katie knew she was still thinking the same things.

Buried in the fresh-smelling covers and pillows, Katie lets herself take a long breath and close her eyes for just a little longer. Somewhere outside her windows, a bird chirps. (*Warbles,* she thinks, composing a note to Madison in her mind.) The last place she lived was the only house left in a whole neighborhood of apartments, and it seemed like somebody was always yelling or playing their music somewhere.

This is good. Very, very good.

Don't get used to it.

She makes herself get out of the soft bed and patters over to the windows in her underwear and T-shirt. Way, way down in the backyard is Ramona, her red hair in a braid that falls all the way down her back, almost to her butt. It's the longest hair Katie's ever seen on a grown-up. Sitting on a bench is an old woman, petting a cat.

The garden looks kind of nice, but what Katie thinks is that she can get to the kitchen and post an email to her mother before Ramona comes in. She brushes her teeth and washes her face. Her dad used to do push-ups every morning, and Katie did them with him, but lately they make her arms feel shaky and she has to quit.

Her clothes are in a neat stack on a chair in her bedroom, everything all clean and perfectly folded. Katie bends her head into them and smells laundry soap. It almost makes her cry. Tears would actually have spilled if she hadn't swallowed fast.

On top of the pile is her favorite sweater, light brown with thin green stripes, and she pulls it on over her T-shirt, along with some jeans that are a little too short. Barefoot, she heads down the first flight of stairs, checking to see which stairs squeak. There's nobody else around.

In the kitchen, there's a bowl of apples and oranges, and Katie snatches an apple, biting into it eagerly. It's so juicy, she has to wipe off her chin, and she puts it aside so the computer keys won't get sticky. At school, they always have to wash their hands before they use the computers.

Katie opens her own special account that Ramona made for her and crosses her fingers. *Be there, be there, be there.*

Nothing. Nothing from Madison, though Katie had not really expected it. Madison might get to go on somebody else's computer at their house or something but not until the weekend. Madison's mother didn't think they'd even get a little bitty netbook until her dad went back to Iraq. The girls would have to make snail mail work.

Also nothing from Katie's mom. Though Katie knows not to expect it yet—her mom is probably still in detox, where everybody is too sick to be using computers—she's disappointed.

The worst is that there is nothing from her dad. He writes her an email almost every week, but there hasn't been one in a while. Not that she's been able to get anywhere to read them.

But seeing that empty mailbox makes her heart hurt for a long, long minute, until she takes a bite of apple and promises she will not think of him again for five hours. Just like everything is normal. She read a book that said whatever you think about comes true, and that scares her. What if she can worry him into being dead?

Instead, she wants to think about her dad being okay, only a little bit hurt, making jokes in his hospital bed.

Feeling nervous, Katie thinks about her mother. She is *not* allowed to talk to her. She gets up, looks out the back windows of the kitchen, and sees that Ramona is still there. The other lady is gone. The smell of bread baking is even stronger here, but it still seems as if nobody else is in the house except her, so she creeps back to the computer and opens a new email.

TO: laceymomsoldier@prt.com
FROM: katiewilson09872@nomecast.com
SUBJECT: safe and sound

Dear Mom,
  I know you can't probably even get to a computer yet, but when you do I wanted there to be an email from me so you didn't have to worry. I'm staying with Sofia's mom in Colorado and it's totally boring but safe, so you don't have to worry. I'm thinking about you every day. Hope you feel better super-fast and we can be together again.
  Love you lots and lots, Katie

She hits the send button. No one will know. It would make her dad really mad. Standing up, she pushes the chair back exactly the same way it had been. Still nibbling her apple to make it last, she wanders through the rooms on this floor, peeking into the big living room and the bedroom that must be Ramona's. An old-fashioned bed with curlicues made of iron sits in an alcove beneath three windows hung with fragile-looking lace. The bed isn't made, and Katie likes Ramona better for it, and for the pair of pants that are flung over a chair, and for a couple of pairs of shoes sitting by the closet door, as if they'd been kicked off.

She ambles through the long hallway, stopping to look at framed pictures of a little girl getting bigger and bigger until she turns into Sofia.

The bathroom is amazing. It's gigantic with black-and-white tiles in diamonds across the floor and a big old tub that you could practically swim in, sitting on sturdy claw feet. One wall is made of glass cubes that make everything look wavy, so right now they are all green and white and blue, like a kaleidoscope. A huge green velvet curtain hangs on rings near the ceiling. Katie pulls it, and it flows on a bar across the glass wall for privacy. "Cool," she says to no one.

The sink stands by itself beneath a mirror with double lines drawn on the edges. No counter, but behind the tub is a built-in dresser with drawers that have crystal handles. Bottles of bubble bath and shampoo and hair stuff are all lined up on top of it. A wicker basket is filled with pins and clips and elastic bands, and beside it is a brush with thick tan bristles that are way too soft to do anything for Katie's crazy hair. She checks it out anyway because the brush is so pretty, looking in the mirror, which she really tries to avoid whenever possible. There is a white patch beside her mouth and a zit coming on her chin, and the stupid brush just skates right over the top of her dry, curly, uncut hair. Ugly! Especially when she thinks of Ramona's hair, which is long, long, and a glittery red. Like Rapunzel, maybe.

She puts the brush away carefully and leaves the bathroom, looking for a trash can for her apple core. A hollowness goes with her. She's bored now. There's nothing to do. She's already read her book six times and she doesn't like computer games, and she can't think about her dad until ten o'clock.

She might as well go outside with Ramona.

EIGHT

Ramona

I'm out in my garden by five a.m., the loaves baked and cooling on the counter. The air is quite sharp so early, and I wear jeans and a sweater, my hair woven into a tight braid, hands in gloves to keep the grit out from under my nails. Sometimes I still have to scrub them like a surgeon when I come inside.

The garden is at the rear of the backyard, filling the space that used to be an old garage. It was falling down when I moved in here eight years ago to live with my grandmother after my divorce. I had someone pull the brick walls down on two sides, leaving one wall with an empty window and another on the north end against the alley. He found some magic way to brace the walls so they are sound, and it looks beautiful like that, as if the earth is taking over, vines growing up the walls, roses twining around the window frame. The floor was dirt to start with, so that meant only digging it out, hauling in a load of topsoil, and then planting. A big project, but I needed something to keep me busy when I wasn't baking.

I'm kneeling in the dirt, carefully thinning nasturtiums, when Katie materializes at the edge of the plot. She's wearing jeans that are too short and a ratty-looking brown sweater that's much too big. Sunlight coaxes golden lights from the bends of her crazy ringlets.

"Good morning," I say.

She yawns. "Hi."

"If you're hungry, there's cereal in the cupboard, or toast, of course."

"I had an apple."

In my peripheral vision I spy the bright blue eyes of Milo, who is stalking me. I grin and point at his tail swishing out of the shadows. I wiggle my fingers on the ground, and he rockets out of the plants, spats my hand with both paws like a boxer, and zooms away, diving into a honeysuckle bush. A squirrel leaps out of it and races down the fence line, chattering in alarm, and as if that is exactly the result he had intended, Milo saunters out and sits regally on the grass, all Siamese elegance, very black points and long nose and long limbs. The king of everything.

"He's really pretty," Katie says. "I've never had a cat before."

"Have you had dogs?"

"Only Merlin. How do you think Merlin and Milo will get along?"

"No idea. We'll just have to wait and see." I am worried, but she doesn't need to know that. I'll enlist my brother's help introducing the two animals. He's done it often enough.

"Do you want to help?" I ask. "I'm just pulling weeds."

"I guess."

The plants are still small and there isn't much to do, but I wander through the rows plucking weeds, thinning the flowers and herbs, picking up sticks and scraps of paper the wind has blown in. An elm tree, ancient and enormous, shades the house and sheds twigs the way a woman sheds hair. Katie follows me, but I can see her heart isn't in it.

I want to talk to her about her dad. I look at the sky, gauging the time to be nearly six. "Let's go out to breakfast. What do you say?"

Her face flares with hope, then she tugs on her jeans. "Er, I don't really have anything to dress up in."

"It's casual, but that's part of the plan. Sofia left me money to buy you clothes. It's not a lot, but we can get you some summer clothes that fit. You must have been growing a lot the last few months."

She nods, tugging the sleeves of her sweater down over her hands. "I can put on my shorts."

"Perfect. Let me change my clothes and wash my face. I'm starving."

The morning is so gorgeous it would be a shame to get in the car, so we walk the three blocks to the main tourist drag, and take seats on the patio of my favorite local café, Bon Ton's. Katie asks for milk when I get coffee. She reads the menu with great concentration, her hand moving over her concave belly. "What are *you* having?" she asks.

It occurs to me that, unlike me, she didn't grow up in restaurants and might be afraid to spend too much. Nothing on this menu will break even my tiny budget. "The works. Eggs, pancakes, orange juice, all of it. Do you like bacon, sausage, any of that?"

"Kind of. Bacon, especially."

"And are you a hash-browns-and-toast kind of person or a pancakes girl?"

"Pancakes."

So we order a massive spread, and when it comes, Katie eats and eats and eats, until her tummy is a small round ball under her too-big shirt. She falls back and puts her hand over it. "That was so good." She burps and slaps a hand over her mouth, laughing. "Sorry."

"It's okay." I sip my coffee, eyeing her long hands and feet. "You must be getting ready to shoot up."

"My mom says I might be six feet."

"I believe it." Oscar is well over that. Thinking of him puts a knot in my chest. I am going to have to tell her about him. First, though, shopping. The child desperately needs a few things.

We get the car and head over to Target, which opens early, and pick up a small assortment of shorts and T-shirts, a pair of jeans and a sweater for evenings.

I'm discreetly assessing where she is in puberty. Soft golden hair under her arms, a little fur on her lower legs. She's wearing a basic training bra and it's doing the trick, so we get a couple more. A part of me shudders away from the idea of her growing breasts in that cesspool where she lived before—all the predators and dangers.

Thank God her mother was arrested. I hope that someday Katie is relieved, too.

When we finish at the store, I drive to a local park and get out, buying us both root beers at a stand. We amble over to a park bench and sit down. "My brother will be bringing Merlin in a couple of hours, and I'm personally going to need a nap before that, but I wanted to talk to you."

Her knuckles go white around the can. "Is my dad dead? Is that why you're being so nice to me this morning?"

"No! Oh, no, honey." I capture her other hand, clasp it between mine. "I would never do that, keep something so important from you."

Her eyes are exactly the same color as the Afghan girl in the famous photo, that green of new leaves. She searches my face suspiciously and frowns, tugging her hand out of my grip. "What, then?"

"It *is* about your dad. Sofia called last night, and he is injured badly. He has some pretty serious burns, and"—I can't seem to help taking in a breath—"he's lost most of his right leg."

"But he's alive."

"Yes," I say, and repeat it so she's sure. "He's alive. Sofia said he's in a coma, but that can be a good thing when someone has been so badly injured. It gives the body a chance to heal."

She stares at me for a long time, then asks, "Is his face burned?"

"I don't know, Katie." This is the second time she has asked this. "We can find out."

Tears well in her eyes, and her mouth pulls down at the corners. "When can I talk to him, do you think?"

"Probably not for a while, but you can email him, and you can email Sofia, too, and she'll keep you posted. Does that help?"

"Yeah." She brushes her hair out of her eyes. "Can we go home now? I want to be there when Merlin gets there, so he won't be scared."

It's my habit to nap in the early afternoon, to make up for rising so early, and by the time I make it to my bed this afternoon, diving into the piles of pillows and covers, I'm wiped out. Milo hears the bedsprings and leaps up to keep me company. I'm out in three seconds. The ding of a text arriving on my phone awakens me. It's Ryan.

Have dog. You are in so much trouble.

I text back:

What does that mean?
He's adorable and completely untrained.
You'll help me, right? You're good with dogs.
I'll do my best. Be there in 20.

I run upstairs and knock on Katie's door. She's not there, and I find her in the kitchen, on the computer. When I arrive, she whirls. Guiltily. "What?"

Must remember to put the safeguards on the computer. Her

innocence is probably fairly tattered given her history, but I can do my best. "Merlin is on his way. I want to shut Milo in upstairs, so let's get things ready for him."

When we get downstairs, the man who has been working on my broken pipe is about to knock on the door. "Hello, Ms. Gallagher. We're finished. You want to come take a look?"

"Wonderful." I follow Henry out. The yard is back to itself, with fresh sod covering the new gashes in the landscaping. "We couldn't do anything about the flowers," he says, "but I figured you'd want to take care of that yourself."

"Thank you. It looks great." Too great. I don't even want to know how much this costs. "Do you want to come in? I have to get my credit card."

"No, no. Cat took care of it. No big deal."

I blink. Two days and a crew of three is a big deal. "I can't let you do that. Please." I can't believe Cat paid. "Come inside. I need to pay for this myself."

"You have to take that up with Mr. Spinuzzi." He holds up both hands and backs away. "It was my pleasure, Miss. You take care now."

Damn it! I borrowed money from him eight months ago when the banks turned me down, and since then he's swooped in like this twice more. He's got to stop.

I need to stop talking to him about anything concerning the bakery, but it's hard. He's been my mentor and guide from the start.

At any rate, it isn't the fault of the plumber. I put my hands in prayer position and bow my head. "Thank you, Henry."

When he drives away, I turn to find Katie standing on the porch, fingering the lilacs in their vases. Such a somber child! "What are these?"

"Lilacs. My grandmother's favorite flower." I gesture with wide arms. "This used to be her house, when I was your age. She left it to me when she died."

"Why you?"

The answer is full of layers, and I say only, "That's a complicated story. Mostly because I was divorced and moved in with her when she got dementia." I smile and tell her a secret. "But it's probably because I was her favorite."

She bends her head into the blossoms. "My grandma was mean to me. She didn't like my mom at all, either."

"Sorry to hear that."

"And it wasn't because of drugs. She just didn't like her from the beginning."

"Unfortunately, it happens all the time." Joining her on the porch, I ask, "Do you want to sweep all this mud off while I make a new sign?"

She nods. I give her the broom and go inside to fetch the markers we use to announce specials on a big black board. Using neon pink and green, I carefully write *Open Saturday morning, 6 a.m.!* and, below that, *Thanks for your patience.* Straightening, I narrow my eyes. "Something should be on special," I say aloud. "To make up for the trouble."

Katie looks at me but offers nothing.

"What's your favorite bakery item?"

A shrug. "I don't know."

"Raisin bread, I think. I make a fantastic raisin bread, with orange-soaked raisins." I clap the lid on the marker. "That'll do it." Suddenly it seems there is a lot to do by tomorrow morning—all the upheavals have knocked me out of my routines.

My brother's blue truck pulls into the narrow driveway, and I can see the dog through the passenger window, sitting in the seat like a human. Katie yelps, "Merlin!" She drops the broom and runs off the porch to greet him, yanking open the door before the vehicle is barely stopped.

He leaps out, making a howling, talky sound of greeting, and Katie falls on her knees. When he licks her face, she flings her arms around his Creamsicle neck.

And sobs.

Merlin tolerates it for about twenty seconds—licking her ear, wiggling forward—and then my brother comes around the truck and grabs the leash. "There's a busy street only one block away, Katie," he says, more harshly than is required. "You've got to be really careful not to let him run."

"Ryan." I frown, using a hand gesture to bring it down a notch. He has no children of his own—a confirmed bachelor—so of course he knows exactly how to raise them. "Give her a minute."

"The way to take care of a dog is to be the master," he says. At least he squats and gives Katie, who's looking at him with a pale, chastened, smitten face, the leash. "He needs you to be the boss. All the time, very consistently. Do you know what that means?"

"Regular," she says.

"Good." He stands. "I've gotta open the pub, but I'll be back to help you train him. Three things to remember: Never let him sleep on your bed. Never give him human food unless he does something to earn it, and never, ever from the table or while you are eating. And third, give him lots of attention. He's a dog who likes it."

"Okay. I can do that."

He bends to scratch Merlin's chest and comes up the stairs to me, handing over a sheaf of paperwork, presumably the dog's shot records. At least that much is done. "Keep him fenced, or he's going to take off. I would suggest you get some identification on him right away."

"Will do." I hug him. "Thanks, Ryan. I know you've got a lot going on, too." He has to fire a bartender at The Banshee, the pub he runs for the family. My father desperately wanted him to call it Gallagher's, but Ryan stood his ground. "Can I make you some dinner this week?"

"Sure. Monday would be good."

"Monday it is."

He turns to go and spies the fresh sod. "Damn." He gives me a sharp look. "That had to cost a pretty penny. Or did your mentor take care of you, as always?"

"I probably deserve that," I say. "But just because Dad hates him doesn't mean he's a bad person."

"Ah, so he did pay?" He sounds incredulous. "Mr. Mafia. Must be nice."

I scowl. "He paid the guy before I knew he'd done it. I'm not going to let it stand. Too many strings."

"Should have thought of that."

Mostly, Ryan and I get along pretty well, but this is a sore spot. He would love to be independent of the family clutch, but chose to stay with the umbrella of the Gallagher Group restaurants. "I raised the money for this bakery myself. I put together the business plan and made it work. You guys always underestimate my brains, which is why I left the Gallagher Group in the first place."

"Yeah, because Grandma gave you the house."

"I got a little luck after a bunch of bad luck. It happens." I glance toward Katie, her back long and stiff. "Let's not do this right now."

"Whatever." He turns away, heads down the steps.

It makes me furious. "What exactly would you like me to do?" I ask in a quiet voice. "Fall on my face so everyone can say they were right about me?"

He only glances over his shoulder. "Nobody wants to see you fall on your face." A sudden flash of humor, the same thing that always saves our tense arguments, comes to the rescue. "Well, maybe Stephanie does."

My sister, who runs the family steakhouse with my father and has not spoken to me since I adopted Cat as my mentor. "And Dad."

"No. He loves you. He just hates Cat."

"Then he should have thought of that when he decided to

keep Dane." My philandering ex-husband, who worked for the Gallagher Group until recently.

"You gotta get over that." Ryan chuckles, shaking his head. "It's been what—eight years?"

"I don't care. As far as I'm concerned, my family chose my ex-husband over me."

He mimes crossing his arms over his chest and sticking out his lower lip, then stomps his foot, in case I didn't get it.

I wave him off, smiling. "Thank you for your help."

"I'll be back later."

Katie moves Merlin away from the truck and comes up the steps, dragging the dog behind her. "I've got to get to work," I say. "Let's check the backyard for escape routes, and you can play with him out there."

We make a bed of old blankets on the sunporch in Katie's room, and she agrees to keep the door closed at night and to leash Merlin if he needs to go outside. The pair head into the backyard, Katie with a book, Merlin snuffling the perimeter like a soldier.

A soldier. Before I head into the bakery kitchen, I stop at the computer upstairs and send a quick email to Sofia:

Katie is fine. Dog is here. Any news? How are you holding up?
Be sure to EAT! Love, Mom

And then at last I escape into the kitchen, where the scent of yeast can help me forget, at least for a little while, that my daughter is in the first real trouble of her life and there is almost nothing I can do to help her.

NINE

Sofia's Journal

MAY 21, 20—

I am writing this as I sit by Oscar's bed. He is almost unrecognizable. No, that is not accurate. Not almost. He is unrecognizable. I would never have known it was him. There are so many bandages and tubes. I can see bits and pieces of his face—his mouth and chin are very swollen and red. His eyelids are a deep, terrible red, swollen and marked. His eyelashes are gone, but the nurse said he was lucky he kept his eyelids, a picture that gives me shudders every time I think about it.

He's a mummy, really. A mummy with one leg. He hasn't come out of the coma yet.

I thought they were going to fly us back to San Antonio yesterday, but he had a bad turn and then something else happened and…I don't know. The chaplain is here often, making sure I'm okay, which tells me how worried they are that he'll die.

He is not going to die. I keep telling him that he cannot give up, no matter what. Katie will be an orphan. Our baby will never see him. He or she will be here in less than two months, Oscar, I tell him. You can make it that long. I know you can.

And if he can make it two months, he can make it forever.

The other thing is, jeez, I am so pregnant! My ankles keep swelling, and I've got a backache that just won't quit. A doctor is keeping an eye on me, and I like her a lot.

In my belly, the baby is doing somersaults or something, I swear! I can feel him banging on my ribs, jumping around, rockin' out. I keep wondering—boy or girl? Boy or girl? I won't let them tell me. It seems like opening a Christmas present too early. I think, though, it's a boy. I'm carrying it high and forward, and one of the other teachers at school did a pendulum thing with a needle before I left. A boy with Oscar's beautiful eyes. His thick curly hair. His hands, which are so huge and beautiful.

When it gets closer to time, I guess I'll have to make some choices. It's hard to imagine having the baby without my mom around, but it's even worse to think of leaving Oscar's side. If I think about it too much, I start to panic.

Which isn't helpful in the least. One step at a time.

I haven't heard a thing from Katie and must remember to send her an email and be sure to be in touch with her. I've been avoiding it because it's so hard to think of what to say, how to tell the truth.

My stomach is growling. I need to go find something to eat. I wish I could find some of my mother's French bread. It helps so much when my stomach gets unsettled like this.

RAMONA'S BOOK OF BREADS

EASY WHITE BREAD

Many people fret about undertaking yeast bread, fearing it will be complicated and mysterious. This is the recipe used for centuries to make classic French baguettes. Children love to make this loaf, and it will give any aspiring bread baker a swelling of confidence.

1 cup lukewarm water
1 tsp sugar
1 T dry yeast
3 cups unbleached white flour
1 tsp salt
1 egg white + 1 tsp cold water

Pour the water into a small bowl and stir in the sugar, then sprinkle the yeast over the top and let stand for 5 minutes. In a big bowl, measure the flour and the salt and stir together. When the yeast is foamy, pour the yeast-and-water mix into the flour and stir together until you can gather it into a blob. On a counter scattered with flour, drop the blob and sprinkle more flour over the top of it, then knead for 5 minutes or more, until smooth and elastic. (The dough should begin to have a texture that's cool and "spankable.")

Gather the dough into a ball and put it into an oiled bowl, turning the ball until it is oiled all the way around. Dampen a flour-sack kitchen towel and cover the bowl. Let rise in a warm place until it is doubled (this will not take as long at high altitudes).

Preheat the oven to 375 degrees, and put a heavy skillet or baking pan in the bottom of the oven with a few inches of water to reproduce the humid environment of a French oven.

Pat the dough down into a long, thin rectangle, then roll the sides toward the middle to shape into a baguette. On a baking sheet covered with scatters of cornmeal or a baking parchment, place the baguette with the seam down and let rest for 10 minutes.

Make 3 sharp diagonal marks across the loaf and bake for 30 minutes, then baste with egg white and bake another 5–10 minutes, until the loaf is hollow when tapped from the bottom. Cool on a wire rack, serve with dinner.

TEN

Ramona

The first task of every afternoon is to refresh the sponges. Turning the radio to a local pop station so I can sing along, I cover my hair with a cap and my clothes with a chef's coat, then wash my hands as thoroughly as a surgeon.

Like any living organism, sourdough must be fed and tended regularly. It's a simple thing, usually just adding flour and water and giving it a good stir to bring in fresh oxygen. Then it is allowed to grow for a bit, usually eight to twelve hours, before it is ready to use.

That means that our sponges must be fed in late afternoon, so we can bake with them in the middle of the night. We use a rotating system, using jars of aqua and clear glass, so that some sponges are resting while others are growing. When Cat helped me plan the kitchen, I designed a storage area specifically for this purpose.

The smell of yeast and vinegar rises as I stir flour into each of four jars with a heavy rubber spatula. Like all mothers, the sponges are unique in texture and flavor. The rye starter is powerfully, almost painfully sour, dark and thick and bubbly. I use it to make authentic German breads, for which I have an established contingent of German shoppers, mostly women who came to the city as service brides—some as long ago as World

War II, others as recently as six months. They're particular but friendly and gratifyingly loyal when they are pleased.

I do this work every afternoon, because I have a very small staff. One baker and two apprentices come in at two a.m., five mornings a week. Each afternoon I set things up for them, making lists and deciding upon loaves for the next day.

With my hands—at last—in dough, tension flows out of my neck, drips benignly to the floor. Thoughts, images, memories swirl without weight. I think of Sofia's baby growing in her belly, and of Katie's long hands, and of my mother's reference to the summer I was fifteen, and of the broken pipe in the front yard, and of learning to bake with my aunt Poppy that fateful summer when bread saved my life. I wonder what passion lies sleeping in Katie's breast.

Finally, the things that really do need my attention surface clearly. Cleanly. When the rustica loaves are ready to rest, I set them aside and wash my hands, then carry my phone upstairs and call Cat.

He answers with a smile in his voice. "Ramona! How did the work turn out?"

"It's great, Cat. But you cannot pay for it."

"Oh, come now. It's nothing. I know you'll repay me. The summer is shaping up to be a busy one, and I know you can't get another bank loan yet."

His voice is persuasive. As I think of my maxed-out credit cards, I'm desperately tempted to accept his offer, but even the thought makes me hate myself. "I appreciate the offer, but I need to take care of this myself."

"Your pride is doing you no favors. We both know how close to the edge you are."

"You're the one who always tells me that it takes time for a business to get on its feet."

"That's true. You've had a lot of challenges the past year with the building, Ramona. Let me help you, just this once."

"It's not just this once, Cat. I owe you thousands and I need to pay you back, not borrow more!"

"*Tesòro mìo,* you don't have this money." He sighs. "I wish you would simply marry me. I could take care of you."

For a long moment, I stand in the middle of my living room, looking down to the view of ancient sidewalks. It feels as if someone has slammed a bat into my temple. "Do you hear yourself, Cat?"

"You know that's what I want. What I have wanted all along."

"All along? From the start, when I came to you for help?"

A slight hesitation. "No, no."

But in that pause, I hear the truth. He's like the rest of them—my family, my ex-husband—patting me on the head, never seeing that I do have the brains and business sense to make a go of this. "Did you ever believe in me at all, Cat?"

"I believe in you completely, Ramona."

I'm shaking my head. "I'll send you a check. Don't come by here anymore."

"Ramona, you're upset. Don't be rash."

"I'm not kidding, Cat. Do not come here. Don't call me."

I hang up the phone and stand in the middle of the room. My sinuses hurt. My chest is burning. I'm blinking back tears of—what? Betrayal? Loss? Anger?

All of the above.

From behind me, Katie says, "Ramona, me and Merlin are going upstairs, okay?"

I whirl, dashing tears off my face. The dog is sitting politely next to her, his dark eyes somehow wise. One golden ear is cocked to a point, while the other has a half fold in the middle, and there is a big freckle on his nose. For the first time I see that he's beautiful. Gold and white patches of smooth short fur cover his body. His paws have gold spats. "Bring him in here for a minute. We haven't properly met."

"Come on, Merlin," she says, and tugs on the leash. He trots over with her, coming to snuffle the hand I hold out to him, then he straightens, giving nothing away.

"Hello to you, too," I say, putting the phone down on the coffee table. I sink down to his eye level, scratching his chest, which I can see earns me a few points. His gaze is steady and wise. I think of the teacher in *Kung Fu,* a TV show I loved as a little girl. "You're an old soul, aren't you?"

He lifts a paw and puts it on my forearm, then leans forward and very delicately licks a tear off my face.

"I can see why you fell in love with this dog," I say to Katie. "He has a big heart, doesn't he?"

She nods, petting his head.

"I guess we need to figure out how to introduce him to the cat, to start the process of getting them used to each other."

"Maybe I can just feed him and then go upstairs? I'm supertired."

"Sure. That's fine."

As we pour some of the dog food we bought into a bowl, she says, "I don't mean to be nosy, but I heard you crying. Is it about...my dad?"

"No. I'm mad at somebody, that's all." Merlin sniffs the food and starts to wolf it down. "I promise that I will tell you everything I know about your dad the very minute I see you after I find out, okay? Will that make it easier?"

"Yes."

I draw a cross over my heart and hold my palm up in a vow. "Promise. Consider it done."

Once I get the dog and the girl settled, I head back down to finish my breads, thinking about Cat, about my brother's snide comments, about the rift in our family, and Dane and my sister Stephanie.

Dane is my ex-husband, a man I probably never loved. He

came into the business as the operations manager for the entire Gallagher Group.

Until he arrived, the restaurants ran independently, more or less. Dane came in and reorganized the structure so that we could centralize ordering, personnel, storage, bookkeeping, and all that kind of thing. He brought us online, organized accounts, essentially brought the structure of the business into the twenty-first century, and it was a godsend. Within a year, profits were up 23 percent.

He was also good with my dad, jollying him out of his stubborn-mule-who-has-to-do-everything-exactly-his-own-way snits. My dad feels an obligation to make sure the Gallagher Group functions well. His father opened the first Gallagher's, out on the highway to the top of Pikes Peak. It's a tourist mecca, beloved, and it shows up on all the postcards—a time machine. My sister Sarah and younger brother Liam run it. They make their own ice cream and pies, and it's bright and full of post-cards and books about Pikes Peak and booths with lacquered things on the tables, the history of the area. It's famous mainly because it's a good place to stop on your way back down, when you're tired and thirsty and want to absorb that terrifying drive.

The other two restaurants are the Erin Steakhouse, which my father opened in the sixties and built into one of the premier restaurants in the city, and The Banshee, Ryan's pub.

I loved the business from the time I was a small girl, and I particularly loved the steakhouse, which my sister Stephanie now co-runs with my father. That was the position I wanted—to learn the business and work with the family—but when I got pregnant at fifteen, my father was so humiliated that it happened in his restaurant that he could never let me back in.

So I worked as a cashier in the summers at Gallagher's Café and Gift Shop. I loved talking to people from all over, loved the pride I felt in being a native of Colorado Springs whenever people expressed their wonder over the beauty of it. Loved it in every way. But I did need to go to college, and there wasn't time for Sofia, college, and a job like that, which was a bit of a drive from home, so I did part-time personnel work for the business. Office stuff, which my mother hated. I had a proficiency for it—not that anyone has ever come out and said that—and I did well enough that I studied business and marketing in school.

Somehow, I ended up managing most of the internal affairs at the restaurants—office work split between three sites, because by then Ryan had opened The Banshee. I was good at managing all the backstage stuff, and I liked it, but it wasn't really what I wanted to do. I prefer the creativity of the food or the pleasure of being in contact with the customers.

But I *was* good. My title was Assistant to the Operations Manager; in actuality, I was doing it all myself. Then the old operations manager resigned, and, rather than put me in charge, my father hired Dane instead. He claimed I was too young—I was twenty-three or twenty-four, I can't remember which—but it was really just a way to dis me again.

Big, hearty Dane, whom my father adored like a son. They're a lot alike—charming, full of laughter, quick with a story or a joke. The difference is that my father is a one-woman man and Dane is a ladies' man of the highest measure, a quick-tongued devil.

I did not like him at all when he came to work for us. I was furious that he'd taken the job I deserved and hurt that my father still didn't respect me. So I did not exactly make Dane's life easy. We spoke only in the most civil of terms for well over a year after his arrival, long after he'd charmed everybody in the family and the restaurants. To her credit, my sister Sarah never really liked him, for the same reason I had my doubts: Such a big personality probably didn't have a lot of substance to it, and, at the very least, he was an egomaniac.

But we made a decent pair in a business sense, and together reorganized everything and eliminated thousands and thousands in repetitive costs. Little things like ordering in bulk and big things like eliminating superfluous positions that could be brought under the umbrella of the operations manager. Him. And me.

The person who adored him from the minute he arrived was Stephanie. He called her Petunia for no reason I ever understood, and she loved it. It's possible that they might have slept together at some point. Despite the fact that I'm the one with the bad rep, Steph is the one who has slept with a few too many men over the years. It is something she used to confess to me at times, swearing me to secrecy, which I honored. Men love her—not that she realizes it. She's been seen with a lot of movers and shakers over time, men with good cologne and clean-shaven jaws. Like Dane.

Not my type. I met a lot of men like that in school and they left me yawning. Which naturally meant Dane worked very hard to capture my admiration.

Three things happened all at once. Sofia got bronchitis one winter and couldn't shake it. She was sick for weeks and eventually went to the hospital with pneumonia. My family, of course, rallied as they always do, and work was covered so I could be with her. Both of us were completely worn out by the end of it, and Dane offered us the use of his condo in the mountains. It was heaven-sent, and I liked him so much better for it.

A little while later, Dane made my father give me Employee of the Year, which I'd never won. He cited all the work I'd done, detail by detail, on the reorg, and two weeks later he said, "Your family does not appreciate you at all, do they?"

Which was exactly the right thing to say.

Then he invited Sofia and me to go skiing. I'd never tried it, and Sofia was desperate to give it a shot. He promised that it was strictly friendship, and I'd been to the condo so I knew there was plenty of room.

Whatever else I say about him now, he was so good with my

daughter. Patient, funny, a good teacher. She could be aloof with people, but she let her guard down wholeheartedly with Dane. We had a great weekend, and I admit there were some sexual sparks. It would be hard not to have them around him—he's just that kind of man. He knows how to look at you. Knows how to pick the things you'll need to hear. The last night I let him kiss me, and he was—surprise!—a very good kisser. It had probably been, at that point, about six years since I'd had sex. I fell. And with Dane, it was sex like I'd not really had it before. Falling-off-the-bed sex. He knew what he was doing.

In the morning I was horrified, and he even knew how to manage that. He said it would be our secret. We'd never do it again. No one would ever know.

The trouble was, we worked together all the time. He'd bend over my shoulder and his breath would brush my neck, and I'd remember something. I avoided him.

I told myself that it would be a fling, that we'd have a good time and that would be that. But affairs are hard to keep secret in a restaurant, and when my father found out, he was not pissed off but *thrilled*. My mother adored him. Sofia loved him. For the first time in about a decade, I had the full approval of my family—maybe even Steph, though she was in the depths of a very tangled love affair herself and never had time to talk.

Dane and I got married. It seemed like the thing to do.

ELEVEN

Katie

S he awakens to the slow, patient wetness of a tongue moving over her fingers. When she stirs, Merlin jumps up eagerly and Katie says, "It's the middle of the night! Go back to sleep!" and pulls the covers over her head.

He nudges his nose under the covers and makes a soft "whuff." Katie remembers that he doesn't have any way to go to the bathroom unless she takes him. Abruptly, she sits up. Merlin backs away, leaping lightly and jerking his head toward the door. It makes Katie laugh. She puts on a sweater—Ramona was right: It's cold in the middle of the night here!—and clips Merlin's leash to his collar. Barefoot on the wooden steps, Katie follows him down, down, down, through the house kitchen and down the back steps into the backyard.

She unleashes him there and stands in the darkness with her arms crossed over her chest. The grass is damp beneath her feet, and it smells like flowers, the purple flowers on the bushes all along the yard. She never knew flowers could have so much smell or that they could be so perfect and beautiful. Even in the darkness, when they are pale gray, she thinks she can see an edge of blurry purple in the air.

Two squares of light fall on the grass from the bakery kitchen, and Katie wanders over curiously. Two women, maybe about the same age as Sofia, are dressed in white chef's coats, with their hair caught back beneath scarves. One is taking care of a big bowl being mixed up by a machine, while the other is shaping dough into long tubes on the metal counter in the middle of the room. Katie's stomach growls.

Ramona comes into view, too, her hair tightly braided away from her face, the same white coat on. Her pants are green and loose, and she's wearing those stupid plastic shoes. Who wears stuff like that? Katie's mother would make fun of her.

But Ramona seems happy, moving around the room, gathering bowls and spoons and stuff, laughing with the other two. Even in the middle of the night.

For one long, pained minute, Katie thinks of her mother in the middle of the night. Two weeks ago. Three. Her face had gotten real bad lately, with scabs and one open spot that got all pussy and disgusting, until Katie brought her mom into the bathroom and poured hydrogen peroxide on it. It bubbled and bubbled and got a little better the next day. But her mom was so skinny that Katie could see there were two bones in her forearms, and she didn't even have any breasts anymore. All she wanted, *all* she wanted, no matter what, was more crank.

Katie realizes she is biting on the inside of her cheek again and makes herself stop. Her mom *will* get better. She's cleaned up before. Katie can remember how pretty she used to be, when she did her hair and put on lipstick, or even when she was in her dress uniform.

She lets go of the fists she made and turns around to look for Merlin to bring him inside. He's sniffing around in the garden.

Ramona had asked how Katie found him, but Merlin had found her. He just appeared on her front porch a couple of hours after her mom got arrested. Katie saw the police coming and ran out the back door to hide in the alley so they wouldn't put her in a foster home. When she came back to the house, everybody was gone. She was scared by herself with no electricity, and all she had to eat was a loaf of white bread and a can of Vienna sausages she'd bought with pennies and dimes she scrounged in the gutters. She had no idea what to do. Where to go.

Then, like an angel or something, Merlin wandered onto the porch and came over to her and licked the tears off her face. She opened the sausages and he ate one, very, very politely, and ate some of the bread, then drank water out of the toilet. She thought he would go then, back to the homeless camps near the railroad tracks, but he didn't. With a sigh, he curled up next to her and went to sleep. He didn't even mind that she wanted to hold on to him.

Now he's digging a little in the flower beds, and Katie is pretty sure Ramona won't like that very much, so she walks over and tugs on his collar. "Come on, Merlin. I want to go back to bed."

He snorts and sneezes, planting his feet in the dirt so he can keep smelling. "Merlin!" she cries. "Come on!"

He doesn't move.

Behind her, the back door opens. "Katie?" Ramona calls. "Is everything okay?"

"No! He won't come in!"

"It's all right. I'll watch him and bring him up when he's done. You go on back to bed."

"That's okay. I said I would take care of him."

Ramona comes outside, wiping her hands on a cloth attached to her belt. "It's really okay, I promise. We've started baking, so I'm awake. You're a growing girl. You need your sleep."

Katie is afraid Ramona will put an arm around her, but she doesn't. "Okay," Katie says. "I'll leave my door open."

TWELVE

Ramona

I go back inside to my baking, peeking through the window every so often to keep an eye on Merlin. He wanders the perimeter, noses through the garden, and finally sits with his paws crisscrossed in front of him in the very center of the small square of grass. Moonlight illuminates his white patches.

"When did you get a dog?" asks Jimmy, an earnest young woman who loves baking bread nearly as much as I do.

"He belongs to Sofia's stepdaughter."

"Cute."

"Yeah," I say, and oil the loaves on the table, then set them aside to rise one more time. Automatically I glance at the big clock on the wall. "These should go in the oven at five."

"Got it. Extra steam?"

I nod and glance out the window again, but Merlin isn't sitting in the grass anymore. I lean to one side to see if I can see him along the fence, but he's not there, either. Frowning, I untie my apron. "I'd better check on the dog."

In chef's clogs, I clump through the back door and down the old wooden steps. "Merlin!" I call, but he probably doesn't even know that's his name yet. I whistle, hands on my hips. There are deep shadows under the lilac bushes, and I think I see him in one. "Come on, baby," I call quietly, mindful of neighbors asleep all around.

Nothing. The first ripple of concern moves down my spine. "Here, puppy! Come on, Merlin. Where's a good dog?"

When he doesn't come out of his hiding place, I go back inside and get a piece of cheese. All dogs love cheese, according to my sister who doesn't speak to me anymore. I am the cat person of the family.

Standing in the yard, I hold it up, wondering how the heck he'll know it's cheese. Maybe dogs smell things like this, I think, and wave it around, making figure eights in the mild night air. "Come on, puppy, where are you?"

A racket breaks out in the back of the garden, and a squirrel bolts out of a honeysuckle bush, chattering in terror. He streaks across the yard and scrambles over the five-foot fence, Merlin following at full speed. The dog is sleek and lethal and doesn't even pause for a breath as he runs for the fence and clears it.

"Crap!" I race for the gate, the clumsy clogs slapping against my heels. By the time I make it through the gate to the gravel alley, Merlin and the squirrel are gone. Looking left, and looking right, I see exactly the same thing: empty darkness.

"Merlin!" I cry, as if he would pay any more attention to me now than he did three minutes ago.

My heart is pounding in my ears. I have to make a choice: I run to the left, out to the adjoining street. No dog either direction, and I can see a fair distance, so I turn around and run to the other end of the alley, past sleeping Victorians, a small parking lot for a clothing boutique, trash cans, garages. The smell of lilacs hangs thick and deep in the air.

At the end of the alley, all I can see are empty sidewalks. Streetlights cast an amber glow through the tree branches. "Merlin!" I call quietly. "Where are you, you stupid dog?"

All I can think of is Katie's face. She trusted me. I'll just go around the block. Surely he'll be somewhere.

But he isn't. I walk up and down the side streets, calling for him, until the edges of the eastern horizon begin to lighten. Defeated, I trudge back home, my arches hurting from the sprints, my body sweaty. Lights are starting to come on here and there. A man with jangling tools on his belt heads for his truck, giving me a nod.

How will I tell Katie her dog is gone?

Another man is sitting on his front porch with a cup of coffee. "Good morning," he says as I pass. His voice sounds oddly familiar, skates along my nerves in a way that makes me take a second look at him. His face, too, seems strangely familiar.

"You haven't seen a dog, have you?"

"I haven't been up very long." His voice is lovely, resonant and calming, like a bow pulling across the strings of a cello. "What kind of dog?"

"He's a mongrel, a tramp. Gold and white, completely charming and wretched."

"I'll keep my eyes open. Where would I return him?"

"Are you familiar with Mother Bridget's Boulangerie? The bakery about five blocks down?"

"I haven't been here very long," he says apologetically. "I'll keep my eyes open."

"Thanks." I wave and head back to face the music. Overhead, pink light kindles on the contrails curving over the sky, and, as if to mirror them, the bare pink granite of the mountaintops blazes. As I approach the bakery that was my grandmother's house, the scent of bread curls out into the morning. I think of Katie, asleep upstairs.

Bring him home, I think. *Please.*

I stand on the sidewalk, my hand on the gate, looking back and forth down the street, praying to saints I haven't spoken to in decades—St. Joseph, because he looks after children, and St. Francis, who is in charge of animals, and Mary, who looks out for mothers.

Soon I will have to help the girls get all the loaves into the cases, start the coffee, write the specials of the day on my neon and black board.

I am still standing there when Katie slams outside. "Where's Merlin?" she demands, her voice already certain that he is gone. "Where is he?"

Taking a breath, I turn to her. "He jumped the fence, running after a squirrel."

Her fists clench. "Is he dead?"

"No! I chased him as long as I could, but he's running the neighborhood. When the Humane Society opens, we'll call and they'll pick him up if they see him."

"How could you?" she cries. Tears are running down her face. "I trusted you with him!"

I expected this, but it's still terrible. "Katie, I was standing right there, and he jumped so high—he cleared the fence in the backyard. We'll have to figure out a way to keep him in."

"I hate you," she says without energy, shaking her head. "I. Hate. You. He was all I had left."

"He's not dead, Katie. He just ran off. We'll find him." I say it aloud as if to bring weight to my desire, as if speaking it so firmly will make it so. I skitter away from the idea of Colorado Avenue, a busy street, and from the idea that if he was wandering on the railroad tracks when Katie found him, maybe he's just a hobo of a dog and we'll never see him again. "We will find him."

Her shoulders sag. "Things don't work out like that for me." She bows her head and opens the door, and I can't stand the sight of her shoulder blades sticking out like folded wings from her back. Leaping up the steps, I put my arms around her, hugging her from behind. "I'm so sorry, Katie."

For one long minute she allows it, then she flings my arms away from her and goes inside.

Now what? I think. But the bread is waiting to be sliced. Customers are even now walking toward us.

For me, always, there is the bread. Which has saved my life more than once.

Ingredients

Before the advent of commercial yeasts, bakers could make a fresh loaf of bread each day only by relying on the levains *and starters they had been keeping according to their traditions. Some of those starters were stiff and required a good deal of water and work to release their essence into the day's mix of flour and water and salt; others were as soft as breasts, divided from the dough of the day before and left in a warm place overnight.*

In some villages, making bread was seen as such a sensual act that only the most devout could perform the task without falling to sin; in others, the bakers were required to go to confession before they baked each day, in order to avoid polluting those who would eat the bread with their desires and failings.

There are many traditions, many flours, many forms, but all have in common their power to seed the fresh ingredients of the new day, to make a ball of flat ordinary powder grow as tall and plump as a mother's belly. Out of such simple ingredients—only flour and salt and wild yeast and fresh water—comes the miraculous holiness of bread.

THIRTEEN

Ramona at Fifteen

The first time bread saved my life, I was fifteen and six months pregnant. I'd hidden the belly as long as I could, petitioning every saint I thought might help to make something happen—not make me lose it, because that would be a sin, but make my period come like it should. I looked up herbal remedies at the library but never could bring myself to try them. No matter how little I liked church, a mortal sin was slightly more terrifying than having a baby out of wedlock.

My mother drove me to my aunt Poppy's in her Pontiac in early June, the day after school got out for the summer. We didn't talk much. She smoked one cigarette after another, L&M Menthol 100's with white filters and a green pack. I rolled the window down every time, but it still made me sick to my stomach, and I leaned on the door frame, feeling the rattle in my teeth. At least nobody smoked at Poppy's house. She'd quit years and years ago.

Poppy, my mother's older sister, lived in a tiny spit of a town between Castle Rock and Denver on the old Littleton highway. I had stayed there many times, loving the freedom of her childless household, the relaxed rules, her bohemian decorations from her travels—statues of elephants and strings of bells and the tapestries she had on the walls. We made trips to Cinderella

City, a big mall in Englewood, and played miniature golf in Castle Rock in the cricket-y coolness of summer nights.

But I couldn't imagine staying there all summer, all by myself, away from my friends and my sisters and my bedroom and my cats. My mother was so angry she'd hardly spoken directly to me since the day she stopped me in the kitchen, put her hand on the belly I was trying so hard to hide, and said, "Oh, Ramona, what have you done?"

We left the interstate at Castle Rock, where Poppy would sometimes bring me to shop at Russ' Drug, have lunch at the B&B Café, and pick up supplies at the single tiny grocery store with its wooden floors and musty smell. A butcher chopped meat at the back, his white apron bloodstained. It made me want to never eat meat again, but Poppy said he was a good butcher and that was worth a lot. There were a few other things in town. A record store, an old-fashioned dress shop—which never had a single customer, that I could tell—and a library in an old school.

Eight miles west of Castle Rock was Sedalia, which wasn't even really a town. There was a gas station and a café on the corner, which was often filled with rough characters, bikers and the like. Before that summer, I wasn't allowed to go there on my own.

From Johnson's Corner, you turned left on the highway, traveled down a handful of small blocks with old houses on them, and then finally came to Poppy's place, which was two stories tall and ancient, with big fields around it. She had a party line— her ring was one long, one short, so you had to listen to find out who was getting phone calls—and I loved thinking of people talking about all kinds of things, right through the phone next to me, while we ate supper or drank our tea or made bread. I sometimes tried to eavesdrop, but the talkers always seemed to hear me pick up the phone, so I'd have to apologize and say I was just going to make a call.

As my mother and I drove up the gravel path to the kitchen door, Poppy came out on the porch. I could tell she was a little sad. Shame pressed down on me again, heavier by far than the belly I'd been hiding. She was short and round, with long hippie hair and a skirt made of India cotton swirling around her legs. She wasn't wearing a bra, and it shocked me; I didn't know any grown women who ever came out of the house without a bra, and she had rather a lot of chest.

A wave of resistance crushed me. "Mom, why can't I stay home?"

"Because," she said. "It's bad for your siblings to see you pregnant. You're the oldest. You're supposed to be a good example."

I wanted to cry. Beg. *It was only one time!* I wanted to say. *Once!* How was I supposed to know?

My mother nudged me, and I climbed out of the car. Behind me, she grabbed my bag and slammed the door closed. "Hello!" she called to her sister. "We made it at last."

"I'm so glad to see you," Poppy said, looking right at me, smiling. She came down the steps and put her arms around me, kissed my cheek. I allowed it, but her breasts squished into my chest, and it was embarrassing. She quickly moved away, only patting my arm.

My mother hugged her with more exuberance, and they rocked back and forth, both of them with closed eyes, as if they were absorbing some magic thing from each other. They were sisters and often seemed at odds to me. Everything about them was different—my mother in her slacks and short hair streaked elegantly, so that it seemed to match the liquid gold jewelry she was so fond of. Unlike Poppy, Lily was always tanned and slim and put on her makeup.

Poppy had run off to India after college in the sixties and spent six years traveling in Europe and even Africa, working when she needed to. She had cooked a thousand kinds of food all around the world, which gave her kitchen an exotic smell.

"How about a grilled cheese sandwich?" Poppy asked when my mother drove away. "I've got to get moving on my sourdough or put it back in the fridge."

"I guess."

She drew me into her kitchen, a room with big windows pouring sunlight into the sink and splashing it onto the table. A collection of blue bottles, large and small, was lined up on the windowsill. Sandwiched between them were small clay pots filled with herbs. When the sun was on them, like now, they made the air smell like root beer and Thanksgiving morning. A rotary fan sat atop the fridge, moving the air around over our heads. Poppy poured me a glass of sweet iced tea with pieces of mint from her garden floating in it.

"You can help me make the bread." She took a jar filled with a noxious-looking substance off the counter. The lower half was a thick gray pillow, looking like some fungus you'd find on Mars. Poppy shook it up cheerfully, then opened it. A strong earthy smell exploded into the air.

I wasn't sure if I liked it or not and put my hand up to my nose, just in case my stomach decided it was time to throw up. But my stomach stayed stable, and I leaned closer. "What is that?"

Poppy held it up to the light. "Magic."

"What kind of magic?"

"It's my own sourdough starter. I've been working on it for months, and I think it's finally getting where I want it to be."

"Grandma has a sourdough starter. She makes biscuits with it."

"Yes, that's from the Callahan side of the family. It's got quite a history." Her mouth went into a straight line. "This one is my own."

"Oh." I sank down at the table, feeling as if my legs had turned into rubber bands. "I'm really hungry."

"Sorry, baby. Let me get you some lunch."

By the time we ate sandwiches and oranges, I was nodding off at the table, and Poppy sent me upstairs to what would be my bedroom for the duration. Her room occupied the front half of the second floor, a wide-open space with a balcony overlooking the train tracks and pale grassy fields rolling toward the burly mountains. My room was in the back, tucked under the eaves, but there was a circular staircase that led to the widow's walk on the roof. One wall of my room was lined with bookcases packed with books, all kinds of books, standing straight up and stuffed in sideways and piled in stacks on the floor. I ran my fingers over them. At least I would have time to read.

The room was stuffy, so I opened the window and the old-fashioned metal blinds, then curled up on the bed. A breeze moved into the room, carrying a faint perfume of roses. I closed my eyes, like Dorothy from *The Wizard of Oz,* and tried to wish myself home.

But I didn't have any ruby slippers, and I couldn't go to sleep, either. Instead, I lay there with my heart feeling like a boulder, wishing I could go back in time, back to last summer when my dad finally let me be a busgirl at the Erin Steakhouse, our main restaurant. It was so much fun. I loved wearing my uniform of black pants and white shirt and little emerald bow tie. It was an ugly uniform, not like the waitress dresses, which were classy but definitely low cut. Not as if I had anything much to put in a neckline like that—I hadn't even had my period for very long, only since May, though it was regular right away.

Too bad.

The baby shoved my lungs up into my throat, and I had to turn over on my other side so I could breathe. Thinking about last summer, so different from this one, made me want to cry again. That was all I wanted, to go back to work at the steakhouse. Or maybe this summer I would have worked at the café out near the Pikes Peak highway, where they sold saltwater taffy in rainbow colors and chicken-fried steaks and zillions of root beer floats to tourists who were going and coming from the top of America's Mountain.

I liked the steakhouse better. One of my jobs was to get the dining room ready, shaking out fresh green table covers over the snowy-white base layer we left on all the time. There were single carnations with their ruffled edges and sharp peppermint scent in crystal vases, so I had to go around and check them, replacing the ones that were getting spotty or brown or droopy. I made sure the table settings were perfect, with pointy napkins sitting in the middle of each place, along with two forks, a steak knife and a butter knife, one spoon to the right of the place, one at the top. The last thing we would do was light all the candles and turn the lamps in the dining room down low.

It was luxe, as my dad always said. He was famous around town for his genius with his restaurant, for his big gestures, his elegant suits that my mom picked out when they went up to Denver twice a year, and his thick, wavy black hair. Everyone liked coming to the Erin Steakhouse, especially for celebrations. We got super-busy on prom nights, when the girls came in with long dresses and corsages, and when parents came in for the graduation at the Air Force Academy, but it was always bustling.

And I loved being in the middle of it. Pouring glasses of water, taking out the giant bowls of shrimp on ice that was the appetizer of choice that summer, making sure the tables were cleared, then reset perfectly. I made tips to supplement the low hourly pay, and together they were enough that I could start putting a little away in a savings account every week.

Now my sister Steph had my job, and I was stuck up in Sedalia with nothing to do but read and wait until I turned into a watermelon.

Curled into a comma on my aunt Poppy's guest bed, I squeezed my eyes tight and put myself back there, last summer.

When I was happy.

Before.

Poppy woke me after dark. "C'mon, sweetie, it's time to get up and have some supper. It's past seven."

Yanked from the faraway world of Nod, I blinked. "I'm not hungry."

"You need to eat." Poppy patted my thigh and stood. "The baby needs to eat."

I closed my eyes, lured back into thick darkness. "Okay. In a minute."

Sometime later she returned. "Ramona, you need to get up now."

I waved her away, tucked myself deeper into the covers. In the depths of my brain, this time didn't exist. My dreams were about school, about my friends, about learning the restaurant business.

After a minute Poppy went away.

In the middle of the night, I got up to pee for about seven years. My mouth was dry, and I bent over the sink to drink from the faucet; then, keeping my eyes half closed so I wouldn't wake up too much, I went back to bed.

That time it was harder, but I got back to sleep.

Until Poppy came in again. I felt her sink down on the side of the bed. "It's morning. You have to get up."

"Leave me alone." I pulled the pillow over my head. Deep in my belly, a gurgle sounded.

Poppy took the pillow from my face. "Now."

I rolled over, belly mounding higher than my breasts, and stared at her. Her hair fell down her back untidily, and she wore an old sweatshirt and jeans. She still didn't have a bra on, and everything about her seemed like a warning—her eccentricities, her husbandlessness, her offbeat everything.

I missed my mother, with her delicate jewelry and crisply ironed slacks. Acutely. "I want to go home."

"I know. But you can't." She held out her hand. "Sit up."

I flung my feet over the edge of the bed and creaked upright. Poppy put her hand on my shoulder. "Every now and then, life throws you something you'd never have chosen in a million years. I know that's how you feel right now."

Bowing my head, I dug my nails into my palms. I would not cry again. Not again.

"You don't have to be happy, Ramona. You just have to live through it. I promise that you are not going to be pregnant and fifteen forever."

"It seems like it."

Her hand moved in that comforting circle around my upper back. "I know. One day at a time, all right?"

A breath moved against my heart at that. I raised my head. Nodded. "I guess I am hungry."

"I imagine you are." She pushed me upright. "Let's go get you and that baby some food, then, shall we?"

The days fell into a pattern very quickly. Poppy had a business out of her home, part farm stand, part bakery. In the mornings she worked in the garden, and she insisted I help, pointing out that staying busy would make time go faster.

She awakened me at five every morning. We ate breakfast together—some herbal tea and toast, or fruit and cereal—while she made up her lists for the day. Then we headed outside in the still-cool air to weed the half-acre plot, accompanied by a couple of her menagerie of pets, all rescues of one sort or another. There was a three-legged German shepherd, a fat gray tabby with eyes like green marbles, an absolutely ancient weepy-eyed little mutt we speculated must be part poodle and maybe shih tzu or Lhasa apso or something. An aloof husky sometimes graced us with her attention, and a handful of barn cats warily approached only if we had something particularly interesting, though they did like to leave dead rodents on the back porch.

"Knock wood, this is going to be a great year for corn," Poppy said one morning not long after I arrived. The little plants were nearly a foot high, and Poppy carefully tugged bindweed from between them.

I knelt beside the squashes, pinching out a dark-leaved succulent that seemed to have roots all the way to the molten center of the earth. "How do you know?"

"Experience, I guess. Hot days, cool nights—that's what corn likes. And peaches, too." She pointed with a spade to a tree draped with netting. "I'll make peach butter this year, and you can take some home to eat all winter."

I grunted. Winter seemed like another world, a lifetime I'd never see. Finishing with the squash, I stood up. "Do you want me to weed between the tomatoes?"

"In a minute. First I want to show you how to tie them up."

She came down the row to me. After the first day, she always wore a bra, though I'm not sure how she knew it bugged me when she didn't. Right now her hair and clothes seemed to make sense—jeans and a sweatshirt, her hair pulled back in a braid to keep it out of her way. Over everything, she wore a colorful bibbed apron with a bunch of pockets, and out of one she took a bundle of long twist ties. She handed them to me and pulled off her gloves.

"Tomatoes like three things," she said, picking up a branch covered with flowers that was trailing toward the earth. "Sunshine, plenty of water, and lots of support." There was a metalgridwork thing around each plant. Poppy used twist ties to attach the branches to the cage. "You try," she said, pointing to the next one. Like it was some super-hard thing to do.

I followed her example, gently tugging a branch over the top of one square of the cage to let the bar support it, then loosely twisting a tie around it to hold it in place.

"Good."

"It's not rocket science."

She grinned. "True. But it matters to do it right." She took the new branch in her hand. "The next thing we do with tomatoes is pinch off some of the blossoms, to get better size on the tomatoes that do grow. Just let one on each cluster stay."

Now, this appealed to me. I walked along the row, looking for flower clusters, and I thought of my grandmother Adelaide, Poppy's mother. "Did Grandma teach you to garden?"

Poppy didn't answer for a minute. "Grandma grows flowers," she said, in a tone of voice that said it was something shameful. "I like to grow things that matter."

"Flowers matter." I thought of my grandmother's irises, which had been blooming a couple of weeks before. Big ruffled flowers on tall stems in colors that reminded me of old-fashioned long dresses—salmon and purple and velvety brown and pale pink. "Her garden makes me think of a ball, with all the princesses dancing."

Poppy stood and raised her eyebrows. "Great imagery, kid."

"Thanks." I moved to the next plant in the group. Two small green knobs of tomato were growing side by side. "What do you do when there are already tomatoes instead of flowers?"

"Pinch one off."

I gave her an exaggerated frown. "But they're so cute!"

"Neither will get enough of what it needs if you leave them both."

With a pang, I chopped one away, let it fall on the ground. "Why don't you talk to Grandma?"

The war had been going on as long as I could remember. Poppy came to our house, and we came here, but Adelaide never showed up at Poppy's, and Poppy never came to celebrations at my grandmother's house. On Christmas Eve, she came to our house to exchange presents and eat fondue, but Christmas Day was always at my grandmother's big Victorian on the Westside of Colorado Springs, and Poppy never came there. Not once in all my life could I remember them being in the same room.

Poppy brushed her palms together. "Sometimes even when someone is your family, you don't get along."

"I get along with everybody."

"Yeah. I hope you always do."

I realized my statement was a lie. "I guess I don't get along with everyone right now, though, do I? My mom is mad at me. *Really* mad at me. She hardly talked to me at all for the last three weeks and didn't say a single thing to me on the way here."

"Oh, honey." Poppy moved toward me as if she would hug me, and I stepped back, putting up a hand to keep her away. She stopped. "Your mom is just sad for you. Someday you'll understand."

"If she's so sad, don't you think she could be nicer? That she would understand that I'm really sorry? That it isn't helping to send me away from everybody for the whole summer?"

"She's doing what she thinks is best for you and the family, sweetheart."

I bowed my head, kicked at a clump of dirt. "Well, I hate it." Some heated thing blistered through my chest. "Did something like this happen with you and Grandma? Is that why you never talk?"

"No," she said with emphasis. "It was nothing like this." She took a breath, looked over the garden. "Let's just say that your grandma is a different person now than she was when my father was alive. Your grandma is not the same person who was my mother."

"What do you mean?"

"I don't want to get into details, Ramona. You have a good relationship with Adelaide, and she's good for you. She wasn't always good for your mom and me."

"So, what, you never forgave her? My mom gets along with her."

"Does she?"

At first I thought it was a real question, then I realized the tone of voice said something completely different. I met her eyes, thinking of my mother and her mother in a room together, a wall of icy politeness between them at all times. "Oh."

"Let's drop this, Ramona. Let it go." She waved me out of the garden behind her. "I need to go to town this morning. Let's have lunch at the B&B Café, shall we?"

"Yes! Can we go to the record store?"

"You can. I've got some errands to run."

I'd been to the B&B with Poppy ten million times. Old men sat at the counter with knobby hands curled around heavy white coffee cups, their cowboy hats and baseball caps and coats still firmly in place. At the tables sat the other customers—church sisters having a sweet roll and a cup of coffee, couples who'd come in to town to go to the grocery store, a sprinkling of men in suits who were the accountants and bankers and lawyers in town. Everybody was always nice. They all gave a nod, and a lot of them recognized me even though I didn't live there but only came in with Poppy.

What I had never done was go in anywhere pregnant. Until my mom found out, I'd been hiding it pretty well, so nobody suspected. After my mom put her hand on my belly that day, it was like the baby grew triple-time, stretching and unfolding like one of my grandmother's irises. Almost overnight, I was huge. Truly, honestly, obviously pregnant.

And this was the first time I was in public. This was the first time I realized that everybody was staring at me, and not in a good way. They looked at my belly, up to my face, and then looked at one another with tight mouths or rolled eyes. I felt as if somebody had written *SLUT SLUT SLUT* right over the middle of my body in Day-Glo orange letters.

"I can't do this," I said to Poppy, and turned around to leave. Her hand on my waist pushed me back into the room.

"Yes, you can. Hold your head up," she said in my ear. "Look right through them and take that seat there."

Ears and face burning, I plopped down, hearing the hiss of whispers start up around us. My hands fell in my lap, below my big belly, and I jerked them up and put them on the table, scooting as close as I could. I didn't look at anybody.

"How are you, Poppy?" the waitress said, putting menus down in front of us.

"I'm well, Marie. You remember my niece Ramona, don't you?"

"I do. How are you, sweetie?"

I kept my head down. "Fine."

"Bring me some coffee, Marie, and an orange juice for my niece."

My ears were buzzing. My throat felt like it would close completely, and when I glanced out of the corner of my eye, one of the old men at the counter gave me a sour look. "Aunt Poppy, can we please just go?"

"Absolutely not," she said in a calm voice. "And after this, we're going shopping."

"Please—"

"Look at me, Ramona."

I raised miserable eyes, hoping she would see that I would die—die—if I didn't get out of here.

"Where do you think the father of that baby is now?" she asked so quietly no one else could hear.

"I don't know."

"Maybe at work, maybe at school? Maybe hanging out with his friends?"

"I guess."

"Probably nobody is making him feel like you do, even though he did exactly the same thing you did. Right?"

I shrugged. "Right."

"You are not a bad person. You're just pregnant. It's natural. It happens all the time, and you are not going to hang your head, got it?"

A little of the heat drained out of my cheeks. I nodded.

"Sit up straight," she said. "Head up. Stare back if anybody stares at you. Got it?"

"I'll try."

She winked. "Good girl." She picked up her menu, then peeked around it. "Have I mentioned today that I'm so glad to have you spending the summer with me? I love you."

I picked up my spine and my chin and my menu. "I love you, too, Aunt Poppy. Really a lot."

FOURTEEN

After lunch, Aunt Poppy had to go to the bank and to see a shut-in. She gave me a twenty-dollar bill from the stash my mother left for me and said, "Walk all over downtown like it belongs to you, and I want you to spend every penny of that money, in three different stores. Got it?"

It made me feel sick to my stomach, but I said, "Okay."

The café was across the street from the courthouse, which had a domed roof. Some people sat on the benches under big trees, and others hurried as if they had some important reason to go inside, maybe to get somebody out of jail or maybe only to get some new license plates. I liked a drugstore around the corner from the courthouse, because it had a bunch of art supplies and notebooks and lip glosses. That would mean crossing the street in full view of all those people and parading right down the whole block.

Hold your head up.

I stood on the sidewalk in the shade, eyeing the bright sunshine across the street. Pickup trucks passed by. A young guy leaned out the passenger window of one of them. "Hey, mama!"

I blushed and marched like a nutcracker, all stiff and sober, down the street in the other direction. I didn't know where I was going. Off the street, out of sight, at least until I could get my courage up again.

Then I heard Aunt Poppy's voice in my head. *Walk all over downtown like it belongs to you.* I straightened up and tried to walk naturally—as naturally as a person could, anyway, with that weight right there in the middle of me. I passed by the dry cleaner's and smelled the starch and scorch of the irons and by the narrow drugstore that always seemed to only stock things for old people—denture creams and elastic bandages and canes. An old man came out of the door as I was going by; he glanced at me but didn't seem to notice or care about my belly, so I kept walking. At the end of the block, I'd cross the street and go around the courthouse on this side, which wasn't as busy, then go to Russ' Drug.

I couldn't really think of anywhere else to stop before that. I wanted to save something for the record store. So I walked down the sidewalk like I belonged there and then turned to cross the street. Traffic was steady enough that I couldn't just dash across—you might not think a little town like that could have so many vehicles, but everybody has to drive on the same street—and I was standing in the sun. A trickle of sweat came out from under my hair and ran down the back of my neck. The baby kicked me, as if he was getting cranky in the heat.

A truck slowed down in front of me and stopped right there, in the middle of the street. It was the same guy who'd yelled at me a few minutes ago. He was way older. The truck bed had a lot of construction tools in it, wheelbarrows and shovels and dusty tarps, and the guy looked as if he'd been working hard. He had light-blue eyes and long hair, and I took one step back.

"What's your name, honey?"

I shook my head, checked to my left as if I was getting ready to cross the street.

"You're not from around here," he said. "I'd remember that hair. You're as pretty as a little angel."

I turned away, ignoring him, hoping for some help from an adult who would tell him to move along. Nobody was around.

"C'mon, sweetie, I won't bite," he said. "My name is Jason. What's yours?"

Finally somebody behind the truck honked. "See you around," the guy said, and pulled away. He hung his head out the window like a dog pretending he couldn't stop staring at me.

The person who'd honked was a woman in a nurse's uniform. She waved for me to cross the street, and I waved back, thanking her, then hurried across.

I made it to Russ' Drug without any more trouble. The air-conditioning felt good after the hot sun outside, and I had twenty whole dollars to spend. There were some people in the store, but I pretended I didn't see any of them, that I was completely invisible, and headed for the stationery aisle.

There were all kinds of things I liked here. Mechanical pencils with their fine, perfect line; labels for jars and file folders; paper for every use—onionskin for typing, Big Chief tablets, spiral notebooks, and, my favorite, sketch pads, which I somehow used only when I was at Aunt Poppy's house. There was something about the place that made me want to draw. Even now I was thinking about the blue bottles and plants on her kitchen window. It seemed like something that would make me feel better, drawing or maybe painting that. I gathered a sketchbook and mechanical pencil and was dithering between the watercolors or pastel crayons when the pharmacist in his white coat came down the aisle. "Can I help you with something?" he said.

"No, thank you," I said politely. "I'm just thinking."

He didn't go away.

"Is there something wrong?"

"Somebody thought you might be shoplifting."

My face burned bright red, all the way up past my eyebrows and around the edges of my ears. "Why? Because I'm pregnant and that makes me a criminal?"

"Now, now, there's no reason to get all excited. Why don't you show me what's in your pockets and we'll be fine."

For a long, hot second, I stared at him, sure it was a mistake. "I come in here all the time with my aunt Poppy. Don't you remember me?"

"'Fraid not." He shifted, folded his hands one atop the other like a deacon. Waiting.

Fighting very hard not to cry, I put back the sketch pad and the pencils. Deliberately, I pulled my pockets inside out, displaying the twenty dollars and a tube of Chapstick. Before he could ask, I pulled the lid off to show it was used. "I've had this."

"Okay, then, we're square. You want to come up to the front, I'll ring those up for you when you're ready."

He walked off calmly. The devil girl inside me shoved everything off the shelf and left it on the floor for him to pick up. I saw it in my mind's eye over and over, twenty times while I stood there, smarting and stinging, with my pockets hanging out beneath my belly and a twenty-dollar bill in my right hand.

The real me tucked my pockets back in, put away my money, and left the store. *I hate you, I hate you, I hate you,* I chanted in my mind. And I didn't mean the pharmacist.

I meant Armando, who didn't even know he'd done this to me. And probably wouldn't care if he did.

Out on the street, I considered trying to find Poppy and clinging to her until it was time to go home. If I told her what had happened, she would be sympathetic.

But the record store was only two doors down, and I had the whole twenty to spend now that I wouldn't buy anything from that guy, not even a fire extinguisher to put myself out if I was on fire. I wanted the art supplies, but maybe we could get them somewhere else, or we might go to Cinderella City one of these days. They at least had a Walgreens there.

I walked to Blue Fish Record Store. It had been there since the hippie days, and looked it, with dusty paisley curtains and a giant jade plant in the window. A yellow cat sunned himself on the windowsill, and I stopped to pet him. He blinked and started purring. "Aren't you hot, cat?" I asked.

"Cats never get too hot," a voice said behind me.

Warily, I turned around. The guy behind the counter was maybe college age, with hair that was long and dark brown, pulled back from his face into a ponytail, like an artist or something. He said, "They're desert animals."

He had a very calming voice. Or maybe it was the music, which was some kind of flutes and drums or something. The air smelled like cinnamon and coffee. "I didn't know that," I said, and then I remembered. "Oh, yeah, like Egypt. They were really a big deal in Egypt."

His smile was kind. "Right." He was writing on file cards, drinking out of a big ruby-colored cup. "You looking for something in particular this afternoon or just in to browse?"

I shrugged. "Browse, I guess."

"I'll leave you alone, then. If you want some help, I'm here, okay?" His eyes were direct, and for the first time all day, I felt as if somebody saw *me* instead of my belly.

"Thanks." I wandered around the bins, flipping through the albums for something I recognized. My dad was a big music fan. He collected records from the fifties and sixties, all kinds of rhythm and blues and rock. I saw covers I recognized—Cream and the Rolling Stones and Albert King.

"You like Cream?" the guy asked.

I didn't know if it would be cool or not cool, but my dad was always saying that Eric Clapton was the best guitarist in the history of the world. But being cool hadn't really gotten me very much, so I told the truth. "They're okay, I guess. My dad likes Clapton."

"How about you? What do you like?"

I lifted a shoulder. Now that I was a few steps closer, I could see his eyes were the color of honey, very clear light brown, and he had that way about him that said he'd been other places besides this. A quietness, a clean and generous curiosity. He was probably a music fanatic if he worked in a record store. "I don't know," I said finally, again telling the truth. "Everybody tells me what I should like."

Something shifted in his face at that. "That's how the world is sometimes." His voice was great—not deep but echoey, kind of, as if it came out of the body of a cello, which I'd played for a couple of years. "What's your favorite record?"

Here was where I should say the Rolling Stones or the Clash or somebody cool, but that would be a lie. I shook my hair out of my eyes. "I don't think I can pick a favorite. I love Cyndi Lauper and Annie Lennox." I lifted a shoulder. "And I really love Bruce Springsteen, and..." I thought about it. "Prince."

His lips turned down at the corners as he nodded. "You have good taste." He smiled, giving me a little wink. "Maybe not Prince, but the others." He sucked his lower lip into his mouth, his hands turned backward on his legs, and he narrowed his eyes. He was skinny, with shoulders like a shelf. His shirt was a cream color with thin purple stripes. The sleeves were rolled up on his forearms. "How about Stevie Ray Vaughan? Ever listen to him? Elvis Costello?"

"I don't think so."

He came around from behind the counter and went down the aisle across from me. He was old, like maybe even twenty-three or so, but I still felt something funny circling around my spine, like iron shavings standing up all ruffled and alert. I pretended to flip through the records on my side, but I couldn't have told you one thing in there.

"Here," he said, and handed me an album. "You can take this home and listen to it, see if you like it." Then he pulled it to his chest. "You do live around here, right? You're not just driving through on your way to Texas?"

"I'm living with my aunt this summer." Almost without my permission, my hands pointed to my belly.

"Exiled, are you?" He said it with a twinkle in his eye, so I could smile back. For the first time all day, I felt like a normal person. I nodded, as if we were conspirators.

"Well, you take that with you, and come in next week and tell me what you think."

I looked at the cover. Stevie Ray Vaughan. "Really?"

"Trust me." He grinned with one side of his mouth and gestured to the empty shop. "I don't think any of the customers will miss it."

"I have to ask my aunt when we're coming back."

"Okay." The phone rang and he headed to the front. "Who's your aunt?"

"Poppy Callahan."

"I know Poppy. She's good people."

I never liked that expression, and it took some of the sheen off his glow. "Yeah."

He answered the phone and I returned to browsing, wondering what I could possibly get now that I had a Stevie Ray Vaughan album in my hand. What could I pick that wouldn't make me look like a little girl? I flipped through the stacks, looking at the Cure and U2 and the other bands I knew the alternative kids liked, but what I really wanted was Madonna. And some voice said, *But he might think you're an idiot.*

I thought of my aunt, telling me to sit up straight at the diner. I took the Madonna album up to the register, thinking only as I got there about "Like a Virgin." Which I wasn't anymore, but that's not what the song is about exactly.

The guy was still talking on the phone. By the way he was writing on a piece of paper, I thought he was taking an order or something. He repeated some names and prices back into the phone, spied me at the counter, and held up a hand, making a face to show that the person was talking and talking.

It wasn't until he came over to ring me up that I saw his left hand was deformed. No, not deformed—messed up, like from an accident or something. The first two fingers were mostly stubs, and the remaining ring and pinkie fingers looked as if they had been shaved. I stared, shocked, then realized I was doing the same thing everybody did to me. And he hadn't!

"I cut them off with a power saw last summer," he said matter-of-factly.

"Sorry, I didn't mean to stare. Everybody has been staring right at my stomach, so I know how it feels." I couldn't look at him.

"Hey, don't worry about it." He took the album off the counter. "What's your name, anyway?"

"Ramona."

He chuckled, the sound low and rich. "I'm Jonah. We rhyme."

It made me laugh, and again that mortification faded. I tried to think of something to say so we could keep talking but couldn't come up with anything.

He looked at the handwritten label on the front of the album and wrote the numbers on a notebook page with a carbon beneath it. I noticed he had perfectly arched eyebrows, dark brown, and they gave his face an elegance. Music played, something wistful with heavy, slow drums. He was quiet, focused on his task.

"What's your favorite album?" I asked suddenly. "You must know a lot of music, working in a music store."

"That I do," he said. His face looked sad—sad enough to cry. "I'll save that story for another day." The bell dinged on the door behind me. "There's your aunt."

"Hello, Jonah!" she sang out. "I see you've met my niece."

"We've been talking music."

"Did you get my order?" Poppy asked. "The Doors?"

He shook his head. "Next week, probably."

"Good enough. I'll bring you some bread."

"I'd like that."

"You ready to go, my beauty?" Poppy asked me.

I nodded. "But I haven't spent all the money."

She put her arm around me. "It's all right. Let's go home and have a nap, shall we?"

On the way out, I waved to Jonah. He lifted his chin and sat back down at his table with his ruined hand.

After we came in from gardening a few days later, Poppy said, "I have to bake. I could use your help."

"I was going to read." I was reading *Mistral's Daughter* for the third time. It never got old, and I'd just started again, so I was in the part where the first woman was an artist's model in Paris. It was very romantic. It made me want to go to Paris and drink absinthe, whatever that was.

"Well, I really need some help, and you're what I've got. You can bake this morning, then read later. Besides, it's good for you."

"Why? You can buy bread in the grocery store. Twenty kinds!"

"None of it tastes like the bread made with your grand-mother's sourdough starter." She plunked a jar of the foamy, smelly stuff on the table. "This has been in the family for more than a hundred years."

"I thought you didn't use hers."

"Of course I do. But I like to experiment with my own, too."

I turned the bottle around and around. "How can it last that long?"

"A mother dough like this can last for decades. Maybe even centuries. This one was carried from Ireland to Buffalo to the Wild, Wild West."

I'd heard bits and pieces of the story from my grandmother. The starter was handed down from mother to daughter, generation after generation. "I don't get how it keeps from getting spoiled."

She scooped out a hefty measure of foamy pale-yellow-white starter and put it in a bowl. "Because," she said, "we refresh it every week so it stays healthy." She turned on the tap, testing the temperature with her fingers. "We add water that's just barely warmer than your fingers." When she got it right, she gestured. "Try it."

I stuck my fingers under the stream. The water was the most bland temperature possible. Poppy filled a glass measuring cup and stirred it into the jar of starter. It foamed up.

"That's kinda cool," I said. "Like a chemistry experiment."

Poppy gave me a half grin. "That's exactly what it is. The yeasts are alive and hungry."

"Do you have to have an old starter to make it work?"

"Not at all. Remember the one I was working on the first day? That's new. I started it." She beat a cup of flour into the mix, then scraped the sides of the container and poured the mass into a waiting clean quart jar, the kind you put peaches in. With a rubber band, she fastened a circle of cheesecloth over the mouth of the jar. "It needs to breathe," she explained, "and a little time to grow. This evening I'll put it back in the fridge."

I bent over and inhaled the tangy scent of the starter in the bowl. "What am I doing to help, then? Mixing the bread?"

"I'll let you work with the sourdough later, but for now let's get some regular yeast breads going. Has your mother taught you any baking at all?"

"My mom? You're kidding, right?" My mother considered cooking to be the devil's way of keeping women chained to the home. Since my dad ran restaurants, she didn't have to cook, and she didn't. Ever. "I can't think of a single thing my mom knows how to cook."

"Oh, she knows. She just chooses not to. First step: Wash your hands thoroughly with soap and dry them on a clean towel." She handed me one. "I keep the thin white towels for the bread and the colored terry cloth for hands."

I followed instructions, watching as Poppy assembled ingredients on the big butcher-block island, which was as old as the house. Bags of flour, white and whole wheat and rye; salt and baking powder and yeast; oil and butter and eggs. "Your grandmother taught us both to cook. Your mother was very good, but she doesn't like it."

The phone rang, and we paused to see who it would be for. *Ring-ring! Ring-ring!* I thought of another kitchen, maybe down the block, maybe way down the road, and a woman picking it up. So weird. They were having a conversation right there.

I said, "My mom says that women shouldn't do housework or cooking, that we need careers so we can be independent."

"It's good to have your own money, work you love," Poppy agreed. "And if you don't like to cook, you certainly don't have to in today's world. But I don't think there's anything wrong with the traditional female arts, either. They're beautiful." She measured out a cup of white flour and poured it over the starter. "Stir that in."

Pleased, I used the sturdy wooden spoon and stirred the flour into the heady sponge, releasing the scent into the air. Poppy turned on the radio, and when "Glory Days" came on, we wiggled our hips. As we cooked and listened to the radio and talked, I was the happiest I'd been in ages.

So, naturally, God had to ruin it. A car came into the driveway, tires crunching over the gravel, and I felt Poppy shift. She gave a hard pat to the dough beneath her hands and wiped her palms on her apron. A woman came to the back door and knocked, even though she could see us looking at her through the screen. "Hello," she called out. "I'm Nancy."

Poppy rushed over to push the screen door open and let in a

woman made of long rectangles—long face, square shoulders, big rectangular hands. Her eyes were big and bright blue beneath hair cut so short it almost looked like a military cut. "Nancy, I'm so happy to meet you in person! Come in, come in!" With a rare fluttering breathlessness, Poppy waved at me. "This is my niece Ramona. Obviously she's the pregnant one, not me."

I frowned at Poppy, whose cheeks were bright red. Nancy smiled down kindly at her—way, way down, because she was very tall, and not just tall for a woman. She took Poppy's hand between both of hers and said, "I'm glad to meet you finally."

"It feels like we've been talking for ages off and on, doesn't it?"

Nancy still stood there for a minute, smiling like a statue of a saint, holding Poppy's hands. Then she turned to look at the counter. "Sourdough?" she asked, lifting the towel over the bowl to sniff. "Mmm! Magnificent!"

"It's my grandma's mother dough," I said, showing off what I had learned.

"No kidding." She inhaled again, deeply, then pointed at the jar with its foamy mass bubbling against the glass. "May I?" she asked Poppy.

"Of course!" She relaxed a little. "You look like you know your way around bread."

"I ran away to Paris as a young woman. Ended up in a *boulangerie* for a couple of years. The baker was old-fashioned, baked everything with traditional *levains*. It was a lot of work, but the bread was fantastic."

Poppy inclined her head. "I've experimented with the old-style starters, but, as you say, it's a lot of work, and most people wouldn't appreciate the subtle differences."

Feeling left out, I said, "What is that? A *levain*?"

"It's a starter," Poppy said. "Some are very stiff and intense. You really need a heavy mixer to work with them, and the risings are very long. It can take a couple of days to go from mixing to baking."

"Days?"

Nancy smiled at me. "It's worth it. There's a bakery in Denver that sells old-world breads. I'll bring some down next time I come and you can taste it."

The baby kicked me in the kidney, hard, and I said, "Ulp!" and slapped a palm to the place, rubbing, then rubbing in front. It seemed like sometimes the baby would move a bit if I rubbed his back. Her back. Whatever.

It. Its back.

Nancy gave me a smile—not all toothy and false but calm and easy. I thought again of the statues of saints at our church; the one I thought of was St. Joseph, with babies in his arms. "Is the baby nudging things out of her way?" she asked.

"I guess. Hurts sometimes, like a little fist is punching me inside."

She came over and stretched out a giant palm. "May I?" she asked, hovering over my tummy.

I don't know why, but I nodded. It was like she carried a force field of quietness and, when she came close, it wrapped around me. Her hand was warm. "I'm a midwife, Ramona," she said, moving her palm. "Do you know what that is?"

"I'm not stupid," I said with a scowl. I had read about midwives in my books. "You deliver babies."

"Right. Your mother and Poppy thought you might be most comfortable with a woman, somebody who has experience with very young women having babies."

"Oh." My heart sank. "Midwives deliver babies at home, right? I don't want to have it at home. That would be gross."

Nancy laughed softly. "It's kinda gross no matter where you have it, honestly, but that's fine. If you want to go to the hospital, I have privileges at all the area hospitals." She straightened. "Do you think you'd be comfortable letting me examine you?"

I looked at Poppy, who nodded. "Okay," I said. I hadn't really thought about this part. "Like when?"

"How about now?" She gestured toward the door. "I brought my bag with me. We can go to your room or your aunt's room, wherever you like."

So that's what we did. I went to my room and Nancy spread a plastic sheet over my bedspread, then covered it with a cotton one and asked me to lie down. She looked between my legs with a metal thing, which I thought would be terrible and wasn't, because she told me everything she was doing, step by step. It felt weird and it was really embarrassing, so I just looked at the ceiling, where the plaster had been shaped into long petals around the light fixture. When Nancy was done, she pressed her palms into my belly and took out a measuring tape to see how big I was.

She slipped off her gloves. "Everything seems to be completely normal, right on schedule. The baby should be born around August twentieth." She wrote something down, then looked at me. "Why don't you get dressed and come downstairs and we can talk a little more?"

"About what?"

"I want to find out more about how you're eating and exercising and your plans for the baby when it's born. Keep it? Allow it to be adopted? What do you have in mind?"

"Keep it?" The idea sent scattershot shards of shock through my upper back. "I'm only fifteen. I can't be a mom yet."

"Okay." She stood. "I can take you to meet some great people who match babies with good families. We need to do it soon, though, so let's go down and include your aunt in the discussion, okay?"

My heart felt hollow all of a sudden. I nodded and she left, but then I just lay there, staring at the ceiling, my hands over the baby inside me. Who would be her mother? I tried to imagine and couldn't.

Within me, the baby somersaulted in a lazy, happy way, turning and turning. Under my palm, some knobby body part—elbow, maybe, or shoulder or heel—moved in a slow, long sweep. For the first time it seemed weirdly incredible that there was a person inside me. A person with eyelashes and lips and fingernails.

To avoid crying, I stood up and put my panties and jeans back on, then went downstairs to talk about my "options."

All I could think about was getting back into my jeans, going to school in September as myself, forgetting this whole mess.

FIFTEEN

Nancy and Poppy mostly talked while I listened, discussing things that didn't even make any sense to me—or maybe I just didn't want to hear them. After a while I left them at the counter, Nancy joining in with the kneading so Poppy didn't require my help anymore. I went to the sunroom—which was shady in the afternoon—and stretched out in the hammock to read. If I left my foot out, I could reach the windowsill and keep the hammock rocking back and forth. The air started to smell like bread, all fresh and homey.

I wasn't concentrating on the book. Outside the window, a plane left a long white trail across the sky, and I wondered what it would be like to go somewhere like Paris and work in a bakery. Or go to India like my aunt. Most of the people I knew were born and raised and died right in the same town, although one of my mom's friends, a realtor who had divorced her husband and wore too much makeup, sometimes went on cruises.

But Paris sounded so romantic. I had travel posters in my bedroom: of Paris and the Eiffel Tower and a loaf of bread and a bottle of wine; of Venice, which also seemed magical; and of Ireland, because we were Irish, and sometimes, when specials came on TV about the Great Potato Famine, it made me sad to think of my ancestor Bridget boarding that ship with a crock of starter in her hands, sailing away to a faraway land and never seeing her family again. I liked to imagine sailing back and stepping on Irish land. It seemed as if it might make my ancestor happy. It looked beautiful with all those green, green, green hills.

Paris, though. Dreamily, I kept nudging the windowsill with my toe to keep the hammock swaying. The baby was quiet, and I rubbed the top of my stomach as if I was rubbing her back, glad for a rest. For no reason I could pinpoint, I suddenly wondered if she would look like Armando. I knew Armando was the father, but I lied to my parents and everybody else about it, saying it was a boy at a party, nobody I knew. Which might shock you, and it sure shocked them, but I just couldn't stand to tell them the truth.

Armando came to work in July, the hottest part of the summer. He was slim but wiry, and quiet at first—like a cat, one of the other girls said. Careful and observant. He washed dishes, which is why we started talking, since I was a busgirl. He flirted with everybody, but it was obvious that he really liked me, liked my red hair and white skin, he said. He had come from Mexico to stay with his uncle, and his English was broken into charming little phrases. He gave me the first nickname I ever had: Zorra, which means fox, for my hair.

Armando. He had the whitest teeth I ever saw and a way of smiling at me that made me forget about the ugly busboy uniform and feel like I was a model—even though he was too old for me and he was flirting with everybody in the whole place.

One of the waitresses, Ginny, a woman with a mouth like a string pulled hard across her face, and acne scars she tried to hide with Cover Girl, started having an affair with Armando. She was too old for him, and she was married, which shocked me, though her husband was a long-distance trucker and not very nice. Part of me was jealous, but part of me was relieved. It didn't entirely stop me from thinking about him before I went to sleep at night, his long eyelashes and white teeth, his hands. In the darkness I imagined him lying on top of me, kissing me, our chests naked and pressed together, skin slipping and sliding.

When school started, I had to cut back my hours to weekends only. Armando and Ginny broke up, he was promoted to line cook, and I didn't see him as often.

Until the Christmas party. I wasn't even thinking about going, because it wasn't the official party, which we'd had the week before. This one was for the adult people at the restaurant; they had it every year. A server threw it in her house in Old Colorado City, which was a slightly seedy place if you got away from the main drag.

If there were such a thing as a do-over for that night, there is a long list from which I would pick. I wouldn't go to work on Friday night, because it was snowing so hard and I was staying with my grandma, who wouldn't be able to drive if it got worse.

I wouldn't listen to the other bus kids about the party or let them talk me into piling into the car that one of the servers was driving over there. I wouldn't change into my new blouse, which was green and sparkly and slid off my shoulders to show a lacy strap beneath it, and I wouldn't wear my tight blue jeans with the fuzzy soft green leg warmers, and I wouldn't let my hair down so it fell all the way to my butt.

It was new, getting looked at. I liked it.

I would change things now. I wouldn't go to the party but would ask to be dropped off at home. I wouldn't give in to the heady, bubbly sense of power that came with the guys coming over to talk to me, and I wouldn't take a beer to look cool. And when Armando came over to talk to me, I would tell him he was too old for me.

But I didn't do any of those things. When Armando asked me to dance, I let him teach me a two-step, which put our bodies close together. After a while, somehow, we were making out, and it gave me the hottest feeling all through my body, up and down my spine and at the base of my skull. Everywhere he touched me, little explosions went off. When he skidded his hands up my thighs, I thought I would faint. He kissed my neck and my chest over the top of my blouse, and then he led me into a bedroom.

I made him promise we would only make out, and that's all we did. For a long time. First in our clothes, and he rubbed my breasts and crotch through them; then he said we should take off just our shirts. I left on my bra, but the heat of his bare skin and his slow, long kisses were more than I could stand, and I took off my bra on my own. That was the moment it was all lost, because his mouth on my nipples was like a comet or an angel coming down with a tablet from heaven—it was the best feeling I'd ever had. I could have stayed there and let him do that forever. Forever.

Then we were both bare, all the way, and he was easing into me, a little at a time, talking to me in a low voice. It was like he always knew exactly when I was going to freak out, because he'd stop pushing into me and kiss me, and lick my neck and stroke my nipples, and I'd relax again.

How long did it take him to get all the way in me? A long time. And let me tell you, all the girls said sex hurt, but it didn't hurt me. Not one bit. It felt good. I even made a sound when he started to move, and he swallowed it with his mouth. "Shhh," he said. "Shhh."

He moved and moved and moved, and a bunch of heat worked its way into my body, but I couldn't seem to figure out what was going on until he started moving really fast, rubbing himself against me, and then my body exploded. Everything was all wet down there, but I didn't care. His body was heavy on my chest and I felt his naked skin, and I didn't think, *Oh, man, I'm an idiot for having sex.*

I thought, *Wow. I get it.*

He whispered things to me that I didn't understand, kissing my face and my neck. Then we were getting dressed, and he combed my hair down and we went back to the party, holding hands.

And that was the last time I ever saw him. He got into a fight after the party and pulled a knife on somebody; he was arrested and then deported. Bye-bye.

What was humiliating was to find out after he left that he had had sex with almost every woman in the whole restaurant, including a lady who was pretty much the same age as my mom and had wrinkles around her eyes. I didn't say a word, and nobody, as far as I knew, realized we went all the way while we were making out.

Now he was in Mexico somewhere, probably having sex with twelve million other girls, and I was going to have a baby. Who was half Mexican, and that might not please some of the people who wanted to adopt.

I would have to tell the truth. But that would mean admitting it was Armando, and that was so embarrassing I could barely stand it.

The farmers' market in Castle Rock started in early July, and Poppy was in a fever getting ready for it. I worked right alongside her, harvesting strawberries and lettuces and spinach. We tied thyme and dill into bundles with yellow string and made chive vinegar with the blossoms that stained the vinegar a reddish purple, making it look like a magic elixir.

And we baked. Muffins; quick breads that we cut into individual slices; whole-wheat rolls; long, thin loaves that my aunt called baguettes, which we made out of my grandma's starter. We carried it all into town in the back of her station wagon at five a.m. on a Thursday morning, and I found myself feeling both apprehensive and excited. I had discovered that I liked being up so early in the morning—liked the hint of dew still hanging in the cool air and the sound of birds getting breakfast and the fact that nobody else was around. Nobody in my family liked getting up early, so unless I was at my grandmother's house, I went along with their schedule. Poppy said I was a lark, just like her, and we didn't have to chatter while we got up and going. We drank tea, split one of the big blueberry muffins, and loaded up the car.

It was fun to be doing something so early, but I was also worried about how the townspeople would look at me. I could hide behind the table for a while, but that would get boring. I mulled it over all the way into town.

"What's on your mind, Ramona?" Poppy asked as we pulled into the parking lot behind the courthouse.

I shrugged, but my hands gave me away, rubbing the growing hill of my belly.

"You don't have to stay for the whole morning. You can go to the library or over to the record store."

My heart gave a little jump. Last week I'd taken the record back to Jonah, and he had given me some more records. He was busy that day, so we didn't get to talk much. He did ask me what I thought of the music. I wasn't sure and told him so. He nodded. "Let me work on it."

Maybe he'd be around today and could give me more suggestions.

I worked with Poppy until the crowds slowed down at around ten-thirty, and then she sent me on an errand to get her coffee, which I bought at a café truck parked on the street. I bought orange juice for myself and carried the change back to Poppy.

Nobody said anything to me, and if they were giving me the evil eye, I decided I didn't want to notice it, so I just made change and helped Poppy hand out food. I even answered questions about the breads sometimes and proudly reported when asked that I had been helping. I could make plain white bread fairly well now and was working on wheat rolls.

When I brought the coffee back, Poppy was talking, so I put the cup on the table and waved to her. When I turned around, there was my mom. It was such a shock to see her that I almost coughed up my orange juice. She wore a white culottes set with a jaunty scarf tied around her neck and gold buttons in her ears. "Mom!"

"Hi, Ramona," she said, and hugged me. I smelled hairspray and cigarettes and Juicy Fruit gum, and the combination nearly made me burst into tears.

But then I remembered her stony face when she dropped me off four weeks ago and stiffened, pushing her shoulder away from me. "What are you doing here?"

"Your birthday is coming up. I thought we could go to Denver and do some shopping."

"Today?" I glanced at the record store. "Like right now?"

"No, we can go later. Poppy said you might want notebooks and art supplies, so I brought a few from home, but maybe you'll want new ones, too."

Against my will, my spirits lightened. "Can we get crêpes at La Creperie?"

She smiled and looked like my mother again. My real mother, who wasn't always so sour. "Of course."

Poppy finished with her customer and came to hug my mother. Poppy seemed happier than my mother did. Easier in her skin. She was wearing a sleeveless pale-green paisley dress that made her complexion and hair appear warmer. My mother noticed, too. "You look great, Poppy. What's going on with you?"

She shrugged. "I'm just feeling good. It's nice to have company this summer." With a wave over the decimated goods on the table, she said, "I'm ready to go get a snack somewhere, if you want to join me. Ramona wanted to hit the record store before we left today, right?"

Gratefully, I nodded. "You can come get me there later."

"Go."

I ambled down the sidewalk and across the street. Sunlight burned the part of my hair, and the air smelled of cinnamon rolls, and somewhere children were playing, their laughter ringing out like the ultimate sound of happiness. The baby inside me moved, somersaulting as if she was happy, too, and something about it put a knife through my heart. She would laugh with somebody else. I would never hear the sound.

I stopped dead on the sidewalk, struggling to keep from crying. I managed not to sob, but tears leaked out of my eyes and down my cheeks and I dashed them away, pretending I was getting something off my mouth. A woman in jeans and a sturdy pair of shoes looked at me in concern, but I moved by her quickly. If anyone offered sympathy, I'd never be able to pull it together.

How did this happen? How was I in this place? How would I decide what do to?

I slowed. *What to do?* Was there more than one answer?

I thought of Poppy's stories of India, of rambling around with her friends, working at an ashram, learning about elephants and saris and things nobody else in our whole family knew. I thought of Nancy's stories the past few weeks about Paris. She was teaching me how to make *levains,* which were a slow way of making bread. I had thrown away two starters already because they didn't catch enough yeast to grow, and just last night I had started another one. It was sitting in a jar on the counter in Poppy's kitchen, where the sun would warm it, but not too much. Maybe this time it would work. Poppy said I couldn't add any yeast, that I had to let it be. So I was trying.

Last Monday we'd gone to the agency for my interview,

which they put on videotape for prospective parents to look at. Nancy said to be natural, to tell the camera what I wanted for the baby, and to say whatever else I wanted. I told the truth—that I was too young, that I had to go to college and wanted to travel someday, so it would be better if the baby went to a home that was ready for it.

On the street in Castle Rock, I faintly heard the sound of music and realized that I'd walked almost to the door of the record store. I felt dazed, as if I'd been crying for a long time, and almost didn't go in, but there was Jonah, putting a sign in the window. He gave me a kind smile and waved me inside. I pushed the door open.

"You look like you're having a rough day," he said, putting a light hand on the place between my shoulder blades. It was brotherly, friendly, I knew that, but that doesn't mean it didn't send a big shiver right down to my hips. Which didn't do as much as you might think to loosen up the thick knot of disaster stuck in my throat. "You want a Dr Pepper?"

I nodded. "Thanks."

There was no one else in the store this time, and we sat on stools by the counter. Jonah gave me a can of soda and opened one for himself. Before he sat down, he changed the music to something somber and moody, and immediately my emotions crowded right up through my throat into my sinuses and eyes. "I think this music is too sad!" I said, and tears spilled over my face. Embarrassed, I stood up, hiding behind my hair. "Sorry. I'm just in a mood."

He reached out and put a hand on my shoulder. "Why don't you sit down and drink your pop? I don't care if you cry. Seems to me a girl like you has a lot of things to work out."

I looked at him. "Why are you so nice to me?"

He didn't look away. His gaze was as calm as morning, direct. "Because you seem like you could use a friend or two."

I bowed my head. "Oh." I had hoped for a better answer, but

that was silly. "I guess I do. Need a friend, that is. None of my friends at home are talking to me right now. I don't know if they'll talk to me when I get back, either." The sadness that hit me out on the street returned. "And I feel so mixed up."

"I bet," he said. "Sometimes I am, too."

"What are you mixed up about?"

That sorrowful smile again. "You first."

I turned my can around and around in my hands. The smell of prunes came out of it. "I guess I kept thinking that I could just have the baby and then go back to my life and it would all be the same." I waited a minute for the tears to go away, then said, "But I don't think that's what's going to happen. At all. Like, I'm not going to be the same person I was."

He nodded.

"I messed things up so much, you know? And now I don't know how to fix them."

"Maybe that's the wrong approach."

"What do you mean?"

"Well, what if it isn't a big mistake? What if this is only something that happened, something that's different from the things most of your friends are doing but not bad. Maybe it's *extraordinary,* to help you become an extraordinary person."

A flare of hope burned through my mind. "I never thought of that."

He half smiled. "Does it feel better to think that way?"

"Yes."

"Then I'd say go with it."

For a long minute I just looked at him, very aware of his hair shining in the light coming through the window, and the hollow of his throat, and his hands lying on his thighs. "Your turn," I said.

"I'm sorry?"

"You said you feel mixed up sometimes. Or did you say that to make me feel better?"

"No, it's true," he said, and picked up his can. He lifted his left hand to display the mangled fingers. "Last summer I lost these fingers in an accident. It was the most ordinary accident, an ordinary summer day. We tried to keep them, you know. Everybody put the pieces on ice, but we were way up in the mountains, and—" He shook his head, put his hand down. "It didn't work out."

I nodded. "And that makes you feel mixed up?"

"No." He inclined his head, as if he was weighing how much to say. "The only thing I ever wanted in my whole life, from the time I was five years old, was to play guitar. I love music like a crazy man, and if I can't play my guitar, I don't know what I'm going to do with myself."

My heart ached for him. "Wow, that's really hard. At least I'm pregnant for only nine months."

He chuckled, and there was such resonance in the sound that I found myself sitting straighter. "But like you said, it changes everything."

"Did you play guitar in a band or something?"

"I just finished Berklee two years ago."

"That's a good school?"

His smile was soft. "Yeah. One of the best guitar schools in the country. Spent the winter touring with a band, and came home for the summer. And here I am, a year later, running the local record store."

I was so much younger than he was that it seemed there couldn't be anything I could possibly say, but I couldn't leave it at that. "Maybe it's just like you told me, though. It's something extraordinary."

He nodded, but sadly, as if he'd said that to himself before and hadn't figured out how to believe it. "Maybe." He started to say something, stopped.

"You can say it."

He leaned forward on the stool, propping himself on his palms, his elbows cocked outward. "Sometimes it feels like there's no point. Why did I have that big dream, just to lose it in a single second?" He snapped his fingers. "Everything gone in the amount of time it takes to fill your lungs with air one time. Years of study and practice. Gone."

I looked at his right hand. Whole. He had made adjustments. "Can't you play guitar with your other hand?"

He went very still, and for a long minute he frowned at me. I worried that I'd said the wrong thing, and began, "I'm sorry. What do I—"

Jonah put his finger to his lips. "Don't apologize. My heart is pounding so hard I think you must be an angel talking for God." There was something so fierce in the air, so strange and brilliant and wild, that I felt it dancing on my scalp and the nape of my neck and over my hands, which wanted to press themselves into his face. He wasn't handsome. I could see that. He had a big nose and a broad forehead and a long throat with an Adam's apple that was too prominent. It was a face I really liked anyway. The honey color of his eyes, his full bottom lip, the thoughtfulness over that high brow. He stared at me intently, and I could see he was thinking very hard about what I said.

"Didn't you ever think of that before?" I asked quietly.

He shook his head. "No." And then he smiled and took my hand. "Thank you, my friend."

The door swung open and in came my mother. I yanked my hand away instinctively, but she'd already seen. "What are you doing, young man?" she said, storming up to the counter. "Do you know how old she is?" Without stopping for an answer, she turned her fury in my direction. "What are you doing, Ramona? Didn't you learn anything?"

I stared at my mother in horror, my entire body frozen with surprise and humiliation. Jonah slowly came to his feet, a quizzical expression on his brow. Before he could say anything, my mother spewed out more of her fury.

"Is there something wrong with you, Ramona? Are you—"

"Lily!" Poppy shouted from the door, hurrying so much that she had to put a hand on her big chest to keep her breasts from bouncing too much. "Mind your tongue, or you'll say something you don't mean."

My heart pounded. "Too late," I said, standing up. My face and my ears were burning, and my knees shook with humiliation. "Sorry," I whispered to Jonah.

He glanced at her, raising his good hand in a peaceful gesture, and said, "I think you misunderstood, Mother. We were only talking." His mild, resonant voice brought a quiet into the room. "She's just helped me figure out something important."

My mother looked as if she might cry. "Let's go, Ramona. We have some shopping to do."

I glanced at Jonah. He gave me a single, nearly imperceptible nod. As I put down my Dr Pepper can and rounded the counter, it felt as if every bone in my spine was on fire; I could barely walk. I didn't look at my mother, who put her hand on my back as if to hurry me out the door. I shook her off, shooting her the purest look of hatred I could muster. When we were outside, I said it, too. "I hate you."

Her chin came up and she marched down the sidewalk, stiff as a broom. "We will discuss it in the car."

"Oh!" I cried. "You can humiliate me to death, but I can't embarrass you? Is that it?"

"Ramona," she said, in a deadly quiet voice, taking my arm in a firm, sharp grip that brooked no resistance. "Don't make me slap you in front of all these people."

There was no stopping the tears then. They poured out of my eyes in a hot, steady stream, piling another humiliation onto the rest until I was pretty sure my heart would stop. It didn't. Instead, my mother marched me down the sidewalk in front of the entire universe, my belly swaying back and forth, so obvious, tears on my face, my mother's hand clutched hard around my upper arm.

When we finally got to the car, I yanked free and flung myself onto the hot hood of the car, not caring that it burned my skin.

"Ramona, stop it. You're hysterical." My mother touched me gently. "The world is not ending, baby. I promise."

"You don't know. You just don't know."

Poppy joined us. "Come on, sweetie, get in the car. Let's go home and you can have a nap. Everything will look better when you get out of this hot sun."

"But I thought we were going to Denver! For my birthday!" I straightened, feeling my hair stick to my wet cheeks and neck. "I was only talking to him, Mom! And I only had sex one time. One time! It's not like I'm having sex with every guy in the universe, ripping off my clothes if they just look at me!"

"I know that, Ramona." Her voice was completely calm, and she opened the door. "Get in the car. We'll go back to Poppy's and have a rest, then figure out the trip to Denver. Okay?"

As quickly as it came, the fury drained out of me. I felt completely empty, exhausted. Like a doll, I fell into the backseat and covered my face with a sweater. In seconds, I was asleep.

At Poppy's, they took me upstairs. My mother set up a fan while Poppy washed my hot face with a cool cloth. I felt about three years old but had no energy to resist.

I slept for a long time, cocooned by the oscillating fan, and dreamed Alice in Wonderland dreams—enchanted apples, and honey dripping from the trees, and bread rising with alarming steadfastness until a baby popped out, laughing.

When I woke, I was starving and thirsty, and I could tell the afternoon was spent. I jumped up to see if my mother's car was still there, but it was gone, which crushed me all over again. I slumped against the wall, tears leaking out of my eyes once more.

But the urgent need to pee took over. I ran into the bathroom and peed like a big horse, on and on and on and on. My disappointment seemed to drain right out of me, and I felt as if I'd eaten that enchanted apple in my dream. My head was filled with gauzy splashes of color.

Poppy was in the kitchen, drinking a glass of tea with floating mint. "Well, hello there, stranger!" she said.

"Did my mom leave?"

"She did, sweetie, but she will come back on Saturday. I think you needed sleep a lot more than you needed a trip to Denver."

I slumped in the chair. "I guess."

Poppy folded up her newspaper. "This gives you both a chance to calm down, too."

"She humiliated me." I pressed the heels of my palms into my eyes. "Completely."

For a long minute she didn't say anything. I could hear the drip of water in the sink. "Even mothers have wounds, Ramona. Your mother—"

"What?"

Poppy inclined her head. "You must promise never to let her know that I told you."

"I promise. What, was she pregnant, too?"

"Not until later, and you know about that already, little love child." It was true—I knew that my mother had been pregnant with me when she married my dad. It was a romantic story.

"What, then?"

"Promise?"

"Cross my heart and hope to die."

"You know those scars on her thigh? She says they're a burn, right?"

Something in me felt sick suddenly. "Yeah."

"Our mother found out she'd had sex and beat the holy hell out of her. She was fifteen, and it left a scar on her heart, too, baby. She was worried about you today. She's been worried about you all year."

"Wait. My grandmother did that?"

Poppy nodded. "I told you, she was a different person then."

My stomach felt upset. "That's terrible."

"It was terrible, and you will hurt your mother if you let on that you know, okay?"

"Okay. I promise."

"Don't be mad at Adelaide, either. Her life was no sweet walk in the park, either."

I loved my grandmother. I didn't want to be mad at her, but I would have to think about this. It was almost impossible to imagine her in such a fury that she would beat her daughter. "With a belt?"

Poppy stood. "I bet you're starving. How about a grilled cheese and a salad?"

"That sounds good." I rubbed my eyes, and the afternoon flooded back to me, erasing anything that happened to my mother a million years ago. "How am I ever going to look Jonah in the eye again?"

"Well, it might not be much of an issue, because she doesn't want you hanging out there."

"He's just my friend."

"You're really vulnerable right now," she said. "And, honestly, sweetheart, so is he. Let it be."

I fell forward, dropping my forehead against my arms, tears flooding the space below. With misery, I asked, "Why can't I stop crying today?"

She came over and rubbed my back. "You're pregnant, honey. It sometimes makes a person kind of crazy." She gave me a paper towel, then pulled out the skillet and a loaf of hearty, grainy bread and the cheese I liked—Gouda, with a hard brown rind. She fixed the meal and I poured a giant glass of water to drink with it. When I demolished every crumb, Poppy said, "You know what I think would make you feel better? Bake some bread."

And for the first time all day, something like relief worked through my limbs. I nodded.

She gave me a recipe and helped me gather the ingredients, then turned the radio to the station I liked. "I'm going to watch TV. Holler if you need anything."

In the purpling evening, with crickets whirring and the radio playing Top 40 songs, I started the bread. My thoughts fluttered around my brain like crazy moths, banging into one another, then flying away, and I let them. I didn't chase a single one.

Instead, I measured. I stirred. I gave the bread space to rise while I sat on the back porch with a barn cat, who leaped on crickets in the grass and then came over and sat on my foot, purring. Soft.

Darkness fell. I went back in to knead the dough, and I could feel that the whirling insanity in my blood was slowing. I pressed the heel of my palm to the fold of the pale-brown speckled ball of dough, over and over, in a steady pattern that worked the stiffness out of my neck as it worked the stiffness out of the dough. Everything crazy drained away, and I was just me again. Ramona.

Changed forever. But still me. I shaped the loaves and set them on the stove where the pilot light helped them rise a little better.

When Poppy and I went to Denver the week before last to get her special flours, I'd bought a good looseleaf notebook and some markers and, on a whim, sheet protectors, slippery and attractive. Now, as the loaves rose, I used the markers to write on the front: *RAMONA'S BOOK OF BREADS*. In the best handwriting I could manage, I copied the white-bread recipe that had been the first one I'd figured out, then I included the one I made tonight.

After that I added dividers to the notebook and labeled one of them *Experiments.* On the following sheet of paper I wrote, *Experiments with levains,* and faithfully recorded my two failed starts. *#3 started on June 20, 1985.*

I put down my pen and waddled over to the counter, where I'd left the new starter. I smelled it, and for the first time there was the faintest hint of sourness. I stuck my little finger into it and tasted it. Still pretty floury, but was that a tiny hint of something else? Something more pleasant?

Cheered, I recorded the observable changes, then put my loaves in the oven and sat in a kitchen smelling of bread until the moon was high in the sky. When the bread came out, hot and rich and perfectly brown, I cut a giant slice for the baby and me, buttered it, and ate it outside under the stars. It was the best thing I had ever tasted in my life.

Only then, alone in the darkness, with bread I had created with my own hands, did I allow myself to think of Jonah and the sharp, sweet thing that had sprung up between us that afternoon, something as wild as an invisible yeast and just as powerful.

RAMONA'S BOOK OF BREADS

SOFT AND DELICIOUS WHEAT BREAD

If you are pregnant or overwhelmed or full of disaster, this bread will cool your overheated spirit. Start it in the late afternoon on a waxing moon and let the evening spirits whisper you into stillness. Such a hearty bread requires a long kneading time, which will dispel a good deal of darkness from even the heaviest heart, and the scent of the baking will untie knots of misunderstanding.

¾ cup milk

1 T honey

½ cup lukewarm water

1 tsp dry yeast

¾ cup water

1 T salt

1 cup sourdough starter

⅓ cup oil

2 cups white flour

6–7 cups whole-wheat flour

Scald milk and let stand until lukewarm. Meanwhile, in a large bowl, mix honey into lukewarm water and sprinkle yeast over the top. Let stand for 10 minutes. Mix milk with ¾ cup of water, add salt, sourdough starter, and oil. Pour into yeast/water mixture and stir well. Add white flour and stir, then begin adding wheat flour 2 cups at a time. When a rough ball has formed, cover with a damp towel and let stand for 20 minutes.

Turn the dough onto a floured surface and begin to knead with firm, sure strokes, until the dough feels smooth and elastic, about 12–15 minutes. Put the dough into an oiled bowl and turn until the entire surface is oiled. Cover with a damp towel and put in a draft-free spot to rise until doubled in bulk, usually an hour to an hour and a half.

Turn the dough out again onto a floured surface and punch it down. Let it rest for 20 minutes, then knead again for 5–8 minutes. Divide into 2 large-size loaves and put each into a well-oiled pan to rise again for another hour. Bake in a 350-degree oven for 1 hour, or until loaves are golden brown and pull away from the sides of the pan. Tip out onto wire racks and let cool.

SIXTEEN

My mother came back on Saturday, a few days before my birthday, as promised, and took me to shop at Cinderella City mall, which had a whole area in the basement where the shops all looked like a medieval village. I loved it down there, and my mom knew it. I didn't want clothes, so she let me pick out earrings, some cute socks with toes, and two records, which I was pretty sure was a way to tell me she was sorry for her fit in the record store with Jonah, not that she said so. I bought Cyndi Lauper's *She's So Unusual*, and then, thinking about what Jonah had said about his favorites, a Rolling Stones album with a zipper on the cover. My mom said, "I love that record," which almost made me put it back, but I didn't.

She never said a single thing about our big fight, or the fact that I was now talking seriously with two couples about adoption, or even if I could come home on my birthday, which was the next Wednesday. Every year, my birthday was always the same: a big party at the pool, then tacos and strawberry shortcake with everybody. I kept wondering if she was going to take me home as a surprise, but when we got back to Poppy's, she hugged me really hard and said, "I can't wait until you're home again. I love you."

I managed not to cry until she was out of sight down the

road, and then, because I didn't want even Poppy to know how stupid I was for hoping, I went to the garden. There were squashes now, yellow and green, and tiny balls of pumpkins along the fence, and cherry tomatoes and big green tomatoes. I kicked at weeds with the toe of my sandal, and pretty soon one of the barn cats came out—stalking me through the corn, reaching out to spat my foot, then dashing into the shadows. It was a little orange-and-white ball of fluff with the prettiest face you ever saw. Some of the barn cats were skittish, but this one didn't mind being picked up. I captured him and put him on my shoulder, listening to him purr.

It was July. The baby would be born at the end of August and I could finally go home. In four days, I would be sixteen.

I could not imagine being lonelier.

Poppy made my tacos and strawberry shortcake on the big day. Nancy came down from Denver to share the celebration, and her present to me was a book about Paris breads and an apron with *Boulanger*—which meant "baker"—embroidered across the chest in script. I pretended to be cheered up by their singing and presents and by opening the gifts my mother had left. There was a bracelet Steph wove at camp and a small statue of a cat from Ryan. My baby sister Sarah, only eight, drew a picture of a unicorn, and Liam made a doll of Popsicle sticks covered with a lot of glue and glitter, which almost made me cry. He's still so little!

My dad signed the card but didn't write anything else, just *Love, Dad*. I guess he's mad at me, too.

Sixteen. Big deal.

That weekend was a festival for the town's jubilee or something. At midday, Poppy and I took a picnic supper into town so we could watch the fireworks from the top of the rock, which didn't look like a castle to me but just another mesa rock like the billions of others around here. I wanted someday to see a real castle, but I was pretty sure it wouldn't look like that.

Anyway, she let me stop at the library first while she went around to meet some of her friends for coffee. It had been so hot that I sometimes read a book a day. We got up early, worked in the garden, baked, or canned, then I read through the afternoon and through the clockwork thunderstorms that rolled in every single day. Nancy brought big fat books she thought I'd like, and I peeled through those, too. Poppy wanted me to read "better" books, something like *Anna Karenina,* but Nancy rolled her eyes. "Please. Krantz is going to feel a lot better right now than Tolstoy."

At the library, I stocked up on glitz and stuffed them all into my backpack and wandered out into the heat of the late afternoon. Black clouds bore down from the west, flashing threads of lightning. Walking rain, smeary against the horizon, marched toward us, and a wind swept my skirt right up to my nose. I grabbed it with one hand and my hair with the other and closed my eyes against a second blast, turning my back to it.

"Better get inside!" a man called, slamming his car door.

Guiltily, I gauged the distance between me and the record store, wondering if I could make it before the rain caught me. Nearly two full blocks, but straight downhill. If I wasn't pregnant, I could have dashed that distance in half a minute. Now probably not.

But maybe only a minute and a half. Twisting my hair, I tucked it under my backpack straps, then kept my skirt in my hands and hurried down the street. I had to stop for traffic at Main Street, and the first of the rain started pattering toward me, splashing on the hot sidewalk and sending up that hot, salty smell. The first drops on my skin were startling and cold. A truck clattered by, and I took the chance to dash across the street.

It was like running into a wall of rain. Drops splattered all over me, on my nose and head, my arms and belly. Even running, I couldn't avoid getting soaked or stung by the hail. By the time I flung myself into the record store, my hair was dripping and my arms were dotted with red marks from the hail. The entryway bell rang and I slammed the door closed again. The hail roared out of the west with a sound like a thousand baseballs falling from the sky, slamming the roof and hitting the sidewalk so hard they bounced as high as my waist. "Wow." I wiped water off my face and turned around.

Jonah was coming out of the back, a stack of records in his hands. He stopped dead still and looked at me with a little frown. I wanted to sink right through the floor.

"Hello there," he said finally, and put the records down on the counter. "You look wet."

I held out my dripping dress. "Kinda."

"Let me find you a towel. Stay right there." He disappeared into the back and returned with a big blue towel. "Might not be elegant, but it should do the trick."

I was starting to shiver as I took the towel and rubbed my face, then dried my neck and arms. Jonah only stood there. "Are you okay?"

My teeth chattered. "Just cold."

He gestured for me to follow him. Overhead, the hail pounded as if there was a war, and I sloshed forward, my feet squishing in my sandals. The books in my bag were heavy, and I suddenly worried that they might be damaged. "Yikes, these are library books!" I peered in to see if they were okay, holding the towel around my shoulders. Jonah disappeared again and came back with a heavy sweater in browns and blues. "Slip this on."

"I don't want to mess it up."

"Don't be silly." He held it patiently. "It's warm."

Taking the towel off my shoulders, I pulled the sweater over my head. I had to tug it down over my belly, but that didn't stretch it out. A heady scent came out of the wool—cloves and oranges and something that made those prickles along my back stand up again. I got goose bumps all over, and without think-ing I lifted it to my nose to sniff it more deeply. It was then that I realized it was his smell, and he was watching me with a funny expression.

He balled the towel up in his hands, tossed it back and forth like a basketball. Looked over his shoulder. "Quite a storm."

"Yeah, it is." I felt weirdly dizzy. We were kind of close. A lock of his hair had fallen out of the ponytail, and I suddenly won-dered what it would look like if it was loose, falling over his shoulders. I wondered how it would feel, that shiny thick brown hair. Even though a rubber band held it back, I could tell it was slightly wavy.

I couldn't think of anything to say, and I sat down on the stool by the counter, pulling the sleeves down over my hands a little bit. After a minute, he put the towel down. "Want a cup of tea?"

"Yeah! Can you make it here?"

"Sure can. Be back in a sec. I'll just start the kettle boiling."

When he was gone, I lifted my sweater-covered hands to my nose and inhaled deeply again, filling my lungs, my body, with his smell. It gave me the oddest feeling—swaying, unsteady, like being in a boat when a water-skier went by.

The music had been rock and roll–ish and now it changed to classical. "Do you know what this is?" he asked when he re-turned, carrying two mugs of tea. It smelled of oranges and spice, and my stomach growled slightly.

"Guitar?" I guessed.

"Right. Very good. It is a man named Andrés Segovia. He's a Spanish guitarist. It's very rich music. I think you might like it." He picked up a small suitcase from the counter behind him, which was scattered with papers and an adding machine and pens and rubber bands and notes. "Do you play backgammon?"

I had never heard of it. Anxiously, I shook my head.

"It's easy. I'll teach you." He glanced toward the weather. "These storms never last that long, but while it's going, we're stuck."

"Okay." It made me feel grown up, a taste of what adults did to pass the time. He opened the suitcase to show a dark felt board with alternating white and brown leather arrows sewn onto it. The pieces were white and brown, too, smooth cold disks he showed me how to lay out around the board. The guitar music danced around us, lilting and then solid, quiet and lacy, thoughtful then passionate. I cocked my head, listening, and suddenly the baby started to move. "I think she's dancing!" I said with a laugh.

"She?"

I shrugged. "It sounds better than 'it.'" She was swirling, doing somersaults. It made me feel slightly off-kilter, and I began to hum with the music, rubbing the elbows and knees and body parts inside my belly. For a minute I was lost in it, thinking of the elbow, her hands, the swirl and sway, as if she really could hear the music.

"That must be pretty amazing," Jonah said. "To have a person inside you."

"It's kind of weird." I looked up. "And interesting. I think she does like the music."

"How about you? Do you like it?"

"Yeah. It's not what I usually listen to, but it's nice."

He nodded and began to tell me how to play the game. I didn't get it at first, mainly because my brain was roaring with a thousand things—like the way he kept his bad hand tucked in his lap and played with his left, and the look of his long throat in the quiet light, and how close our knees were.

Finally, though, because I didn't want to look like an airhead—which I wasn't at all—I concentrated and played for real. Although I didn't win the first round, I got close.

We played again. And as we played, our eyes on the pieces, we talked. About when my baby was due and how long he'd been living back in Castle Rock. I told him I liked watching MTV, and he said he did, too—but only sometimes. Sometimes, he said, the values were too materialistic.

"That's what Poppy says." And a sudden wrenching sense of guilt twisted my tummy. I looked outside and the sun was beginning to peek through. "I guess I need to go find her pretty soon. She'll be worried."

"She'll understand about the rain."

I nodded, not at all sure that was true.

"Sorry you got in trouble last time," he said, and his voice seemed deeper, richer.

"My mom was being weird," I said, unable to look at him.

"Parents only want to take care of their kids, Ramona."

To my horror, a welter of tears built in my throat. "I don't know how long she's going to stay mad at me about this. It's terrible how she looks at me now."

"She loves you. I could see that."

I pressed the tops of my fists together. Nodded.

Poppy came in then, the bell over the door banging loudly. "I thought I might find you here."

She didn't sound mad, but I stood up anyway. "It was raining really hard. I didn't know what to do."

Hiking her bag over her shoulder, she came up to the counter and leaned her elbows on it. "Backgammon! I haven't played that in a long time."

"It's fun. Do you have a board at home?"

"I could probably get one next time we go to Denver." She inclined her head. "You like board games, don't you?"

"My family plays them a lot."

Jonah collected the disks and settled them a few at a time into their places. He did it without much thought, but I saw the moment when he made to use his missing finger and three of them fell out of the space where the finger should have been. They clattered onto the counter, and one rolled away and fell on the floor, and I leapt up to grab it, chasing it under the lip of the counter before capturing it. "Got it!"

His cheekbones were red when he held out his hand, palm up. "Thanks."

"We'd better get our errands done, Ramona," Poppy said. "Will we see you tonight at the fireworks, Jonah?"

"I'm not sure. Some family friends are coming in today, and I've been summoned to my mother's house for dinner." He gave her a wry smile. "You know my mother."

"I do, son, I do. Enjoy."

I started to take off the sweater, but Jonah stilled my hand. "It's chilly out there. You can bring it to me when you go to the farmers' market next week."

"Okay, thanks." I didn't look back as we headed out, but I felt twenty feet tall, cloaked in Jonah's sweater, and I kept wondering as we walked through town if anyone would realize it was his, that he'd loaned it to me.

Poppy had to run a million errands before the fireworks. When she stopped at a friend's house to take her some bread, I was too tired to go inside with her, and I begged off and curled up in the backseat for a nap. Jonah's sweater was almost too warm, but I kept it on, letting the scent of it fill my head as I drifted off. Beneath my hands on my belly, the baby was quiet, as if she was sleeping, too.

Suddenly I thought of her as whole. A person who was going to grow up and have favorite foods and hate to wear certain things and love to dance. I thought of her at three, with chubby feet and hands, and a pain like twelve knives went through my heart. I would never see her at three, or twelve—or at sixteen, like me. Opening my hands, I pressed palms and fingers in a net over my belly, feeling her. As if in response, a knob moved against my palm. From the corners of my eyes, tears leaked in a slow river into my hair.

What if I didn't want to give her away?

The thought stayed with me, beating like a heart, through our picnic in the park, where we ate cheese sandwiches and sliced tomatoes from our garden. Little kids spun around in circles and screeched for the fireworks to start and held sparklers far away from their bodies.

Poppy asked, "Are you all right, sweetie? You're awfully quiet."

"I'm just thinking," I said.

She looked at me for a long moment. "If you ever want to talk, let me know. I'll listen, I promise."

"Thanks."

It wasn't until dusk started filling the air that I saw Jonah, loping toward us across the grass. He was as graceful as an antelope, with that same long-legged thinness, and his hair was loose for the first time. It made my stomach hurt the way it caught the last bits of sunlight, going golden and soft. He looked exactly like the prince in a fairy tale to me, even dressed in jeans and a button-down shirt with the sleeves rolled up on his forearms. He carried something. It seemed as if he was looking right at me, and I pulled the sweater sleeves down over my hands, wishing I didn't have to give it back.

"Hi, Poppy," he said. "Ramona."

"Hey," I said, and stood up to pull the sweater over my head.

"No, no. Don't worry." He smiled. "You can wear it awhile longer. Looks better on you than on me, anyway."

I hugged my arms around my body. "I like it. It's warm."

He held out a cassette tape. "I made you a tape of the classical guitarist you were listening to this afternoon."

"Oh!" I felt dizzy, taking it. Like maybe he really did like me or something. "Thank you."

He glanced at Poppy, gave her a wink. "Rare that a teenager likes classical music, right?"

She nodded. "Thanks, Jonah. That was thoughtful. Give your mother my regards."

"Will do." He saluted us both and sauntered off.

Poppy put her hand on my upper back and rubbed a warm little circle. "Too bad he's way too old for you. He's a good man, I think."

"Yeah," I said. "Too bad."

SEVENTEEN

One afternoon at the end of July, I walked down the road in Sedalia with a pink umbrella over my head in case it rained. Which it seemed like it would, any second. Dark purple clouds covered the sky about twelve feet over my head.

Back in Poppy's kitchen was a war party made up of my mother, my grandmother, Poppy, and Nancy. A war party determined to convince me how stupid I was for wanting to keep my baby. I'd asked them to come so we could talk about the whole thing, hoping they would listen to me, but all they had done was bring lists of all the reasons I should give the baby up.

As if I didn't know all those reasons. As if I didn't get it.

From the day in the record store when the baby started dancing to classical guitar, I knew I didn't want to give her up. We went to Denver that week to meet with the adoption people, and on the way there I told Poppy and Nancy the truth about the baby's heritage. They said they didn't think it would matter, that I should keep the information to myself.

So I did, but it made me feel icky.

Then I had a nightmare that I was walking around a park with a baby in my arms—my baby—and she was laughing. A woman came up to me and yanked her out of my arms and walked away really fast. Somebody said, "You will never see her again."

When I told Poppy about it while we were weeding the garden the next morning, she said, "It's normal that you should have conflicting emotions, sweetie. It's a big thing."

I said, "But what if I don't want to give her up?"

She looked at me. Pinched off a handful of squash blossoms, and inclined her head. "Is that what you're thinking?"

I took a breath and nodded. "My mom is going to be so mad at me."

"She won't be happy, that's for sure, but this is not her decision to make. We can help guide you, but ultimately you have to make the choice yourself."

"Will you help me talk to my mom and my grandma?"

"Can we think about it for another week or so? Let's me and you and Nancy talk about it before we bring the others into it."

So we did. Nancy brought me books on single parenting, on mothering a baby—and also the statistics on the lifelong earning loss for teen mothers. Poppy talked about her travels and how much she had hoped I would follow in her footsteps. That pained me. I wanted that, too.

But would it be enough?

My heart felt torn in two, and for that long week I thought and thought and thought. I thought about it while I gardened and while I listened to music.

And while I kneaded bread. Especially then. I was learning now to combine flours for new flavors—a bit of buckwheat added specks of purple to a white loaf, and spelt made it taste a little spongier. I folded eggs into a brioche dough and imagined myself as a world traveler, living in Paris, learning to bake bread there.

But I kept seeing the baby strapped to my chest in a Snugli.

I braided sweet breads and painted them with egg whites, breads so beautiful that Poppy sold them for an extra dollar. I imagined going to school and facing everybody when I had a baby at home. It would be embarrassing, but would it be any worse than going back without the baby?

At the end of the week, my mother and my grandmother drove up to Poppy's house. Before they got there, Nancy, Poppy, and I baked zucchini bread, made coffee, and set the table in the kitchen with a cloth embroidered with tiny mirrors around the edges. Nancy had all kinds of papers and folders of information for me to use if I wanted. She had stayed completely neutral and factual, and for that I was grateful.

Poppy went upstairs to change and came down wearing a dress, with her hair tied back in a braid. She had put on lipstick, which she never did. It was weird to see her so nervous.

"Can you tell me why you and Grandma don't talk?"

"Maybe someday," she said. "I'll talk to her today. I promise we'll be nice. This is about you."

"Thank you."

I spent a lot of time with my grandmother back at home. I was her first granddaughter, and I knew, along with everybody else, that I was her favorite. When I saw her climbing out of the car in a dark-blue dress belted smartly at the middle, my heart swelled to the size of the Empire State Building, and I ran down the steps. "Grandma!" I cried, and flung myself into her arms.

She caught me tightly, fiercely. "Oh, child, I'm so glad to see you! Let me look at you." She held me at arm's length, studying my face and then looking at my belly. "You are prettier every day, Ramona. You're as beautiful as my own mother was. I'm so sorry you're having to go through this. It's not your fault that men can't handle themselves around a beauty."

"Mother," said Lily. "Please. Let's go inside."

We all sat at the table, with Poppy putting down the neatly sliced zucchini bread and pouring the coffee. "So, what's this all about, Ramona?" my mother said.

I took a breath, squared my shoulders, and said, "First, I want to ask you to listen to me all the way through before you say one word."

My mother's face turned into a mask of solid rock. She pressed her coral-lipsticked lips together.

"We're listening, honey," Adelaide said.

"Okay. I asked you to come here so that we can make a plan that would make it possible for me to keep the baby."

"What?" my grandmother said, and slammed her hand on the table. "Did you put her up to this, Poppy? Is this some woman-power thing?"

"Let her finish, Mother," Poppy said. "Everybody needs to let her present her case."

My mother's lips didn't move one tiny bit, so I looked at my grandma. "I want to keep the baby. I can do it if you guys help me. I can still go to school and finish my education and then find a job."

"Go to college," my mother said.

"But, Ramona—" began Adelaide.

"Please let me finish. Look, I'm not an idiot. I know it will be hard. I know this is not a great thing, that you all had other dreams for me. I had a different plan in mind, too, but maybe this is just how things are supposed to go. Maybe it's fate or something that this baby is important to my life." I looked at my mother. "Think about when you were pregnant with me."

Adelaide and Poppy looked at my mother. Who had the stoniest, coldest look on her face that I'd ever seen. "No, Ramona. The answer is no. I am not going to let you throw your life away like this."

"It's not your decision."

She crossed her legs and lit a cigarette, daring Poppy to say a word. With her thin arms crossed over her chest, she blew a stream of smoke out into the kitchen, and the smell of it choked me. "It is my decision," she said. "You are a minor, and I am still your mother."

I stood up. "But this baby is mine!"

"Oh, for God's sake, Ramona! Come down off your cloud. Wake up! This isn't some little toy you get to bring home, or a kitten who will be so cute on your bed." A lock of hair at the edge of her bangs quivered, and I thought she wanted to shake me. "It's another human being, who will depend on you for absolutely everything. A newborn consumes every tiny bit of energy you have. You won't even want to watch television, much less go to school."

"Mom, I know all this. I've been reading and studying, and I know it will be hard. That's why I asked you here—I need your help."

My grandmother reached out a hand. "Please sit down, sweetheart. Listen a minute."

I flopped onto the chair.

"You have to go to school. You know that's true. The world is changing, and a woman needs a way to support herself. Men are not all that reliable, frankly, and you need a way to take care of yourself. You need a good education."

"I agree. That's why—"

"And you need a chance to ripen yourself, grow up, find out who you are, before you start trying to guide another person."

"I have you guys, a really good family. She'll have four mothers, not just one."

"Three. I will not do this." My mother stood up and stormed out of the kitchen.

"Lily, come sit down," Poppy said.

But it all went downhill from there. My grandmother turned on Poppy, blaming her for the decision, and I shouted that Poppy was on their side, and Adelaide shouted that not everyone was as screwed up as Poppy, which made Poppy furious, and Nancy reached for her and pulled her back when it seemed like she might hit my grandmother.

That was when I grabbed the umbrella and bolted out the front door. "I'm getting out of here. You're all crazy."

"Ramona! Get back here!" my mother screamed from the yard as I took off.

But I ignored her.

I walked along the red dirt road with the umbrella over my head, hoping that it wouldn't start to lightning, because I would have to go back. And if I would do something as stupid as walk in the rain with a lightning rod of an umbrella over my head, maybe they were right, anyway.

It was very quiet. The fields stretched for empty miles in every direction, rolling fields of grass that had gone a pale yellow in the summer heat. Behind the fields rose the mountains, their lower half dark blue and furry-looking, the top half buried in the pillow clouds. A bird sat on a fence post, whistling. It looked lonely.

I walked and walked. The air tasted like rain. I knew I should go back, but I didn't want them to talk me into anything. I needed to decide for myself. It was my life. Either way, something was lost. Either way, something was won. I needed to figure out which was the best answer for me.

A car came along the road behind me, and when I looked back, I saw an old Mercedes, the kind with little fins on the taillights. It slowed as it approached, and I frowned, looking steadfastly ahead. What if it was that creepy guy from town?

Beside me, a calm, honeyed voice said, "Where you headed, my friend?"

Jonah! I turned, brushing bangs out of my eyes. "I don't know." I sagged. "Away from my mother."

"Hop in. We can have a cup of hot chocolate at the truck stop."

I desperately wanted to, but things were bad enough today

without me getting in trouble. And I had to think of the baby. "Sorry, I can't. My mother is mad enough already. Thanks, though."

"Your aunt called me." One elbow hung out of the car and his hair was tied back with a leather string, which seemed sexy somehow. "She said you were pretty upset and might need a friend to talk to."

"Oh." I still didn't move right away. It might be kind of overwhelming to be in a closed car with him. But Poppy was right: I needed somebody impartial to talk to, and he had the most patient eyes I'd ever seen. "Okay."

I walked around the car and got in just as it started to rain in heavy splotches, so big they made a fat sound as they hit the roof. The car was old but still beautiful, and instinctively I touched the dash. "Is this wood? I never saw a car with a wooden dash before."

He nodded. "She's a beauty. My first car, and I haven't had a reason to get another one. I fixed her up myself."

"Cool."

Cocooned in the car with the windshield wipers slapping back and forth, the rain pounding, the gravel crunching beneath the tires, I felt myself relax. The song "Fernando" came on the radio, and I made a soft noise. "I love this song."

He turned the music up.

"Do you like it, too?" I asked in surprise.

"It's wistful," he said. "You like emotional music. Music that tells a story."

"I guess I do."

"Let me ask you: When you hear a song, do you see pictures, or do you feel it in your chest, or none of the above?"

For a minute I curled a long strand of hair around my finger, thinking. "Pictures. I see like a little movie. And when it's sad, I feel it in my heart. Also when it's happy, I guess." I wondered if that was the right answer. "How about you?"

"I see it in colors. This song is silvery, and green in this part. It's reddish brown in the drums."

"Oh, my gosh! I can see that! The flutey sound is silver, right?"

He looked at me, a genuine smile opening his serious face. "Yes. Exactly."

We pulled up in front of the truck stop. There weren't many other cars, and the rain was pouring down. "Ready to make a break for it?"

I grinned. "I am if you are."

"Ready, set, run!"

We bolted out of the car, dashing toward the door with our hands over our heads. Jonah got there first and pushed the door open to usher me inside. We found a booth in the nonsmoking section, and when our waitress, a tall curvy woman with a lot of long blond hair, came over, Jonah said, "I'll just have a coffee. How about you, Ramona?"

"Hot chocolate, please."

"Tell me what's happening," he said when she left.

I looked out the window at the smeary view. "My mother is so mad at me, I think she'd like to shake me. She wants me to give the baby away. So does everybody else."

He folded his hands in front of him on the table, the right over the left, hiding the ruined fingers. "I take it that you might not want to?"

I leaned forward, my own hands in front of me. "You know that day you played the classical guitar music in the shop? I could feel the baby dancing. I don't think it was real to me before then that there is a person inside me."

His eyes stayed on my face. He nodded.

"I'm confused," I said. "Maybe they're right. They love me. I know they love me, right?"

"They do. They care about you more than anything else."

"But I think I"—I touched my fingers to my mouth—"care

about this baby more than anything else. It's like the way it happened doesn't even matter. The baby is mine. It's like she's here for a reason or something."

The waitress brought our drinks in heavy ceramic cups with a pitcher of cream. "You want something to eat with that, sweetie? I used to get such an acid stomach from chocolate when I was pregnant."

I looked up. It was the first time anyone had treated me like a member of a club, a club of women who were pregnant or had been. "I think I would, actually. Pie? Do you have apple pie?" I looked at Jonah. "If that's okay. I don't have any money with me."

"Oh, he's rich, sweetheart," she said, and winked at Jonah. "He can handle it."

Jonah flushed, just as he had the day he dropped the backgammon piece. "I'm pretty sure I can manage a piece of pie. As a matter of fact, bring me one, too. With ice cream. You want ice cream, Ramona?"

"Yes!"

"Be right back."

I stirred my hot chocolate. "Have you ever had to make a really big decision? How do you do it?"

He took a breath. "Well, you have to weigh the alternatives and consider what will make you happy. And what will make you miserable. Then trust your gut. Make a choice and be real with it, no matter what happens. Once you choose, don't second-guess yourself."

"I kept thinking that I was just going to go back to school and be the same old person I was, but everything is changed now. I think what I have to do is imagine who I'll be ten years from now and think about what I will want then."

"Good plan. You can talk it out with me if you want. See how it plays."

I took a breath and shook my hair out of my face. "Okay, this might be stupid, but this is what I think. I think if I let her go, I'm going to wonder every single day what she's doing and what she looks like and if her parents are being good to her.

"I think if I *don't* give her up, I'm sometimes going to be mad about taking on too much responsibility so young. I think I'll be sad about not going to Paris and Ireland and all those places, and I bet it's going to be kind of hard to find a boyfriend if I'm a single mom." I sipped my chocolate. It was so good to take my time to say these things out loud. "But I don't think I will mind as much about those things as I will mind not having my child with me."

"So your gut is saying you want to keep the baby."

"My heart and my gut and my entire soul."

He nodded, his eyes very kind. "It sounds to me like you know exactly what to do."

"How do I convince everybody else?"

"You'll figure it out."

The waitress brought our pie. We ate it, talking and not talking, peacefully.

When Jonah drove me home, I sat in the car, gathering my courage for a minute. "Thanks, Jonah."

He touched my upper arm with one finger. "You're welcome."

For a long minute we were facing each other, hidden from view by the rain, and I looked up at him, seeing his mouth, wishing with all my heart that we were not separated by so many years so that I could kiss him. I took a breath, swept by a vision of what that would be like.

"You're not going to have any trouble finding boyfriends, Ramona. You're a very pretty girl."

I almost stopped breathing. "I am?"

"Yes," he said, and leaned away from me. "Better get inside before they come after you."

My mother was sitting on the back porch, smoking, sheltered from the rain by the roof. One of Poppy's big multicolored sweaters was wrapped around her shoulders, and she looked small inside it. Her makeup was worn off, even her lipstick. She blew a lungful of smoke into the air. "Come sit down with me, Ramona."

I paused at the top of the step. "Please don't yell at me anymore."

"No," she said. "I just want to say a few things. I need you to listen to me."

With a sigh, I sank onto the chair next to her, my hands going around my tummy like a circle of protection. "What?"

"I'm sorry I got so upset, Ramona. I think what's getting lost in all of this is the fact that I love you. And whatever anger I'm feeling, it's not directed at you but at the circumstances. Does that make sense?"

"It feels like you're mad at me."

She smoked, stroked my hair. "I know. But what I'm really upset about is the way your life has been turned upside down, in ways you can't even imagine yet. Whatever you do with the baby, this has ended your childhood."

"It is changing me."

"Yes. You're growing up very fast. I didn't want that for you—I wanted to give you things I didn't get to have. Going away to college and maybe traveling and finding work you love."

"You wanted to go to college?"

"Good God, yes. I was the smartest girl in my school. I wanted to study architecture and become the best designer since Frank Lloyd Wright." She shrugged. "Honestly, I didn't know how to make that happen—it wasn't like people in my family went to college, you know—but if I'd kept working rather than getting married, I might have figured it out."

Instead, she met my father the summer she was nineteen and they were married the following year, with a baby—me—ripening in her belly. "You could go to school now. I know lots of moms who do that."

She put her cigarette out in a flowerpot. "Maybe," she said, but I could tell she didn't mean it. "I have a lot to do with you children and the business."

"That's Dad's business, though, right?"

"No," she said, and met my gaze. "It's ours. We're a good team and I love him and I'm not sorry I started a family. But that doesn't mean I don't have higher aspirations for you. Will you think about that, Ramona? You will be so much freer to make your own choices if you let this baby go to a family that is aching to have it."

"I'll think about it," I said. "But I want you to think about how you would have felt giving me up for adoption. Never seeing me ever again. Not looking at me now, never knowing how things are with me."

Her eyes grew bright blue with tears, and she squeezed my hand with her own. With a little shake of her head, she pressed the fingers of her free hand to her lips.

"I'm going to keep her, Mom," I said. "Will you help me?"

She gave the saddest sigh in the world.

And then she nodded.

One mid-August afternoon, I was as restless as a cat, unable to sit down for more than six seconds anywhere at all. Poppy watched me carefully and asked if I felt anything that might be labor or if I had a backache.

I snapped that I did not, and she put me to work in the kitchen, baking a loaf of straightforward sourdough from my grandmother's starter. The smell of it eased me, and as I was kneading the dough, I did start to feel the oddest sensation, like a ripple moving from the outside of my belly inward. It didn't hurt, but when I put a floury hand against my apron, my stomach was as hard as a boulder. The sensation went away after a minute, and I finished the kneading. Just as I put the loaves on the rimless baking sheet we used for baguettes, I felt it again—a long, slow ripple, like a gathering. I said, "Poppy?"

She came into the kitchen. "Feeling something now?"

"Maybe. But I don't want to leave the bread."

"Babies don't care about bread. We'll put it in the fridge to proof and bake it tomorrow." She laughed and hugged me close. "I'm so proud of all the things you've learned this summer, sweetheart. Do you have any idea how much I love you?"

A big tight fist grabbed my belly and squeezed hard. "Ow! I think this might be the real thing. Feel it."

She put her palm on the rigid rise. "Yep. We'd better get moving."

"This is too early, though! Will the baby be okay?"

"Honey, she's due in eleven days. This is not all that early for a first-time mother."

Sofia Adelaide Gallagher was born in the hospital birthing room at six minutes before midnight. My labor was as ordinary as they come—progressing through each step as if to illustrate a textbook. Because Nancy was such an experienced midwife, I didn't have any stitches or tearing, and I had not wanted any drugs, so I was exhausted but clearheaded when Nancy put Sofia's slick body on my belly while she cut the cord. I put my hands on her back and said, "Welcome." Maybe it was just the angle in which she was lying, but I swear she smiled up into my eyes and made a soft noise of happiness.

Later, when both of us were cleaned up, I was finally alone with my daughter. She was a solid seven pounds, with little folds of skin on her arms and feet, and plenty of meat on her calves and tummy. I touched her tiny shoulders and toes and nose and ears. She had a lot of dark hair, which was all soft and crazy, but it made her seem much bigger than a newborn. Her eyes were enormous and blue, and as she nursed—taking to it like an old hand, Nancy said—she gazed up at me with curiosity.

"I know," I said. "I'm amazed, too. It's kind of crazy that we haven't seen each other 'til now, isn't it?"

She paused in her gulping, and we locked eyes, and I felt everything in me shift, turn upside down.

Forever.

I stayed with Poppy for two weeks, learning all the stuff a mother has to do, while my parents got things ready for my return home. Until they saw her, two days after she was born, everybody was still disappointed that I'd kept her, but now they were all as much in love with her as I was.

Not that she was a good baby, necessarily. She fussed when her clothes irritated her, and she didn't like the heat, so she preferred to be carried outside at night. She nursed so much that I thought I was doing something wrong, but Nancy said that was just how babies ate.

One early evening, Sofia had fallen asleep and I was out in the garden collecting squashes and tomatoes and corn into a basket. My breasts were so big they were in the way, but I secretly liked the full milky enormity of them. My stomach was still a little poochy, but I could get into my old clothes, and the happy thing was, by nursing I could eat a lot and all the pregnancy pounds melted off right before my eyes.

I hadn't been alone much since Sofia arrived, and it felt great to just be in my own head for a little while. The garden smelled of damp earth and tomato leaves; overhead, the sky grew streaky red and pale gold as the sun headed toward the mountains. Crickets whistled, and somewhere in the corn was a cat rustling through the stalks. I plucked a big red tomato and admired it. In that moment, thinking of my daughter and all that had happened this summer, I was happy.

Car tires crunched on the gravel drive. I walked to the edge of the corn rows to see who it was, expecting Nancy, who had become one of Poppy's best friends.

It wasn't Nancy. It was Jonah, in his old Mercedes. He got out, his hair falling free over his shoulders. Everything in me went still, as if every cell was holding its breath. I hadn't seen him at all since the day we ate pie together, and I knew that was by design.

"Hello," he said, tucking his shirt into the back of his jeans as he came toward me.

"Hi."

"I hear you had a baby girl."

"She's so beautiful. You should come in and see her."

"I came to see you," he said, and gestured toward the path between the corn and tomatoes. "Can we walk a little?"

"Yeah. Yes." I felt dizzy with the smell of him, the nearness. We had not walked side by side like this before, and I was aware of his legs, and the swing of his arm so close to mine, and the sound of his low whistle.

Midway into the garden, he stopped and turned to look at me. "I came to tell you that I'm going back east. It's time to stop wallowing and get on with things; I found a teacher I think can help me."

A sharpness of tears pricked my eyelids and I forced myself to say, "Oh! Um, when do you leave?"

"Now," he said, and smiled down at me kindly. "I'm on my way out of town, and I couldn't leave without telling you how much—" He stopped and looked off into the sunset-mottled sky. His hair caught that red light, and I ached to touch it. He put his hands on his waist, looked back to me. "How much you helped me."

"I did?" On one hip I held the basket of vegetables, and the free hand fluttered up to my throat. "Me?"

He glanced over his shoulder toward the house, which was hidden from me by the corn, and took a step closer. "You." He took my hand and lifted it to his chest, pressing my palm into his breast. "Meeting you changed my life, Ramona. I thought you should know that."

"How?" I whispered, but I wasn't even sure I'd be able to hear him, my heart was pounding so loud.

"A hundred ways," he said, "but mainly by showing up."

"You helped me," I said. "I think you are—"

He shook his head and lifted his other hand to my face. "I'm too old for you."

His palm was warm, and I could smell his skin, which made

all the words fly out of my head. I could only stand there, looking up at him. Waiting.

"I wish I wasn't," he said, then he put a thumb under my chin, lifted my face, bent down. His full lips touched mine, just lightly. It was almost reverent, the way he kissed me, and I felt it right in my heart. My eyes filled with tears as I kissed him back.

After a moment, he turned his head a little and kissed me more deeply. I could feel his fingers against the lobe of my left ear, and his lips were full and soft, and his tongue was hot and close. Beneath my hand, his heart was pounding as hard as mine was. It went on and on in the sunset-washed light, in that time between day and evening.

At last he raised his head. His hand stayed where it was, and he looked right into my deepest soul with those gold eyes. "Take care, Ramona."

"Can't you write to me or something?" I said, my heart suddenly torn in two pieces. "I'll miss you!"

"It wouldn't be a good idea," he said, and I could feel his genuine regret.

His hand slipped from my face, and he lifted my hand from his chest, putting it on my own chest. "So long, Ramona."

"So long," I said, dizzy with all of it. I stood there until he climbed into the car, until I could no longer see the taillights in the dusk.

Knead and Set in a Warm Place to Rise

"Breadmaking is one of those almost hypnotic businesses, like a dance from some ancient ceremony. It leaves you filled with one of the world's sweetest smells . . . there is no chiropractic treatment . . . no hour of meditation in a music-throbbing chapel that will leave you emptier of bad thoughts than this homely ceremony of making bread."

—M. F. K. FISHER, THE ART OF EATING

NINETEEN

Katie, Present Day

*R*amona lost Merlin!

Katie can't breathe for the fury and terror in her chest, and she careens around the house to the backyard, the last place she saw her dog. In the middle of the grass, she turns in a careful circle, calling him. "Merlin! Merlin!"

She knows it's her own fault that he got away. She was so tired and she wanted to go back to sleep, but she's probably just like her mother—not very good at taking care of things that depend on her. The thought makes her want to cry. "Oh, Merlin! I will take care of you. I promise. Please come back."

"It's going to be okay," says a woman from the garden. "He's only running. He's a smart dog."

It's the old lady who was sitting beneath the tree last night. Katie frowns. The woman is cutting flowers from the border of the garden, where all the tall purple and blue and brown and peach flowers are—some of the prettiest flowers Katie has ever, ever seen. She's dressed as if she just got up, in a thin white robe with little sprigs of flowers on it and a scarf over her hair.

Still, her words ease some of the heat in Katie's throat. "How do you know?"

"I saw him." The woman clips a flower, leaving the stem long, and holds it up next to the others in her basket. "On my way over here."

"He was running?"

"Rolling in stinky stuff, actually, but really, he's exploring the neighborhood. That's what dogs do." She holds up a flower that's exactly the color of the flesh of a banana, edged with a dark nutmeg brown. The petals are as ruffly as a dress. "What do you think of this one?"

"Are you allowed to pick those flowers?"

"Oh, yes. Ramona and I have an understanding."

"I've never seen such amazing flowers," Katie says, letting her guard down for one second. "I've never seen anything that even comes close to being so beautiful."

The old woman smiles, and Katie sees she has a missing tooth. As if she remembers just in time, the woman gives a very lighthearted giggle and covers it with her hand. "Sorry. I haven't put my bridge in yet, have I?" Her eyes still twinkle. The color is a bright, powerful blue. "If you like flowers, Lily can teach you."

"Who?"

"Ramona's mother."

Katie shivers suddenly. From behind, she hears her name being called. "I have to go."

The woman nods. Katie turns and runs around the outside of the house, hoping against hope that Merlin has returned.

TWENTY

Ramona

When Katie flees toward the backyard, I reluctantly get busy, too. The girls and I fill the cases with our overnight creations, bringing the glorious scent of bread into the front room. Jimmy starts the coffeepot and when all of that is finished, I take a wet towel to the porch and erase the board. When it's clean and dry, I use my best handwriting and write with neon-blue marker:

WELCOME TO
MOTHER BRIDGET'S BOULANGERIE!

Today's Specials

Gougères
Raisin Walnut Pain Grenoblois
Sourdough Wheat Rolls
Assorted Muffins

As I'm finishing, a voice says behind me, "Hello!"

I turn to see a man—the man I saw on his porch while I was looking for Merlin—coming up the walk with a dog on a line. The dog is cheerful, tongue lolling.

"Merlin!" I dash down the steps. "Where have you been, you naughty boy?"

"Careful," the man says, "he's been rolling in dog perfume."

The odor slams me, and I cover my nose. "Gross, Merlin!"

The dog sits down, utterly pleased with himself. A big dark mark smears the white fur at his neck, and he's panting from the good workout, grinning broadly, showing all his teeth and a long slobbery tongue. He's being held loosely with what appears to be a man's striped green tie looped around his collar. I'm so happy to see him, I want to cry.

"Thank you, thank you, thank you," I say, looking up. "You have no idea what a huge disaster this was about to be."

The man nods in a genial way. He's long-limbed, very lean, and wears a corduroy coat over his jeans. A rose, dewy and perfect, hangs out of one pocket, such a whimsy that I grin and am about to remark upon it, when I notice his left hand. Two of his fingers have been cut off at the knuckles.

In swift, sharp recognition, I think about his voice and look up at a face that was once the most remarkable I'd ever seen in my life.

Jonah.

He looks back with honey-colored eyes, his expression only gentle, revealing nothing. My lungs have gone airless, and I can't think of what to say, and maybe he doesn't realize that the forty-year-old woman standing in front of him is the pregnant teenager who once had a most embarrassing, painful crush on him.

"Um," I say, "well... thank you very much." I reach for the tie. My hands are shaking. Visibly. "I'm... uh... we... um..." I touch my throat as if that will help clear the words stuck there. "We have fresh bread. Can I send some home with you?"

"That would be nice," he says in that resonant tenor, so unique. I can feel it between my shoulder blades. "Thank you."

From behind me, one of the apprentices says, "Oh, there you are, Ramona! I was worried. Do you want us to finish?"

"Yes. I have a little emergency here, but I'll get him cleaned up and help in a few minutes."

I can't look at him. "Please," I say, "come and choose a loaf."

His hand captures mine. "It is you!"

I look up into those beautiful eyes. "Jonah."

His gaze is unwavering. "I thought it was you yesterday morning at the café." He inclines his head. "I just didn't think…" He shrugs, tucks his hands behind his back. "I didn't think it was possible that you could still look so much the same."

I'm drinking in the details of him, the line of his jaw and the symmetry of his eyebrows, which I had forgotten, and that full lower lip. I can't think of anything to say, as if I am still sixteen. "The café?"

"You were with a young girl."

"Oh, Bon Ton's. I guess I didn't see you."

He's grown into his angularity, I think, become a man of unusual but compelling attractiveness. It occurs to me that I'm staring, mouth open, and I put a hand to my throat again. "Sorry. I'm being an idiot. I'm just so astonished."

"Me, too. I'm sorry to be forward, but you are still so very beautiful."

A rustle moves down my skin. "So are you."

He shakes his head, gentle smile on a generous mouth. "I have never been beautiful in all my life." His fingers pinch mine a little. "Except to you."

I am not sixteen anymore. I am forty, and a mother and a business owner. I straighten, conscious of the curves baking has given my body, of the lines he must surely be able to see in my face in the bright sunlight. "That is not true."

He inclines his head, almost wistfully. "It is, actually. But thank you. You, on the other hand, look remarkably the same."

"Oh, not at all," I protest, gesturing downward. "I'm fat."

"You were considerably bigger when I knew you."

I laugh, and it breaks up some of the airlessness I'm feeling.

"I suppose I was." Suddenly I think of Katie's terror, ongoing as I stand here. I hold up a finger. "One second. This is not my dog." Clomping around the side of the house, I call Katie's name. I wait for her, then call once more.

She comes thrashing along the bushes, sending a shower of loose lilac petals raining down on us both. As she emerges from the cool, shaded cove, she is so thin and her hair so wild that I think of some enchanted, untamed forest creature. She looks at me with such an agony of hope that I am unable to speak. I take her hand and lead her into the morning sunshine, where her smelly dog waits.

She cries "Merlin!" and rushes to him, skidding down beside him on her knees like a baseball player diving for home plate.

He gives a woof and a lick to her face, and then looks over her shoulder at me. I swear he winks.

"You found him?" Katie says to Jonah.

"He was sniffing around in my garden. Your mother was looking for him—"

"She isn't my mother!" Katie snatches the tie out of Jonah's hand. "She's not even my grandmother!"

"Katie," I say mildly. "There's no reason to be rude. Take Merlin in the backyard and hose that mess off his neck. I'll be with you in a few minutes and we'll take him upstairs for a bath."

"Whatever." She takes the tie, and then something comes over her. She looks back at Jonah. "Thank you."

"No problem." As she disappears into the cave of bushes again, he says, "She's not yours?"

"No, she's my daughter Sofia's stepdaughter." I take a breath. "It's a long story, but I'm sorry she was rude."

"It's all right." He shrugs lightly. "You have flower petals all over you."

I laugh nervously and brush my shoulders, the top of my head. "Thanks."

"I can see this is a bad time," he said. "But I'd love to have a cup of coffee sometime, catch up."

I'm captured by the faint hints of ginger and peaches that come off him. "Yes," I say. "I would love that. I'm free after two."

"I'll come back then."

A wistfulness pierces me as he turns to walk away. "Jonah," I say, breath high in my chest.

He turns, waiting.

"Do you want some bread? It's fresh. You should try it now."

He pauses, comes back. "Yes, I would like that."

I lead him inside, call to Heather, one of the college students who rotate the front-end shifts. "Give him a loaf of whatever bread he would like."

"Sure." She smiles and whips a piece of parchment from the dispenser. "What's your pleasure, sir?"

Jimmy rings a bell in the kitchen. "Call later," I say to Jonah. "I've gotta go."

By the time Katie and I get Merlin bathed and dried off, we're both starving. We feed the dog, then Katie takes him out on a leash to poo. Afterward she leads him upstairs to sleep on her sunporch.

When she comes back into the *boulangerie* kitchen, she's had a shower and put on clean clothes, the ones we got at Target, and says, "I'm sorry I was rude to that man."

"Thank you for the apology, but I was a little upset with you. He did something good."

She bows her head. The hair, a mass of curls and waves, stands out from her head like a caramel-colored hat. "Sorry." The word is sullen, but I'll take it.

Heather rushes into the kitchen. "Are we out of raisin bread already?"

I glance at the clock. Is it only eight-thirty? "Check on the cooling racks, but if none are there, we're out."

She scrambles through the racks, pulling out a handful of sourdough baguettes, still warm enough to give off a heady scent, and torpedoes of multigrain. Then she cries out as she discovers two loaves of raisin bread. "Thank goodness! It's Mrs. Klamkein. You know how she is!" And she scurries back to her customer.

I like hiring college students for the front, and I admit to hiring a certain wholesome, fresh-faced sort of girl for the position. It makes the breads seem more appealing if the clerk looks like she has been raised in the Swiss Alps on a diet of milk and honey. Sofia was the first, with her smooth olive skin and enormous blue eyes.

I wish she would call me. What is she doing? It must be nearly dinnertime in Germany. She must have more information by now. "Let's take our breakfast upstairs, shall we?"

Katie is standing with her arms akimbo, biting her lip as she eyes the pastries left in a pile on the table for the staff. Little *pains au chocolat,* big flaky croissants, a few muffins of various sorts. "Can I have any of these?"

"Of course! And I have some boiled eggs upstairs, maybe some strawberries, though they are not at their best yet."

She reaches for a croissant and looks it over, puts it carefully on her plate. I pluck a *pain au chocolat* from the pile and put it on her plate, too. "You'll like these, trust me."

We carry our breakfast upstairs to the kitchen, and I pour Katie a glass of milk and start a fresh pot of coffee for myself. "I want to check email to see if Sofia has written anything."

"Can I check mine after you?"

"Sure."

While I'm waiting for the coffee, I pull up my email and scroll through the meager offerings. A reminder from my dentist, a note from a friend in Alabama.

And, yes, an email from Sofia. I scan through it very quickly to see if there is anything disturbing, then read aloud to Katie. "Listen. Sofia says,

"'*Hi, Mom,*'" I read aloud in the most upbeat voice I can manage. "'*Sorry I didn't call, but there isn't much to report. We're still in Germany—we might be flown to San Antonio in a couple of days. Maybe Tuesday. I sit by Oscar's bed and read him books, because they say that he might be able to hear me and, at any rate, it doesn't hurt. If Katie will send me an email, I'll read that to him, too. Tell her he is doing okay, and we will know a lot more when he wakes up. The amputation is just above the knee, and they say there are really good prosthetics now, so not to worry about that.*

"'*As for me, I'm doing fine, so don't worry. There is a really great group of women here, and the nurses are excellent, and I have a cute little room, and really—the food is great! You'd be so happy to taste all these breads, I just know it.*

"'*Give yourself a kiss, and tell Katie I hope she's settling in okay. Love you both, Sofia.*'"

While she listened, Katie has shredded the croissant into a billion tiny pieces, a fact she seems to notice only when I finish. Her face falls when she looks at it. "Dang it."

"That's all right. Go get another one."

"Are you sure?"

"I'm the boss, remember?"

The very faintest of smiles touches her mouth. "Sorry. I tear things up sometimes without even thinking about it. Once it was my friend's Valentine's Day card to me! She got really mad."

"I guess she would!"

When she dashes downstairs, I turn to the keyboard and write, very quickly,

Thanks for your email, sweetie. Sounds like you are very tired, so get some rest and we'll be okay. Katie will send you an email in a little while.

Please find some time to call her when you can. She's really
worried and not able to express that.
  Love, Mom

I hear Katie tromping up the stairs and hit the send button,
noticing only as I do so that there is more than one set of feet on
the stairs. "Your mom is here," Katie says, gesturing. "She
brought doughnuts, but I got a muffin instead. Is that okay?"
She holds it, normal size but bursting with raspberries and
blueberries beneath a crown of streusel, in her hand. "It just
looks so great."

"Yes." I smile. "That's actually a muffin I started baking when
Sofia was a teenager. She needed a fast breakfast, and that's a
good muffin for it."

Katie bites into it. Widens her eyes. "It's good!" she says,
mouth full.

Lily breezes into the kitchen, wearing crisp white capris and
a sleeveless green blouse with a big collar. Her earrings match, as
does her green-and-white watch. "Good morning, ladies," she
says, putting the Dunkin' Donuts box on the table. "How are
things?" She breathes in deeply. "I see you made coffee. Mind if
I have some?" Without waiting for me to answer, she takes a cup
out of the cupboard and pours herself some coffee. "You want
some, Ramona?"

I nod, thinking suddenly of Jonah standing outside on my
sidewalk this morning. It seems incredible. Miraculous, even.
How is it possible that he's living this close to me? I mean, I
don't know even a tenth of the people in that five-block radius,
but still. It seems I would have noticed him.

I wonder how his life has gone, if he has children, if he married, and think again of the whimsical flower in his pocket, his
beautiful eyes. It shook me, seeing him, and as Lily pours coffee,
she is hauling me out of the record store again, and the life I
thought I was going to have is gone, leaving my world upside

down. The emotional echo still has surprising power, and suddenly I am my sixteen-year-old self, overwhelmed and lost and clinging to the kindness of a young man far older than I.

Smiling to myself as I stir sugar into my cup, I think, *Today he didn't seem old at all.*

Lily opens the box of doughnuts, and I think of her fury, her fear, that summer. As a mother now, I understand it—a heart broken on one's own behalf is one thing. A heart broken for the losses of a child is a yawning sorrow that cannot be eased by anything except the happiness of the child. For a moment I am her, looking at me pregnant and hysterical, and love floods me. I press my fingers to my diaphragm, take a breath.

Across the table, Katie is silent, peeling the boiled eggs I'd put out in a blue bowl for her. Her eyes flit from my mother to me, gathering data in a way that is much too old for her.

"Mom," I say. "Will you take the butter out of the fridge and bring a couple of knives?"

She's happy to have a task, and I have to remember this—she doesn't move around my kitchen as if she owns it because she's bossy. Well, only partly because she's bossy. The real reason is that she likes feeling useful and part of things. Why do I have to be so mean about it? I am kinder to almost everyone in the world than I am to my mother. "We had an email from Sofia this morning," I offer.

She pulls out a chair and sits down with us. "How are things going?"

"Don't really have much information yet. You can email her, too, if you like. Katie, after breakfast you should send an email for Sofia to read to your dad."

She pulls the *pain au chocolat* apart, seems to remember that she doesn't want to shred it, and puts it down. "What am I gonna say?"

"Just tell him that you moved here, that you have a dog. Ordinary things."

"Cheerful things," Lily says. "If he knows you're okay, he can focus on getting well and coming home sooner."

Katie nods. "Oh. Okay. I'll tell him about Merlin and about him jumping the fence."

"He did?"

"Yeah," I say, but wave a hand to forestall a recounting right this minute. "Long story, Mom."

With two delicate fingers, she picks out a strawberry-frosted doughnut and puts it on the saucer she took out of the cabinet. "I'll send her something, too. Promise. Don't you want a doughnut, Ramona? I brought an apple fritter just for you."

"I'm living in a bakery, remember?"

"You don't make doughnuts, though, do you?"

"No." I take a deep breath in, blow it out.

"Hey," Katie says, saving me. "There was an old lady outside earlier who said you know a lot about flowers, Mrs. Gallagher. Are you Lily?"

"I do know a lot about flowers. What would you like to know?"

"What old lady?" I ask.

"I don't know. She didn't tell me her name." Katie gobbles the last of her muffin, brushes her fingers off. "But I think flowers are so pretty. I would like to grow some, maybe?"

"That's a wonderful idea!" Lily's face lights up. "Ramona, would you mind if I take Katie to look at bedding plants this afternoon?"

"Not at all." Maybe I can steal a nap.

Or have coffee with Jonah.

RAMONA'S BOOK OF BREADS

HEARTY BERRY STREUSEL MUFFINS
Makes 30–32

This is a muffin for those crazy mornings when you need calories in a hurry. The yogurt and nuts add protein, the whole grains add fiber, and the fruit adds nutrients as well as general seduction for picky children. The streusel can be left off to save calories, but, trust me, you're better off with one good one. Serve with boiled eggs for a super-fast breakfast.

1 cup white flour
½ cup spelt flour (or add another ½ cup white)
1 cup whole-wheat flour
1 cup oats
1 T baking powder
1 tsp baking soda
½ tsp sea salt
1 cup honey (or raw sugar)
1½ cups plain yogurt
1 6-oz. container raspberry or blueberry yogurt
½ cup milk
3 T canola oil
2 tsp vanilla extract
1 large egg
1 cup each fresh blueberries and raspberries

STREUSEL

¼ cup flour
3 T brown sugar
¼ cup chopped, lightly toasted walnuts, pecans, or almonds
1½ T butter, melted

Prepare muffin tins with paper or oil. Prepare streusel first and set aside.

For muffins: Mix dry ingredients well. In a separate bowl, mix all wet ingredients except berries, and beat together well. Pour the wet ingredients into the dry mix and beat firmly and quickly just until thoroughly moistened. Add berries and fold in gently. Divide batter into greased or paper-lined muffin tins and bake at 400 degrees for 15 minutes. Cool for 15 minutes in the pan to set the berries, remove from pan, and cool on wire rack.

TWENTY-ONE

Sofia's Journal

This evening I went out walking. There are flowers everywhere, and I'm thinking about Grandma Lily and her ten million tulips and forty different kinds of dahlias. She and my grandfather went to Holland last year, and she came back with so many pictures of flowers I finally had to stop her from showing me every single one and naming the species and genus and whatever. I don't know. I'm not a gardener. Or a cook, for that matter. Sometimes I wonder why the family gifts skipped me. I like looking at flowers and heaven knows I love eating good food, don't get me wrong.

Oh, I suppose I like quilting. My mother would rather have her hands cut off than knit or sew anything, but I like it. Maybe I should get some yarn and crochet while I'm talking to Oscar. It would be soothing.

I've just had some supper at the hospital cafeteria—a plate of roast pork and cabbage with a very nice rye bread I should remember to tell my mother about. I ate it with butter, even though I've been trying hard to be good and not gain ten million pounds with this baby. But I needed something a little luxurious.

It has been a very discouraging day. Everything the doctors are not saying is written on their faces when they talk to me. They are pretending hope and optimism, but I can see how the mask slips the minute they turn away. They feel sorry for me.

I have been sitting with Oscar all day, talking until I'm hoarse, reading to him when I run out of things to talk about—the newspaper, a magazine article. Tomorrow I'm going to the library to see what I can find to read aloud, chapter by chapter.

No matter what, he's got a long road ahead of him. He will have to learn to walk again, of course, but the burns are the thing. The blast came from the front, so his head and face and chest took the brunt of it, and I have to admit I'm afraid. It's strange to know his face will not be the same face I have loved. Is a face who we are? I know it isn't, but that's how we recognize one another and ourselves, by the marker of a nose and the shape of eyes and lips and chin.

I am worried about how he will take it, seeing that his face is ~~ruined~~ different.

Until I feel calm, I can't call my mother. She'll pick up my terror, and I can't stand to have her worrying, too, not about me when she has so much to deal with already.

My entire body feels like I've been soundly beaten, as my grandma Adelaide used to say, so I guess I'll finish up and go back to my room and get some sleep.

Oh, Oscar, Oscar! I'm so sad this happened to you. I hope I can find the right words to encourage you and let you know that you are loved, no matter what. You have to live, for me and for your daughters. We need you.

Now I'm crying and need to just get myself to bed. Tomorrow, though, I am going to get some yarn in beautiful colors.

Enough.

TWENTY-TWO

Katie

K atie feels shy going with Lily, but the older woman is so happy to be talking flowers that Katie finds herself swept along. In Lily's big green Nissan, they drive to a greenhouse that's set back from the street, and the minute Katie walks inside, it seems as if everything in her whole body lets go with a sigh.

Just inside the door, she stops. The light is a pale, soft color over the endless tables of flowers in every color and size and shape, the most beautiful thing she has seen in her entire, entire life. "Oh, my God."

"Haven't you ever been to a greenhouse before, hon?"

"No," Katie whispers. She breathes in the smell of earth and leaves and something damp. She can't take her eyes off the rows of colors. "It's amazing."

"You go wander, then, and I'll do the same. Take your time."

Katie floats between the tables, looking at little pink and white flowers called impatiens that are flat and seem as if they're smiling, and big white daisies with yellow centers, and even a long table of cactus of so many kinds she's never seen before. Around her she can feel a soft, rustling awareness, as if the plants are talking in very quiet whispers. What do plants think about? She smiles and moves down the aisles, lightly touching a ruffled dark-red thing and fluttering her fingers over a bush covered with tiny white flowers. She looks at a big vine, with really bright pink flowers that look like they are made of paper, and marigolds, which she knows.

There are so many flowers and plants! So many differently shaped leaves and petals, so many different smells. It's exactly what she'd want heaven to be like.

It's not until they get outside, carrying flat boxes of bedding plants Lily says she'll help Katie plant, that Katie realizes she has not thought about anything. It's as if her brain just turned off.

Weird. But good weird.

That night she writes to Madison again, though Madison has not written one single letter yet. Not even an email.

Dear Madison,

Today I planted flowers for six hours with Sofia's grandmother, and it was the most fun I ever had. My arms are super-tired and I got a sunburn a little bit, but now I had a long hot bath in this beautiful bathroom here and I feel like I could sleep for six years.

I like it here. I wish you could come visit. We could go to the flower show Lily told me about, which has all kinds of flowers and people try to win prizes. She's going to take me.

My dad is doing okay. He doesn't have a leg and he has burns, but Sofia says he's all right. I wish he would wake up and write to me, though, so then I would know he was going to be okay.

I haven't heard anything from my mom yet, but I guess I will sometime. WRITE ME BACK! What are you doing this summer?

Your BFF,
Katie

TWENTY-THREE

Ramona

Not twenty minutes after my mother leaves with Katie, I'm cleaning the kitchen when the bakery phone rings. Tucking the phone between my ear and shoulder, I say, "Mother Bridget's Boulangerie. This is Ramona." I shake the dish towel over the sink.

"Hello, Ramona," he says. "This is Jonah."

I think of the first time we met. "Our names rhyme. That's so funny."

"It is." There is warmth in his voice. "Do you have time for a cup of coffee or something? Is this a good time?"

"It's perfect. Shall I meet you at Bon Ton's in about a half hour?"

"Yes. I'll see you then."

Leaving the rest of the chores, I dash upstairs and take a ten-second shower to rinse the sweat and work of the day off my body. I think about running up and down the alleys looking for Merlin, and the baking, and the email from Sofia. Soon I will need some sleep. When I wipe the steam off the mirror, there are bluish circles beneath my eyes, and I can see worry lines at the corners of my mouth. I purse my lips and relax them three or four times, but the lines don't go away. There is Sofia's tragedy, right on my face.

I brush the flour out of my hair and put on some lipstick. The green sundress hides some of the extra weight I carry around my middle. Before I leave, I lock Merlin upstairs so he'll be safe, then head out to meet Jonah.

The café is only three blocks away, and I am a little early, but Jonah is there already, sitting at an outdoor table with a view of Cheyenne Mountain. A tree shades the table from the high-altitude sun. When he sees me, he stands, and for a moment I pause, feeling oddly nervous. What will we even say to each other after so long?

Then he smiles, and a part of me that is still sixteen melts ever so slightly. I give him my best smile as I come forward. He extends his hand, but on impulse I stand on my toes and hug him instead. It's a quick fierce greeting, old friend to old friend. His neck smells of ginger, and his hand comes around me, touches my back lightly. I close my eyes, swept into another time, another me. "I'm so glad you could come," he says, letting me go.

"Me, too." I sit down and the waitress hurries over.

"Coffee?"

"Please."

"Well," I say, and lean back, inclining my head to take in the details I was too rattled to register earlier. He's wearing jeans and a thin cotton shirt that buttons up the front, with long sleeves he's rolled up his forearms. His hair is still the same thick dark chestnut, wavy and shiny. His face is so much the same it's eerie, but he's somehow grown into the angles. There is a gravity that was missing. Finally I say, "You really don't look very different. I can't believe I didn't recognize you in your yard."

"It's been a long time." He folds his hands on his belly. "The advantage goes to me, because you have such distinctive hair."

I pull a thick section through my palm. "I grew it out again only about four years ago."

"Was it short?"

"It's been everything. Long, short, in between. Super-professional. It's like some big experiment in social adaptation." The waitress brings my coffee. "When my daughter was small, I had so much to do that I cut it all off."

"I like it long."

"Yours was long once, too," I comment.

"Yes. Back in the rebellious days."

A pause falls. I stir sugar and milk into my coffee, wondering where to start, how to begin the reacquaintance. "So, how long have you been in the Springs?"

"Not very long—only a few weeks, actually. I flew here at Christmas, found the house, and started the renovations, then moved in about a month ago."

"I've always liked that house, the garden," I comment. "My sisters and I liked the balcony in the back. It must have a wonderful view."

"It does. It was not in great shape when I found it, but the bones were good. I've been in the L.A. area for a long time, so I'm very happy to be back in Colorado."

I nod, wondering if it would be too forward to ask if he is a musician. If he is not, perhaps it would be unkind. "What brought you back here?"

"Work. I'm the director for a children's charity, Hearts Abound. Their headquarters are here."

"I know it well. We have donation jars in the bakery." I smile. "You're *the* director?"

His smile is gentle, amused. "Yes."

"Wow." I widen my eyes. "Impressive."

"How about you, Ramona? Is the bakery yours?"

I laugh, thinking of all the struggles we've been facing. "Yes. It was my grandmother's house. She left it to me when she died six years ago, and I jumped at the chance to create the bakery."

"The bread is terrific."

"Thank you. Which one did you choose?"

"Cranberry walnut."

"Ah. One of my favorites." I lean forward. "But the girls will tell you I say that about all of them. The sourdoughs, the raisin bread, the oatmeal."

It's only then that I realize he's looking at my mouth, my throat, and there is something in his face that touches me, like the flutter of bird wings. "Which is your true favorite?" he asks quietly. His voice moves down my neck like a whisper.

The atmosphere has shifted, the air growing taut between us. "I'm not sure." I smile and give a tiny shrug, maybe flirting the slightest bit. "Depends on the day."

He nods. Our eyes meet, lock. The waitress swings around with coffee, breaking the moment. I am relieved.

"Your daughter must be grown. What is she like?"

The dark cloud of her life moves through me, aches.

"I'm sorry," Jonah says. "Is that a sore spot?"

"No, no. I'm sorry." I shake my hair away from my face. "Sofia is a delight and a fantastic person. She's pregnant with her first baby, so I'll be a grandmother in a couple of months."

He laughs. "You hardly look old enough to be a mother."

"Oh, please. Thank you, but, believe me, I feel plenty old enough." I fold a sugar packet into precise quarters. "The trouble is, she's in Germany right now with her husband, who was wounded badly in Afghanistan. They're waiting to stabilize him before they move him to San Antonio."

"I'm sorry. That must be terrible."

I'm about to make some comment that will excuse him from the burden of this darkness, but I find myself saying simply, "It is. And Katie, the girl you met, is his daughter. So she's feeling it."

"Burns?"

I nod.

"I hate this war. Is it all right to say that to you?"

I bow my head to hide the unexpected and intense emotions that rise at that statement. "I hate all of them." I lift my head, sigh. "It used to be so much easier to make pronouncements, you know? It feels complicated now. I do wish we lived in a world that used some other method to solve problems—it's so wasteful, on every level—but this is the world we live in."

"Well said." He inclines his head. "Now I find myself remembering the way you always said the most unexpected things."

"Did I?"

"You must have an old soul."

I snort, in a very old-soul way. "My family would disagree with you on that."

His chuckle is warm. Inclusive, somehow. "They just don't see you clearly. It's hard for families to see one another sometimes, don't you think?"

It's my turn to incline my head. "Yes. And that's what I remember about you—how kind you were to me. I always felt so . . . honored in your company."

"I'm glad." Again there is that moment of connection, weaving between us like the first notes of a symphony.

I break it, picking up the menu. "You know, I'm a little hungry. Would you mind if I ate something?"

"Not at all. I'll join you."

In the end, I sit with him over a late lunch for more than two hours. In silent agreement, our conversation is carefully superficial, about public things, nothing too dark or charged. He makes me laugh with stories about his work, and I tell him about the bakery and my cat, Milo.

As we talk, our bodies move ever so slightly closer. He bends over the table and I lean in. I find myself watching his mouth move and looking at the long line of his throat, admiring the shine of his hair in the late-afternoon sunlight. Something that has been sleeping low in my belly wakes up, stretches up my spine, spreads across my upper back.

He wears no ring, but that doesn't always mean anything. It's hard to ask straight out, to reveal that I might be thinking of him in that way.

Finally, the waitress apologetically asks us to leave. In surprise, I look around and see that the place is empty. "We closed an hour ago."

I laugh, glance at Jonah. "Sorry. We're old friends. Time got lost."

Beyond the low iron fence, we pause. He looks down at me. "Did you marry, Ramona?"

"Yes. And divorced."

"Ah."

"You?"

He meets my eyes. A light is there. "The same."

I nod, holding his gaze.

"I wonder," he says, "if you and—Katie, is it?—would like to come to dinner sometime? I'm a good cook, I promise."

Is Katie a chaperone or is he being kind? "I would love that. Yes." I lift a finger. "One caveat. I get up at two in the morning, so I prefer earlier rather than later."

"Do you have days off?"

"Sunday and Monday."

"What about tomorrow, then? I'll cook, and you can bring Katie and her dog, and we'll eat on the porch. Five-thirty early enough?"

Something like hope blooms in my chest. "Yes."

To cope with my unusual hours, my habit is to take two naps each day—a short one after the morning rush and a longer, deeper one late in the afternoon. When I get back to the house, Katie still has not returned.

Milo and I go to my north-facing bedroom and curl up on the bed. A breeze sweeps the curtains up and down in a little dance, and the air feels fresh on my tired skin. Milo covers my belly with silk and purr. I close my eyes and think of Jonah, his adult face, his still-kind eyes, and something that was missing when he was younger: an unmistakable sense of presence and power. I drift off.

That's where I am, suspended somewhere between past and present, when a voice arrows into my consciousness.

"Ramona," it says. "Wake up, I need to talk to you." A hand is wrapped around mine. Struggling to surface, I say, "Jonah?" before I realize where I am. And when.

And who it is in front of me. Not Jonah, of course, but Cat. Who sits intimately on the edge of my bed, holding my hand. I bolt upright, yanking my hand away. "What are you doing? Get out of here! I told you I don't want to talk to you."

He tsks. "Ah, no no no. Don't be silly. You were angry at my high-handedness, but that's nothing to worry about. I'm sorry." He puts his hands over his heart. "*Mea culpa.*"

In the cascade of quiet light coming from the windows, he looks as roguish as a pirate—which is, of course, the charm. It has been my curse to be surrounded by big personalities, starting with my father and my grandmother, then Sofia's father, and then my ex-husband, Dane.

But I am tired of being buffeted by all of their wishes. Swinging away from Cat, I put my feet down on the floor and push my hair out of my eyes, my fingers automatically going to the end of my braid so I can brush and rebraid it. "No. You need to go."

He hasn't moved, and I see, unexpectedly, that he is filled with regret. I waver, feeling that familiar pluck in my chest, a need to make sure everyone else is happy.

No. Steeling myself, I walk around him, unweaving my braid as I go, so my hair is falling down my back, which is a mistake I would not have made if he had not awakened me. My hair is like a siren call to him, irresistible, and he follows me into the kitchen, watching from the table as I pour out the old coffee and draw fresh water for a new pot. "You really don't want me to talk to you at all?"

I frown over my shoulder. "Right." I pour beans into the grinder and push the button, releasing that most elegant, reviving scent. I breathe it in.

He comes up behind me, putting his hands on my shoulders, his forehead against my hair. "Ramona, *tesoruccio mìo*, give me another chance. I have been an ass, I know it, but just forgive me, huh?"

For the first time I realize that his feelings are strong, that perhaps I have been leading him on in a way, leaning on him because I am lonely without my family. And he, being the man he is, took my continuing friendship as encouragement.

Gently, I turn and put my hands on his dear face. "Cat, I'm grateful to you for all the things you've done for me." I rub his smooth jaw with my thumbs. "But I am not in love with you and I never will be."

"I don't need for you to be in love with me." Urgently, he takes fistfuls of my hair into his hands. "I love you enough that it doesn't matter. We can be happy. Prosperous. It's a foolishness that women now have to prove themselves, even if they fail, when they don't have to."

I drop my hands, smiling gently. He genuinely doesn't understand, and nothing I say will make any difference. "You need to go, Cat."

And to my surprise and dismay, he bends his head and gathers me into a bear hug. "No."

I endure it for one minute, then push him away, and it's only then that I hear the footsteps on the stairs. He's still clinging to a fistful of my hair, and there might be tears in his eyes when my mother comes into the kitchen, carrying a flat of bedding plants. She halts, taking in the tableau. A slide show of emotions moves across her face—surprise, then dismay, then fury, and then something I can't quite identify. She's looking at Cat, not me.

And then she does look at me. Squarely. Her nostrils flare ever so slightly before she rights herself, almost visibly slipping into her cloak of blankness.

"I'm sorry," she says smoothly. "Are we interrupting?"

"Don't be ridiculous," I say, scowling at him. "Cat was just leaving."

"Hello, Lily," he says. He, too, is a master of the cloak. His is debonair and charming. "You look wonderful," he says, and means it. We all know he does. It is his gift, that he sees the best in all of us and gives it back to us like a shiny apple—all women, everywhere, and he genuinely admires each one. When I am with him, I forget the ten extra pounds I am carrying, forget the lines etching themselves into my face, and become as gloriously beautiful as a mermaid. Is that what my mother feels, too? If he is so devastating now, how much more was he at twenty-five, when he pursued her as if she were a queen to rule over his kingdom?

"Thank you," she says coolly, putting the flowers on the table. "How are you?"

"Very well, thank you."

I've never seen them in the same room together. Cat and my father are sworn enemies, so there would be few chances for Cat and my mother to cross paths. Looking at them—she so trim and well tended, looking much younger than her years, he so big and sturdy and beautiful—I think they must have been a stunning couple back in the day. What happened there? What made my mother choose my father?

My mother brushes her hands delicately, gives me a glance

loaded with meaning. "Katie is on her way up with some dahlias. Would it cause any trouble if she came to my house for supper? She wants to help me plant some more, and I told her I'd make her a banana pudding."

Katie comes into the room then, looking flushed and as happy as I've ever seen her. In the new clothes—clothes that actually fit her—she doesn't look nearly so awkward. "We bought zillions of flowers!" she cries, and puts geraniums on the table next to the dahlias. They are Martha Washingtons, with their extravagant magenta petals edged with white. She points to a box of bachelor's buttons, too. "Lily let me buy these to plant in front of the bakery, if that's okay? To replace the stuff that got messed up in the repair."

"No problem." I glance at my mother, widening my eyes to say, *Where did you find this sunny child?* Her mask cracks slightly and she grins. "Katie has an aptitude for flowers. I didn't think you'd mind."

"Not at all." I frown at Cat, who is still standing there in the middle of the kitchen. "Thanks for everything, Cat," I say pointedly. "I'll see you later."

He lifts a finger. "Right. So long, ladies. Enjoy your flowers."

"I'm hungry," Katie says. "Are there any more doughnuts?"

"No more doughnuts," I say.

"Have a sandwich or something, sweetie," Lily says.

Our eyes meet over her head. My mother's eyes say, *This is not finished.*

"It isn't what you think," I say aloud, crossing my arms.

She raises an eyebrow in disappointment, and it is as devastating as it was when I was seven or fifteen or twenty. "Really."

Katie is in the fridge, comfortably taking out sliced turkey and mustard, and I'm glad, at least, for that. "What's not?" she says, oblivious to the undercurrents.

"Nothing, kiddo," I say. "You want some iced tea?"

. . .

My cell phone rings later, as I am refreshing the sourdough starters. I glance at the unfamiliar number and debate whether I should answer. I'm not interested in talking to solicitors. "Hello?"

"Mom?"

"Sofia!" I head out into the backyard. Merlin follows me. "What's up? It must be very late there."

"It is." Her voice sounds squashed. "Past midnight. I couldn't sleep. How's Katie doing?"

"She's with your grandmother, planting flowers."

Sofia gives a soft laugh. "Gram must love that."

"Yeah." For a long moment I listen to the silence, the phone pressed tightly to my ear for fear I might miss some clue. Between us, the air rushes, sounding like the ocean that divides us. "What's on your mind, honey?"

"I don't know. I don't want you to worry about me, okay, because I know you have other things on your mind, but you're the person I really need to talk to. Can you promise to just let me fall apart without needing to solve my problems?"

"Do I do that?"

"Yes. You're a fixer. That's your entire impulse, and it's okay, but it's not going to work for me right now."

"Okay. I promise." I rub a hand over my belly. "Fall apart."

"I don't know if he's going to live. He has so many things wrong and he's really burned. I don't know if he'll *want* to live. I don't know what to say when he's lying there to—" Words give out and a puff of air comes through instead. I can see her in my imagination, hand pushing through her thick dark hair, making the bangs stand up. "I don't know what I'm calling you for."

I take a breath and try to find the right non-fix-it words. "Because you know I love you. Because you know I'd rather hear your voice than any other on the planet. Because I'm thinking about you and it's really good to hear from you."

"Yeah. All those things. The funny thing is, Mom, there's no list to make this any better. I don't know what to do," she says, and begins to cry. "I have to be strong. For him. For Katie. For my own baby. And I have no idea how. I don't know if I'm that strong."

Tears well up in my own eyes, but it's absolutely critical that she not hear them. I blink and look up at the tops of the lilac bushes. "Close your eyes."

"Okay."

"Now imagine for one minute that you're standing in the backyard with me. There's a soft breeze, and it smells almost too much of lilacs. Somebody nearby is watering their lawn, and the sprinkler is making that *tick-tick-tick* sound. Milo is sitting at your feet."

"Okay. This is good." Her voice is still wavery but better.

"Now imagine, sweetheart, that I am taking your hand. Can you feel it?"

"Yes."

"I'm right there with you. I'm always holding your hand. I am always here, whenever you need me. You are not alone."

"Imagine that I'm putting my head on your shoulder now, and just let me do that."

I close my eyes and imagine that I truly can hold her, that her face is pressed into my neck, soaking my shirt. Tears pour out of my eyes, down my face, as Sofia cries in my ear.

After a time, she sniffles hard. "Okay. Thank you. I love you, Mom. I'm holding your hand."

"I feel it. Get some sleep. That will help, too."

"Light some candles, or have Grandma do it, okay? We need them."

"Consider it done. I love you, baby."

"I love you, too," she says, and hangs up.

Holding the phone in one hand, I rub the yawning ache in my chest with the other. My hair falls over my shoulders—too long for someone my age, I know it is—but there is no cutting it. It is the thing that is most myself, no matter what anyone else thinks. At moments like this, it's like a cape shielding me from the world.

My poor girl. My poor, poor baby.

Merlin has been sitting with me, and now he jumps up as if he's been called. He trots across the garden, walking carefully between the rows of new squash and corn, and heads for the open corner. There is an altar there that my grandmother erected years and years ago, and Merlin lies down alertly before it, paws neatly placed in front of him, his head high, as if he is listening.

"What are you doing, you funny dog?"

He looks over his shoulder at me and woofs softly, then looks back at the altar. Curious, I follow him. A garden statue of a saint I don't remember stands amid a low border of alyssum. In the dimming evening, the flowers almost seem to have a light of their own, and I swear I can hear humming. It triggers an old hymn in my mind, something we used to sing with guitars—"Alleluia."

Merlin lets go of a soft, joyous woof and his tail wags slowly. I sit down next to him in the cool grass, thinking I could do worse than pray for my daughter here in this sacred space where my grandmother said her own prayers so often. "Are you listening? Help her. Help him." I stroke Merlin's thick fur, trying to even think of what to ask for. "Let them find peace and happiness."

The song is running insistently through my mind. So I begin to sing aloud, for my daughter.

TWENTY-FOUR

Katie

TO: Sofia.wilson@horaceandersen.edu
FROM: katiewilson09872@nomecast.com
SUBJECT: a letter you can read to my dad

Dear Dad,

I'm writing this from my stepgrandma's house. I guess you already know Lily, because she's Sofia's grandma, too. We have been planting flowers in Lily's garden all day, but more about that in a minute.

I don't know if you've ever been to this house, but it's really, really cool. There is a lot of wood and a stone fireplace with two sides—kitchen and living room—so everybody can enjoy a fire! It's kind of up in the hills, and Lily (don't get mad at me for calling her by her first name, okay? She doesn't like to be called Grandma) says they had it specially built in the '70s when their restaurant was the number-one steakhouse in the whole state. Like, they hired an architeck and everything.

The restaurant is called the Erin Steakhouse because their family is Irish, which you probably already know. We went there for dinner, and it's pretty cool, up on top of this bluff so you can see all the lights in the city and the mountains. It was kinda old school, but the food was really good. I had a steak, and baked potato with butter and sour cream, and a salad with little blue cheese crumbles on it, and big dinner rolls. I asked Lily if Ramona comes here, but she said no. Kinda mad like. I get the feeling Lily is mad at Ramona, but I like them both, although I got really mad at Ramona for losing my dog last night. It turned out okay because a man found him and brought him home.

Which I guess I haven't even told you about Merlin! He's a really cute dog, with white and orangey fur and a freckle on his nose. I love him.

The last thing I want to tell you (I can't believe how long this is getting! I'm glad I wrote you first) is about the flowers. We went to a greenhouse and it was filled with flowers in every color. Pink and yellow and white and blue and even green. Inside, it felt like a different planet, like I could breathe ten times better. Lily let me buy a bunch of things, some marigolds, which are orange and brown, and dahlias, which she says come in a lot of different kinds, and she has a bunch of them and they will start blooming in a few more weeks, she says, so I'll take pictures and send them. She let me take one with her camera, and although she couldn't figure out how to upload it, I did and it's attached here for when you wake up. Me and the garden.

Anyways, everything is okay here, but I really miss you, Dad, and I can't wait until you come home.

Love, Katie

Katie is writing on the computer, which is on a built-in desk right next to a balcony looking down into the living room. It's the best thing she's ever seen in a house. In fact, the entire house is amazing, with the ceiling at all angles and hidden window seats piled up with pillows. Lily showed Katie to a room at the end of a long, long hallway and said she could use it whenever she was over. It used to be Ramona's room, but it's been decorated since then with turquoise and green rugs and a bed that's kind of low to the ground. The window is really high, looking down a rocky ledge and over the mountains. The first time Katie looks out, she feels dizzy, but the view is of mountains upon mountains upon mountains, like velvet cutouts in layers and layers of blue.

Although it makes her feel like a traitor, and a super-spoiled traitor at that, Katie thinks this room is ten times better than the one over the bakery, and that was the prettiest room she'd ever had before this. It scares her even to think it, as if maybe not appreciating it enough might make it go away.

So she acts all bored (*Nonchalant,* she writes in her mind to Madison), like she's seen these kinds of things a million times, even though she could stare out that window forever. It makes her feel quiet inside. And when Lily asked if she wanted to spend the night, it was really hard for Katie to say, "No, thank you. I have to take care of my dog."

"Oh, honey, Ramona can take care of Merlin. We can call and ask. If you want to stay, that is."

But she decides to just have dinner and then go home. She loves being able to get on the computer and surf around. She writes an email to Madison, telling her about the day, and then, looking over her shoulder just in case, she opens another email.

TO: laceymomsoldier@prt.com
FROM: katiewilson09872@nomecast.com
SUBJECT: from Katie, saying hi

Hi, Mom.

Just checking to see if you got email yet. I'm having a good time here, so don't worry about me. Sofia's grandma is really nice to me and she helped me plant a bunch of flowers today, but I miss you a LOT.

She chews on her lip, thinking. What else can she say to her mother? By now she's probably feeling pretty crummy. Katie has seen her get off meth before—three times, as a matter of fact. Once she lasted only a couple of weeks, another time it was a year—that was when Katie lived with Sofia and Oscar. It wasn't bad living there; she just felt like a traitor about her mom. So when Lacey stayed clean for a whole year, and Oscar was deployed again, he let Katie go live with her mom, as long as she promised to let him know the minute Lacey started using again.

Don't think about that now.

She writes:

> I know you probably don't feel very good, but remember: You can do it! You got clean before and felt really good, remember? Once you get out, I can come and live with you again. I love you! Lots! Lots! Lots!
>
> > Your daughter,
> > Katie
>
> PS—Dad got hurt really bad in Afghanistan. Probably nobody told you, so I thought you should know.

She wants to write more, wants to pour out her worst fear about her dad—not that he will die but that he will look like a soldier who used to shop at the commissary, his nose burned off, the skin of his face all pink and white and stiff. If he looks like that, how can she love him? It makes her shudder.

And that makes her feel like the worst person in the world, that she would be afraid of her dad having a messed-up face even more than she would be afraid of him being dead.

From the kitchen she hears voices, a man's and a woman's, and hurries to send off the email. Lily calls up to her, "Katie, my husband and daughters just got here with a beautiful peach pie. Why don't you come down and have some with us?"

"Sure. I'll be right there."

She closes down the computer and heads down the big sweep of stairs, which are made of wood and all open, with a view out the top windows of more mountains and pine trees. She feels as if she's in a movie, and it makes her stand a little straighter, imagining she's a singer like Taylor Swift, coming down the stairs of her beautiful house. She's so absorbed in the fantasy that she starts when a woman comes around the corner from the kitchen. She has streaky blond hair cut in a very straight line at her shoulders, with straight bangs across her forehead, and Katie knows right away she is Ramona's sister, because they have exactly the same eyes. "Hi, Katie," she says, holding out a hand as if Katie is a grown-up. "I'm Stephanie, Sofia's aunt. And this," she turns, to introduce another woman behind her, also blond with giant blue eyes like Sofia's, "is my sister Sarah. She just got home from India, so we're celebrating."

"Hi." Katie lifts a hand. Sarah wears a glittery red scarf around her neck and looks exotic. Interesting. For a minute Katie wishes to look exactly like her. "Cool scarf," she says.

Sarah takes it off, winds it around Katie's neck. "It's yours. I have a million of them."

In wonder, Katie touches it. "Really?"

"Hello there, pretty girl," a man with a sweep of silver hair brushed back from his face says in a booming voice. "I am so happy to finally meet you."

Lily says, "Katie, this is my husband, James. You can call him Gramps if you want. Everybody else does."

"Beware," Stephanie says. "He's a terrible tease."

The man winks at her. "You takin' good care of Ramona over there, toots?"

"I guess." Katie shrugs.

"Leave the poor girl alone," Lily says.

"Where's Liam?" Stephanie asks. "I hardly see him lately."

Lily waves a hand. "Nobody does. He's working or he's holed

up in that studio of his, or he's out with some woman. Not that I ever see any of them."

It's as big a family as she's ever met, and they're all so nice to her. Why, then, does Katie feel so mad all of a sudden?

TWENTY-FIVE

Ramona

On Sunday afternoon, my brother comes over to help me with a few small repairs around the old house and to help Katie train Merlin. The dog is utterly meek and mild in my brother's hands, and Ryan exclaims several times, "Dang, this dog is smart!"

After lunch, Katie goes upstairs to read. Ryan and I take tall glasses of iced tea to the backyard. He kicks his long legs up on a lawn chair and slides down, a baseball cap tipped down over his eyes. "How's business?" he asks, too casually.

"What did you hear?"

"That you're very thin on credit."

"How did you hear that? Hardly anyone knows!"

He makes a noise. "Come on, Ramona. Everybody knows everything about everybody in this business. There are spies everywhere."

I take a breath. "It's true. Please don't tell Dad and Steph. I'll work things out."

Not looking at me, he nods. After a minute he asks, "You ever think about pooling resources with the Gallagher Group, now that Dane is gone?"

"Oh, yeah, right. Like they would welcome me with open arms."

"Did you ever think about it? All those resources, the central ordering, the accounting department . . . Could be sweet."

"No. The whole point is to prove that I'm not the idiot bimbo they all think I am."

"Nobody thinks that! Only you do."

I shake my head. "Ryan, you don't, but believe me, Dad doesn't think I could run a truck around the block. If I have to admit that I'm over my head with this bakery, all that is reinforced."

He sits up and pulls his cap off. Black hair, exactly like my father's, falls across his brow. "It's going to be better to just lose the whole thing? Including Grandma's house?"

"No." For a long minute I swing back and forth on the glider, my bare feet grazing the top of the grass. "I am drowning. That's the truth. It was a good business plan, and I had plenty of capital and plenty of experience. It wasn't as if I heedlessly dove into something without knowing what I was doing."

"I know that."

"The old-house building stuff has been more of a problem than I anticipated, but I probably could have managed that if the economy hadn't tanked. I lost so much capital and lost value in the building and—"

He reaches for my hand. "It's been hard for all of us, Ramona. I know so many small businesses that have gone under. It's not your fault. What I want you to do is recognize that the answer is not to go under out of pride or stubbornness."

"I don't think I'm stubborn."

He laughs. "An unstubborn Gallagher has never been born. What can I do, sis?"

"Help me brainstorm. Help me come up with ways to generate more income without a lot of extra overhead."

"That I can do."

By the time he leaves to open the pub, we have mapped out an entire list of possibilities. I can use the Internet to offer the breads to a different set of customers, perhaps using frozen doughs, and I'm going to brainstorm some more ideas about that with Jimmy and my Web designer.

There are a lot of intense athletes in the city. Runners who train for the Ascent to the top of Pikes Peak every summer and other extreme races at high altitudes. Cyclists who ride the mountain passes to train for their races, whatever they are. They burn a bazillion calories and need high-quality carbs. They would love my healthy breads. Ryan and I come up with two plans to get the word out to them: I'm going to look into the possibility of offering my wares at race events, and I'm also going to take Katie with me to the trailheads and offer samples.

The final idea is to open on Sundays, with a skeleton staff. I'm tired as it is, but desperate times call for desperate measures. And you don't get into the business for the short hours.

Armed with a plan, I take a good long nap.

It will work. It has to.

Katie absolutely refuses to go to Jonah's house. She wants to stay home and read and not talk to anyone. Maybe she wants to get online. But, really, she's thirteen. I'm going five blocks. She deserves to be alone sometimes.

I'm somewhat disconcerted since the invitation was for two of us, but at five-thirty, I head for his house. I've bought a beautiful bottle of wine, tied with a ribbon, and I'm bringing one of my best loaves of bread, the rustica, made with a slow European *levain*. It takes three days to make this bread properly, and the taste is worth every second—the crumb filled with classic sourdough holes, the crust perfectly crisp and golden. I bake it in the wood-fired oven that was so costly and so right, and we sell dozens of loaves every day.

The light is angling deep gold over the mountains as I walk to his house. It falls in dappled patterns over the aged sidewalk, squares of crumbling concrete with grass growing between them. Impossible to avoid stepping on the cracks, but some girl-hood part of me always tries, so I don't break my mother's back. The skirt I chose, an ethnic print in soft purples and greens, floats around my calves. My toenails are painted peach.

Stephanie and I stayed overnight with my grandmother often. She loved walking and taught both of us to love it, too. After supper, we'd amble around the neighborhood, winter or summer, and admire the gardens or the new paint. We had our favorite houses, about which we would make up stories.

Jonah's house was a favorite with all of us. In recent years it has grown a little weary, but it boasts two things that were of particular interest to my sister and me. There is a square tower with windows looking in all directions, and a balcony juts out from the back, overlooking treetops and mountains. We thought it was wildly romantic.

The house sits on the corner of a pair of quiet backstreets, on a vast, grassy lot bound by a turn-of-the-century wrought-iron fence. As I come around the corner, I see Jonah sitting on the porch, wearing jeans and a simple long-sleeved shirt. His feet are tucked into Tevas, and he looks exactly like what you might imagine a well-tended fortysomething native Coloradoan would look. Healthy. Tan from taking his exercise outdoors.

But there is also something not quite so obvious that gives off an aura of elegance. Wealth. Perhaps it is his well-cut hair or some scent he wears. I can't decide.

At the foot of the steps to the porch, I halt. "Hello," I say, and touch my diaphragm. "I'm sorry, but Katie wasn't able to come. I hope that doesn't put you out."

For one long second I am afraid he's going to call dinner off. There's a wall that comes up, chills the air. He doesn't speak immediately.

I lift a hand. "I can see this is not a good thing. Sorry. I just didn't have a phone number for you." I'm backing away. "We can reschedule."

He steps down to grab my waving hand. "I'm sorry. That was rude. Please stay."

"Are you sure?"

"Yes." He lets go of my hand. "Come in. Please."

Giving him the wine and bread, I say, "If you put that in the oven, it will be warm for dinner."

"Thank you." He lifts the loaf to his nose and sniffs. "Mmm. That's nice, isn't it?"

I smile, a little of my nervousness bleeding away. He holds out a hand and I reach for it, letting him pull me up the steps. "Thank you for coming, Ramona."

"You're welcome."

He opens a white-painted screen door and gestures me inside. The house is an updated 1920s bungalow, and within it's been very carefully renovated, with polished hardwood floors and a wall or two removed to give a sense of more space. "Oh, it's lovely!" I exclaim. "My sister and I always wanted to see inside. Have you changed it a lot?"

"Yes." He opens a bottle of wine that's sitting on the counter. "It's a quirky place, as you see. It needed to be opened up, but I kept the general feeling."

"It's hard when you have an old place, balancing grace and convenience." I trail my hand over the walls, touch a cabinet, put my hand flat on the counter. It's uncluttered to the point of spare, with no plants in the windows or statues sitting on the low tables. Art with a South American feel graces the walls. "Have you been to Peru?"

"I lived in Argentina for a few years." He puts the bread in the oven and stirs a pot on the stove. "After I left New York." He pours wine into oversize glasses and gestures toward the dish of cheese and fig preserves ready to carry out. "Will you take that?"

Finally, I notice there is music playing quietly. Spanish guitar. "'Asturias,'" I say, and smile.

"Yes." He inclines his head. Lifts one shoulder, and I understand that he is every bit as nervous as I am. "Let's go out on the porch, shall we?"

The air is as soft as down against my skin as I sit. He puts the dish of fig preserves on a small table between us and holds up his glass. "To old friends," he says.

"To old friends." Our eyes meet over the wine, and I'm suddenly filled with a wild sense of happiness. I laugh. "How wonderful, Jonah! Cheers."

His eyes crinkle. "It is wonderful." He takes a stick of cheese and dips it into the dish of preserves. "Try this," he says, offering it to me with his left hand, the one with the damaged fingers. I take it, touching his hand lightly.

"Mmm. This would be very nice with Bridget's sourdough."

"I love that you became a baker. You fell in love with bread so much that summer."

"Poppy was a good teacher. And it was magical, you know?" I shake my head. "It's funny how you can get so off track."

"I ate nearly the whole loaf of bread you sent home with me."

"Really? That's wonderful." I feel a little shy. "How about you, Jonah? Did you learn to play the guitar with your other hand?"

"I did," he says. "Alas, I could never capture the same . . . gift, though. That's why I ended up traveling. In Argentina, I fell in with some composers, and that's where I stayed for a long while." He smiles, dipping the cheese. "There was a woman, of course."

"Of course." I smile. "Did she break your heart?"

His mouth tilts sideways as he meets my gaze. "I'm afraid it was the other way around. In the end, I didn't want to stay there, and she wouldn't leave her family to come to America." He shrugs. "It was a good time in my life. Learning to compose."

"You did?" I'm immediately enchanted. "Classical music?"

"Spanish influences, guitar and cello. But mostly I wrote scores."

"Wrote? You don't anymore?"

He shakes his head faintly. "Things...got in the way."

Something in his face makes me ask, "Do you miss it?"

In the house, the music shifts to cello, a slow long bowing of singular beauty. I watch as he turns his glass of wine in a circle on the table. His untouched thumb is long and graceful, and he looks restlessly toward the mountains. "Sometimes. Not very much anymore."

Rising around him like heat waves, invisible but bending the air, is his sorrow over that choice. Much too large for this moment, so I say, "We go where we should, I suppose." I lean toward him. "It smells as if you have become a wonderful cook. What have you made?"

Immediately the air shifts. He smiles. "Pasta. With prosciutto and asparagus and fresh peas and sun-dried tomatoes. Are you hungry now? Would you like to eat?"

"Whenever you like."

As I watch, his body softens and he leans back in the chair, then looks over at me. "Let's wait a little. Drink this wine and then go inside. I love this time of day."

"So do I."

He says, "You were a godsend to me that summer, you know."

"Was I?" I laugh. "What I remember is chasing you shamelessly."

"You did," he agrees, and raises his glass to me. "It was the best thing that had happened to me for a long time. You can't imagine how healing it was." He pauses. "Or how difficult."

The air has gone quiet, falling into the purple hush of dusk as the sun slips suddenly behind Pikes Peak. Something electric buzzes between us—or maybe that's just me. "I'm sure it was terribly embarrassing."

"Not at all. It—" He bows his head briefly. "But you were so very young."

All at once I am standing in my aunt's garden in the red light of a summer dusk, nearly fainting as he bends over to kiss me. It has been almost twenty-five years, but the moment rushes back to me as perfectly detailed as if it happened ten minutes ago. The heat of it rushes down my spine, and again it is like he is a magnet and my body is made of iron shavings.

I raise my glass. "To your kindness, sir. It was a very hard time for me."

He touches my glass with his own. "So tell me about your daughter. What is she like?"

"Sofia." Even her name makes me happy, and the corners of my mouth curve upward as I look out to the ocean of grass surrounding the ship of a house. "She's very, very, very smart, like my mother, and has a mighty will, like my grandmother. She's quite beautiful, dark hair, blue eyes. Curvy but in no way fat. She's a terrific person."

"So," he says in his mellow voice, "she's smart like your mother and stubborn like your grandmother. How is she like you, Ramona?"

"Hmmm." I think, *Only you would ask that question,* and ponder it for a moment. At first, all I can come up with are the ways she is not like me. "She's not a baker, or even really much of a cook thus far. She's a lot less at the mercy of events than I've been in my life, and she's wary about relationships with men, smart. Not my strong suit."

"How is she like you?" he repeats.

"She has my sense of wonder," I say at last. "And a sense of the absurd. And she loves music."

"Do you still?"

"Absolutely." I smile. "Maybe I should make you a tape."

He laughs, eyes crinkling at the corners. "I was sure I could school you in good musical tastes. Arrogant."

"No, I loved it. I still have that tape, actually. A few years ago I had my brother burn me a CD of the same songs so I could listen to it." I stick my feet out in front of me and cross them at the ankles. "I could probably recite the whole playlist."

He relaxes, too, but in the manner of a cat, alert in the dusk. "I remember 'Malagueña.'"

"Yes. And 'Asturias,' and Segovia's Cello in C." I gesture with my half-empty glass toward the soft strains of guitar coming from within the house. "I'm hearing bits and pieces of it playing now."

He nods, looking slightly abashed. "All my favorites. I wanted to play them for you, and that was as close as I could come."

Tears spring to my eyes, and I look away, trying not to let them show. It's been such a long day, I'm dangerously emotional, and the thought of how things might have been different for me if we'd been able to—

Ridiculous.

"Did I say something wrong?" he asks.

"Not at all." I take a breath.

He rises. "The mosquitoes will be out soon. Shall we eat?"

"Perfect."

I wander in with him and take off my shoes at the door to spare the beautiful floor the scraping flap of my sandals. The wood is cool on the soles of my feet, and, as ever, the temperature drops the second the sun goes down. I should have brought a sweater. "Can I help?"

"Not at all. I only need to stir it all together." He gestures. "Have a seat."

A table, Arts and Crafts style, is set with three places. I gather one and take it away, which is my restaurant training, and he smiles.

Jonah serves his pasta in a big bowl, along with the bread I brought, warmed in the oven. He slices it expertly with a serrated knife. "Well done," I say.

"I am good in the kitchen," he says. "It's my hobby."

"I hope you're not a snob about it."

He laughs. "Probably I am. But not always."

The wine has eased my nervousness enough that I lean forward comfortably. "Now tell me about you, Jonah. Do you have children?"

"No." He does not quite meet my eyes. "I have spent my time on travel and debauchery." He raises his fork and looks at the food. "And learning to cook."

"Ah, so that's where that aura of world-weariness comes from." I smile and take a bite of the pasta. My mouth is filled with a dozen flavors and cues, tomato and cream and the texture of the penne, the saltiness of the prosciutto. I widen my eyes and look at him, putting my fingers lightly against my lips as my tongue and teeth release more and more of the flavors—there, cracked pepper, and then the elegance of asparagus. Jonah watches me, a small smile turning up the corners of his lips.

When I swallow, I put down my fork. "I'm almost afraid to take another bite. It couldn't possibly be that good."

He laughs, and the sound is as sexy as the music, as the food, as his dark hair falling down on his forehead. "I think you'll find it holds up."

And then there is only eating. My bread with Irish butter, and his magnificently orchestrated pasta, and the wine, so velvety and rich. I eat more than I should and, sitting there with my empty plate, I put my hand on my tummy. "I wish I had two stomachs," I say, and laugh. "I'm eyeing that little bit of sauce there and all I want to do is bow my head and lick it up."

His face is faintly flushed. He laughs, too. "Thank you. It's a pleasure to cook for someone who appreciates it so much."

"Did your wife like your cooking?"

"I hadn't become serious about it then, but she was an actress. She had to stay very thin."

I grin. "Are you implying something, sir?"

His eyes sweep over my body. "No way." He stands and collects the plates. "Would you like coffee or something?"

"No, thank you. I suppose I'll need to get back soon, check on

Katie. She hasn't been here long, and that house can be kind of creepy at night."

"Sure? Maybe a round of backgammon?"

I smile. "No, thank you. Really." I feel fizzy and relaxed, aroused and wary. "I've had a very good time, Jonah."

"So have I."

His phone rings on the counter, spinning in a circle. "Sorry," he says. "I forgot to turn it down." He looks at it for a moment, hands loose, as if he knows who it is. I wonder with a stab if it is a woman. Maybe that's why he's so formal with me, keeping his distance in a way I can't quite name.

"Well," I say. "Thanks for everything."

He walks me to the door. "Sure you don't want to stay for another glass of wine?"

I nod with regret.

I'm aware of my skin, aware of the ginger-and-peaches smell of him, aware of the darkness and crickets beyond the door. A shiver rushes up my spine, and I want to kiss him more than I have wanted anything in years.

I bend to put on my sandals, and when I straighten, I realize he's been admiring the view of my cleavage. For a minute I linger, and then something makes me bold. "Are you involved, Jonah?"

"No," he says.

So I stand on my toes, put my hands on his shoulders, and lift my face, which he bends down to kiss. Our lips brush, and then again, and I take the half step closer to bring our bodies into light contact. He puts his hands on my wrists, and we both turn our heads. There is such tenderness in the kiss that I feel my spirit filling with air and light and promise.

Then he gently takes my hands away and steps back, pressing my hands into a prayer, palm to palm. Hair falls down on his forehead, and his eyes are so acutely sad that I feel I could weep. "I'm sorry," he says. "I can't do this right now."

Something makes me touch his cheek. I nod. "Okay."

We simply go out on the front porch and I look at the starry sky. "Good night, Jonah."

"Good night. It was good to see you."

I look back at him over my shoulder. "You, too."

RAMONA'S BOOK OF BREADS

MULTIGRAIN CRANBERRY WALNUT BREAD

This is a wonderful bread, chewy and very flavorful, and it uses a slower fermentation period to expand those flavors. Plan to begin a day before you want to serve it. It also uses a sourdough sponge. Any starter will work just fine, but if you happen to have a hearty rye starter, it will be especially lovely here.

TO BEGIN:

1 cup cranberries, soaked for an hour in hot water

PREPARE THE SPONGE:

1 cup sourdough starter at room temperature

½ cup bread flour

½ cup whole-wheat flour

½ cup ground walnuts

1 cup cranberry water, poured off the cranberries (add a little plain water to make a full cup, if necessary)

2 T molasses

1 scant tsp yeast

Mix together all ingredients and knead for a few minutes, then wrap tightly in plastic wrap and allow to rise at room temperature for 2–4 hours. It should be very foamy.

TO MIX THE DOUGH:

Sponge, from above

1 T oil

1½ cups walnuts, broken into pieces

1 tsp sea salt

¼–½ cup whole-wheat flour

1 cup soaked cranberries

A stand mixer or bread machine is highly desirable for kneading, because this begins as a very sticky dough.

If using a mixer, put in the sponge and sprinkle with the oil, walnuts, and salt; knead on low for a couple of minutes. Let rest for 30 minutes, then knead again for 10 minutes, or until the dough starts to pull away from the bowl. If it continues to be sticky after the first few minutes, add flour a little at a time, no more than ¼ cup at this stage. Turn out onto a floured counter and gently knead in cranberries. Let rest again for a half hour.

If mixing by hand, turn the sponge onto a floured surface. Oil your hands and knead the oil, walnuts, and salt into the mix until a rough dough forms, then let stand for 30 minutes. Sprinkle dough with flour, oil your hands again, and begin to turn and fold, turn and fold the dough, adding flour a little at a time until it is less sticky. Gently knead in the cranberries and let rest for half hour.

Dust with a little white flour if needed and form the dough into a rectangle. Put this in an oiled 2-quart container (a 4-cup glass measuring cup works well) and mark where the dough will be when doubled. Roll the dough to coat it on all sides. Cover and let rise until doubled.

Deflate the dough, cover tightly, and let stand overnight in the fridge.

In the morning, turn the dough onto a lightly floured surface and roll it into a rectangle that is about 8 inches long. Roll it into a loaf and tuck the ends under. Put the loaf, seam down, on a baking sheet lined with silicon or parchment and cover with oiled plastic. Let rise in a warm place until doubled.

A half hour before baking, preheat the oven to 400 degrees. To mimic the humidity of French ovens, fill a large cast-iron skillet with water and put it on the bottom rack of the oven.

Uncover the loaf and let stand for 5 minutes, then slash the top of the loaf diagonally three times and put it in the oven. Immediately turn the heat down to 375 degrees and bake for 45–55 minutes, until the loaf is golden and sounds hollow when tapped from beneath. Cool on a wire rack.

TWENTY-SIX

Nearly every night I wake up at some point and lie in the dark, staring at the ceiling. Sometimes I think of Sofia. Sometimes I worry about the business. I think of the baby, wondering how he or she is doing while Sofia is so stressed out. I worry that the birth will be hard on her. I was going to be there, her coach, and I'm very disappointed that it might not happen now.

I take refuge in work, getting up to bake, often finding Jimmy there already. She's an insomniac, and the hours of a bakery suit her well. Together, we bake and talk about everything in the universe, from men and children to food to politics and music.

By the time dawn tumbles through the windows, the darkest worry is tucked away. It is the time of year I love the best, May sliding into June. My grandmother's garden is exploding into blossom, and I love the way the light falls, illuminating valleys you never see the rest of the year; the burnished look of morning on the grass; the hot afternoons broken by dramatic thunderstorms that wash the air and give us cool, cricket-spun evenings.

It is on one of those dramatic afternoons, as clouds roll in over the mountains with menace, that my sister Stephanie shows up at the bakery. I'm alone, refreshing the last of the starters, when she storms through the back door, letting the screen door slam behind her. She makes so much noise that I think it's Katie and Merlin and raise my head to reprimand them.

Instead, there's Steph, in a pair of jeans and a turquoise tank, silver jewelry around her neck and wrists and swinging from her ears. Her hair is pulled back in a ponytail and she looks athletic and hearty, like an Olympic skier. "Steph!" I say in surprise, because it has been ages since we've spoken.

"Are you sleeping with Cat Spinuzzi?"

Of course that's what this is about. Because she couldn't just come and *talk* to me. She has to show up with her temper turned to scald. It's the only way she deals with me these days. I sigh, scraping the last of the starter into a clean jar with a rubber spatula. "Not that it's any of your business, but no."

"That's not what I heard."

It never helps for two Gallaghers to get pissy at the same time. Wars erupt that way, wars that last as long as . . . well, this one between my sister and me. Eight years, more or less. Since I inherited the house, which was the final nail in the coffin of our relationship. It *infuriated* her. As calmly as I can, I say, "Mom saw Cat over here a couple of weeks ago and jumped to conclusions."

"I don't believe you." She crosses her arms. "I saw you with him at the Sunbird one night, had to be a year ago."

"It's none of your business, but what difference does it make, Stephanie? Honestly. I mean, we're grown."

"Is that a yes? God, I can't believe you! You'll do anything to get what you want."

"Excuse me?"

"Oh, don't pretend you're not using him, just like you use everybody else!"

"That's not true!" It's no easy thing to keep my anger

burbling on low. "Cat's my mentor, the person who stood in my corner when the rest of you stuck with my cheating, lying skunk of an ex-husband."

"That was business. Dane was a hell of a manager and we were lucky to have him. He single-handedly shifted the fortunes of our company, and you know it. We couldn't fire him, and it would have been stupid anyway."

"First of all, he took the job our father should have given me, and *you* know it. Secondly, he didn't single-handedly shift the fortunes of the business—I was there, too. And, third, if Dad had fired him, I wouldn't have quit, and I could have had the position he kept."

"It's not always about you! You think the world is supposed to stop every time you get a hangnail, for God's sake!"

"Actually, that *was* about me. It was my husband, my job, my rift with the family."

"God, Ramona, when are you ever going to grow up?"

"Says the woman who is still working for her daddy!"

"I'm not working for him. We're partners. As you would have been if you hadn't turned your back on the restaurants."

"Yeah, he calls you his assistant. That's not partners." I shake my head, trying to imagine cooling waterfalls and tinkling bells, as a therapist once suggested. "Why are we having this same stupid fight? Did you just wake up and think you had to come give me some shit, see if you could make me feel even worse than I do already? I mean, my daughter's husband is lying in a hospital bed halfway around the world with burns over most of his body and a leg missing, and my daughter is pregnant and alone with him."

Her mouth goes hard. I hate to say *bitter,* but that's how she seems lately, all tight and vinegary and hard. I wonder what happened to her. What has gone wrong in her life to make her such a hard-ass? "See how you do that? Even Sofia and Oscar's tragedy is all about Ramona."

The barb, curved like a scimitar, curls right through my heart. "Score, Steph," I say, and carry the jar to the dishwasher. "Anything else you want to rub into my wounds? Maybe we could get to the part where I'm a loser with men."

"Oh, stop!"

Merlin trots into the kitchen urgently and rushes over to me, licking my hand. He sits on my foot and woofs softly at Stephanie. The gesture is so loyal and kind it brings tears to my eyes, and I bow my head to hide them. "Thanks, Merlin."

It calms Stephanie, too. "Look, I didn't come over here to yell at you. It just—" She shakes her head. "It just seems like you never think about anybody but yourself. Didn't you realize that it might really upset Mom and Dad for you to have a relationship with Cat Spinuzzi?"

I close my eyes and sigh. Merlin leaning on my leg seems to bring some centering magic. "It's over. It has been for a long time. And I didn't plan it. It just happened. Hasn't anything ever swept you away? Ever?"

"No." She meets my eyes, and we both know what she's thinking: *It ruined your life, and I'll never let it ruin mine.*

What I want to say is that I miss her. Not this priggish, judgmental bitch, but the other side of her. The one who makes me laugh so hard I can't talk. The one who will tell me when I should get rid of an ugly blouse. The one who walked ten billion miles with me when we were children and spun a hundred thousand fantasies.

"I don't want to fight," I say. "If you want to come sit on the porch and have a croissant, I'll talk. But I'm not going to fight."

For a long minute she stares across the space of the stainless-steel counter, and I think she might relent. Then she turns and stomps out of my kitchen.

Lost to me, still.

And I am feeling like maybe the most flawed human on the planet, riddled with as many holes as a wormy apple. It is a feeling I have known intimately at various times in my life, but I realize it's been mostly missing since I opened the bakery, even if my family has me on the outside.

I truly miss Sofia. Her company, her commentary on the world, her face.

The only thing I can possibly do is bake, but Merlin isn't allowed in the bakery kitchen, so I whistle for him to come upstairs with me, and I pull out ordinary amounts of flour and yeast and water and salt. The eternal, essential ingredients for bread.

"Whatcha doing?" Katie asks, wandering in from the living room. She has her finger in a book and that sleepy look that comes from reading all day. It's one of the things we have in common, and I gave her permission to go to the library as often as she likes. Her taste runs counter to the vampires and werewolves that are so popular right now, to sweet books set in sweeter times, like *Anne of Green Gables* and historical novels from the seventies. I'm sure her real life has been full enough of bloodsuckers and men turned to slobbering dogs.

"I think I'm going to make some cookies," I say. "Want to help?"

"Yes! I love cookies."

"Let's see what we have. Chocolate chips, oatmeal, butterscotch?"

"Can we do all of them together?"

Laughter breaks through my self-pity. "Definitely."

The tourist season is upon us at last, crowds of families trundling into town in their RVs and sedans and rent-a-cars. The motels are full, the streets busy. Over the past week we sold virtually everything we baked, and no matter how I increase the order, we run out of muffins very quickly. Both of my assistants have added a day, and Jimmy volunteered to come in on Saturday nights, too, so we can open on Sundays. I'm going to take the service shift myself that day to save on payroll, and Katie will be my runner. She's very excited about that, since there is some exotic dahlia my mother told her about that she wants to buy when they go to the flower show next month.

The Army flew Oscar to San Antonio earlier this week, and it makes me feel better to know Sofia is within a two- or three-hour plane ride again. She called when they arrived, talked to me and to Katie, and everyone seems to be sleeping better over this.

On Thursday afternoon, the tourist traffic has slowed enough that I take a cup of tea and a sandwich out to the front porch to go over some paperwork, while the day clerk cleans the bakery cases and polishes the glass for tomorrow. Katie is somewhere reading, as usual. It pleases me immensely that she loves books so much, and I went to the library with her the last time, finding something I could use to escape, too. At night, I'm reading before sleep again, a habit I'd lost somewhere along the way.

Now I settle on the wide Victorian porch with a cup of lemon-scented tea and a tomato and cheese sandwich on bread sliced from the last loaf of sunflower wheat. The world has taken on that hush that arrives before a thunderstorm, birds silent, traffic muffled. Clouds move ponderously over the sky, hiding the sharp blue of Colorado summer. As I eat my sandwich, I admire the shifting colors—slate and pale blue and eggplant, with the odd, distant thread of white-gold lightning. The clouds make me think of elephants or rhinos plodding over the day.

A flash of broader lightning crackles into a valley, and, as if he's stepping through a rent in the atmosphere, Jonah comes around the corner. It's the first time I've seen him since the evening at his house a couple of weeks ago. Several times I've thought about calling or walking by, and each time I stop myself, for a million complicated reasons.

Or, really, for one: I don't want to be the smitten one, chasing him this time.

Now he is here, wearing a pair of jeans and a long-sleeved ivory Henley. His belly is flat, and he has a loose-limbed confidence I find very appealing. At the gate, he pauses to appreciate the flowers exploding from the earth where there was once a big gash in the landscaping, then looks up and sees me sitting there.

His expression brightens notably enough that my stomach flips—*he likes me, he likes me!*—before I remember that I don't need anything in my life that's volatile or exhilarating or that might turn everything upside down.

"Hello," he says, standing at the foot of the stairs. "May I join you?"

I take his measure. Shrug as if I don't care one way or the other. "Sure."

He climbs the steps and sits in the chair on the other side of the table. "How are you, Ramona?"

He is close enough that I catch a waft of his scent, and it plugs directly into every lust cell in my brain. *Limbic memory,* I tell myself as awareness prickles to life on my shoulders. Memories from another me. "I'm good. Busy. How 'bout you?"

"Getting used to the new world."

"Hmmm." I wait. In the distance, a rumble of thunder rolls.

He's looking at me now, his eyes touching my throat, my hair. "The light suits you. It makes your hair glitter."

"Thank you."

He pauses, as if considering. "There is going to be a string quartet in the park on Sunday evening. I came to see if you might like to go. With me."

Inclining my head, I say, "I'm not sure. Honestly, I'm getting mixed messages. That's not very comfortable."

"Right." He nods, takes a breath. "If you will come with me, I'll explain."

"If you're involved or finishing something or whatever, I'd rather not get in the middle of that."

His smile is wry. "Nothing like that, I promise."

"All right. I would love that," I say. "To go. With you."

"Good," he says, recovering. "I'll bring a picnic. I'll come over at around five and we can walk from here. How does that sound?"

"Perfect." I smile as he stands up and find myself tossing my head slightly so that my hair, which is loose, swishes down my arm. He notices.

Over the days when he did not call, I wondered if I'd imagined a mutual attraction. But no. He gives himself away as do I. Eyes lighting on breasts, thighs, lips. The way he swallows when I push my hair away. The way he meets my eyes, not so long as to be odd but long enough to make a connection, to create a spark.

"I have some work to do," he says. "I'll see you on Sunday."

"Yes" is all I can manage.

TWENTY-SEVEN

Sofia's Journal

SAN ANTONIO
JUNE 3, 20—

Oscar is awake! It's too early to call anyone, so I am writing it here.

I couldn't sleep, so I went to his room in the middle of the night. He was just lying there as always, the machine blipping and beeping and clicking. It hit me with a big wave of depression that it's been three weeks since he was injured and he might not ever come out of this coma, and I need to find some people to help me decide how to manage that possibility.

Grandma Adelaide used to always say that it was a sin to despair (though I think she did sometimes, anyway, which just goes to show that we're all human—and she never did manage to heal her relationship with her own daughters, so I guess she had reason. My mother tried so hard to help fix that situation, but neither Grandma nor Aunt Poppy ever did really forgive her for whatever she did when they were young. Sad).

Anyway, despair. A sin. I can't despair is what I was telling myself. Gotta stay upbeat for Oscar and the baby but most of all for myself. I will set the tone. It feels like a lot, I won't lie, but this is what we do for each other, isn't it? If it was me lying in that bed, unrecognizable for my injuries, I would desperately want Oscar to be sitting there, talking to me, telling me jokes, telling me he loved me.

I had printed out Katie's email, and I stood close by the bed. "Good morning, Oscar!" I said. "I'm early today, but the baby was kicking me awake, so I thought I'd get some coffee and come over. Can you smell it?"

Holding the email, I took a sip and rubbed at a foot sticking out. "There he goes again, like he's a kickboxer, Oscar!"

It's hard sometimes to keep doing that, talking like he can hear me. It makes me feel silly sometimes. So I held the letter from Katie. "Your daughter is sounding very happy and really grown up," I said. "Listen to this."

I read him the email, trying to put lots of enthusiasm in my voice.

And, at the end of it, nothing.

I went to sit in my chair. And, okay, I was crying a little bit, mainly because I was homesick and sad and wanted to be back with my mother in her kitchen, watching her make bread, or with my grandma in her spectacular garden that Katie is enjoying.

And I heard a groan from the bed! I jumped up and said, "Oscar?"

He made another sound around all the tubes and bandages. It was hard to tell at first, but his eyes were open a very small slit. I got so excited, I ran out into the hall and got a nurse, who got a doctor, who confirmed that he is actually waking up.

I still don't know a lot. It's not like he recognizes me yet or anything. They are not sure how long it will take before he's all the way awake, but this is a start. My heart is about twenty times lighter!

I can't wait to call Katie.

TWENTY-EIGHT

Ramona

That evening Katie and I print flyers on the computer and duck out very early on Friday morning to drive up to the trailheads where I know serious runners and hikers go to train—Barr Trail, Waldo Canyon, Red Rocks Canyon.

Taking a lesson from my aunt Poppy, I've made trays of samplers—mini-muffins and scones and slices of my favored breads, with little sides of butter in paper cups. As the runners come off their trails, they're hungry and ready to eat anything. Katie holds the tray while I pass out the samples and offer a coupon. We run through our cache in no time.

She's an excellent helper. One of the things I like about her is the way she flings herself into a task. Watching her from the corner of my eye as she explains the various forms of muffins, I can see that it's good for her to be here, to have people around to love her and take care of her. The hair is still crazy, but no one has yet been able to talk her into a haircut. When she helps in the bakery, she wears a white cap with every bit of hair tucked under it, a compromise I thought she'd resist. She only shrugged and pulled it on. It shows off her pale-green eyes, the olive smoothness of her skin.

Back at the bakery, we have a lot of work to do to get ready for an extra day of sales. Katie is a great runner, dashing into the

front with a tray of muffins, dashing back with whatever emp-
ties there might be. Heather is training her how to use the cash
register, how to protect the breads and pastries when bagging
them, how to make small talk. Customers like her, especially the
old folks.

She's making change for one of our regulars, a slim beauty in
her sixties, when Sofia calls on my cell phone. "Hi, Mom. Is this
a good time? Is Katie around?"

It's hard to tell whether the news is good or bad. I glance over
at Katie, wrapped double in a baker's pale-green apron. "She's
here. Is everything okay?"

"It's good. Um, Oscar's awake. I wanted to tell Katie in person."

"Oh, my God, Sofia! That's fantastic! Let me get her."

"Mom." Her voice is serious. "There's more to this. I'll call
you when you're up by yourself, okay? Tonight."

"Sure. Anytime, Sofia. Anytime you want to call me, I am always here."

"Thanks, Mom. I know."

"Let me get Katie." Holding the phone to my chest, I duck behind the counter and crook my finger, then point to the phone.
"Sofia is on the phone." I smile. "Good news."

Her eyes widen, and she pulls off her cap as if her hair is some
magic protection. She takes the phone through the side door to
the porch. "Hello?"

I leave her to it, rubbing the dull spot between my ribs where
worry lives. What is the rest of the story? I hate it that Sofia is
alone, pregnant and afraid. Maybe, I think, going back to the
kitchen, I should close the bakery and go to her. Katie and I
could help her—

Great idea, says some cynical voice, *and what will you live on?*
The bakery might be in trouble, but at the moment we are still
afloat, and it is the only revenue stream I have.

But I *hate* it that she's so alone. It makes me feel helpless. As I return to the tasks at hand, I poke the problem from a dozen directions.

Katie bounces back into the kitchen. "He's awake! My dad is awake!" she cries, and for the first time ever, she flings her arms around me. That's when I realize that she's grown taller than me this past week or two, and her arms are powerful with all the gardening and baking. I hug her back. "Sofia thinks it was my letter that helped him wake up."

"Hooray!" When she lets go, I point upstairs. "By all means, you should write him another one right now."

She leaps toward the stairs, then whirls around. "What time are your aunts coming over?"

Poppy and Nancy are coming down for dinner. "Five. I know it's early, but I have to get to bed."

"I know. I just wanted to get it in my head. Do you think I should put on something nicer?"

"Sure." I smile through my worry. "We'll make it a celebration of your dad's awakening."

"Thank you!" She whirls around and dashes for the stairs, and I think of Tinker Bell, moving like a dragonfly, feet barely touching the floor.

TWENTY-NINE

Katie

W hen Katie signs on to the Internet to write to her
dad, there is an email from her mom. Katie's heart
leaps into her mouth, and she opens it as fast as she can, looking
over her shoulder in case somebody comes upstairs and catches
her.

TO: KATIEWILSON09872@NOMECAST.COM
FROM: LACEYMOMSOLDIER@PRT.COM
SUBJECT: GETTING BETTER ALL THE TIME

HEY BABY!! I WAS SO HAPPY TO SEE A EMAIL FROM YOU, SORRY
THAT YOURE DAD IS WONDED, BUT HE IS STRONG, HE'LL GET BETTER
FAST YOU WAIT & SEE. DOING GOOD HERE. ON THE STRATE ROAD
FOR 23 DAYS NOW, WHICH IS THE BEST I'VE DONE FOR A LONG
TIME. MET SOME NEW FRENDS HER AND HOPE YOU CAN COME SEE
ME SINCE THEY AINT GONA LET ME SEE YOU ANYTIME SOON, MAYBE
IF YOU CAME WE COULD GO TO THE PARK OR SOMETHIN AND TALK
ABOT LIFE, I'M LOCKED UP AT SUNNYSIDE, WHICH IS A JOKE, CUZ ITS
DARK HERE, BABY, DARK WITHOUT YOU AS MY SUNSHINE,
REMEMBER WHO YOU ARE, SWEETS, AND DONT FORGET YOU'RE
MAMA LOVES YOU AND NEEDS YOU AND THINKS ABOUT YOU ALL THE
TIME. I DREAM ABOUT YOU ALL THE TIME, I HATE TO ASK CUZ I KNOW

YOU AINT GOT ANYTHING YOURSELF, BUT MAYBE SOFIES MOM'S GOT
SOMETHING, SO IF YOU CAN SEND ME SOME MONEY, IT WOULD
REALY HELP A LOT. CANT BUY NO CIGARRETES WITHOUT CASH, AND I
COULDN'T EVEN GET NO TAMPONS, YOU BELIEVE THAT? THEY GIVE
YOU PADS, BUT NO TAMPONS, WHICH IS TOTALLY F'ED UP IF YOU
KNOW WHAT I MEAN. I AM GROWING OUT MY HAIR AND THERE'S A
GIRL HERE DOES MANICURES, SO MY HANDS LOOKING BETTER,
AND YOU KNOW ME, I LIKE LOOKING GOOD, JUST LIKE MY BABY
GIRL. WRITE ME SOON NOW, HONEY, AND I LUV YOU.
   MOM

Katie stares at the email for a long minute, feeling strange.
Kind of dizzy and a little bit sick to her stomach. Looking over
her shoulder, she hits the print button, then closes her email and
takes the printed page upstairs. She sticks it inside her notebook
and then puts it out of her mind. Tonight she wants to be happy.
She wants to celebrate her dad waking up and the aunties she's
heard so much about coming down to dinner.

But even as she puts on the green halter dress Lily bought for
her, she can feel the cold tentacles of Lacey sliding around her
ankles.

THIRTY

Ramona

I awaken from my nap by a quarter to four, take a shower to get a fresh start on the evening, then head into the house kitchen to start a simple supper of veggie tacos and strawberry shortcake for dessert. Poppy and Nancy are vegetarians, and I take pride in trying to find excellent recipes for them. This recipe is from the Green Gate Organic Farms cookbook; it uses grilled sweet and hot peppers, onions, broccoli, and squash, with goat cheese. I wonder if Katie will eat them and check to make sure there's something else for her to eat just in case. Earlier, I made a tomatillo salsa and left it to brew in the fridge.

My mother is the first to arrive, bringing fresh tomatoes from the store and a bunch of cilantro clipped from her garden. She's wearing crisp capri slacks in lemon yellow with an orange and yellow striped tank. Her earrings are whimsical lemons and oranges that match her bracelet. I wish I had inherited this dressing gene, but I did not. I think of Steph in her turquoise tank and jeans and sandals, her hair cut in a mod, angular style. She's the one who got it. When we were teens, she was the plump one, always draped in oversize T-shirts and jeans. I can't remember now when she started looking so together all the time; it's been long enough that I can't remember much about her adult self other than this one.

Maybe I am as self-centered as she says I am if I can't call up her transformation period.

"Cute jewelry," I say to my mother, hoping to start the visit on a high note. We haven't really talked since the day she found me in the kitchen with Cat, and I'm irked at her for telling Stephanie, but tonight is not the time to bring that out into the open. I'm jumpy, thinking of Sofia and Oscar and what her news might be, and between those emotions are the juicy plum edgings of Jonah's arrival in my world.

Which I am keeping to myself.

"Where's Katie?" my mother says, putting her bags on the counter.

"Upstairs."

"Good. I've been wanting to talk to you."

"Mom. This is not the time."

She puts a hand on her hip. "Haven't you learned one single thing about men all these years, Ramona?"

In a rush, I think of her driving me to Poppy's house, of her storming into the record store, of a dozen other times she thought the worst of me without giving me a chance to explain. Putting my knife on the counter, I face her, unaware that I am mimicking her posture until I feel my hand on my hip. "Has it ever occurred to you that you could give me the benefit of the doubt?"

She makes a noise that would be a snort in anyone else. "You are going to stand there and tell me that you are not having an affair with Cat Spinuzzi?" Cocking her head, she adds, "Do you think I'm blind, Ramona?"

"Actually, I am going to stand here and tell you that. But you know what, Mom? I'm forty years old and single. And I don't appreciate your speculation or the fact that you discussed it with my sister. My love life—or lack thereof—is none of your business."

"Well, you know, Ramona, you haven't exactly shown the greatest discernment in the area of men."

"Oh, is that right? Which man are you thinking of, Mom? The one who fucked me when I was a child—"

"Watch your language!"

"—or the one I married, the one everybody approved of so much and who ended up being as faithful as a tomcat? Everyone sure seemed to like him when I married him." She opens her mouth, but I hold up a hand. "I'm not doing this. I'm a successful, independent"—not quite true, but I'm on a roll now—"divorced businesswoman who raised a fantastic daughter."

"With help!"

"Absolutely I had help. Thank you." I step toward her, keeping my voice low. "But I'm tired of apologizing for a mistake I made when I was fifteen. I'm sick of being treated like a teenager. It's ridiculous."

"That's not what I'm talking about today, and you know it. Cat Spinuzzi is one of the biggest womanizers in this town! You want to be just a notch on his belt?"

"Mom! Stop. That's not what you care about. You care that it will infuriate Dad, but I'm not sure why it matters anyway, since all we ever are is polite to each other."

"And who started that?"

I sigh. "I'm sure I did. But it's not like that with Cat, anyway." I shake my head, realizing it won't matter what I say. "He's my mentor, and that's all." I hold up a hand. "I swear on all that's holy."

"That's not what I saw."

I want her to shut up and leave the subject alone. I want to retreat into silence. I want to stonewall her. But if this pattern is going to change for any of us, somebody has to start. "Mom, will you listen? Please?"

She takes a breath and crosses her arms—shutting me out physically if not mentally—and I do something it has never occurred to me to do. I step forward and put my hands on her arms, gently taking them apart. "Really listen."

Her shoulders ease the smallest bit.

"He *was* my lover for a while." *The truth*, I say to myself. "Maybe a long while."

Her mouth tightens. "He's much, much too old for you."

"I know. But he's also charming and kind, and he's very good to me. He made me feel good about myself when I was feeling like the ugliest, stupidest, most pathetic woman on the planet. Does that make any sense to you at all?"

"Yes." Her eyes cloud. "I'm so sorry you felt that way. I hope you don't anymore."

"I don't. He gave me that gift, Mom. But I also realized that he is too old for me and I was using him to avoid facing my real life. So I ended it. Well over a year ago."

"I see." She presses her lips together. "Thank you for telling me."

The doorbell rings and I shout, "Come in! We're upstairs!" To my mother, I say, "Can we keep this between us, please? Please?"

She nods but doesn't look at me.

Whatever. It's a start. It's the best I can do for now.

Nancy and Poppy fell in love that summer I stayed in Sedalia, and they credit me with their long and happy partnership. It's been a boon for both of them. They're now in their late sixties but quite vigorous from daily yoga and the walking treks they take all over the world. Poppy is still plump and busty, but she's taken on muscle in her calves and shoulders from all that exercise. Her hair is steel gray and clipped to her shoulders, and tonight she is wearing a simple athletic top and hiking pants with Tevas. Nancy, tall and rangy and very tan, wears a straight blue-and-white-striped shift. She reminds me of Julia Child, with that same vivid zest for life, and as she comes in bearing bags and boxes, she fills the entire room with a soft violet light.

"Hello, hello!" she cries, bending to kiss my cheek. "It's so good to see you! Lily, you look terrific as always. That color is excellent for you." She puts her parcels on the table and inhales deeply. "It smells great. Is that our dinner?"

"Yes." I laugh, hugging Poppy and feeling all the tension flow out of me. "What's all this?"

"Well, we thought we should welcome a new member of the family in a proper fashion. Where is she?"

"I'm not sure. She was getting dressed. Let me call her."

But before I move to the door, her herald arrives with his tail in the air, happily snuffling the hands that reach for him. "Oh, who's this?" Poppy cries, getting down to look him in the eye. He sits politely, as if he is well trained, and licks his lips but doesn't lick her.

Nancy smiles fondly. "What a mutt!"

And there is Katie, leaning like a garden creature against the doorjamb, her wild hair springing around her head. She's wearing a sundress my mother must have bought her. It's made of some airy fabric the color of new leaves, a shade that brings out her eyes and flatters the warm tone of her skin and makes her look even more like a dragonfly. "He rescued me," she says. "His name is Merlin."

Nancy smiles and offers a hand. "You must be Katie. I'm Nancy." She gestures toward the table. "We brought you a few things to welcome you."

A split second before she speaks, I realize Katie is in haughty mode—that nose tipped up in the air. "I'm not an orphan, you know. My parents can buy me things."

"Katie—" I begin, but Nancy gently waves her hand my way.

"Absolutely. I've met your dad and he's fantastic—I can't wait to see him again." She gestures toward the bags and boxes. "This is the extravagance of women who never had daughters of our own to spoil. We do the same thing to Ramona and Sofia."

"It's true." I nod my head. "No matter how I protested, they spoiled Sofia rotten."

Katie looks to Lily, as if for permission, and my mother gives a slight nod. Katie eases forward. "What *is* all this?"

"Open it and see!" Poppy says, and brushes dog hair from her shirt. "If I'd known about the puppy, I'd have brought him something, too."

Katie opens the parcels to reveal outdoorsy clothes and shoes and gardening gloves in two colors, plus a big book, used but in good condition, on dahlias. "Oh," Katie breathes, "this is beautiful. Did Lily tell you about how much we've been planting? And we're going to go to this flower show together in a couple of weeks."

"What are some of your favorites?" Poppy says, drawing the girl to sit beside her. I glance at Nancy over their heads and smile. They've always been so good at nurturing.

We eat heartily—even Katie loves the tacos, much to my surprise. Afterward we take cups of herbal tea down to the backyard, and only then do I bring up my idea. "I'm worried about Sofia," I say. "She's due to deliver in a few weeks, and I think she needs somebody with her."

The aunties and my mother all sit up straight. "What are you thinking?" Poppy asks.

"I'll go," Lily says, and only I catch the flicker of dismay that crosses Katie's face before she hides it, bending over to pet Milo, who has followed us down, weaving through human and chair legs, brushing his tail along the backs of knees.

I give my mother a look, one she misses. "I think it would be better if it was Poppy and Nancy. They like to travel, and they can go hiking or whatever. And Nancy is a midwife."

"Retired," Nancy says.

"Officially," Poppy laughs, taking her hand. "I'm in! How about you?"

"Of course. Whatever we can do to help." Nancy inclines her head. "Is that all right, Lily?"

My mother's mouth is pinched. "Well, I'm no midwife, but she is my granddaughter."

"Mom," I say, standing. Something brushes over my face and, thinking it's a spiderweb, I swipe at it with a shudder. Instead, I feel something almost silky moving over my skin, like a scarf. For a moment I am reminded of my grandmother and even fancy I smell her perfume. Wishful thinking. "Can I talk to you for a minute?"

Not happy, she follows me, and I'm so mad at her by the time we make it to the kitchen that I could cheerfully slap her. In a low, fierce voice, I say, "Did you happen to notice that there's another girl who might need you right now?"

"What are you talking about, Ramona? I'm only expressing a preference—"

I put my finger to my lips. "Katie worships the ground you walk on, Mom. She needs you."

"Oh." She looks over her shoulder, and when she looks back, tears glisten in her eyes. "I'm so sorry, Ramona. I wasn't thinking."

"It's all right. Let's just go fix it."

But Katie has gone upstairs by the time we return to the yard. "She said she'd be right back," Nancy says.

Of course she isn't, and after a while, during which we hammer out a plan for Nancy and Poppy to head to Texas, my mother goes upstairs to see if Katie wants to spend the night. She declines.

A small wound, I think. She'll heal quickly enough.

· · ·

I've finished pouring white and wheat flour into the vast kneading machine for our first round of baking this morning when
Sofia calls. It's just past three, and I take the phone into the
backyard again. "Hi, honey. How's it going?"

"Not good, Mom. Oscar is awake, but he doesn't want me
here."

"What do you mean?"

"He told me to go home. And it wasn't even a nice kind of go
home, where he asked me to go home and be safe or take care of
Katie or anything like that. He won't even look at me." Her voice
thins. "He's so angry."

I have no idea what the right thing to say might be. *Listen*, I
think, *just listen.* "That must be crushing."

"It is. I've been waiting and praying for him to wake up. I
have been sitting right beside him and reading aloud and trying
to be encouraging, and now he's finally awake and he can't even
stand the sight of me?"

"I'm sure that's not what it is, Sofia. He might be shocked and
upset and angry, but not at you."

"I know. I keep telling myself that, too, but it's hard. I'm not
tough, like you."

I laugh a little. "I'm a real tough marshmallow, baby. What if
I can send you some backup?"

"Are you coming?" Her voice is filled with hope.

It pierces me. "I can't, honey, not if we are going to have any
money at all. I can't leave the business right this second, and
there's Katie."

"I know. I understand. But I wish you were here. It would
make it so much better."

"How about a couple of aunties instead? Poppy and Nancy
will come if you want them to. They're so excited about it."

Her voice is quiet. "I know you love them, Mom, but they are
kind of eccentric and this is an Army hospital, and...I don't

know." She starts to cry softly, then swears. "Damn! I keep telling myself that crying doesn't help, but I can't seem to stop anyway."

For a minute I'm wondering about my choices. Would it be better to leave somebody else in charge of the bakery? Bring Katie with me to Texas to look out for Sofia?

No. Impossible. "I would love to be there with you, Sofia. I hope you know that."

"I do. And you know I love the aunties. I just wish it was you."

How did I get so lucky to have this child who likes my company? Who needs and wants me? In a deliberately upbeat tone, I say, "Remember, Nancy is a midwife, and it won't be so bad to have someone with medical training around. Oscar loves Poppy, too. Maybe that will help."

"Maybe." She takes a breath. "When are they coming?"

"They have to get things arranged—maybe a week or two. I'll let you know."

"Okay. I guess I should let you get back to work. What kind of bread are you making today?"

I tell her the names of the breads, the oatmeal sunflower and millet whole wheat and the sharply sour rustica. But what she wants is distraction and a sense of normality. "Oh, guess what? I met a guy from a long time ago, from when I was pregnant with you."

"No way! The sweater guy?"

I blush to the top of my bra. I'd forgotten that I told her all about the sweater, which I do still have tucked away in a trunk of things I've kept. Sofia loved to go through it with me and have me tell stories about each thing. My roller skates, a scrapbook I made at church camp one year, an autograph book and pictures. And the sweater. She used to like to put it on. "Yeah. How weird is that? He found Katie's dog when he got out of the yard one day and brought him back."

"So is he still hot?"

I should never have brought this up. It feels girlish and idiotic to be talking about him so soon. As if it has the potential to be something.

My mother is right. I should know better by now.

But this is my daughter, who needs distraction. "Yes," I say. "Way out of my league!" I laugh to show it doesn't bother me, but I'm thinking of his house, the music playing, his calm, elegant manners.

"Nobody is out of your league, Mom. You're probably out of his." A voice murmurs nearby and Sofia says something muffled. "Hey, I have to go. The doctors are going in."

"Love you! Let me know if you need anything."

"Kiss, love, bye!"

I stand in the dark garden with the phone in my hand and send a prayer to my baby across the miles. *Be well. Be safe. Be strong.* A wind moves across the moonflowers, making them bounce, and my cat comes streaking out of the garden. For a minute it almost looks as if someone is standing there. Then a cloud shifts and the area is too dark to see.

The bread is waiting.

Jimmy is at the door with a frown. "We might have a problem." She holds out a wooden spoon. "This is Adelaide's sponge."

Even before it gets to my nose, I can tell it's gone too sour. "Ay yi yi." With the tip of my little finger, I scoop out a small taste, put it on my tongue, and turn to spit it right out again. I should never have refreshed it when I was so angry at my sister, and I'm still rattled over Sofia. "Tell you what. Do what you can with the others and I'll get this washed and refreshed this afternoon."

She nods. "Any ideas what to put in place of the rusticas, then?"

"You know, Jimmy, I'm going to let you decide."

One pierced eyebrow lifts in wary surprise. "Me. Decide."

I laugh. "Yes. It's time. Choose something and let's go with it."

"Cheese and herb focaccia," she says, testing. She's been dying to make focaccias part of our repertoire.

"Perfect." I carry the starter to the counter. Even the color is off, a vague pink, stained with my lingering fury at my sister. Later it will have to be washed, but for now I have to focus on what to fill the cases with this morning. Baguettes, I think, the best and simplest bread in the world. I wash my hands and dive into the comfort of flour and salt, yeast and water, the eternal, essential cornerstones of bread.

RAMONA'S BOOK OF BREADS

CARING FOR YOUR MOTHER DOUGH

Starters are sturdier than they appear, despite all the legends of miners sleeping with their starters against their bodies overnight to keep them from freezing. Still, some tenderness is required.

To care well for a mother dough, take it out of the fridge and refresh it once a week. The starter may have a layer of liquid, which will vary in color from light yellow to dark brown. This is the natural alcohol produced by the yeasts and is never to be feared. Stir it into the starter vigorously, measure out half of the starter, and put it in a fresh jar. Use the other half in some baking, or throw the other half away (or give it away). To the remaining dough, add 1 cup flour, 1 cup water, and stir vigorously. Let it stand overnight and return to the fridge.

If a starter has gone too sour or weak, stir it vigorously, measure half into a large, clean jar, and add 1 cup of lukewarm water and stir it in. Then add ½ cup rye flour and 1¼ cups unbleached white flour. Stir and let stand in a warm place where you can keep an eye on it. You should see plenty of activity within a couple of hours. By morning, even the most bitter of mother doughs should be refreshed and ready to work again.

THIRTY-ONE

Katie

W hen Katie gets up, Merlin is already outside in the backyard with Ramona. Shimmying into a pair of shorts and a T-shirt, she pads down the stairs as quietly as if someone might hear her. In the cool, still-shadowy kitchen, which smells a little of the supper they ate last night with the aunties, she turns on the computer. While it boots, she peeks out the kitchen window to be sure Ramona is still there. From below come the sounds of the girls setting up the bakery cases for the day. It's only five a.m. With a rush of longing, Katie thinks of how the dew will still be all over everything, making diamonds out of flower petals and stalks of grass. She loves to help pull weeds first thing, then have breakfast and some tea. Ramona says she is a natural lark, whatever that means. Lily is more of an owl and does her gardening in the evening, but she has to wear long sleeves and put on mosquito repellent, which stinks so much that Katie doesn't understand why she wouldn't get up early.

When the computer comes up, she opens the email from her mother and reads it again. When she first read it, she felt her throat get all clogged up with tears, and it was just depressing—how her mom doesn't know how to spell, and how she writes everything in capital letters as if she's yelling. Which is kind of how she is. Noisy. Like a hurricane or a tornado.

What Katie didn't get until she came here is how nice it can be to have everything all calm and ordinary—reliable. Like right now she could open the cupboard and there would be cereal, and on the counter are some bananas and oranges, and there's milk in the fridge. A long time ago life was like that, when Katie's mom and dad were still married, but even before Lacey came back from Iraq as a different person, she didn't always have that much food in the house. She liked to be skinny and she wanted Katie to be skinny, too, so they would practice going without food for lunch or sometimes dinner.

Katie never liked it. She got too hungry. Even thinking about it now, she gets up and takes a banana off the counter and peels it and eats it just because she can. While she eats, she reads the email over and over.

Her dad is awake, which is a good thing, but Sofia made it sound as if it could be a super-long time before he's well, which only makes sense.

That made Katie think about where she would be living. It's one thing to be here with Ramona for the summer, but how can Katie stay here? She thinks again of Lily volunteering to go down to Texas, and the same stupid pang goes through her chest. *She is my granddaughter,* Lily said. Until then Katie had been thinking maybe she finally had a grandmother of her own, but that was dumb. Why would any grandmother care more about a strange kid than about her own blood?

Katie's only true blood are her mom and dad. She has to take care of those relationships. This won't last. She has to keep remembering that.

This. Will. Not. Last.

Clicking the email reply, she writes:

TO: laceymomsoldier@prt.com
FROM: katiewilson09872@nomecast.com
SUBJECT: It's all good here, too.

Dear Mom,

    I loved getting an email from you. It sounds like you're doing really well, and I hope you can keep getting better and better. I'm working in the bakery, just little stuff, running things from the front to the back, and I get paid for it. It's not like a real job, because I'm too young, but I like it a lot.

    I've been learning all about flowers. Dahlias have hundreds of different species, did you know that? And they are so beautiful! Lily, who is Sofia's grandmother, has a lot of different kinds in her garden. Some have little curled petals and some have spiky petals and they come in every color you can think of. I really like gardening. We have a vegetable garden in the backyard here, too, but I like the flowers best.

    I have saved up $20 and can send that to you first thing tomorrow. Please quit smoking! I know it's hard, but it's not good for you. Write soon.

    Love,

    Katie

PS—Dad woke up from his coma, so he's going to be okay.

THIRTY-TWO

Ramona

I'm ready to go way too early on Sunday evening, even after changing my clothes four times and then putting on makeup and changing again. Katie, sitting at the kitchen table to cut out pictures of flowers from a gardening magazine, finally says, "Why are you so jumpy?"

I halt in my tracks, looking down at the fourth shirt I've put on, a simple V-neck T-shirt, dark blue to maybe hide the little tummy that pushes over the top of my jeans. "Does this make me look too fat?"

She narrows her eyes. "Kinda. What about the green one you had on first?"

"I like it, but it seems kind of hippie-ish?"

"It's a good color."

I inhale and exhale slowly. "Okay, I'm changing." In my bedroom, strewn now with all my dithering, I pull off the navy-blue T-shirt and shake out the printed green-and-orange peasant blouse I chose first. It shows off my collarbones and drapes kindly over my tummy, and Katie is right: It's a good color. I pop out into the kitchen. "Better?"

"Yes," she says definitively. "And you should wear the sandals with those jewels on them."

"Oh! Good idea!" I scramble in the hall closet through the forty thousand shoes that live in the darkness there, breeding. Someday I have to find some time to declutter this house. Maybe I can get to it in 2042. Sliding my feet into the shoes, I clip-clop over to the table and sit down with her. "Thanks."

"This is the guy who brought Merlin back? You're going on a date with him because he returned the dog?"

"Um . . . no. Here's the thing—don't say anything to Lily or to the aunties if they're here, but he's somebody I knew a long time ago."

"Wow. That's kinda weird. Merlin went to his house. Just like he came to me."

I blink at her. It's true. "How weird."

She rubs her foot over his back. "I don't think he's really a dog."

"Really?" I laugh. "What, then?"

"I dunno. Maybe an angel or something." She looks over the top of the picture. "Why would they care about you going out with that guy?"

"*They* won't. I will. This is my secret."

She lifts a shoulder. "Okay."

"You sure you're going to be okay?"

She raises those droll eyebrows, her eyes with too much knowledge. "Seriously? I'm almost fourteen. And it's not like I've had highly supervised environments."

I laugh. She's so old for her years sometimes. "Well, I'll have my cell phone, and you have your dog angel to protect you. And my mom can be here in ten minutes."

She focuses too intently on cutting out a photo of a cactus dahlia the color of a baby's fingernail. "Whatever."

Still wounded, then. I wonder if I should address it or let it be.

Leave it. Her defenses are up and prickly.

The clock reads four forty-five. He won't be here for another fifteen minutes. I fold my arms. "Did you write your dad another email?"

"Yes. And Sofia wrote me back. She said to tell you she'll call when they get more information." She smears purple glue over the back of the photo and sticks it on a notebook page, smoothing the wrinkles out neatly, then writes *Cactus Dahlia* in colored pencil beside it.

I think of my book of breads, and just as I am about to tell her about it, the doorbell rings downstairs. Widening my eyes in Katie's direction, I put my hand to my throat. I whisper, "That's him."

Leaning over the table, she whispers back, "You should probably go let him in."

I grab my purse, swipe lipstick over my mouth, and drop it in the bag. "There's plenty to eat and drink. And you can reach me—"

"On your cell phone. I got it."

Laughing, I unthinkingly drop a kiss on the top of her head. As if she is my own. She gives me a look over her shoulder, and I waggle my fingers, not taking it back. "Have fun," she says, her green eyes unreadable.

I fly down the stairs, my hair a wild flying cape behind me, and halt at the foot. Jonah is on the porch, framed by the old glass in the front door. Behind him is the thick dust-gold of late-afternoon sunlight. His jaw is clean and he's looking toward the west, and for one long second I let myself fill up with the pleasure of just looking at him. Then he turns and sees me through the door and smiles.

I open the door to him and step out. "Hi." It sounds breathless.

"Hi." A wistful sort of smile touches his mouth. "Hope I'm not too early."

"No, I always get ready too early, since I have a tendency to be late for everything. It used to drive my ex-husband crazy." I look up at him. "Oh, sorry. I'm really not one of those people who

talk about their exes all the time. I mean, not that we're...
uh..." My hand flutters up, then down. I will myself to shut up.

He takes a step closer to me, picks up my hand. "Are you nervous?"

I laugh ruefully. "What was your first clue?"

He lifts my hand, carries it to his mouth, and kisses the palm.
It quiets me. He says, "I was nervous, too. But I have the opposite trouble—I have a hard time thinking of what to say. My tendency is to pontificate about something, on and on and on.
About exciting things like the mathematical grades in composition, say, or obscure eighteenth-century violinists."

"Oh, please, sir, do say more!"

"Exactly." He indicates the picnic basket in his other hand.
"In this case, I made way too much food, in the event we couldn't
think of anything to say."

"That's not ever a problem with me." I smile then, and we
seem to sway forward without moving, into a space only the two
of us can occupy. He lets my hand go, sparing us the awkwardness of knowing when to clasp and when to release.

The park is only a few blocks away, and within a minute or
two we join the flow of people headed for the outdoor concert.
"You opened this morning for Sunday traffic, right?" he asks. "I
saw the flyers."

"Where did you find one?"

"At the organic grocer in Manitou."

"Do you run, then?"

"There are hikers there, too."

"Not that early."

He inclines his head. "I do. Ran track in high school and
never gave it up."

"Are you one of those extreme people? Running the Ascent
and marathons and all that stuff?"

"Not at all." He grins down at me. "You sound as if you'd turn
around and go home if I said yes."

"Let's just say I've had a few encounters with runners of the extreme variety. Takes a particular kind of personality."

"True. How about you? Everyone here seems to have a sport. Do you?"

"Who has time?" I shake my head. "I'm a small-business owner."

"An extreme sport of another sort."

We reach the park and find an open expanse of grass beneath a tree. From the hamper, Jonah produces a green-and-white-checked tablecloth and flings it up and into a parachute that falls wide on the grass. "After you," he says, gesturing. We settle cross-legged on the cloth. He's wearing sunglasses, and I take mine out of my purse, too, dazzled by all the light splashing into the park. Overhead, the elms and cottonwoods rustle in a breath of wind, and from where we sit, the mountains are huddled like a football team, burly and blue.

As Jonah begins to take things out of the hamper, the musicians are warming up on the stage, which is curved like a seashell for the acoustics. The crowd is a genteel sort—I see several Mother Bridget regulars, tidily attired in their SPF-50 hiking shirts and tear-resistant pants. The women sometimes don a skirt with their Tevas, but mostly the shop of choice is REI.

Twice, people stop to say hello to Jonah. One is a balding genial man who is a bassist with the symphony; another is a Celtic drummer with a long, graying ponytail and an embroidered shirt. They both nod to me politely. Jonah says, "This is my friend Ramona."

Meanwhile, he lays out cheese and crackers; deviled eggs; chocolate cake with frosting; three kinds of sandwiches, cut into triangles; bananas and clementines; and two glasses for the bottle of wine he has tucked away. Seeing there is still more in the depths, I say, "Whoa there, Curly. I'm worried about the bottomless pit. Are you expecting the sixth brigade to join us?"

He chuckles. "I told you. I couldn't stop." With his long-fingered right hand, he picks up a deviled egg and offers it to me. "Start here. I have been told my recipe is the best."

For a moment I'm tempted to lean over and let him feed it to me, but I open my hand and he puts it in my palm. It's cold, and the filling has a good strong color. It is also artfully swirled into the bowl of white. "Mmm," I say, as I bite into it. "That really is great."

He has been waiting for me and now pops a whole one into his own mouth, and I find myself watching. Sun glances off his glasses, touches his long throat. I find myself rubbing a palm on my knee. He catches me looking. "Do I have egg on my face?" He wipes the corners with a cloth napkin.

"No," I say quietly. "What else should I try?"

He smiles ever so slightly. "Everything."

"See, there you go, teasing me." I hold the egg in my hand. "You promised to tell me your story."

"I did." He opens a bottle of San Pellegrino and pours it into glasses for us. "I told you I was divorced and that I have no children. Which is true."

"But?"

"But I did once. A little boy. His name was Ethan, and he was born with congestive heart failure. He died when he was five, waiting for a heart."

"Oh, Jonah!" I think of Sofia at five, and my eyes fill with tears. "I'm so sorry. That must have been terrible."

"Yes," he says matter-of-factly. "It was the worst thing that ever happened to me." He looks at me and seems to be choosing his words carefully. "Life is not served by staying stuck in that time, but in a way I think I've been standing right there for a long time. Do you know what I mean?"

"I think so. Is that why you divorced?"

He takes a breath, sips the sparkling water. "Yes. She took

refuge in a conservative Christian church. It didn't work for me."
He clears his throat, looks at me. "She found God. I lost him."

I remember standing in the record store as he struggled with
the loss of his music, the way that sudden, inexplicable twist
of fate ended his dream. *Sometimes it feels like there's no point.*
My heart splits, and I see the hollow points of connection. "It
doesn't seem fair to lose two things that you love so much."

He bows his head, and for a time he's quiet. Finally he looks
at me. "Exactly."

"How did you cope?"

He gestures toward the food. "I started volunteering with the
organization that helped us so much. I learned to meditate, to
keep things very smooth and even and ordinary."

"That's where the music went," I say aloud.

He smiles. "Yes."

"And women?"

"No, not all of them." He swallows. "But you...the other
night..." He pauses. "It seemed like too much."

For a moment, I let hope rush through me. "And now?"

"It's too extraordinary that we met again. I like you."

"Me, too." I feel faintly dizzy. "Like you." I ask, "Can I try the
cake first?"

"If you wish. And, certainly, wine." He pours a ruby red into
goblets.

"Is this allowed in a public park?"

A single, careless shrug. "I doubt it." He hands me a glass. "To
serendipity."

"And picnics," I say.

We sip, and I choose a slice of cake and a fork. Jonah says, "So
tell me about your husband."

I tsk. "Dane. We were not married a terribly long time. Only
seven years, and I don't think it was really meant to be." I sigh.
"He's kind of a big personality, and I got swept up into it."

"Are you friendly?"

"No. Our divorce caused a rift between me and my family." I lick a tiny bit of frosting to wash away the bitterness I can still sometimes taste. "He was unfaithful, and I kicked him out, quit the restaurant. Sofia was in college, her first year, and I had no idea what to do with myself." I held up a finger. "Oh, and did I mention my grandmother was sinking into dementia? Bad year, all in all."

"I guess!"

The expert in me eyes the crumb of the cake, and while bread is my specialty, I can see how perfect this is—moist and dense, with a thin layer of white frosting that turns out to be white chocolate. The whole thing explodes in my mouth, chocolate upon cocoa upon vanilla. "Oh!" I put my hand in front of my mouth. "You made this?"

He smiles. "Like it?"

I take another bite, close my eyes, pinpoint vanilla bean and the layers of chocolate all jammed into a feathery crumb. "Wow. Yes. Fantastic." I open my eyes, look at the cake. "There's something...can't quite catch it..."

"Nutmeg."

"Ah. Of course. Mmm. Is it your own recipe?"

"Now, that I can't claim. I found it in a cookbook somewhere. Tweaked it a bit, but mostly it wasn't mine."

"You are a fantastic cook. You should be a chef."

"No. Too much hard work." He takes a plate from the basket—a real plate, painted blue and yellow in an ethnic pattern—and puts sandwiches and watermelon and more deviled eggs on it. "Have some supper now that you've had your dessert."

I grin.

On the stage, the musicians begin to play. Jonah makes a plate for himself. "So what was Sofia like as a little girl?"

"Oh, she was wonderful. Always bossing the animals around and playing school. She had this giggle that killed me every time. I was finishing high school and all my friends were dating

242   BARBARA O'NEAL

and going to the prom, and I didn't care. I just wanted to be with her every minute I could." Licking frosting off the fork, I say, "God, this is so amazing."

A woman approaches. She's very long-legged and glossy in the way of women who have been wealthy their entire lives. "Hello, Jonah," she purrs. "I thought that was you."

His shoulders look rigid. "Hello, Alex." His voice is calm.

She looks at me, head to toes, and then dismisses me. She squats in front of him, showing her sleek calves and a tasteful glimpse of cleavage. "How have you been?"

"Good. This is my friend Ramona. Ramona, this is Alex."

"Hello," she says, holding out a hand with a topaz the size of a bread box on her finger. "Jonah and I have a long history."

"Ah. What a coincidence," I say. "So do we. When did we meet, Jonah?"

His smile says everything I need to know. "Twenty-five years ago."

"Old friends, then, huh?"

I look at Jonah, and he looks at me. "Not exactly."

She shakes her hair, smiles. "Well, you know where to find me," she says. Wiggling her fingers, she sways away.

"Please tell me that was not one of the Real Housewives of Vail," I say. "I would hate to think I had been rude."

He laughs. "Well done."

"A love affair that ended badly?"

"Never even an affair. We dated a little, but she's not...the kind of woman I like to spend time with."

I pluck a sandwich from my plate. "Gorgeous and rich isn't a combination that works for you?"

He frowns. "High maintenance. Wrong values."

"What are the right values?"

"Human beings before things. Earth before consumption." He lifts a shoulder. "Time is precious and should be respected."

For a moment I look at him, thinking, *He really is the person I thought he was all those years ago.*

Onstage, the cellist begins to play a solo. The bow strokes are long and melancholy, as if to underline Jonah's words. *Time is precious.* I look at Jonah's hands, his neck. Notes weave into the gilded evening, sailing almost visibly through the air to land in my chest, caress my throat. "What *is* this?" I ask.

"This one," he says in a rough voice, "is mine."

I close my eyes, overcome and embarrassed to show too much, and let the notes settle into the crooks of my arms and the bones of my spine. Tears fill my eyes and spill over. Embarrassed, I blot them with a napkin. "Sorry. It's just so beautiful. I can't help it."

"Don't apologize. I'm touched that it moves you." He takes my hand and pulls me closer, his thumb moving over my inner wrist. I scoot a little nearer and can hear him humming beneath the cello—not singing along but adding harmony or counterpoint. It makes me want to cover him with my body, press him into the grass, and kiss his throat. The brush of his thumb, slow and light, sends sparks leaping across my skin, and I can feel the movements beneath my hair on the nape of my neck, on my temples, beneath my arms.

I lift his hand, his marred hand, and press it to my face. "Will you play for me someday, Jonah?"

His breath leaves him on a sigh as he bends in to my invitation, sweeping his other arm around to create a circle that encloses us. His breath smells of chocolate as he leans to kiss me, and when his mouth touches mine, delicately at first—such full lips—my skin and brain are so tingly that I almost feel as if I will faint. I reach for him, for the brace of his shoulder, and grasp the fabric of his shirt as he—or I, or both—makes a low sound, angles his head, and our tongues touch. It feels like an act we invented this minute, something so rare and strange and incredible that I want to hang in this cello-wound moment, just touching Jonah's tongue, for at least a year.

But our bodies move, our lips, our tongues, exploring and breathing and sliding and swirling. We breathe. His hand is hot on the back of my neck, and I am holding too tightly to his shirt, and all my resolve to be distant and aloof and to guard myself is gone.

I pull back to look at him. His lion eyes look down at me and we move in to kiss again, this time eye to eye. "I can't believe I'm kissing you," he whispers.

"I know. It's like a dream."

The music trails away behind us. He straightens, tucks a lock of my hair behind my ear. "My hands are shaking."

"Everything in me is shaking," I say, and frown. It feels like too much. I think of him in the record store when we were young, asking why his dreams had been stolen. I think of the music he composed, the music played here tonight, and it is highly emotional. I think of his house, so austere, stripped clean of things to care about.

And now our hands are shaking with emotion. Too much. I think, *This is not going to be good for me,* and I cannot afford to be caught in a dramatic love affair. Too many people are depending on me. I must be the center that holds.

"Maybe," I say, "we should play backgammon."

He straightens. "Yes. That's a good idea."

He walks me home when the concert is over. Music unhinged me earlier, but we grounded ourselves in the game and food and laughing. Now I feel the evening coming to a close, and I need to make sure we do not take this anywhere.

At the porch steps, I turn to look up at him, feeling suddenly without words—or maybe with too many words, all crowding in, tumbling over themselves. "Everything I'm thinking of to say sounds false."

He picks up my hand and kisses my knuckles. "Don't say anything."

I nod. He releases me and I say, "Good night, Jonah."

For a moment he stands quite still. Overhead, a nightingale whistles in the trees, and moonlight filters through the branches, dappling his face, his hair. I want to take him inside and tuck him close, smooth away that sorrow I now understand, but it could ruin me.

"Good night," he says, and walks away.

Inside, I sink down on the bottom stair and let the shivering take over. It feels as if I have been fighting. Bending my head, I hear the mournful sound of his sonata, and it makes me dizzy. This is better, that we should be only friends. He is too much, the feeling is too much, and if I fell from such a distance, I don't think I could bear it.

On legs that feel wobbly, I turn and go upstairs, to the things I can believe in. My cat. A young girl who needs me. My daughter, who might even now be writing me an email.

But as I sink into my bed, what I think of is the way his mouth tasted, the smell of his skin. How do you stop a thing once it begins?

Punch It Down

When the dough has doubled, the belly filled with carbon dioxide and madly multiplying yeasts contained by the skin of gluten, the baker must punch it down. This is not an actual fist, a true punch, but rather a deflation. Turn the dough out onto a hard surface and gently press down to let the air out. The excess carbon dioxide is gently squeezed out, and the yeasts are more fully distributed through the dough so that the loaf can be shaped and set to rise into the true shape of the bread it will become.

THIRTY-THREE

Ramona

The second time bread saved my life, I was again nursing wounds inflicted by a man.

I didn't date much after I had Sofia. There wasn't time, for one thing. I was busy with school and work, and any hours I had left between those things were spent with my daughter. By the time she started kindergarten, I had saved enough to buy us a small house not far from my grandmother's, and I was the assistant operations manager for the Gallagher Group, a job that paid well even if it was boring. It earned me a place in the family business. I had great benefits for Sofia and me. All around me, I saw people who had far less. If I hated my job, I was only one of billions, and at least mine was clean, honest work. Outside work, I was a classroom mother, I baked elaborate and beautiful things for Sofia's parties, and I read a lot in the evenings.

Dane came to work for the company when Sofia was seven or so, and I didn't pay him much attention. I didn't pay attention to any man, and that's why they mostly left me alone. Once in a while I dated somebody for a bit, but there were always conflicts with my job or my daughter or my own finicky tastes. My mother urged me to find a husband, to be less judgmental, but it seemed to me that unless a man was on the level of the greatest

soul mate of all time, the complications he would bring would
be too much.

Dane joined the Gallagher Group as general manager. A
tall, charismatic man with a failed marriage behind him in
California and a cheery good nature, he almost immediately
raised the profits in the company by 10 percent, and by the end
of two years that number was 30 percent. But it was his personality that made him such a star. He counterbalanced the Irish
furies and tempests generated by my family. He had a way of
smoothing even the fiercest of disagreements, easing difficult
chefs and my father with the grace of a medieval diplomat. I noticed this quality first, when he managed to defuse a furious
clash between my father and a distributor he felt had done him
wrong. I gave him a thumbs-up in the kitchen afterward. "Good
work."

He lifted a brow. "She speaks!"

"Very funny," I said, but that was the start of it. Once he
found my weak spot, he pursued me in a way that was flattering
and heartening. His zest for life was practically irresistible, and
I was as drawn to him as everyone else in the business was. He
was like a cool, burbling fountain in the midst of our tropical
passions.

He was good to me. Sofia adored him, as all children did, and
he loved her in return. My parents approved. I liked him and I
thought he was sexy, but here's the thing:

We had sex. A *lot* of sex.

I was hardly a virgin, considering my status as a mother, but
there I was in my mid-twenties, with every hormonal juice
pumping through my system urging me to get physical and
have a billion babies, and I just wasn't.

Dane swept me into a deliriously sexual relationship. He was
a terrific lover, as thoughtful and sensitive to the needs of a
woman as he was to the emotional needs of chefs or distribu-
tors. There are some people who have a genius for giving you

what you need, and Dane is one of them. He knew my grandmother loved to be flirted with. He knew my mother loved to be thought the most intelligent person in the room, that my father respected hard work and didn't trust anyone who came from money.

We married when Sofia was almost ten, in a ceremony with lilacs filling the air with their heady perfume. Sofia was my maid of honor, and my mother, Stephanie, and Sarah were bridesmaids. It says something that my brother was one of his groomsmen. Liam didn't care.

The only person who never approved was Poppy. She tried to keep it to herself, but when I announced we were going to marry, she sat me down and tried to talk sense into me. She all but said she suspected it would be impossible for Dane to be faithful, that he was not the kind of man who would make me happy for the long term, but I couldn't hear her. I was swimming in a juicy fountain of great sex and had somehow won the approval of my family, as well. Not only that, Dane loved and cared for my daughter as his own and didn't mind that I wasn't interested in having more children at the moment.

We married.

We were happy.

Or maybe that's a lie. Maybe I always knew, on some subtle level, that we had struck a bargain. His income helped create a good life for my daughter—buying clothes and trips and experiences that she could not have had if I had remained a single mother. He agreeably nourished my appetites for attention and good sex and facilitated the ease between my family and me.

In return, I never noticed that he sometimes disappeared for a very long time. That he took business trips rather a lot. That certain women seemed to dislike me for no real reason.

I don't know. That sounds so cynical. Maybe I did just like being married. Maybe, as hard as it is to admit it, I honestly did love him.

No. I didn't. I have never loved any man, not really. It's my failing and my protection.

Either way, it turned out that Poppy was right. It was impossible for Dane to be faithful, as his first wife had discovered. One of his lovers—yes, there were evidently several over the years—would not let him go when he gently tried to break it off. She went nuts and showed up at our door, stalked me and him for a month, and generally made a nuisance out of herself. She made it impossible for me, or Dane, or even my family, to sweep it all out of sight and pretend it had never happened.

The only blessing was that Sofia had already left for college. She was in her first year at a teacher's college in the western part of the state, a long, long drive that she made only every other month or so, and during the winter snows not even that.

It helped protect her from the ugliness.

It also left me completely and utterly alone. I couldn't face the pitiful, or smirking, or even smug looks that followed me at work, so I turned in my notice. I kicked Dane out of the house.

And there I sat, most of the autumn, drowning in humiliation and loss. I'd seen uncles fall into bad habits with alcohol, so I didn't indulge my desire to drink entire bottles of wine, but I developed other self-destructive behaviors. I stayed up all night playing games on the computer. I watched endless movies on cable. Twice, I went out with friends and ended up in a one-night stand, not something I'm proud of.

The only people from the family I would speak to were Poppy and my grandmother, who was weaving in and out of dementia, so she often forgot that I was getting divorced. Forgot, for that matter, that I had ever been born and mistook me for one of her sisters or daughters.

It was bread that saved my life. For the second time.

While I was throwing things out one night, I found my old notebook, *Ramona's Book of Breads*. The sight of my hopeful handwriting on the cover, the memory of those dire days in an earlier part of my life—days I had survived, after all—went right through my gut. I sank down on the floor, pulled out of my dervish whirl, to open the cover. And remember.

Almost without thinking, I carried the book to the kitchen and pulled out those simple magic ingredients. Flour, salt, yeast.

But nothing had gone on in that kitchen for months. I'd been eating Lean Cuisines and peanut butter crackers almost exclusively. The flour had bugs in it, and the yeast was ten years old.

I pulled on my jeans, washed my face, and drove to an all-night grocery. With a genuine sense of delight, I bought white bread flour, and whole wheat, and a paper bag of rye. Instead of envelopes of yeast, I bought a brown jarful. Below it was kosher salt, looking so official, and I put that in my basket, too. Something I'd forgotten, something alive, stirred within me. I carried it all back home and dumped it on the counter.

I baked all night. Stirred yeast into sugar water and watched it grow, then stirred yeast and sugar water into flour and salt and dumped it all on the counter and kneaded it far longer than was required. My hands remembered things my brain had forgotten—the way to turn and fold, the feeling of dough going smooth and clammy below the heels of my palms.

When morning came, I called Poppy and asked her if she had any of her starters left. "Of course," she said. "But you could get some from Adelaide today if you want it."

"She probably hasn't refreshed it regularly."

"Get some," she said, "and I'll teach you to wash it."

The starter was salvageable, but just. It had taken on the taste of disuse and the world narrowing in. I gathered the old crock and my grandmother from her house and brought her to mine, and even as I began to work, the mother dough lightened, began to sweeten.

I divided it into three sections. One I darkened with malt sugar and rye and my own sorrow. One I washed according to Poppy's instructions, to bring it back to a version of itself that was as close to Bridget's original as possible. The other I used to bake a loaf of bread that I buried in the backyard at Adelaide's, to signify the end of this life and the start of the new one.

It was easier to care for my grandmother in her own home, so I sold my little house and moved in with her, and I continued to cook that whole long winter. My grandmother sat with me, sometimes staring with vacant blue eyes into the far distance, where perhaps she saw to the other side. At times she kneaded with me, her veined hands and crooked fingers still finding comfort in the shaping of loaves.

Poppy arrived one Sunday evening, alone, and found us in the kitchen. She halted at the doorway. In her hands were two Bell jars of starter—one pale and smooth, the other brown and full of holes. She stared at her mother without moving for a long time, long enough that I wondered if she would turn around and leave. The only time I could remember them speaking was the day everyone came to Poppy's farm when I was pregnant. I still didn't know why, but I could guess it had to do with Poppy being gay, with Adelaide's fearsome unhappiness as a mother, or both.

Adelaide was having one of her lost days. I'd given her a chunk of dough to press and fold, and it occupied her for hours. Like me, she seemed soothed by the smell of yeast and baking crust, and she loved the classical music I played. We often worked side by side in that kitchen for hours and hours without even speaking.

"Grandma, look who's here," I said.

She turned. "Hello, Poppy," she said, with the surprising perfect clarity that could sometimes arrive. "Are you going to bake with us?"

My aunt, as mighty as any woman I had ever known, crumpled. She carried the jars to the table, put them down, and bent to hug her mother from behind. "I love you, Mom. I hope you know that."

Adelaide closed her eyes. "You wouldn't have been keeping my starter alive all these years if you didn't, would you?" She curled a hand around Poppy's arm and pressed her cheek into her daughter's.

They rocked back and forth for a long moment, and Adelaide said, "Will you tell Lily that I'm sorry?"

"Yes," she whispered. "But it doesn't matter."

"I ruined her dress. Never could get the stain out."

"I know." Poppy straightened and went out to the backyard. When she came back, we baked rolls with each of the mother doughs and tasted them all side by side.

THIRTY-FOUR

Sofia's Journal

SAN ANTONIO
JUNE 10, 20—

I've just come from the most depressing hour of my life. I sat with Mica Reed, one of the other wives, while she cried. Her husband didn't make it. He's been here longer than Oscar, but he was much more seriously injured, with burned lungs, which I think was the main problem, and a lot of internal injuries. It was always a very slim hope that he would make it, but he's been hanging on for so long you know that's what he was trying to do. Live. He never regained consciousness, so the mind was willing but the flesh was too wrecked.

What I hated was that, the whole time I was sitting with her, all I was thinking about was how bad Ralph's wounds were in comparison to Oscar's, making this mental list that was just horrible. Head to head, lungs to lungs, skin to skin, missing limbs to broken bones to lost digits.

You think, going into this, that you know how it will be if your husband (or wife) gets injured or killed. It happens all around you, so you start to get that it really could happen, but the only way to stand it is to keep believing in some strange protection that's going to take care of your person. Keep HIM safe, above all others.

And there are all those crazy stories about soldiers who survive three deployments, then come back and get into a car wreck or a bar fight or get cancer and die at home. The truth is, any of us can die at any moment, but who can live with that, ever?

Oscar is alive. He isn't talking to me still, but he's alive, and he's actually getting a little better. I see the faces of the nurses and doctors. They're not as grim. They smile at me now, and not with pity like they were before.

Tonight I went back in there after sitting with Mica, and I told him that Ralph died, that he left behind five kids and a wife who can't stop crying. That he tried to stay alive but he couldn't get through it. I told him that his children are waiting for him to stop feeling so damned sorry for himself and get well.

Oscar just stared through his mummy bandages at the ceiling. Never even said a word back to me.

I don't know what to do. Maybe I should leave him here, go home and let him work it out, whether he's going to live or not.

But I can't, not yet.

Not yet.

THIRTY-FIVE

Ramona

I am lying awake, doom heavy in my gut, when my cell
phone rings. Snatching it off the side table, I answer,
"Sofia?"

A man's voice says, "It's Jonah. Did I wake you?"

"No." Sitting up, I peer at the clock. One a.m. "Is everything
all right?"

"I'm outside."

I think of walls falling down, letting all the good and all the
bad come rushing in. "I'll be down in five minutes."

"Thank you."

I tug on my jeans and a sweatshirt, splash water on my face.
Staring at my bleary eyes in the mirror, I promise myself that I
won't get too tangled in this. The last thing I need in my life is a
man with a yawning wound. There are quite enough wounded
people in my world already.

But, once upon a time, he was so very kind to me that I cannot possibly turn him away now.

He's sitting on the front-porch step and turns as I come out
the door. In a quiet voice, I say, "Hi. Is everything okay?"

He stands. He's wearing a T-shirt and jeans, and his hair is
brushed back from his face as if he's been running his hands

through it. "Yes. I'm not sick or anything. I just thought you might be awake."

Tugging the door closed behind me, I sit down on the step and reach for him. "Sit. Tell me."

He perches beside me and picks up my hand, places it against his thigh, palm up. "This line here is the one that says we've known each other in many lifetimes."

His light touch makes me shiver, makes me conscious that I am not wearing anything beneath my sweatshirt. "This line marks the day we met, all those years ago." He holds up his hand and places his palm against mine. "I know you were worried about my sad story, Ramona. Maybe it seems the timing for us is terrible again, but it isn't."

"It is, though. I'm overwhelmed by my life right now."

"Mmm." He looks at me. "Is that really why?"

His thumb is moving on my inner wrist, igniting a million nerve cells. It moves higher, through that center line, and I almost think I can see phosphorescence wherever he strokes my skin. "I don't know."

"I think you're afraid."

I let go of a humorless laugh. "Yeah, well, with good reason. I've not had good luck in this department."

"That doesn't mean you'll always have bad luck." He curls my fingers and covers them with his other hand. "I've been writing music for three days. Nonstop, practically. It's terrible. It's wonderful." He pauses, looking into the darkness. "It's Ethan."

"Your son."

He nods. "The thing about a sick kid is that they don't live in the sick part. They're still growing and making funny faces and learning to talk, all those things. He had his favorite toys and breakfasts and cartoons, you know?"

"Yes." Again I think of Sofia at five, her black curls and wicked eyes. "What did he love, Jonah?"

"Fish. We had a saltwater tank, and it was his joy. He knew the name of every fish and coral in that thing. They're beautiful, so colorful and peaceful, and it always seemed to me that something like that could heal you."

"I believe that."

He nods again. Starts to say something and then stops. "I hadn't written anything since he died. Not one note."

"Maybe you needed time to grieve."

"It's been fourteen years, Ramona. The trigger was you."

I give him a smile. "Ah, so I'm a muse. That's cool."

"I've noticed you do that little joking thing when you're feeling something strong."

I look down.

He pushes back my sleeve, strokes up and down my inner arm, and an answering swirl of nerves moves up my spine, around my ribs, across the tips of my breasts. I pull away, tuck my arm against my body.

He chuckles. Scoots close to me. "You like me, Ramona."

I bend over my knees, my hair falling down around me like a tent. "I do, but that's besides the point."

"What is the point?"

His arm comes around my shoulders, and our hips are touching. "I can't remember."

He says, "I came here to kiss you."

"I think we shouldn't." I close my eyes, trying not to think about it, so of course all I can do is think about it. The taste of him. My wish for the feeling of his hands on me. "It just feels too...big or something. I am so bad at relationships."

"Me, too." His fingers are brushing my hair from my neck, and then his lips fall there, on my nape, which makes me shudder. He feels it. "Sit up," he says quietly.

And as if my body belongs to someone else, that's what I do. I sit up and fall into the crook of his arm, across his lap, and he kisses me. Sweetly at first, full of tenderness. Gentleness. I feel safe here, against his chest, in the dark. His hand is on my face, smoothing over my cheek and chin, my neck.

Light shimmers in the darkness behind my eyelids. I find myself leaning into him more, curling my hand around his neck, touching his ear. We press closer together, and I am dizzy. I reach beneath his shirt to touch his skin, hot and smooth, and his hand circles my waist below the sweatshirt.

At last he raises his head. "Do you remember when I kissed you?" he says. "In your aunt Poppy's garden?"

"Yes. I thought I would die."

"Me, too," he says. His hand moves to my hair. "I thought about you for years, wondering how you were, what you were doing."

In my back pocket, my phone rings, and I sit up, urgently digging it out. "Hello?"

"Hey, it's your baker," Jimmy says. "I'm standing on the other side of the streetlight and don't want to interrupt anything."

I laugh and wave at her. "That's fine. Come on over."

As I hang up, I stand and hold out a hand to Jonah, relieved in a way that this conversation can be finished. I'm feeling aroused and sad and nervous and giddy and need a little time to sort it out. "That was my baker. That's her, over there." I point across the street.

He stands. Bends in and captures my neck and kisses me again. "What happens if you let go, Ramona?"

I only look at him. Even the thought makes me feel faintly ill.

He smiles. "I'll talk to you soon."

Business is good. The Sunday morning openings, combined with juicy crowds of tourists flooding the streets—some of them looking for me specifically, thanks to an arrangement of trades I've set up with local motels and hotels—have created enough cash flow that I'm starting to feel as if I really might have a chance to hang on to the bakery.

Katie is thriving. She loves the job and loves getting money, although she never spends more than a few dollars, and that is nearly always on flowers. I ask what she's saving for and she shrugs it away. "I don't know. I just like having it."

Which makes sense.

Sofia so fiercely resisted the aunties coming that I gave in and didn't push it. She's now eight months pregnant, and as desperately as I had hoped to be there with her when the baby was born, it's beginning to look like that will not happen.

Every week, Lily, Katie, and I gather together a care package to send her, filled with all sorts of whimsical and delicious and funny things—a Gumby doll I find at Goodwill, a collection of Far Side cartoons, pretty magazines, chocolates from the Rocky Mountain Chocolate Factory. Whatever seems happy and upbeat, to let her know we love her.

There is, beneath everything, a dogged sense of things being out of kilter. It feels as if I must keep my guard up, alert to whatever is coming.

Katie sends her father emails nearly every day, which Sofia reads aloud to him. She brightly assures Katie that it's helping, although Katie asks me plainly one afternoon why he isn't writing back to her.

It isn't a question I can answer.

And there is Jonah. He comes to visit sometimes on these soft purple evenings. We sit on the porch. We drink ginger tea with lemons or pale lager poured into my grandmother's old-fashioned pilsner glasses frosted with gold leaves. Sometimes we play cards or backgammon with Katie or listen to music. For now he respects my limits. He doesn't try to kiss me.

He brings me presents. A CD of a cellist named Adam Hurst; a clutch of roses cut from his garden—headily scented flowers in red and pink and white, one with peppermint stripes that smells wildly of oranges; a book of poetry that he reads to me in the darkness with Milo sitting on his lap, tail flicking.

And, although I should not, I find myself baking special things for him, discovering his pleasure in dark malty rolls with caraway seeds, in sourdough so sharp it needs butter just to be chewable. He likes lemon bars dusted with powdered sugar, and chai tea made with honey and fresh spices.

On Wednesdays and Sundays, he invites Katie and me over to his place for supper. She is enchanted by him, by the stacks of books in his library, the clean elegance of his furnishings, his collection of photos of cherry blossoms in Japan, taken by his ex-wife. Katie looks at them for a long time. "I've never seen anything like that," she comments gravely. "How could I see it?"

"In the springtime," I say. "I'll take you down to Pueblo and you can see the crab apples blooming."

For a long time, she looks at me. "I'm sure," she says, glancing away, "that I'll be living with my mother by then."

It stings oddly. "If that's what you want."

She narrows her eyes. "Of course I do. Who wouldn't want to live with their own mother if they can?"

"I know. But I don't want you to get your hopes up, Katie. Your mom has a long road ahead of her."

"I can help her."

"That's not your job, sweetheart. Your job is to devote yourself to your own life. To flowers, and staying healthy, and—"

She stands up, haughty and still too thin, partly because she's growing about a half inch a week. "I can do both." With dignity she says, "Thanks for supper, Jonah. I'm going to walk home now."

"Katie! You don't have to go. I'm—"

She gives me a cold, hard stare. "This is none of your business. And you can't be my mother, understand? I don't need another mother." She lets the screen door slam behind her.

For a long moment I stare at the blank place of her leaving, feeling oddly embarrassed. Jonah puts his hand on my shoulder. "Let her go. She'll be all right."

"When I was her age," I say, "I really loved my mother, but she drove me crazy."

"I was a mama's boy. Not in the sissy way you hear it, but I wanted to please her. When she needed something, it was always me she asked." He gives a chuckle. "She still does, come to think of it."

"So she's alive."

"Yes. That's one of the reasons I wanted to come back to Colorado. My brother and his wife and all his kids are still up in Castle Rock and my mom lives in Boulder in a really nice apartment house for seniors."

"How old is she?"

"Eighty-three and still out on cruises every winter."

I laugh. "That will be my mom."

He leaves me alone, heading for the kitchen to collect the dishes. I imagine him as a boy, fetching groceries or pulling weeds to please his mother, and it pierces me in some way I don't want to examine. I watch him, the singular grace in his long back, the smooth efficiency of his movements in the kitchen. His hair is wavy and has grown too long in the back, capturing light on each bend. It is thick and inviting hair, and I'd like to touch it. Something I've been pushing down hard rises to the surface, whispering, insistent.

He looks up, as if he feels my gaze, and before I can look away, he smiles. "What are you thinking, Ramona?"

There is something haunting and wistful on the stereo. "What is playing, Jonah?"

"This one is mine. Do you like it?"

I touch my chest, close my eyes, feeling that yearning rise higher and higher, pushing through my limbs. "Yes. It's like you."

He closes the door and comes around the counter, draws one of my hands to him, puts it on his shoulder. "How is it like me?"

"A little haunted. Deep. Gentle."

"Is that how you think of me?"

"That's some of it." I close my eyes again, hearing the essence of him. "The picture is your face that day we were in the car on the way home from the truck stop, do you remember?"

He nods. "It was raining."

I look up at him, touch his mouth with my finger. "I was so in love with you. I wanted to kiss you so badly."

He recaptures my hand, presses his mouth to the center of my palm. "I remember that your hair was damp, and you were wearing a green shirt." A smile touches his lips. "I could see your breasts a little through it. You have such extraordinary skin."

"Do I?"

He bends, presses a kiss to my neck. "Yes." His hands slide around me, over my waist and back, down around the curve of my bottom. "We're adults now," he says. "We can do whatever we want."

"Yeah?" I look at his mouth, sway against him. "Like?"

"Depends. Do you trust me?"

"Yes."

"No," he says, and smiles. "But that's all right." Holding my gaze, he slides a hand down my leg and crumples the fabric of my skirt, pulling it upward until my leg is bare and his fingertips are skimming over the skin, up the back of my thigh to my buttock. One finger slides beneath the elastic. It feels decidedly more intimate to have our eyes locked as he does this, and I glance away. He stops.

I look up. He smiles, bends, and captures my lower lip, suckling it for a moment, and I feel a jolt of heat. I reach for his shoulders, wanting to pull him into me, and he resists. "Fold your hands. And keep your eyes on me," he murmurs. His hand begins to move again, lightly skimming over the infinitesimal hairs on my body, along the back of my thigh, around my buttocks, beneath my panties.

It's hard to keep my eyes locked with his. To keep looking deep into the honeyed irises. I feel revealed. Anxious. I capture his hand, and he smiles.

"My turn."

He stands straight and looks at me. I reach for the buttons of his shirt; he doesn't move. I unbutton it, then put my hands on his chest, not looking down, just feeling it. Nipples and hair and ribs, belly and belly button, sides. He takes one of my hands and puts it over his erection, holding my gaze, and I take one of his hands and put it on my breast. "Shall we go upstairs?" I ask.

"Oh, no. Not tonight." He shrugs out of his shirt. "My turn again."

This time he tugs the bottom of my tank top and pulls upward. I lift my arms and he skims it off, tossing it aside, then takes off my bra. Only the tips of his fingers touch me, circling my shoulders, stroking my breasts, curling around to cup them, brushing over my nipples. It's very difficult to stand there, looking into his eyes, and I see that he's struggling, too. His nostrils flare.

"I don't think I can keep looking only at your eyes," he says, a dark glitter in his own. "But don't move, all right?"

Caught in the dream, I nod ever so slightly as he leans over me, cups my breasts with a sigh, and kisses them, as lightly as he has touched me all over. Every nerve in my body is on alert, and when he grazes my forearm, I shudder.

He pulls me into a kiss, and our bare skin brushes. His hands run up my back, down. I wrap my arms around him, pull his head into me, feeling as if I might dissolve right here.

And it's a thousand times better than I could have imagined. His scent envelopes me and ignites every sensor on every square centimeter of my skin. His hands leave trails of red lava over my back, my shoulders, my neck. When he kisses the bare flesh of my shoulder, moving mouth and tongue over my skin, I pull up his shirt in the back to touch his skin.

"Jesus," he whispers, "I love kissing you." His hand moves on my neck, my shoulder, over the square of skin on my chest. "Touching you." I even like the hectic way he looks when he says it, color high across his cheekbones.

He resumes kissing my neck, my throat, which makes my spine soften, and I'm exploring the skin of his back, his sides, his ribs, feeling ripples as my fingers cross the terrain, his thick, cool hair, feeling the shape of his skull as his hands slide lower. He pulls himself up to my mouth and kisses me again. His hands are still, his erection pressed into my thigh.

He shifts, lifts his head. He's breathing hard. "That's as much as I can stand and still stop."

I'm flushed from breast to thighs. "We aren't stopping!"

"Yes, we are." He gives me a wicked little wink. "Second base." He shakes out my tank and bra, gives them to me.

"Why?"

"Because I won't want you to leave, and you will have to get up and go, to Katie."

I nod.

"And because," he adds, "I want you to see that you can trust me."

"Trust you? I do!"

"You don't trust anybody," he says definitely, and smooths his hair away from his forehead. "And with good reason."

It strikes me that I am falling, *really* falling, and that recognition alone is good enough to make me straighten. I sink to the stool. I struggle with what I should say. My hands are shaky, and I'm swollen with the wish to make love.

He doesn't fill up the space with anything, only lets me think through what he's said, what we did. I feel like flash paper, as if I will go up in a single blast at the flame of his hands, and I shift away. "I don't know how anymore. To trust anyone."

"There is one way to know some things."

"How?"

"Ask yourself what you want. And then go for it."

"But that doesn't always work."

"No?" He's sitting on a stool now, his long body relaxed and sexy, but it is that face I always want to look at—his beautiful, wise eyes. "Give me an example of something you wanted and it didn't work out."

"Oh, thousands of them," I say, rolling my eyes. "Let's start with Sofia's father. I wanted him and I ended up—" I don't want to say *screwing up my life,* because there is so much that's good. "It ended being a very dark time for me. Out of something I thought I wanted."

He nods, his finger sliding down my arm. "What did you really want, though? At fifteen, did you want sex? Or did you just want to kiss him and be with him?"

To my horror, tears spring to my eyes. "I had no idea what I wanted except to be held, to kiss him. I didn't know all the stuff that we would do."

"Right. He wanted sex." His hand twining around my wrist is so gentle I can't bear it. "You wanted kisses. Big difference."

I feel slightly sick to my stomach and look at the door. "I think I should go."

He stands with me, puts his hands on my shoulders. "Don't panic, Ramona. It's only talk."

"No. It's you. It's . . . me." I look around the room, at the clean serenity, the undisturbed quiet. "It's all of this. I have to go now."

Jonah captures me from behind as I am running away, his arms coming all the way around my body. He puts his face into my hair. "Don't run." His body feels reliable against my back, solid and real, and I find myself leaning into him, letting go of… everything. My head fits into the cradle of his shoulder, and his cheek presses into my ear.

"This is scaring me, too, Ramona. It feels dangerous and unreliable, as if it could really hurt."

I put my palms on the arm that circles my throat. "Yes," I whisper.

"But it also feels magical. Like my blood is filled with glitter. Like a spell was finally broken."

His voice in my ear has color and texture and richness. I close my eyes and it flows down the side of my neck, into the hollow of my throat. I think, *I am in love with him.*

He's rocking me gently as he says, "Do you know how I see you?"

"Foolish?"

"Generous. Independent. Loving." He kisses my neck. "So loving."

I turn in his arms. "What do we do, then, Jonah? I don't know how to leap without fear of the consequences anymore. I don't know if I can."

"No leaping," he says, and kisses me. "Just one step at a time."

I raise my eyebrow. "Well, I *did* like second base."

He looks at my mouth, presses forward subtly. "Me, too."

I leave him, walking home through the dark beneath whispering trees. Once he is out of my sight, the cool night air washes the smell of him from my skin, my nose, and I am left with a hollow terror.

I have not been in love. Until now I thought my love was channeled in other directions, into my child and my breads and my family. With Dane, I said I was, but it didn't feel like this— as if all these years I'd been living in moonlight and had no idea there was even a sun. Until Jonah arrived. Jonah feels like sunlight, and my light-starved skin craves him.

It's one thing to live in moonlight and never know there is a sun. But once you know, how can you ever be happy with night again?

In the dark of my neighborhood, I put my hands over my stomach, feeling my heart flutter in panic. He's too much. It's too dangerous. There are too many other things I should be thinking about—Katie and Sofia and my bakery.

And yet, as I am settling into sleep with Milo purring against my side, it isn't fear in my mouth. It's longing. It's love. The color of it is soft purple, woven with the gold of Jonah's eyes.

THIRTY-SIX

Katie

F or two weeks, Katie has been walking to the 7-Eleven down the street and buying a money order with whatever she has saved. If she doesn't spend some money, Lily and Ramona will be suspicious, so she buys candy and some scrunchies for her hair and little things like that. Lily bought her a soft knee pad for the garden, and Katie let Ramona think she bought it herself with tips she earns in the bakery. It made her feel bad, but then she thought of her mother alone in the rehab unit, looking for Katie's mail, and she hardened her heart.

Everybody here has somebody to depend on—some even have a lot of different people. Katie's mom has only Katie. When Ramona puts together a care package to send Sofia, Katie asks if they can do the same thing for Lacey. Ramona looks all soft and sad when Katie asks, but then she says, "Sure," and they fill a box with things a woman might need in jail. ("It isn't jail," Katie says. "Okay, a hospital, then," Ramona replies.) Soap that smells like flowers, small bottles of shampoo, tissues in small packs, gum and candy. When they put the box in the mail, Ramona touches Katie's shoulders. "You have a good heart, sweetie. And you are a very good daughter."

"Why isn't my dad talking to me, do you think?" Katie asks as they walk back to the bakery. The only free time Ramona ever has is in the late afternoon and evening, so the air smells of roses and supper, and the sun, which sets so much earlier here, is already falling behind the mountains. It's beautiful, and Katie loves it a lot. Maybe more than any other place she's ever lived.

And that makes her feel bad, like a traitor. A ripple of annoyance rushes down her neck, which happens a lot lately. She feels grumpy all of a sudden for no reason, like there's a band of anger right over the top of her eyebrows. Since there's no reason for it now, she rubs the place and waits for Ramona to answer.

"I'm sure he's just focused on getting well," she says. "Sometimes when a soldier has been badly injured, it takes time for him to come to terms with it."

"A lot of soldiers kill themselves when they get out of the hospital."

Ramona looks down at her quickly. "What makes you think that?"

She shrugs. "They talk about it in schools on the base. Two girls I knew in El Paso had parents who committed suicide when they came back. One of the girls just got out of the hospital."

Ramona says nothing for a long while. It's so quiet Katie can hear their footsteps whispering over the old sidewalk. "Your dad has a lot to live for. You, and Sofia, and the new baby."

"Yeah," Katie answers without much enthusiasm.

"Are you excited about the baby at all?"

"I don't know. It doesn't seem real." She kicks a stone in her path. "And it's not like we'll all live together, anyway." Saying it out loud makes her feel that pinch in her chest.

"You probably could if you wanted to."

She nods. "My mom needs me, though."

"What about your dad?"

"He has Sofia and the new baby. My mom doesn't have anybody."

They stop at the gate to the bakery, and there are Katie's dahlias, growing in happy clumps all along the old wrought-iron fence. They look like women in beautiful blouses, cheering, with hands up high and big smiles on their faces. Katie touches her favorite, a red flower with rolled tubes of petals, called Figaro.

"Well," Ramona says. "Nothing has to be decided right now."

Katie knows that Ramona wants her to go live with Sofia and her dad and the new baby, which sounds good in a way, but the thought makes her feel so guilty that she rushes away from it and goes inside.

This morning, Ramona is out doing some shopping and errands. Katie writes her mom a letter on paper, just as she has been doing sometimes to her friend Madison in El Paso, even if Madison hasn't written back even one time.

Dear Mom,

Here is a little more money. Sorry it can't be more, but I have to be careful or everyone will be suspicious and then they won't let me talk to you at all.

I hope you liked the care package, which you should be getting soon, if you haven't already. We weren't sure what you'd like, so I just grabbed things that might make you happy.

Katie pauses, rubbing her bare foot over Merlin's soft ribs. He sighs, hard, and falls back to sleep. It's always so hard to know exactly what to say. She doesn't want to sound like she's too happy, so she doesn't talk about the flowers too much, and she doesn't want to seem like she likes Ramona more than her own mom, so it's hard to talk about that. Finally she says,

I've been writing emails to Dad every day. I'm going to take swimming lessons pretty soon, too, and I've grown so tall you won't believe it!

Love,
Katie

She puts the letter in an envelope and leaves it open so she can seal it after she puts the money order in it. This one will be the best so far—almost thirty dollars—and she feels pretty proud of herself. When Ramona takes her nap this afternoon, Katie will mail it.

Then, since she feels like she should, she gets online to write a cheerful email for Sofia to read to her dad. In these emails, she can sound as happy as she wants, so she tells him about the suppers at Jonah's house, which she loves, and about how she and Lily are going to a flower show at the City Auditorium in July, which is the biggest flower show for dahlias in almost the whole country. Oh, and about hitting five foot eight.

And then, because the day is so gorgeous and who wants to be inside in the summertime, she goes out to the backyard garden.

THIRTY-SEVEN

Ramona

I'm counting bags of flour when Katie comes into the storeroom and breathes, "Can I talk to you?"

She looks pinched and scared. All day long, I've had a feeling of impending doom. Is this it? "What's wrong? Did you get bad news about something?"

"No, um..." She looks over her shoulder, where the apprentices are working. The dishwasher is humming, music is playing—cheery sounds. "I just think I...uh...might have started my period?"

"Oh!" I'm surprised. She's young, but Sofia was barely fourteen. Katie is only a few months behind that. None of which is any help to a young girl who probably wishes very badly that her mother was here for this moment. "Okay. Let's go upstairs and I'll show you where everything is."

"Okay."

I'm frantically wondering as she trails behind me into the upstairs bathroom if there are any pads or only tampons, which would not be the easiest thing for a girl to manage her first time. There are a few supplies in the bathroom, though, and I show her how to use them, then leave her to it. Merlin waits with me. When Katie comes out with clean clothes and an abashed look on her face, I smile.

"Congratulations," I say, as my mother said to me. "I have friends who took their daughters to lunch to celebrate this, but I'm guessing you might be more in the category of let's-keep-it-between-ourselves. Is that right?"

"I don't know," she says, and I see the wonder in her eyes. "I'm surprised, that's all, but I guess that makes sense with how I've been feeling lately."

"How is that?"

"Grumpy sometimes, for no reason."

I laugh. "Yeah, that would be the feeling. Sometimes. Not always. I have to get some work done this afternoon, but you'll need some better supplies. What if I call Lily and all of us go out to a nice little supper somewhere? Would you like that?"

Her smile is both shy and winning, and it catches me at the base of my throat. "Can we maybe go to Nosh? Grandma—I mean Lily—took me there for lunch one day."

"That's perfect!"

"I'll be upstairs," she says, and dances away. Merlin stays in the kitchen, staring at me, as if I need to know something.

"What?" I rub the top of my belly, aware that the sense of doom is still there.

He shifts, foot to foot, the old kung fu master waiting for me to decipher his brain beam.

I shake my head. "Sorry. I don't know what you want me to do."

And there on the table is a letter addressed to Lacey Wilson, Katie's mother. It's wrong, I know it is, but I open the envelope and read the letter, then fold it up and put it back exactly where it was. If that deadbeat female was anywhere in my realm, I'd strangle her to death right this minute.

And yet what can I do? Leaving the letter in plain sight on the table, I rub Merlin's head. "Thanks. Go take care of her. I have to get to work."

As I come around the corner of the stairs, into the bakery,

Jimmy gives me a weird look and cuts her eyes behind her. "There's a health inspector here. He's coming to look at the work the pipe guys did."

"Good." It has taken much longer than it should have, but I would never say that. I walk forward to greet him. He's a balding man in his fifties, with the harsh mouth so many bureaucrats sport. "Hello." I hold out my hand. "I'm Ramona Gallagher, the owner."

His grip is limp and unfriendly, and I'm suddenly worried. They do sometimes show up to surprise you, to keep things on the up and up, and I've had inspections plenty of times. But there's something sour about him. A no-carb person, I'm betting, one who would find croissants a sin against the belly. "I'll just have a look around."

"Okay. We'll get to work." I give Jimmy a meaningful nod and take my clipboard into the storeroom to check off supplies. I'm wondering where the dog and the cat might be; they rarely come in, but they have been known to slip by the doors. I once found Milo crouched under the dishwasher, a dead mouse at his feet. When I came into the kitchen, he sauntered away, plainly pleased with himself.

For obvious reasons, animals and professional kitchens don't mix.

I take a breath, write down an order number. He's here to check the pipe work. I've kept up with everything I am supposed to do, and we've had inspectors all along the way; there is nothing wrong with my kitchen. I would put money on it.

He combs through the front and then comes into the kitchen, X-ing things off on a big sheet. I've finished the orders and have begun to assemble the next day's menus when he returns to the room, a grim look on his face.

"I'm sorry, but I have found a problem. You want to come with me, ma'am?" He looks genuinely apologetic. "Your hot-water heater is leaking through the top."

"What? That's impossible. It's only a couple of years old."

"It looks like it might have been damaged at some point. There's a lot of evidence of water leaking over a long period. Mold, some other issues." He shakes his head. "It's a miracle it hasn't stopped functioning completely."

"How long can you give me to fix it?"

Again he looks regretful. "I'm sorry, Ms. Gallagher, but I'm going to have to ask you to close until this situation is resolved. It's too dangerous to run it the way it is, and you can't be open without hot water."

I close my eyes. Swear.

He gives me a sheet of paper with the order and his telephone number. "Call me here, and I'll make a point to get right back and clear you to open."

"Thanks." I promise myself that I am not going to cry in front of my own employees.

Who are grouped in an apprehensive little knot, facing me, as he leaves. Jimmy looks sick, and so do the dishwasher and apprentices. "What do we do?"

"Fix it. I'm sorry, you guys, but there won't be any work until they let me open again. I'm guessing at least a couple of days. Maybe more."

Heather gets tears in her eyes and wipes them away with a corner of her apron. "This makes me so mad! I wanted to buy the good bag of fireworks this year."

I can't bear for them to be cheated. "I'll give you half pay. I wish it could be more."

Heather blinks. "Really? Even though you won't be open?"

"Yeah."

"I'm cool," says Roberto, the dish kid. "I'll just go chill with my girl until next week."

I put them to work shutting everything down for a few days, and I head into my small office overlooking the backyard to make phone calls. Katie and Merlin and Milo are out there, moving through the vegetable garden. It's hot this afternoon, and if I were her, I'd be upstairs under a fan; instead, she's walking through the rows, pinching blossoms from tomatoes and squashes into a basket, talking aloud to Merlin, who walks beside her, his long pink tongue hanging out.

With a sigh, I turn my attention back to the less-thrilling task inside my office. I'm trying not to panic, which won't help any of us, but this is a huge blow. Lost wages, lost income, huge outflow of cash. I need advice.

The first person I call is my brother Ryan, but he has no ideas. "Call Dad."

The last time I asked my father for advice, he said I should have thought of how hard it was going to be before I opened a restaurant to compete with him. Which is how he sees the bakery: in competition with the Gallagher Group restaurants.

And yet I'd rather call him than Cat, who is probably angry with me. I haven't taken any of his calls or even listened to the messages he has been leaving.

Gnawing my lip, I juggle the two possibilities and wonder if my sister is right that I use people.

Steph. Steph will know what I should do.

I punch in her number before I can chicken out, and she answers on the second ring. By the background noise of radio and horns, I can tell she's in the car, which explains why she answered so readily. "Stephanie Gallagher speaking."

"Hi, Steph, it's Ramona."

"Ramona?"

"Yeah. I need advice on how to get my hot water fixed as fast as possible."

She's silent. Then, "Why not ask your sweetie?"

"Because, as I told you, he isn't my 'sweetie' at all, and I've been trying hard to set boundaries between us. Unfortunately, I now have a huge problem and I need some advice. He's been my go-to guy. I'd rather ask other people."

"You're kind of putting me on the spot."

"How?" My mouth goes tight, and I think of the inspector's pinched face. Deliberately, I move my lips around, making them soft again. "Come on, Stephanie. We have to get over this."

A horn honks loudly and she swears. "Look, I'm in Denver and the traffic is really heavy. I have to go."

"Steph! Please, I'll do whatever—"

She hangs up on me. For a moment I'm so breathlessly angry with her that I want to fling the phone across the room. Instead, I take a breath and dial my father's telephone number.

He answers, "Hello. This is James Gallagher."

I start to speak, but his message goes on. "I'm in a meeting for the rest of the day, but if you leave your name and telephone number, I'll get back to you as soon as possible. If this is an emergency, please call my assistant, Stephanie Gallagher, at 555-6820."

I punch the off button and look out the window. Merlin is dancing around the grass as if there is a person playing tug-of-war with him. Katie is sitting on the bench, talking to him. Curved up against her is Milo. *Traitor,* I think.

There's nothing to do but call Cat.

Turnabout is fair play: He doesn't answer my call.

No help for it—I'm going to have to go see him in person, and right away. As I walk through the bakery, Jimmy holds up two jars of starter. "You want me to put everything in the walk-in?"

"Leave the rye and malt. I'm still feeding it. The rest . . . yeah. Put it away."

In the muffled quiet, I wonder if this is it. If this is the thing that will bring me to my knees. It's Thursday. There is a very minute chance someone will have this hot-water heater in stock nearby and can install it tomorrow, but I've spent my life in restaurants, and I know I'm telling myself a big fat lie. It will be Monday. Maybe Tuesday.

My stomach aches. No revenue coming in on Friday, Saturday, Sunday, Monday. Maybe even Tuesday?

I have no idea how we are going to survive.

Going to the back porch, I call through the screen, "Katie, I have to run some errands. Do you want to go or stay?"

She walks toward the window. Merlin has given up and is lying in the shade. "Are we going out to dinner later?"

I forgot, in all the madness, to call my mother. "Absolutely."

"I'll stay here, then."

Leaving her in the yard, I don't even bother with changing anything except my shoes. I trade clogs for a pair of sandals and head out wearing printed cotton chef's pants and a pale lavender chef's coat. If I hurry, I can catch Cat while he's reconciling the books for the day. In the car, I punch in my mother's number and ask her if she can meet us at Nosh for dinner, to celebrate the whole advent of womanhood. She's very excited and we make plans to meet there at five-thirty.

I glance at the clock. It's only one-thirty. I might be able to squeeze in a nap at some point if I can get this all in motion in time.

Oh. But I don't need a nap, do I? Since I won't be opening in the morning. Damn it.

Cat is always doing the books at this time of day, and I find him in the corner booth at his restaurant. A couple of guys are standing around, waiting for orders, and he scribbles something, hands it over, and one scurries off. He doesn't look well. His face is drawn and waxy, his hair a bit too long. Has he been eating? Sometimes he forgets. If there is no woman in his life, he sometimes drinks too much, forgets to take care of himself properly.

When he catches sight of me in the shadows, one dark eyebrow lifts. He waves away the guy who has been waiting and says to me, "What are you doing here?"

"I need advice."

For a minute, he only looks at me. He shakes his head. Gestures. "Come talk to me."

When I stand at the side of the table, he looks at my attire and says, "It must be big if you came out without changing."

"Hot-water heater rusted out. I've got to get it replaced as fast as possible."

"What do you need from me?"

I lift my hands, show my palms. "No money, no phone calls, just advice. Who would you call and what would you do?"

"I'd kick some asses is what I'd do." He growls and throws a pencil down on the table. "That hot-water heater is only a couple of years old."

The first ripple of hope touches me. Maybe there will at least be a way to recoup the lost revenue. Eventually. "That doesn't actually help me today."

He nods. "Let's go to my office, see what we can do."

"You don't need to make the calls and I don't need any help financially." I say it again so it sinks in. "I really need to do this myself. So if you could just give me advice and maybe the best people to call, I would appreciate it."

He inclines his head. "Okay. I still need to go to the office to get the names you need. Is that all right with you?"

I relent, smiling. "Yes."

"Come on, then. You want Parker to pour you some wine or something?"

"No, I'm fine." It occurs to me that I've missed him. We spent a lot of time together, and now I haven't seen him at all for weeks. I miss my friend. "How are you, Cat?"

He steps behind his desk and looks at me. "I had a touch of food poisoning a few days ago. I know you were worrying when you came in. You get this little wrinkle on the side of your mouth."

"You don't look well," I return honestly. "Sure it was food poisoning?"

He shrugs, flips through a Rolodex, and writes some names and numbers down. He hands the paper over to me. "You sure you don't want me to call somebody?"

"Yes." I smile. "But thank you. You have been so good to me." I lower my gaze, nod almost imperceptibly.

He points to the paper. "You let me know if you have any trouble, all right?" He winks. "I know people."

"Thanks," I say, and give him a hug.

THIRTY-EIGHT

When I return, Katie has left a note on the table that she's gone to the store. It makes my heart hurt to think of her writing a money order to send to her mother, but this is something I have to let her work out on her own.

In the meantime, I call the numbers Cat gave me and arrange for someone to come in and look at the problem. He promises to be here in an hour, which isn't going to leave a lot of time to get ready for dinner. Realizing that I'm still wearing my work clothes, I jump in the shower—which is served by a regular household water heater upstairs—wash my hair, and shave my legs in some kind of nod toward the big day. Leaving my hair rolled up in a towel, I put on a workaday sundress and some flip-flops, pour a glass of iced tea, and whistle for Merlin to follow me out into the backyard. He trots along happily. "Why didn't Katie take you with her?"

He looks up, woofs softly, and I nod as if I understand. "I'm so glad you showed up to take care of her."

Sitting on the bench in the shade, I comb out my hair and let it dry in the air, which makes it smell like fresh laundry. The garden is faintly wilting in the heat of the day, and somewhere behind me a lone cricket is singing. Everything else is on siesta. As

I should be. I lean back and put my head against the tree behind me, closing my eyes for a minute. Just a minute.

Merlin woofs softly and I imagine he's talking to someone, but I'm far enough gone that my brain spins out a funny little dream. My grandmother sits beside me on the bench, smelling of talcum powder and freshly ground coffee, which she loved with an unholy passion. "He's a good dog."

"Yes. He takes good care of all of us. Old soul."

"He is that." A breeze ruffles her short white hair, then she turns and puts her hand on mine. "You need to call Sofia. Right now."

I jolt upright, having almost fallen sideways. Merlin lifts his head and solemnly waves his tail. Blinking, trying to clear the fuzziness from my brain, I think I can still smell that lingering scent of talc and coffee beans. I rub my face vigorously, pick up my phone, and check the time. It's four, making it five in San Antonio. Sofia will probably be at dinner.

Still. While I am not as superstitious as some people in my family, getting a direct edict from a dream is not something I can ignore. Especially with that lingering sense of doom in my belly. Taking a long cold drink of tea to clear my head, I punch the shortcut that dials her cell phone.

She doesn't answer. Instead, her voice says, "Hi, it's Sofia. Leave a message or send me a text."

"It's your mother. Give me a call, okay?"

To be doubly sure, I also text her:

Thinking about you is everything okay?

To my surprise, the phone dings quickly.

Not a good time to talk crazy day. Oscar is not good. Will call in my morning. Too tired to talk right now.

What does that mean, crazy day? I text back:

Is the baby okay?

False labor today. Braxton Hicks. But we are fine. Fine. Don't worry.

My phone trills, the actual ringer, and it's the repairman. "Meet you in front," I say, then text to Sofia:

Okay. Anytime. Any hour. I'm here. I love you.

As predicted, the heater has to be ordered, and although they're hoping for delivery tomorrow, it will probably not be here until Monday.

It's what I've been expecting, but it doesn't make it any easier to hear. I nod, valiantly trying to be an adult businesswoman and not burst into tears. *What would Cat do?* I ask myself, and it gives me the courage to cross my arms over my chest and say, "This water heater is only a few years old. What happened?"

He frowns. "It looks like it might have been damaged when it was installed, honestly. See this?" He points out the rusted wound. "That's been coming apart for a long time."

"So, workmanship, then?"

He nods. "Considering how much this is going to cost you, I'd sure talk to a lawyer about getting some of it back. Not that it'll help today."

"Right. Thanks." I hold out a hand and he shakes it firmly.

"I'll call you as soon as they call me."

As I'm writing out the bad news on the sign in front, Katie walks up. My mouth drops open. "You cut your hair!"

"Do you like it?" Shyly, she swings her head, and her hair, a tumble of loose, healthy curls, swings around her neck. The colors of caramel and toast and some brighter streaks of lemon from her days in the garden are shiny, laced throughout.

Impossible not to reach out and put my hands in it. "Wow, Katie, it looks terrific. Can I take a picture to upload to Sofia and your dad?"

She poses, inclining her head and smiling directly at me. I snap a couple of shots with the phone and tuck it in my pocket. "Lily will be thrilled."

And when she arrives to drive us over to the restaurant, she makes as much of a fuss as I did. Katie is wearing a lime-green tank and jeans, with pretty sandals on her feet, and with the haircut and her height, she looks about sixteen. Still coltish and gamine with that angled face and elfin eyes, but much older. "You look gorgeous," my mother says. "Did Ramona go with you?"

"No," she says. "I decided I wanted to surprise you guys, so I went to that place down by the grocery store."

So independent, I think, and I'm proud of her for it. "I love how you think for yourself."

"Thanks."

Nosh is a downtown eatery that serves small plates, and my mother loves it. We order a selection of plates to share, vegetables and meat dishes and even the duck, which my mother insists upon. I'm trying to keep my mind on the celebration instead of the doom hanging over me. In the back of my mind, I wonder what's happening with Sofia, what the unease I feel might be.

As for the bakery, I keep playing with possibilities, but not one is realistic thus far. The one thing I know I will not let stand this time is Stephanie's refusal to help me. This has to end, although I'm not sure how.

We toast Katie discreetly, celebrating what we call her special day without saying any more. She's glowing with good health—amazing what a couple of months of good food and fresh air can do for a child.

Midway into the meal, Lily says, "Have you heard from Sofia?"

I have a mouthful of food, which gives me a chance to think about my response. "Yes," I say, and drink a sip of water. "She texted me this afternoon." I pause, glance at Katie. "She didn't say a lot. Just that she had some false labor today and things were really overwhelming."

"I hate her being there all alone." My mother delicately nibbles a spear of endive. "When are Poppy and Nancy going to get there?"

"They aren't. I thought I told you. Sofia didn't want to deal with their eccentricities."

"I don't think they're eccentric," Katie said.

"Maybe a little," I say.

Lily snorts. "I love my sister, but she's been a hippie since the day she was born. That's not what Sofia needs right now."

"You sent *me* to live with her."

"Sofia's pregnant," Lily says dismissively.

"So was I, as you may recall."

Katie looks between our faces. "You lived with Nancy and Poppy?"

"Only Poppy. That was when they met, the summer I was pregnant with Sofia. Nancy was the midwife who came in to deliver her."

"And that was when they fell in love? Cool."

This is the thing I like best about this generation of children, all those Sofia's age and younger—they don't even think about mixed-race or same-sex relationships. Or any variation therein. Love is love. "It was. They've been really happy together."

Maybe sensing the tension at the table, Katie asks, "When were you pregnant with her?"

"I was fifteen."

"Why did you get pregnant? Didn't you use a condom?"

I chuckle. "No. I should have. But they weren't as easy to get then, and we didn't talk about it so openly."

She gives a shrug and stabs an asparagus spear. "That seems kinda dumb."

For some reason, it makes me feel acutely emotional. Never full of regret, because how can I regret the single most perfect gift in my life? But I have a sense of time shifting, offering a glimpse of a different life. Another me.

And I think of Jonah kissing me. I think about Sofia sitting at the bakery counter, rubbing her hand over her belly just before the phone call came. I think of never meeting Katie. "Things happen for a reason."

Katie looks at me, her eyes too old for her face. "Not everything."

"No, I don't believe that, either," Lily says. "People make choices. That makes up a life. Choices. Decisions."

"There's some fate involved, Mom. You have to admit."

She shakes her head firmly. "No."

I let it go.

After a few minutes my mother says, "That child can't be alone any longer. I'm going to go to Texas."

"When?" Katie asks, looking stricken. "We have the flower show next week."

"Hon, there will be another flower show. Your dad is really in bad shape, and Sofia is too pregnant to be handling that all alone."

"But we've been planning it for a whole month. I put it on my calendar with a big star and everything."

I reach across the table to put my hand on hers. She yanks it away violently, almost knocking over a glass of water.

"Get a hold of yourself, young lady," my mother says coldly, and I remember being led down the street in Castle Rock, hysterical.

"Mom, she's disappointed."

"You made a promise," Katie says, her voice gaining volume, "and now you're breaking it."

"Lower your voice."

I hold up a hand between them. "Hey, everybody, this is supposed to be fun. Let's eat and not get tangled up in anything else right now, okay?"

"I don't see why you can't wait for a few more days."

My mother puts down her fork. I can see she's trying to rectify the situation, but she says exactly the wrong thing. "You'll understand when you're older."

"Oh," Katie says dangerously. "Understand how adults never do what they say they will? Ever?" She stands up, blinking back tears, then flings her napkin on the table and hurries out of the room. I see other diners giving her looks of disapproval, and I want to slap each and every one of them soundly. I want to tell them they have no idea what she's been through, how strong and brave she is.

"What is wrong with that girl?" Lily says.

"Mom, she's thirteen, her whole life has been turned upside down, and she's hormonal as hell. Not everyone is as icy as you are."

She glares at me. "What is that supposed to mean? Control is not the same as icy, Ramona. That's what you, with all your dramas, never seemed to understand."

I force myself to take a long breath and reach for her hand. "I'm sorry. It's been a very emotional day." I pause to steady my voice. "Please go to Texas. I'm half crazy with worry over Sofia, and I cannot go. I can't leave the bakery right now."

"Oh, Ramona," she says, and grasps my hand. "I'm happy to do it. Now, go find Katie and tell her I'm sorry. See if you can smooth it over and bring her back to the table."

But Katie returns on her own, with dignity in her stiff shoulders. "I'm sorry," she says. "I was being ungrateful. I don't know what is wrong with me lately."

"It's all right, sweetie," I say. "Let's order dessert, what do you say?"

THIRTY-NINE

Sofia's Journal

JULY 8, 20—

3:00 A.M.

I am so tired you would think I'd fall over in a dead sleep, but I've been tossing and turning for hours. Every time I close my eyes, I hear Oscar screaming again. He sent me away, but I stayed close by. It seems only fair to bear witness to everything he is going through.

They had to do what they call debriding the burns today. Which means pretty much scrubbing all those raw wounds. It's the worst thing I can think of, and however I might imagine it, from the sounds he was making, it was so much worse.

And for the first time today, I saw his face. His beautiful, beautiful face, which is now ruined beyond recognition. His nose is burned off, which gives a monsterish look to his face, and I'm crying as I write that because I never want him to know how horrifying it was to see that this first time. I will get used to it, and I love him for himself, not his face, not his body, or anything external. I love his fierce, kind spirit, his need to take care of everything and everyone. He's the original father of the world, watching out for animals and children and his men. If there was no war, he would *be a fireman or a cop or something like that; it's just his personality to take care of things, to shoulder the hard line of the law.*

I keep thinking, though, of the first time we met, in a bookstore coffee shop by the Citadel. I'd bought some new picture books for my classroom—my very first class of my own!—and he was there supposedly to meet a woman. I noticed him right away. He was wearing his uniform, which gets some women all excited, although you get used to it, growing up in a military town.

But there was Oscar, well over six feet tall, with those pretty green eyes and curly hair and cheekbones like a cat. I noticed him, all right. And when he caught me sneaking a peek at him over my shoulder, he winked. The way he smiled, showing those big, strong, white teeth, made you know he was the kind of person who would always be in charge of everything. He'd never be at a loss.

Of course, that isn't true of anyone, right? He couldn't control Lacey, who cheated on him over and over again until he finally gave up.

And he sure can't control this. Which is part of the trouble. He wants to protect me from it all, wants to make me go home so I don't have to see him this way.

We fought about it. I stood beside his bed and started singing a kid's song that drives him nuts, "The Wheels on the Bus." I don't know why he hates it, but he does, so I started singing it over and over and over.

Finally he looked up at me and said, "Why are you doing that?"

"Because I want you to start acknowledging my presence. I want you to talk to me. If you won't, I'll sing. And I can come up with a lot of crazy stupid songs."

He stared at me. Hard. And here is what's true: His eyes are just the same, the most beautiful color of green. Not exactly light green, but like a pool in a forest, still enough that you can see yellow rocks in the depths. Katie has his eyes, and I'm praying and praying that our baby has them, too.

*I touched the very tips of his fingers, where they are unburned.
"You can't give up on us, Oscar. We love you."*

*He kept looking at me, and a million things were moving in
those irises, but he still didn't speak.*

*So I started to sing again. He tried to ignore me, closed his eyes
as if that would make me go away.*

After about seven rounds, he growled, "Enough!"

"Talk to me and I'll stop."

*"What do you want me to say, Sofia? That everything is going to
turn out okay? It would be a lie. My face is gone and I'm crippled
and I haven't got a clue what to do if I'm not a soldier. Maybe I
should have considered that before, but I never thought—"*

I stood there, listening.

*He turned his face away and there were no tears, but his voice
was raw from not speaking for so long. "I can't talk yet, Sofia. I just
can't stand it. Don't ask it."*

*The nurse came in then and apologetically said it was time to
take care of the wounds. "It's pretty grim," she told me. "You need
to wait down the hall."*

But I could still hear him screaming.

God, I have to call my mother. I wish she could be here.

FORTY

Ramona

After dinner, Katie heads upstairs and I find myself pacing, restless, hoping Sofia will call. It's odd that I will have nothing to do for days on end. It's so strange I don't even know how to start to fill them. In the warm night, I sit out on the front porch and think about calling Ryan. Or Sarah, who has been slammed with obligations since she returned from India. Maybe she could come over and tell me about her travels.

Finally I pick up the phone and do what I have been resisting most of the day: I call Jonah.

"Hello!" he says, and sounds genuinely happy to hear from me. "What are you doing up so late?"

It's nine. I laugh. "Well, I don't have to get up in the morning, so I'm living decadently."

"No work tomorrow?"

My breath gusts out of me. "It's been a bad day. I was wondering if you might want to come by and sit outside in the backyard with me."

"Now?"

"Yes. If you're not busy or whatever."

"I'll be there in twenty minutes. I have to finish some business, but I'll be over right after that."

I go to the kitchen and gather things for us—a shawl to put

over my shoulders, an old blanket to sit on, and tidbits from the kitchen. An orange and two small pastries that should get eaten, and my phone in case Sofia calls. I wash my hands and face and spritz on a bit of perfume that he has said he likes. Not all men do these days, but I buy unique things from a shop in Manitou sometimes, handmade perfumes with colorful names.

I wait on the front porch, shawl around my shoulders, and when I see Jonah coming up the walk, everything in me rushes outward to meet him. Physically, I stand and go down the steps toward him. He's wearing a light-colored shirt, open at the neck, and jeans, and again I feel that little shock: This is *Jonah*!

He greets me with a kiss. "Hi."

Taking his big hand, I say, "Let's go to the backyard."

I lead the way, walking on the old, crumbling sidewalk between the house and the lilac bushes. Our arms brush the cold leaves.

We sit down on the glider, and he says, "Do you want to tell me about your day?"

So I pour it out to him, the waking up to dread and my worry over Sofia, and the terse texts followed by nothing, and then the big disaster of the hot-water heater and the fight with my sister who would not help me and the fear of calling my father, who wasn't in, anyway.

"Pretty lousy day."

I nod. "And I just can't shake this feeling that something is really wrong somewhere."

"I know that feeling." He takes my hand. "I've been thinking of quitting my job."

"I thought you came here to do it."

"It's a good organization. I like it, and it feels good to do work like that, but I've been asked to submit some possibilities for a score. A friend of mine is pulling it all together, and—" He shrugs. "It seems like it might be worth a try."

"Jonah, that's great news. I'm happy for you."

"Thanks." In his pocket, his phone buzzes, and an expression of weary sadness moves on his mouth. He doesn't answer.

"I don't mind if you answer."

He shakes his head. "It's my ex. She calls nearly every evening. I don't have the heart to tell her to stop."

"Why does she call?"

"So we can say a prayer for Ethan." He takes a breath. "It seems to help her."

"That's very generous. Pretty sure I'm not that nice."

He glances over his shoulder. "Would you ever want more children?"

"No." The word is absolute, and I mean it most sincerely. "I'm going to be a grandmother any second. That will be plenty."

"I can understand that."

"Do you want another child?"

"I've never considered it. But sometimes lately I think it wouldn't be so terrible."

"You're older than I am!"

He laughs, low and deep. "That's true. But there are a lot of children in the world who just want a place to land, something safe and warm."

"Katie was so skinny when she got here that I was horrified."

"Exactly."

"So you would adopt?"

He looks at me. "Yeah. I couldn't—"

I smile softly. "You won't love any child less. It doesn't matter if they belong to your blood."

He puts a hand over his chest. "It's hard to imagine."

"I know. But that's how it is. Life happens to you."

"Speaking of that…" He puts his feet down, stopping the glider, then stands up, pulling me gently to my feet. "It's time."

"For?"

"The natural thing for two lovers to do is to make love." He pulls me into his body. "I've been thinking about you all day, and the day before that and the day before that."

And for the first time, it does seem right. It's not a decision made in the heat of the moment, although when he gathers me close and kisses me, I find myself melding into him, our skins dissolving one into the other. His hands press down the cloth of my dress, moving surely across the landscape of my back, cupping my bottom. I press upward into him, head bending backward to accommodate his tongue. My hands are roving, too. Over his back, down his arms, hands open along the outside of his thighs. I feel the air on the back of my bare legs and realize only as his hands move beneath my skirt that he's tugged it up. "Is Katie asleep?"

"Yes," I say, but the sound is strangled, because he's sliding those clever fingers between my legs, and I make a noise, then step away. "Let's go upstairs."

He smiles and follows me, and I lead him up the back stairs, through the dark kitchen, and into my bedroom, which is messy because it always is. At least the quilt is pulled up over the pillows and the clothes are mostly piled on one chair. I close the door and reach for him.

"It's too dark," he says.

"My room is messy." I think of how tidy his house is, everything in its place, all the clutter stowed. If he even owns any clutter.

"I don't care," he says, laughing. "I want to look at you, not your bedroom."

Reluctantly, I turn on a lamp, and I'm even embarrassed by the fact that there is a scarf around the shade, a peachy color I love so much I want to put it everywhere. I turn back to find him looking at me soberly, and he reaches for the buttons of my dress. I start to help him, but he says quietly, "Let me."

He takes his time, unbuttoning each button, and then he pushes the light dress off my shoulders and I'm standing in my panties and bra. I kick the dress aside and move toward him. "I used to imagine that you were in my room with me," I say, unbuttoning his shirt. "That you were lying in my bed and our chests were bare."

"I used to imagine a little more than that."

I take off his shirt and lean in to kiss the hair across his chest, inhaling the scent of him, so concentrated here. His skin is warm. His hands skim down my hair. His mouth presses into my temple, and it feels holy and quiet and perfect. He pushes down my panties until I can kick them off. Last is my bra, and he's slow with it, his hands grazing my breasts, but then it, too, is gone, and I'm standing naked before him, clad only in my hair.

His eyes glitter as he pulls it around, great swaths of hair that fall over my shoulders and arms, breasts peeking out. "You look like a painting, a pre-Raphaelite woman."

And in that moment I see myself through his eyes, and it's much sweeter than the reality. I hold out an arm. "Come to me, Jonah," I say, and he comes, tumbling me backward to the bed, where we start to laugh and kiss and kiss and laugh, tangling limbs, naked chests pressed together. I wrap my legs around his jeaned hips and push him up to look in his eyes. "There's something wrong with this picture."

He goes to his knees and gestures. "A little help, maybe?"

Laughing, I reach for the buttons and skim him out of his jeans and underwear, inclining my head as his flesh leaps out. "Nice," I say, and circle it with one hand. He allows it briefly, then he's covering me with his long elegant body and our mouths join, and the mood shifts. I feel it, as if there is light edging around the bed, soaking into us, almost a sound. He touches my face, whispers my name, kisses my neck, and I kiss his chin and his neck, thinking of the self I was at fifteen, wanting him so much it practically flattened me every time I saw him.

And it has not changed. I'm breathless with wanting him,

craving the union that comes at last when he pulls me closer and touches me with his fingers to smooth the way. Then he bends over me, bracing himself on his elbows so I can look up at him.

Jonah.

"Keep your eyes open," he says, and slides into me. It's the most intense moment of connection I have ever had with another person. It feels as if our bodies blur, that I am him and he is me, and our skin is melting into each other's. Still I keep my gaze on his deep-gold eyes, until he leans down and kisses me and seals us together, moving us so tightly into a unit that I know it cannot ever come apart. "Jonah!" I cry, and then I'm tumbling into the union, and from here it feels we are eternal, that we have been together in some way for all of time, traveling as a pair.

When we are finished, I keep my arms tight around his neck, panting. Our skin is slick with sweat and I can feel his heart pounding against me, mine practically shattering my ribs. Suddenly I'm shaking head to toe, and he simply gathers me up, enfolds us within the blanket, and caresses my back. "Shh. Shhh. Shhh."

Finally my body seems to absorb the shock of it. "Jonah! Oh, my God!" I put my hands in his hair, on his face. "I can't believe it."

He smooths hair away from my face. "I know."

I lift up on one elbow, touch his mouth, his chin, his throat. His eyes are calm and deep. Tender. "That was so much...it was..." I shake my head. "Maybe it was just me," I finally manage. "But I've never felt anything even remotely like that in my life."

"It wasn't just you. I've been waiting for that for a very, very long time."

I fall against his chest, nestling my head into the hollow of his shoulder. "Me, too." I close my eyes, breathe in. "Me, too."

FORTY-ONE

Katie

Katie awakens in the dark with a deep, throbbing pain in her low abdomen. It's just her period, she knows that—she's heard her mom complain about cramps often enough—and she takes it as a badge of honor.

But she didn't expect them to be like this, as if there is a fist with giant knuckles in her belly, twisting and turning very slowly, each knuckle rubbing along some sore place. She pulls her knees up to her chest and tells herself to go back to sleep. It's no big deal. Only cramps.

Maybe she should go down and ask Ramona for some help. Katie's embarrassed, but it was okay this afternoon, and Ramona was really nice, showing her all about the whole business.

It is still hard to get used to, though, the feeling of something between her legs like that. Tears well up in her eyes, and she dashes them angrily away. All these emotions are so stupid! She feels like they're something outside her, demons taking over her mind and body. She got so mad at Lily over dinner and she tried to hide it, the red tide rising through her so she was like a cartoon character with steam coming out of her ears.

It *isn't* fair, though. Lily knew how much Katie was looking forward to the flower show, and it won't be the same with

Ramona, who doesn't even like flowers that much! The loss of it makes more hot tears stream out of her eyes.

A wave of knuckles rolls through her belly, and she makes a noise and flings back the covers. Merlin trots over and they pad downstairs, but before she gets to the bottom, she hears voices. Ramona.

And a man.

In Ramona's room.

Wrapping her arms around her middle, Katie turns and goes back upstairs and climbs into bed. She wishes for her mother.

Merlin appears at the side of her bed and woofs softly for permission to come up. Ryan told her never to let him on the bed, but sometimes he feels like her only friend. Tonight she's so miserable she just doesn't care about any stupid dog-training rules. She pats the bed beside her and says, "Come on, baby."

Even though he jumped a fence, he always does a funny thing with his chin to jump up onto something like this. He does it on the couch, too—a tap with his chin to the surface of the bed, and then again, and then he readies himself and leaps. It's so cute it makes her laugh even now. He turns in a circle on the bed, putting his spine to her and his head down on her pillow so she can put her arms around him. He's warm and soft and smells of starlight. Katie presses her tummy into his back and strokes one velvety ear, trying not to think about her cramps.

When they got back from dinner, Katie had gone upstairs, feeling a tangle of completely unfamiliar and unpleasant emotions. Lily had just blown her off, and it stung, and although she got it—she wasn't stupid!—she felt as if nobody ever put her first. Her dad always had the Army. Her mom always wanted her drugs. Ramona and Lily have Sofia and the new baby to worry about.

Hugging her dog, crying like a little kid, Katie wonders if anyone will ever put her first.

FORTY-TWO

Ramona

Jonah and I lie entangled, talking, for hours. Few things in my life have ever been what I imagined, but this comes close. We talk, and talk, and talk. He tells me about his years of restless travel, through South America and the East, and the woman he thought he would marry in Argentina. He speaks fluent Spanish, and to my delight he murmurs it against my ear, whispering in that beautiful tongue. I tell him about running restaurants and the pleasure I find in bread, the earthy depth of it. Few things make me feel as joyful as the sight of a loaf of golden bread coming out of the oven, the smell filling the air with a peace unlike any other.

We also talk about little things. Like movies and how airplanes stay in the sky and whether toenails should be painted. After a while we make love again, moving more slowly this time, examining each other more closely. Just before we fall asleep in each other's arms, he says, "This is serious, Ramona. You know that, don't you?"

I think of us as old people on a porch. I reach for his hand, place it over my heart. "This makes me so happy it scares me to death."

He kisses my forehead fiercely. "Maybe we could just be happy. Things are not always doomed, you know."

I laugh softly. "I forget that sometimes."

Nestling closer, I will myself to accept happiness. No drama, no disaster, no big fights, simply fitting together, like puzzle pieces.

I don't know what time it is when the ringing of the phone jolts me from sleep. Bolting upright, I grab it off the nightstand and croak, "Hello?"

"Were you sleeping, Mom? I'm so sorry. Usually you're up by now."

"It's a long story. Let me grab my robe and I can talk." I mouth "Sofia" to Jonah and wave him down to sleep. Feeling slightly self-conscious—but not as much as I might have imagined—I pad across the room and grab my robe, then slip out of the room and into the kitchen. "Sorry, honey." My voice is craggy, but there's nothing I can do about it. "I'm so happy to hear your voice."

"You were whispering. Do you have someone there? Is it the sweater guy?"

"Sofia! No!" Then I realize it's silly to lie. "Um. Yes."

"Mom!" Her voice is genuinely excited. "You're so cute! You have to tell me all about him."

"I promise I will. But not, uh, right now."

"Why aren't you baking yet? It's four."

"Had to close for a couple days," I say as lightly as I can. "Hot-water issues. That's enough about me. Tell me how you are, what's going on. How's Oscar? How are the Braxton Hicks?"

"Oh, Mom," she says, letting go. "This is so hard." And then I do the part of mom work that is easy: I listen while she pours out her story. She's terrified and lost and hopeful and in love with her broken husband. She's worried about her baby and about Katie and about being alone during the birth.

At least I can offer some good news. "I know you didn't want Poppy and Nancy, but what about having Gram come to stay with you? She really wants to be there, hold your hand."

"I wish it could be you."

"You have no idea how many times I've tried to work that out, but it just isn't possible. Not if I'm going to have a livelihood."

"I know. I do know, honestly. And it would be great to have Gram. I need somebody. I'm really lonely."

"I'm so sorry. I wish I could spare you all of this."

She takes a breath and I can see her in my mind's eye, squaring her shoulders. "How's Katie? She sounds so happy! I've never known her to be this way. You're such a good mother."

"Oh, it's not me she loves. It's your grandmother. They have this whole flower thing going. To tell you the truth, she's pretty sad about Lily leaving to be with you."

"Then have her stay with Katie. I'm a grown-up. I'll be okay."

"Even adults need help, sweetie. I'm here for Katie. She'll be fine." I lower my voice. "We actually celebrated her first period today. How exciting is that?"

Sofia bursts into tears.

"Honey! What's wrong?"

"I'm just so glad she's with you. Imagine, Mom, how that would have been in that crack house she was living in. I'm so grateful. Thank you."

"She's wonderful, Sofia, and she's been a big help to me." Merlin has come into the kitchen and sits down in front of me, one paw on my foot. "I think her dog needs to go outside, as a matter of fact. He's sitting here staring at me."

"I should let you go, anyway. I have to go sleep for a while. I'm a basket case, as you can tell."

I chuckle. "Sleep will help. And this is a very emotional period anyway, even if you didn't have all this stuff going on."

"Have Gram give me a call when she knows when she's getting in. I'll make arrangements for her. And tell her that I am so grateful that she's coming."

"I will." We hang up and I sit for a minute in the quiet

kitchen, worrying about my baby, so many miles away, alone and lonely, wanting her mother with her. Is there any way to make that happen? Could someone fill in for me?

But even if I could get coverage for the bakery, it feels wrong to create any more upheaval for Katie. She might be irritated at Lily, but the simple cornerstones of normality are so important for her healing—the flowers, regular mealtimes, her dog, her bedroom. She is thriving, like a plant in the right soil, and it feels like my job to be a fence around her.

Merlin lifts his foot and taps my toes lightly. "Sorry," I say with a chuckle. "You need to go outside. I forgot."

But when I stand up, he jumps up and heads for the attic, not the stairs to go to the yard. It sparks fear in me. "Is there something wrong?"

He woofs and jerks his head, as if to say, *Come on.* Following him, I wonder traitorously if a cat would ever do this. He leads me into the attic room, where Katie is curled up in a ball under her covers. "Are you all right, Katie?"

"No," she says. "I have really, really bad cramps and I don't know what to do."

I stroke her forehead. "Aw, I'm so sorry. It won't always be like this, but when it is, what you need is ibuprofen and a good hot bath."

"Now?"

"Yeah. It'll help."

"I'm not going down there. You have a man in your room."

That throws me, and for a minute I have to think about all the ramifications. "Yes, I do. I'm sorry if that upsets you. I thought you were asleep."

"I don't care."

"It's only Jonah, and he's asleep and the door is closed. A bath will make you feel better. I'll make sure he doesn't come out."

"No. It's embarrassing."

I wonder if I should kick him out, but that feels wrong, too.

"Well, I can't force you, though it would really help. Hold on and I'll get you some Advil."

Sullenly, she flings back the covers. "I'll take a bath," she growls, as if she's doing me a favor. "I feel gross anyway."

"Good choice." I scrub Merlin's head. He licks my wrist. "Give your dog some extra love. He came to get me."

When I get back to my room, an exhausted Katie sleeping upstairs, the sun is beginning to come up over the horizon. In my bed, Jonah is asleep, naked, his white shoulders flung out of the sheets, one foot sticking out at the end of the bed. Milo is asleep at the small of Jonah's back, and when I come into the room, he stretches out one black paw and begins to purr audibly.

At the side of the bed, I pause, looking down at my sleeping lover in the soft gray light. His grizzled jaw, his tousled dark hair, his beautiful mouth. I want to bake bread to commemorate this emotion, create something beautiful just for him. Whispers of what it will be waft over me as I admire him—almonds, perhaps. Walnuts. Honey to make the crust the color of his hair.

My entire being is alive with a thrumming. With sunlight.

I press my fingers to my mouth. I am so in love. And like every woman in love through all of time, I crawl in beside him, quietly, so that I can watch him sleep. I look at his ear and the white skin on his shoulders. He has not even one freckle.

His eye is open, looking at me. At this angle I can see the crow's feet around his eyes. There is silver in his morning beard. He blinks, closes his eye, and lets go of a breath. Blindly, he reaches for my hand, draws it across the covers to his mouth, and kisses my fingers—one, two, three—then tucks it under his chin as if it is his own hand. We both doze for a while, but it's no good. I'm awake. I poke him. "I want to go eat breakfast."

"Do you get up this early every day?"

"Yes! I run a bakery. The bread doesn't bake itself."

He sighs. "Okay, I thought you might be my soul mate, but that would mean I could sleep in."

A zing of disappointment touches me. "Really? How late do you want to sleep?"

"Six?"

"It's five after six."

"Ah, good, then." He moves over, tucks me into his body, and makes love to me one more time.

We shower together afterward, and I realize as I'm soaping his body that I am happy. "This might be one of the better moments of my life thus far."

"Yeah? Like top five? Top ten?"

I make swirls of soap in his chest hair. "Hmmm. At the least the top twenty."

He laughs.

I leave a note for Katie on the table, though I doubt very much she'll be awake before we return. In the cool, bright freshness of seven a.m., we head out for Gertrude's, an upscale breakfast spot on West Colorado Avenue. I don't usually go there, but Jonah loves it. We have to wait just inside the door while they make a table ready, and he holds my hand. A spritely little rose he plucked from my garden is sticking out of his shirt pocket, and there is that luminosity of sex all over his skin, shining out of his eyes. I see women eyeing him, and it makes me proud and possessive.

And suddenly I am completely aware of this exact moment— the smell of potatoes browning on a grill, the clatter of someone putting dishes away, the low murmur of polite patrons— because, as I look up at Jonah, I realize that I have fallen over into another state of being and there is no returning from it. Whatever happens, I can't un-fall in love with him. Whatever thing was born so long ago, that summer when I was pregnant with Sofia, has now sprouted, coming to vigorous life.

The protective person in me, the one who has made so many mistakes, wearily warns against it, but even she knows this is already in motion. She says there could be things lurking, says that we don't really know each other.

It doesn't matter. Now, in this very moment, when I am forty years and eleven months into my life, I am in love with Jonah.

He catches my gaze and lifts my hand to his lips. "It was that expression that used to haunt me when we were young. No one, ever, has looked at me like that." Tenderly, he rubs his thumb over the palm of my hand. "Am I giving it back to you the way I hope I am? I had to hide it then."

"You are not hiding it now."

An older woman, tucking her hair under a sun hat, gives us a look. "You two must be newlyweds," she says.

He tucks my hand close to his ribs. "Something like that."

RAMONA'S BOOK OF BREADS

SUNSHINE FRUIT AND HONEY BREAD

Sometimes a recipe is born from a moment, and this is the recipe that I came up with after my first night with Jonah. Filled with light and juice and tenderness, it is one of my favorite things. Try it with a cup of sweet chai.

2 cups all-purpose flour

1 tsp baking powder

1 tsp baking soda

½ tsp kosher salt

½ cup butter, softened

½ cup raw sugar

½ cup dark honey

½ tsp vanilla extract

½ tsp orange extract

2 tsp grated orange zest

2 eggs

1 cup raspberries, whole

⅓ cup slivered toasted almonds

Juice of 1 orange, mixed with enough powdered sugar to make a thin glaze

Preheat oven to 325 degrees. Grease a 9 x 5-inch loaf pan. Whisk together the flour, baking powder, baking soda, and salt. Cream butter, raw sugar, honey, extracts, and zest. Add eggs one at a time. Mix in the dry ingredients until just moist, then very gently fold in the raspberries and toasted almonds. Bake for 55–60 minutes, until a toothpick comes out clean.

Cool for 20 minutes, then tip bread out onto a wire rack and cool thoroughly. Drizzle the top lightly with glaze.

FORTY-THREE

Katie

A long bar of hot sunlight wakes Katie. She notices right away that the cramps are gone. She still feels kind of grouchy, but maybe that's from not sleeping enough last night. Lily told her that teenagers need ten solid hours of sleep a night, sometimes even twelve when they're growing.

She changes into jeans and a cute little halter top Lily got her, then heads downstairs to find the note from Ramona. She's left some *pain au chocolat* on the table, too, and Katie honestly doesn't mind. She's been noticing that Jonah really likes Ramona, and he's a good guy. Katie likes that he cooks, that his house is so clean, that he's so ... classy. From all that Lily has let slip, Ramona has had a broken heart for a long time, so this is a good thing.

She pours a glass of milk to go with the *pain au chocolat* and carries both to the computer nook. There are three emails there this morning. One is from Sofia. One is from Madison, her friend in El Paso. The third is from her mother. She reads them in order. Sofia's is short. She talks about Oscar and thanks Katie for writing emails every day. They help, she says; he listens carefully.

Katie writes back, *Why won't he reply to my emails?*

Then she reads the note from her friend. It's been less than two months, but already that friendship seems like something from another life. Madison tells her all about meeting a boy at the swimming pool, about sneaking a cigarette from her mother, about getting a bra in a B cup!

Katie can't believe this has been her best friend for seven years.

Last, she reads the email from her mother.

HI KATIE BABIE!

YOUR OLD MOMMA IS SURE PROUD OF YOU FOR GETTING SO MUCH MONEY TO ME. YOU MUST BE WORKING REALLY HARD. WHAT ARE YOU DOING TO GET MOOLA. IM WORKING MY PROGRAM BUT I HATE THIS STUPID PLACE AND ALL THE STUPID THINGS THEY MAKE YOU DO. IM LOOKING BETTER THO YOU WOULD BE HAPPY TO SEE THAT MY FACE IS CLEARING UP. WHATS GOING ONE WITH YOU? HOW IS YOUR DOG? HAVE YOU SENT MORE MONEY YET.

I WAS THINKING YOU SHOULD COME SEE ME. THEY'LL LET ME OUT FOR AN HOUR IF I WANT TO SEE MY CHILD, AND THEN I HAVE TO COME BACK IN, BUT I COULD DO THAT EVERY DAY IF YOU COULD GET HERE COME RIDE THE BUSS DOWN AND STAY WITH THE PETROSKYS. THEN WE COULD SEE EACH OTHER AN HOUR EVERYDAY. I SURE MISS YOU BABY AND WANT TO SEE YOU SO, SO, SO BAD. I THINK THE BUSS DOESNT COST THAT MUCH MAYBE RAMONA WOULD PAY. WHAT DO YOU THINK OF THAT IDEA? WRITE BACK AND TELL ME.

LOVE MOM

For a long time, Katie sits right there without moving, feeling a weird hollowness in her chest, like all her air has been sucked out. When she takes a breath, it doesn't go away.

She doesn't want to go to El Paso to see her mother. She'll just keep sending money and hope that keeps her from insisting. Katie had been thinking of telling her mom about getting her first period and all that, so her mom would be included (she was feeling guilty over dinner that Ramona and Lily were acting like mothers, though she was happy that they did).

Instead, now she writes,

Hi, Mom. Merlin is good. I'm good. I sent some money yesterday, so you should get it pretty soon. I've got a big flower show on Monday, so I might not be back to talk for a while, but I love you lots. Katie

FORTY-FOUR

Ramona

Trying to make lemonade from lemons, I pay Katie to help me scour the bakery on Friday and Saturday. It is a good use of downtime, and it keeps Katie occupied. The money will no doubt all go to her mother, but that is her choice. Obviously she's using some of her bakery earnings for things she wants—I noticed her fingernails were painted pale blue one day, and she had on a cute pair of sandals another. When I commented, she said, "Goodwill! Only two dollars, can you believe it? They're a tiny bit too big, but my feet are still growing, right?"

On Sunday, Lily asks if Katie would like to ride up to the airport with her, but she refuses and hides out in her room all afternoon. Leaving her to her sulk, I tackle another task on my to-do list: having a conversation with my sister.

I've been thinking about this since our conversation on Thursday, when she point-blank refused to help me. We've been on the outs long enough, and I'm not going to leave it alone anymore.

But how to catch her so that she can't run away is another trick entirely. I consider and discard a couple of possibilities: showing up at her town house some morning (but that would mean talking to her before she has coffee—never a good idea); going to the trailhead from which she walks every day at three

316 B A R B A R A O'N E A L

p.m. (but she is much fitter than me and would just outwalk me).

I settle on catching her at the steakhouse in mid-afternoon, when she'll be performing any number of catch-up tasks for the week. My father is driving my mother to Denver, so he'll be off-site.

Perfect.

As if I am attiring myself for battle, I choose my outfit carefully—a simple sundress that makes me look a little less curvy, hair pulled back in a half French braid that flows loose partway down my back, sandals. Silver bracelets, like war gear.

I drive over there to arrive at exactly two fifteen, one of the deadest times in any restaurant.

The Erin Steakhouse was established in 1964. A long, mid-century-style building with angles and plate-glass windows on a bluff, it offers spectacular views of the city from one side and the Front Range from the other and has been one of the premier restaurants in the city for more than forty-five years. People book tables with a view in order to propose. Graduating seniors are feted; Air Force Academy cadets and their parents celebrate here. And the number of prom dresses that have paraded through the establishment over the years has to count in the tens of thousands. It is the star of the Gallagher Group, my father's flagship.

Or was. As I pull into the lot this afternoon, I am startled to see how dated it looks. With the critical eye I have developed under Cat's tutelage, I mentally pull out the dusty, aging junipers and replace them with pots of cactus and yucca, cover the too-jaunty green shade of the paint with something more fitting to the landscape. Forest green, maybe, or a rosy sand to match the earth.

And the sign, I think, touching it as I walk by. The sign definitely needs help.

It isn't a place I come to very often, but the Erin is still associated very much for me with the summer I was fifteen.

As I walk in, a hostess comes forward, and I wave her away. "I'm looking for Stephanie. Is she here?"

"Can I tell her who is looking for her?"

"I'm her sister," I say, putting my finger to my lips and smiling as if this is a happy moment. "I'd like to surprise her."

The girl is instantly conspiratorial. "Oh, sure," she whispers, and comes close to me. "She's over in the corner. Do you see her?"

I nod and make my way through the sparsely occupied tables. It does seem that there should be a little more business during a Sunday lunch, but this has always been mainly a dinner restaurant. The presence of customers is part of my plan to keep Stephanie mellow, so I'm glad for any of them.

My sister is neatly dressed in a white cardigan and sharply creased black pants. Her jewelry is a single thin gold bracelet and the amethyst ring that belonged to my grandmother. In this, she and Sofia are both like my mother—elegant, always perfectly groomed, though Sofia has a more passionate and expressive personality, which perfectly illuminates her Irish-Mexican DNA.

Steph is bent over a stack of papers, and I can see she's doing scheduling. "Aren't there computer programs for that now?" I say, sliding into the booth.

I've caught her off guard, as I'd hoped, and before she can erect her mask, I see the exhaustion around her eyes, the fleeting surprise. "Ramona!" she says, staring. "What are you doing here?"

I fold my hands on the table and look around. Inside, it's even more dated, with a decidedly Vegas-circa-1973 feeling. It has to be hurting the restaurant. I frown. "Is the menu still the same here, too?"

She raises an eyebrow and gathers papers into a stack. Nods. "Wow."

"That's not why you're here."

"No." I sit straight and look her in the blue, blue eye. "I'm tired of this long war, and I want to end it."

Irritably, she says, "What war? Don't be dramatic."

I think of Jonah, wonder how he might manage a conflict like this. Trying to channel his calming tone, I say, "Maybe it isn't a war. Maybe it's just been a disagreement, a different way of looking at things. What I know is that I—" I pause, bite my inner lip. "I miss my sister. I hate it that we never talk, that you're so mad at me. And I don't know why, so I can't fix it."

Color has been creeping into her cheeks as I talk. She has always had perfectly smooth skin, and it shows this color as delicately as a princess. "I'd rather not have this conversation here." She glances over her shoulder. "Now."

"I know. But the thing is, I'm not leaving until we talk today. And if you get up to walk away"—I smile brightly—"I'll follow you."

In a low voice, she says, "Why are you doing this?"

In a voice just as quiet: "Because you came to my business and yelled at me as if I were a child. Because I asked for your help and you completely dismissed me, and that is not what families are supposed to do."

"Oh, what families do!" Her eyes narrow as she leans over the table. "You can do whatever *you* want, *whenever* you want, and then when you want us you can just come waltzing back and expect everything to be forgiven?"

"What did I do to be forgiven for, Steph?" I touch my chest. "What did I do?"

She makes a huffing sound of disbelief and looks over her shoulder again. "Let's start with you screwing your father's worst enemy."

I shake my head. "That was after."

"How about leaving the restaurant, leaving us in the lurch?"

"That's true, I did do that." It's harder to be calm than I expected, and I have to look away, take a deep breath, and imagine the cool air of the mountains bringing down the temperature in my lungs. "But we both know that it wasn't okay for the Gallagher Group to keep Dane when he had been so repeatedly, shamefully unfaithful to me."

She rolls her eyes. "For God's sake. It was years ago."

"But we're talking about what happened years ago." I lean forward and say again, "What did I do *then* that I need to be forgiven for? Tell me and I'll make amends."

"You always get whatever you want, with a snap of your fingers. You just sail through everything, and everyone loves Ramona."

I blink. "Sail through? Through what? Through being pregnant at fifteen? Through—"

"You always go back to that, like you're the only person who had big problems as a teenager. Everybody does. Get over it."

For a minute I want to storm away. Instead, I stand my ground. Quietly. Firmly. "You said I sailed through everything. I don't see it that way. I think I've had kind of a challenging path."

"No more challenging than anyone else."

I lean back against the ugly green leather banquette. Maybe that's true. "I don't know how to atone for that. Can you forgive me for sailing through everything? For not having a harder road?" I frown. "I don't think any of that is what this war is about."

"Don't call it war," she says, and taps her stack of papers crisply against the table. "I just get tired of you being the center of everything. Plain and simple."

"Talk to me."

She meets my eyes. "Too late." She swings her legs out of the booth and stands. "Now, if you'll excuse me, I have work to do."

Before she walks away, I say, "Well, thanks for that, anyway.

And if you need any help bringing the Erin into this century, I can probably help."

She only glares over her shoulder and clip-clops into the kitchen.

Heading back to my car, I think, *At least I gave it a shot.* Maybe it will be like water against stone, but it is a beginning.

Because it's that kind of a day, Katie is still in her room sulking when I get home. "Hey," I say, knocking on the threshold. "You about ready to go to Jonah's for Sunday-night supper?"

"I know you guys want to be alone," she says, barely looking up from her thick book. Merlin sprawls on the floor of the screened-in balcony, panting hard.

"I love your company," I say. "And maybe your dog would like to get out of this oven, hmmm?"

She glances over the top of her book. "We'll go outside."

"No, you should come with me. Jonah's making his fish tacos, and you really loved them last time."

"I don't want to go, Ramona!" One foot is crossed over the top of her knee, and the foot wiggles furiously.

I wait.

"Did any of you ever think that I might want to see my dad? I mean, he is my dad, and I can be very helpful." Tears glitter at the corners of her eyes. "Why didn't Lily even ask me if I wanted to go with her?"

If living with my family, especially my mother, has taught me anything, it is to take a deep breath when a teenager flings an accusatory question on the table. It writhes between us like a rattlesnake, tail wiggling dangerously. "It would be terrible for you there, Katie. Sofia is in the hospital all the time, and there wouldn't be anything to do. You would spend time in the room with your dad, but that would get old fast. He's not well. He wouldn't be talking to you—"

"I know that! I'm not a baby."

My temper flares. "Well, you sure have been acting like one. Everyone is bending over backward to give you a better life, and you—"

"Nobody asked me if I wanted a better life!"

"No, because sometimes you have to trust adults to make good decisions on your behalf."

"But I can't act like a baby?"

In that instant I remember how illogical Sofia could be at this age, given to circular arguments and emotional pleas that didn't follow any rules I could discern. Putting my hand on her knee, I say, "You can if you want to. You can sulk up here as long as you like, too, but please take care of your dog." Merlin has come over to the side of the bed, panting, and I stroke his head. "I'm going to Jonah's. You are welcome to come with me if you leave your mood behind."

"I'm not going." But she does fling her legs off the bed and put on her flip-flops. "We'll go read outside."

"Don't forget the bug spray."

She rolls her eyes. "I know, I know. West Nile virus."

As I escape into the dusty gold air of late afternoon, I am not unhappy to be leaving her to her sulk. It occurs to me that nearly everything in my life is teetering on the edge of disaster, but I'm also happy. How is it possible that things can be so beautiful and so awful, so rewarding and so exhausting, all at once?

As I walk down the narrow sidewalk, passing tiny front gardens planted with flowers I can't name, it seems easy to count my blessings. I'm relieved beyond measure that my mother is on her way to San Antonio, is in fact probably there. I'm relieved that if I had to have a big problem with the water heater, it came this weekend instead of two weekends from now when there is a festival. I'm glad for the good weather and my hair and living in such a beautiful place.

Any second now I'm going to burst into song. Raindrops on roses and whiskers on kittens.

As I round the corner to Jonah's house, the reason for my happiness is standing in his yard, watering the flower beds with a sprinkler hose. He's tall and fit, his muscled runner's legs showing beneath long khaki shorts. Something about his ankles is sexy, and it makes me smile.

And maybe it's unfeminist of me to be so pleased by a man's company, to find happiness in falling in love, but there is no denying the reality. I am thrilled to see him, every single time. "Hello, gorgeous," I say, coming up the walk to stand beside him. "What are those flowers?"

"The purple ones are phlox. I wouldn't choose them myself, but the garden here is old, and I like the way it all works together." He gestures toward a climbing pink rose, which is blooming in a profuse cascade above a bank of something blue, and a line of yellow flowers below that. "Somebody really loved this place and spent a lot of time on it. I like to honor that."

"It is beautiful. I have sometimes wondered why you chose this place, in particular."

"Aside from the fact that it was obviously fated, you mean?"

I smile up at him. "Well, it is modest, and you could have probably chosen anything in town. There are some spectacular places around the city."

He moves the spray over the blossoms, back and forth, back and forth. "There are. I looked at some of them." There is something still in him when he says, "How much does one person need, really? This is plenty."

"Can I kiss you for that, please?"

"You can kiss me whenever you like." He points the sprinkler in the opposite direction from us and I lean in, standing on my toes to press my mouth to his. His hand wraps around my waist and hauls me close. "Mmm," he says, smacking his lips. "One of my favorite things. Kisses from Ramona."

I let him go and follow him across the lawn to turn off the water. It's a thick, established bluegrass, and it gives off coolness that brushes my ankles. Over the top of the house, the mountains draw a zigzaggy dark line against a sky made of pale lemon clouds and layers of airy blue meringue.

"Listen," I say.

He turns. Cocks his head.

The world is very still. Far away, a child calls. A bird is singing in the foliage. Water drips from leaves to the ground. "Could you write music from that?"

"Oh, yes. With you at the center. Could you bake bread from it?"

My mind springs toward ingredients—lemons and honey and almonds. "Yes."

"Let's call it a challenge, then, shall we? I'll make music. You make bread."

And they all lived happily ever after, I think, smiling. "Deal."

In my pocket, my phone rings.

"M om?" Sofia's voice is thin and wavery.

I give Jonah a glance of alarm and lift a finger, turning my back and walking toward the edge of the property. "What is it?"

"Oh, my God, Mom," she wails, and begins to sob. She says a jumble of words, but they're unintelligible, and my panic is threatening to close my throat.

"Honey, slow down. Breathe. I can't understand you."

"Oscar. Tried. To. Kill. Himself."

I press my palm into my belly. "Oh, baby. Oh, no."

Jonah comes up behind me, touches my shoulders. It startles me and I turn around, shaking my head in alarm. "Wait," I mouth. To Sofia, I say, "When did this happen? What did he do? I mean, isn't he in intensive care?"

"He got a bunch of pills from somebody. Nobody is talking, but it's part of some soldier pact or something, that if one of them gets badly injured and says some magic phrase, the others will take care of them."

I think of Oscar, his beautiful eyes and kind heart, taking this terrible action, and I understand, *really* understand, how desperately badly he must be injured. "How is he now?"

"He's all right. They pumped his stomach and he's asleep

now." She is choking on her tears. "I thought I was doing the right thing, I thought he'd be okay if he knew I loved him, but it's like this is making it worse, and I'm so exhausted and strung out and he's still not talking to me—" She breaks down and cries hard.

I just sit on the line with her, murmuring quiet, soothing things. "Go ahead and cry it out, sweetheart. I'm right here."

Jonah takes my hand and gestures, pulling me to the porch. He pushes me into a chair and brings me a glass of wine, offers cheese, which he sets down on the table beside me. The light is still perfect, slanting into the grass on almost solid bars of gold lines, but nothing is beautiful when my daughter is sobbing so inconsolably. When her sobs slow a little, I say, "Did Gram get there?"

"She's on the way from the airport."

"That's something. Do me a favor, baby."

"What?"

"Lean on her. Let her take care of things—she's good at getting results, so let her. Stop trying to hold up the whole world and go to sleep for a few days."

"What if he tries again, Mom?"

What I want to say is that she can't stop him if he really wants to kill himself. Instead, I say gently, "You have to keep yourself strong for the baby, Sofia. Exhausting yourself will hurt all of you. Oscar needs you to be strong. Have you eaten?"

"Yes. One of the nurses brought me a Reuben a little while ago." She laughs slightly. "My appetite doesn't seem to be suffering in the slightest."

That single, rueful laugh reassures me. "Good. What I want you to do is let Gram take over when she gets there, and you go to sleep, deal?"

"I'll try. Are you going to tell Katie?"

A rock thuds onto my heart. "I don't know." I think of her pretty haircut, her shining eyes, her normal teenage sulking.

"She is thriving, happy, growing so strong. I hate to undermine that."

"She's had enough trauma in her life, don't you think? If he"—she chokes on the word—"dies, that's one thing. But let her just be happy right now."

"You're right."

"Okay, I'm going to bed. I'll call you again tomorrow and let you know how things are going."

"I love you, Sofia. And you are handling all of this so well."

"Thanks, Mom. Love you."

I hang up the phone and the sun slips suddenly behind the peak, plunging the porch and yard into dusk. The colors of the flowers are subdued, as if someone turned all the internal lights to dim.

I think of Oscar laughing and toasting Sofia at their wedding, both of them so lovely and healthy and young. I think of his smooth neck, so deeply tan, and his golden forearms, and the way he looked at my daughter, with such a fierce love and protectiveness that I knew I could trust him.

Grief bows my head. My lungs feel squashed and I can't quite get a breath. Jonah's soft footsteps come across the porch. "Are you all right?"

I shake my head, trying desperately not to break down, but I think of Katie, of Sofia and the baby she's carrying, and of Oscar himself, so deeply in despair that he would leave them all.

I reach for Jonah's hand and press his knuckles into my forehead. Tears flow hard down my face—silently, at least, though I can feel my shoulders shaking. He kneels and strokes my back. Nearby, sparrows are singing in mad conversation, and it is this sound that brings me back to myself. Jonah hands me a handkerchief and I blot my eyes and nose, looking for the birds. "Where are those birds?"

He points to a cone-shaped juniper. "The sparrow condos. There must be forty birds who live there. They love the berries."

"It wouldn't suck to be a bird, would it?"

"Summers wouldn't be bad. Winters would be a drag."

I nod.

"Do you want to talk about it?"

In a weary voice, I recount the story. "My mother will be there soon, and she'll handle everything. I just feel so terrible for him."

"Why don't you drink your wine and I'll go get Katie and we can all watch a movie after dinner?"

"I don't know. Maybe I should go home."

He holds my hands, rubbing his thumbs over the heels of my palms. "If that's what you want. But maybe you don't have to hold up the whole world, either."

I half smile. "Were you eavesdropping?"

"I was." He stands up. "At least come have some supper now. There isn't anything you can do for anyone else right now. You might as well let me take care of you."

I look at him, nod, and let him lead me inside.

FORTY-SIX

Katie

Monday is the flower show, and Katie is so excited she wakes up very early and takes a shower so she can be ready. Ramona is downstairs in the bakery, talking to someone, and Katie heads down there. "Hi!" she says cheerfully. "Do you want me to make you some coffee?"

Ramona is in deep conversation with a man wearing blue coveralls. He has a big toolbox and he's working on the hot-water heater. "Thanks, hon, but I'm kind of busy right now."

"Okay. What time do you think we'll leave?"

"Leave?"

A ripple of worry crosses Katie's belly. "For the flower show?"

"Oh, Katie, I forgot!" Ramona comes forward, stepping over the toolbox. "I can't go. There's no way. They're installing the hot-water heater today."

"You promised."

"I know. I'm sorry." She shakes her head, waves a hand at the workman. "Sometimes, emergencies come up, Katie. That's just how life is. Maybe he'll finish in time and we can go before the day is over."

"No! That's not fair! First Lily bailed on me, now you?"

"I'm not bailing, Katie. My business is closed and I have to be here to supervise this!"

"Why can't Jimmy do it? Or Heather?"

Ramona gets a steely look on her face, and before she even speaks, Katie knows she's lost this round. "Go upstairs. Right now. I'll meet you there in two minutes."

Katie stomps up the stairs, Merlin panting behind her, and sits down with her arms crossed. When Ramona comes around the corner, Katie gives her the hardest glare she can muster.

"Oh, stop it," Ramona snaps. "You're acting like a two-year-old, and I'm tired of it. If I could go, you know I would take you."

"Everybody and everything is more important than I am," Katie says, and she's shocked that she actually said it out loud. "I'm sick of coming last."

Something odd crosses Ramona's face, and then it's gone. "Well, that's hardly true, but what if I call Jonah? Maybe he would take you."

"Forget it!"

Ramona stands there for a little while, and Katie sees that she looks tired. She knows that Ramona is worried about the bakery, and for one long second she feels kind of guilty. Finally Ramona says, "Suit yourself. I have to get back downstairs."

Katie sits there fuming for a few seconds, then she jumps up and stomps—loudly—down the back stairs to the garden. The sun is not hot yet, so she yanks out some weeds and flings them across the yard. Milo bolts out from beneath the umbrella leaves of a squash plant and leaps on them as if they're bugs or snakes, but Katie doesn't even laugh.

She is mad. Doesn't anybody care about her feelings?

"Hey there." The old woman looks over the fence. This morning her hair looks almost like smoke. She has a necklace with red stones around her neck, and she's wearing an apron with little cherries all over the front of it that is just like one Ramona has. "Who are you so mad at, sugar?"

"Everybody!" Katie growls as she yanks out a tumbleweed.

Right now it is sturdy and green and the roots probably go all the way to Malaysia. It comes free with a big clump of dirt and goes sailing across the garden, where the clump slams against the fence. "Lily was supposed to take me to a flower show and she had to go see Sofia, who is in Texas. And then Ramona was supposed to take me"—she yanks on another weed—"but she has to be here for the stupid furnace guy or whatever, and she won't go, either." This whole weed comes up more easily than the other and doesn't fling nearly as satisfyingly. "Nobody cares what I think about anything or that I've been looking forward to this for about ten years!"

"Lily is always trying to make up for being mean to Ramona when she was pregnant."

"Really?" Katie straightens, holding her dirt-speckled hands at her sides. "How was she mean?"

"She sent her away to her aunt's house for the summer, let Ramona's dad give her sister the job Ramona loved, and then they fought over whether Ramona should give up Sofia for adoption." The old woman slaps her gloves together, sending a puff of dust into the air. "Between you and me, I think she feels guilty that she was so mad at Ramona for not giving her up."

"Because she loves Sofia so much now."

"Relationships are complicated. Lily was mean because her mother was mean to her."

"Really?"

"Beat the holy hell out of her when she was fifteen. She has scars from it still. She never got over it, and never forgave her mother, either."

"That's sad." Katie thinks of her own mother. "I have forgiven my mother. But she never beat me, even when she was high."

"Remember, though, that sometimes you can love and forgive somebody, but you might still want to keep your distance."

"What do you know about it? You don't even know my mother!"

The old woman nods. "That's true. I wasn't speaking in particular, just in general. Maybe Lily was right not to forgive her mother, even if her mother wanted her to."

Katie feels that tangle of anxiety and sorrow and relief that always comes up when she thinks about her mother. Looking at a rosebush, she frowns and suddenly remembers the flower show. Maybe she'll go on her own. She's thirteen! She can ride the bus. Nobody cares where she is, anyway.

"I have to go," she says to the old lady. "See ya."

Ramona is still in the kitchen, talking to the workmen as they bang around inside the utility closet. Katie dashes up the back stairs quietly and fires up the computer. She'll check Google maps to see where it is, then take a bus, which she used to do in El Paso all the time. It comes only a block away. Her dad used to always say what a great sense of direction she has, and it's true. It's like a map lives in her brain and she moves around it without ever losing her place.

She collects the information she needs: the bus schedule and the address of the flower show. She can look at all the flowers and come home. For a minute she wonders if she ought to tell Ramona that's what she wants to do, get her permission, but Ramona doesn't care how Katie feels, so why should Katie care how Ramona feels?

There's an email in her inbox from her mom, but Katie leaves it for later. She feels a little guilty, but she has a plan and not much time to catch that bus. She runs upstairs, changes into a pair of shorts and a T-shirt, then gathers all the money she's saved and sticks it into her pocket.

Merlin follows her up the stairs and then back down, and she has to scatter a bunch of treats all over the floor to get out of the kitchen without him. She slips down the front stairs and out the side door—and then she's on the sidewalk. Free!

When the bus comes right on time, she's exhilarated, paying her fare and getting a transfer. "I can get to the Broadmoor on the southbound bus, right?" she asks the driver, who is an older black woman.

She just nods.

There are not many people on the bus, and whatever city Katie goes to, it always seems to be the same ones: poor people who don't have cars, and teenagers, and disabled people who probably can't drive. Katie sits in the middle, by the window, and thinks of herself as a brave and interesting girl, off to an adventure. In her backpack is a newspaper with the address and information on the flower show in case she gets lost, and it shows photos of a zillion kinds of flowers. She can't wait.

At the downtown bus station, there are a lot of homeless men shuffling along, but Katie finds an older woman and sticks close by her, as if the woman is her mother or aunt, a trick her dad taught her. She has also learned that grandma women are the ones to ask for directions, and if a bus is crowded, she can sit beside them. Race doesn't matter—a white old woman or a black old woman or a Navajo old woman each offers the same protection.

Now she climbs onto the second bus and thinks about Lily, far away in Texas with her dad. It makes her feel a ripple of sadness. Why does everybody get to be with her father except her? She brushes the feeling away and shows the bus driver the ad for the flower show. "Where do I get off for this?"

He's a middle-aged man with a crew cut, and he's chewing gum, like a cop. "Sit right behind me and I'll tell you."

She rides to a ritzy part of town and admires the mansions on big plots of grass, and then they drive around a big hotel with the mountains very close behind it. The driver says, "This is it, kid. Go right—"

But Katie has spied the signs. "I see it!" She leaps up. "Thank you!"

Adjusting her backpack, she hurries toward the door, and even from twenty feet away she can see flowers through the door. Her heart begins to sing, and she can't stop smiling. The woman at the door sells her a ticket and says, "That is one happy face. We don't usually get a lot of young people on their own."

Katie can't stop looking into the room. "I've been looking forward to this for weeks," she says, and takes her ticket, putting it carefully into a pocket of the backpack.

And then it's as if her heart is filled with helium, because she practically floats around the show. There are little tickets and giant ribbons on the award winners. Typed cards tell the genus and species and—thank heavens—common names. She writes the names of the most beautiful ones in her notebook, which Lily said would help her remember things about gardens from year to year. She falls in love with a rose that looks like a fairy collapsed in a pile of silky red and yellow and silvery skirts, and with a spray of tiny green chrysanthemums, and she loves the orchids, which look like butterflies about to take off and fly around the room.

But it is the dahlias she has come to see, and when she finds the award winner—a pale peach-and-pink beauty that is bigger than her head, she starts to cry. A white-haired lady next to her says, "It's really something, isn't it?"

Katie can only nod, riveted. And in that instant she doesn't care if she gets in gigantic trouble. It's worth it.

For the rest of the afternoon, she takes notes and makes drawings. She asks questions and discovers that everyone wants to tell her their theories of growing. It's like a tribe with a special language, and she feels a creeping sense of excitement. Maybe this is where she belongs. Can people have jobs growing flowers?

All the money Ramona paid her for cleaning the bakery— which is sixty dollars, because they were at it for most of the day Friday and Saturday—isn't a ton of money in a place like this, where she can buy tiny potted plants and special bulbs and even some books. She's very hungry and has to buy a hot dog and a

Coke, which uses up five dollars. The rest she spends all on dahlias.

And then, because there is no way to get the box of potted plants home on the bus without hurting them, she asks a middle-aged woman close by if she has a cell phone and could dial a number for her.

"You go ahead, sweetie."

Katie takes a breath and dials the phone. When Ramona picks up, she can tell she's been hurrying. "Hello?" she says in an anxious voice.

"Hi, Ramona. This is Katie. I came to the flower show and I know you're really going to be mad at me, but I need a ride home. Can you come get me?"

"You are in so much trouble."

"I know."

"I'll be there in about a half hour. Are you okay? Is everything all right?"

Katie feels like she might cry over that. "Yes." Then, "Ramona?"

"Yes?"

"I'm really sorry. It was just something I had to do."

"We'll talk."

FORTY-SEVEN

Ramona

A fter the long, sick worry of the day—over Sofia and Oscar, over the whereabouts of Katie, over my chilling calculations of how much cash flow has been lost through this debacle—I find myself in the bakery kitchen at midnight. The hot-water heater was installed but, much to my vexation, the inspector did not make it here, no matter how I begged, meaning yet one more day of lost revenues.

But I have the mother doughs, all breathing and alive, waiting for me. One by one, I take the mothers from the fridge, stir the hooch vigorously back into the sponge, throw away half, and refresh it with whatever materials it demands. The cornerstone, Adelaide's mix, likes white flour. The one I've been experimenting with, a dark rye I want to mix with malt sugar and molasses, likes half white, half rye. The *levains*, those old-world sourdoughs, like a hint of whole wheat mixed with white, to give them some solid food.

In the still kitchen, with darkness lying over the world outside, I stir and smell and taste the mothers, tending to their good health so their offspring will be healthy and strong, so that the sponges can grow vigorously to leaven the breads they season. Adelaide's sponge is a stringy, powerful girl, and her acidity leaves giant holes in the bread, for that traditional sourdough look. Meditatively, I pull the elastic strings upward, watching the texture as the bands spring back down, almost like a thick rubber band. The smell is sharp.

I cannot sell bread, but that doesn't mean I am forbidden from making it. Choosing the Adelaide daughter, I quickly put together a sponge with salt water and white flour and put it in the mixer, with the dough hook turning.

I am not exactly thinking as I work, though I am aware of images skittering by, like goldfish in the depths of a pond—a flash of Sofia, of Oscar, of my mother, who called to let me know she was there and had everything under control.

It's the picture of Katie, waiting outside the flower show with a box of blooming plants, that surfaces most insistently. When I drove up, I was furious over the worry she caused me, fury that hid the terror over what might have happened to her.

And, in part, some of that terror stemmed from the truth about her father that I am hiding. How will it help her to know her father tried to kill himself?

Except that I promised to tell her the truth, no matter what.

When I pulled up to the building, she was standing against the wall in the sunshine, her skin golden, hair a mass of ringlets in toffee and yellow and gold. She had the flowers in a box in front of her, a parti-color shrub of beautiful blooms, and she was gazing down at them with a pensive expression, part astonishment and part pleasure.

"Get in," I said, and she hung her head but nestled the flowers carefully in the backseat before she got in the front beside me.

For a long time, neither one of us said anything. Then she said, "Thank you for coming to get me. I would have ridden the bus back, but I didn't want to hurt the flowers."

I nodded, mouth set so that I wouldn't say anything I didn't mean. Finally I managed, "You know that I worried about you, don't you? I couldn't find you, and I didn't know where you were, and terrible things went through my mind."

"Like what?" She made a noise. "It's not like there's some big river to drown in or a lot of creepy neighborhoods or gang-bangers around."

I looked at her, once again realizing what her world had been, what it is now. "It takes only one bad person, Katie."

"I know." She slumped.

"Why didn't you at least leave me a note? You always leave notes."

"Because I was mad, okay? You all let me down on this flower show, and it was important to me."

"It's not always about you, Katie! There's a lot going on. It was a flower show, not your only chance to go to college."

She crossed her arms over her chest. "It mattered to me," she said.

And neither of us said anything the rest of the way. I sent her to her room and made her put the flowers on the back porch in the shade. Her dog licked her face and cheerfully followed her upstairs, though I swear he gave me a conspiratorial look over his shoulder.

When the dough is finished, I put it in an oiled bowl, cover it with a damp flour-sack towel, and make a pot of coffee. My dilemma ping-pongs back and forth across my brain. *Tell her. Don't tell her. Tell her. Don't tell her.*

Ticktock, ticktock.

Herself comes down just before five a.m. "Can I help you with anything?" she asks, all meek and mild.

"No, thank you."

She leans on the counter. "What is that?"

"Oatmeal and whole wheat with sunflower seeds."

"Oh." She chews on her inner cheek. "I had a bad dream about my dad."

A ripple of unease disturbs the calm in the room. "What kind of dream?"

"That he died. That he didn't want to live."

Tell her. Don't tell her.

I shape the loaves carefully, rolling them into country rounds, my eyes on the flour. "Mmm."

"I'm kind of scared to see him," she says. She's rolling onto the outsides of her feet, then coming back to the soles, back to the outsides. Over and over. One hand is gripped around the other wrist. "I used to be really scared of this guy who was badly burned when I was little."

"I didn't know that," I say. "Tell me about him. How old were you?"

She shrugs. "I dunno. Maybe five or six or something. He came to the grocery store by our house. He had all this pink skin that was like muscles on the outside of his body, you know?"

The visual is acute, and I nod. For a minute I stop shaping the loaves.

"He didn't have any hair on the top of his head—no eyebrows, nothing—and he wore sunglasses all the time, so I think his eyes must have been bad. But the worst part was that he didn't have a nose. It was gross." She pauses. "I thought he was a monster. I cried whenever I saw him. What if my dad looks like that?"

I take a breath and give her the only possible answer. "You'll know what to do."

She folds her left hand into her right, and her feet come to the floor. "I'm going to plant my flowers."

Maybe I'll tell her over dinner.

Or tomorrow morning.

. . .

At midday, I'm rearranging the walk-ins when Katie bounces into the kitchen. "Your dad is here."

"My *dad*?"

"Yeah." She turns and points. "I brought him back."

I'm up to my elbows in bleach and rubber gloves, and I blow a lock of hair off my face. Sure enough, there's my father, dressed in his workday uniform of black suit with white shirt. No tie in the heat of the day. He looks good. "Hey," I say warily. "What's up?"

"Came by to talk to you. Got a minute?"

"Sure." I strip off my gloves. "You want something to drink? I can have Katie get us some tea from upstairs."

"That would be good. Thanks."

I give Katie a glance. "Will you?"

"'Course."

He looks around. He's never been here, because he was sulking. "You did all this design?"

"I had help, but mostly it's my idea, yeah."

He points to the oven yawning on the wall. "Wood-burning, huh?"

I nod.

"Smart." He nods, too, looking around, and I can read the approval on his face. "Great kitchen, kid. Looks good."

"Thanks." I point to the backyard. "Let's go outside, huh?"

In the years since my divorce, my father and I haven't had much reason to have long conversations. I see him at family gatherings—at Christmas and birthdays and that kind of thing—and we exchange the usual pleasantries, but that's about as far as it ever goes. When I was a child, he was the classic patriarch and not particularly chatty, so this is not a big change.

But it's weird that he's here. "So, Dad. What's up?"

He wiggles his nose, a habit born from allergies as a child. "I've got an offer here for you, Ramona."

"What? An offer for—"

"Let me finish. Ryan told me that you have trouble."

"Oh, great." He was the one I thought I could trust. "He had no right to—"

"Ramona. Please."

I take a breath. Nod.

"A lot of small businesses, especially restaurants and food service, have failed. You have resources in the family, and you don't have to be one of them." He takes out a manila envelope. "I've put together an offer. Take your time, look at it later. Maybe we can talk."

I shake my head. "I don't want to do that."

"Ramona." His steel-blue eyes are sharp. "Don't let pride lead you to a fall."

Katie comes with the tea. My father winks at her. "I hear you've been planting a lot of flowers."

"I have. Do you want to see them?"

"Maybe before I go. Give us a minute."

She nods.

I hold the envelope in my hand, smarting. Mad at my brother. Mad at the economy. Humiliated.

My dad drinks his tea. "I'm proud of you, Ramona. You've got guts."

"Thanks," I say, sure he's saying that only because my brother told him something.

He clears his throat. "Also, I'm sorry."

"For what?"

His mouth moves, and he keeps his gaze trained on the corn growing in the garden. "For not firing Dane. I should have. The job could have been yours."

"Did Ryan tell you everything? I'm going to kill him."

"He didn't tell me anything. I figured it out all by myself." Now he does look at me. His mouth twitches in amusement. "I was wrong, okay?"

"Okay. I'll take a look, Dad. No promises."

"None expected."

But right after his visit, the inspector arrives, and we're finally cleared for opening. I call my employees to tell them the good news. We'll be open for business tomorrow morning. Jimmy asks how dire things are. "Should I be looking for another job?"

"I won't lie." I sigh over the phone. "It's bad, but with a little luck we can make it up next weekend." There is a festival that brings in tens of thousands of people, and with all the promotions I've done over the past few weeks and the trades I've made with motels and hotels in the area, surely we can make up some of it. "We'll get our A game on and do the best we can."

"Yay, team."

"You're my quarterback."

Tattooed and pierced and be-ringed, Jimmy snorts. "Whatever, Coach."

That's when I take the envelope into the office and open it. There is a single sheet, outlining an offer to bring Mother Bridget's Boulangerie under the umbrella of the Gallagher Group for a sum that would put me well out of debt. Ownership would go to the corporation, but I would be the general manager of the bakery.

Autonomy and possible complete failure?

Or community and possible success?

How can I give up now? For the moment, I put the offer back into the envelope and slide it into the small wall safe.

I've invited Jonah over for dinner, since I won't have any time for the next five or six days, and it seems fitting to celebrate the green light for the bakery. As Katie and I prepare the meal, we're listening to her favorite, Lady Gaga, and I find I like dancing around to it, singing lyrics I know by osmosis. I've roasted some corn in the oven and cut the kernels off into a big bowl, then sprinkled sea salt over them.

Katie helps me toss the salad and squashes the avocados for guacamole. She, perhaps by virtue of living in El Paso, likes things much hotter than I can tolerate, and I caution her to go easy with the jalapeños.

"Wimp," she says, grinning.

"I just like the roof of my mouth."

I slice cold roast chicken and lay it out on one of my grandmother's plates, because I've been thinking of her and roast chicken was one of her favorites. Her recipe for roasting chicken is heavenly, but this is one I bought at the local organic-foods store, already cooked and studded with big flakes of black pepper. It's been busy, and I'm not much for cooking main meals. That was always Stephanie's great pleasure. Nibbling on tidbits of tender chicken and crackly skin, I think of the Erin again, the dated, sad look of it, the tired menu. Why hasn't she done anything about it? It's probably that my father is too stubborn to listen to her.

When everything is ready, we carry it all down to the backyard, where I've spread a tablecloth over the table, fastened down with rocks to keep it from blowing away. Merlin is playing in the grass, tossing around a ragged toy almost as if he is playing with someone. "That is one crazy dog."

When Jonah arrives, he brings wine and sparkling cider, big yellow daisies, and a CD for Katie. "Thought you might like this," he says.

She looks at him with suspicion. "You know I don't like classical, right?"

He grins, plucking a tortilla chip from the ceramic bowl. "What makes you think it's classical?"

"That's what you guys listen to all the time."

"Hardly!" I protest, and launch into the story of Jonah and the record store and the music we shared.

"And when was that, 1980-something?" Katie asks.

Jonah laughs. "Old school, right?" He uses the tongs to serve himself salad, wipes a little vinegar from his hands with his napkin, and says, "Just give it a try. If you don't like it, no problem."

After dinner, Katie, who has been very meticulous about doing chores since yesterday, clears the table, leaving the wine. "See you lovebirds laaa-ter," she says, and dances upstairs to read in the living room.

"Finally," Jonah says, and scoots closer to kiss me. His hand slides under my shirt at the back and moves in a circle that sends a shiver through my middle. Again I think, *How can I be both so happy and so worried? So content and so frantic?*

But maybe that's what life is—a mix. As we swing on the glider, I tell Jonah about Katie's trek to the flower show, and he tells me about the composition he has been working on. "Have you baked me a loaf of bread yet?"

"Is that what you're working on? Something that sounds like a summer evening?"

"With Ramona at the center."

"I suppose I should get busy, then."

"Time enough," he says. "Time enough."

FORTY-EIGHT

Katie

W hen she finishes cleaning up the kitchen, Katie signs on to the Internet to play around a little. She has two new emails. One is from her mother, the same one she saw yesterday. The other is a new one, also from her mother. In the subject line is *SORRY!* Katie's heart does this weird thing, a double bump.

She opens the email.

TO: katiewilson09872@nomecast.com
FROM: laceymomsoldier@prt.com
SUBJECT: SORRY!

OH HONEY, I JUST HERED THE NEWS BOUT YOUR DADDY SO SORRY.
YOU'RE PRACTICALLY AN ORPHAN NOW ARENT YOU? I WISH I COULD
CALL YOU AND MAKE SURE YOUR ALLRIGHT BUT YOU NOW I CAN'T
AND THAT I AM THINKING ABOUT YOU. COME SEE ME AS SOON AS
YOU CAN AND ILL HUG YOU AND HUG YOU ALL BETTER. YOU KNOW
YOUR MOMMA IS THE ONE YOU CAN DEPEND ON YOU CAN JUST
RIDE THE BUS, RIGHT TO THE OLD PLACE, WHERE I WAS B4 AND
THEN WE COULD GO WALKING IN THE PARK OR SOMETHING MAYBE
GET ICE CREAM, WHICH I KNOW YOU LIKE.
    LOVE MOM

Katie's hands are shaking as she reads through the note a second time. What does that mean, *practically an orphan*? It feels like her throat is closing up, maybe so she won't scream. She opens the first email to see if it says anything else, but it's only the usual thing. Nothing.

She closes her eyes. Something black buzzes right beneath her skin, at the back of her neck and down her arms.

Don't let him be dead.

But of course he wouldn't be. Ramona had promised to tell Katie the truth about her dad at all times.

But what if...?

A pain tears across the top of her stomach, and she can't even breathe right. Merlin comes over and urgently puts his head in her lap, as if he has heard some sound she didn't even know she made. He looks at her with whiskey eyes. For a second, Katie can't even move enough to pet him.

What would happen to her if her dad was dead? Where would she live?

After a long minute, she puts her hand on Merlin's head and threads his gold ear through her fingers, like the satin on a blanket. He licks her wrist. Slowly, patiently.

Go down and ask Ramona, a little voice in her head says, all reasonable.

But what if they're making out or something? They are so lovey-dovey it's embarrassing, and although she knows they're trying not to do anything in front of her, Katie had once accidentally seen Jonah slide his hands under Ramona's skirt. Barf.

She'll just make a lot of noise going down the stairs. Standing up before she can change her mind, she says, "Come on, Merlin."

FORTY-NINE

Ramona

J onah and I are swinging lazily back and forth on the
 glider, hardly even talking, when Katie comes crashing
down the stairs and yells out, "Ramona!"

There's something in her voice. I straighten, taking Jonah's
hand for courage. "Here I am!"

She is in high huff, but there's something so wild in her eyes
that I stand up, reaching for her even before she clenches her
fists and cries, "Is my dad dead?"

"No!" I bolt forward and put my hands on her thin arms. At
least there is some flesh to them now. "No, he is not dead."

"Promise?"

"Yes. Why are you asking?"

"My mother sent me an email and it sounded like my dad
was dead, because I'm almost an orphan."

I look over my shoulder at Jonah, who nods imperceptibly. I
should never have kept this from her. The weight of my betrayal
is gigantic, even more so since the adults in her life have let her
down over and over. Her dad, too. "There *is* something I need to
tell you, Katie."

She slides out of my grasp, almost visibly building armor.
Merlin comes and stands at her side, like a page or a bodyguard.
"What?" she asks in a harsh voice.

"There is no easy way to say this." I gather my breath and squeeze my hands together. "He's okay, but he tried to commit suicide."

Even in the evening light, I can see the color drain away from her face, leaving her as pale as the moonflowers she planted against the fence. "When?"

"The night before last."

"When did you find out?"

"Sunday night."

"And you didn't tell me?"

"I was just—"

"You promised you would tell me anything I needed to know." Her shoulders are shivering faintly. "I think this counts."

"Katie, I was trying to find a gentle way. I didn't want it to upset you. I didn't want you to feel so squashed—"

"He's *my* father, okay? Mine. Everybody else is related to him by marriage, but he is my own blood, and I had a right to know that right away. Right away."

"You did. I'm sorry. I made the wrong decision, but I was trying to protect you."

"I don't want to be protected!" she screams. Her fists are at her sides, balled up tight at the end of rigid arms. "I hate you! All of you! This makes me sick. I should be with him. He wouldn't do that if I was there!"

She bursts into tears, and I dive forward to put my arms around her. With a wild roar, she flings her arms upward to break my grip, a classic self-defense move. I stumble backward slightly, still reaching for her, and she bolts.

"Katie!" I cry, and run after her.

At the door, she halts, holding up a hand, palm out, her breath coming in ragged gasps, her face wet with tears. "Don't. I want to be alone."

With effort, I clasp my hands, step back. "I'm sorry."

She flings herself inside and I stand in the gilded light, staring after her. Cool air comes up from the grass. Somewhere, someone is playing music.

Merlin nudges my hand, licks my palm, then stands there looking at me. "She will not welcome me right now, sweetie." I open the screen. "Go with her."

He pauses, his tail low, his wise old eyes transmitting some message I don't understand. I wish I spoke Dog. "What is it?"

His tail waves slowly, and he looks back up the stairs.

"I know. Go to her. Take care of her."

He trots up the stairs, and I close the screen door. Jonah comes up behind me, his hand making a comforting circle on the top of my back. I step away. "I need to think. To be alone."

"I see."

My head is hurting as I think about all the things I should be taking care of and I'm not. Katie. The bakery. Sofia. Every one of the failure tapes I've been hearing off and on through my life is playing at full volume in my head.

"I was remembering the day your mother came into the shop and was so upset. Do you remember?"

"Oh, yeah. I was so humiliated that she misunderstood everything, that she made me feel like such a slut."

"And yet," he says in that smooth amber voice, his fingers touching my bare neck, "she was worried for a reason. There was a lot of electricity between us. You were so lonely and I was"—he takes a breath, blows it out—"lost. Sad. It could have been dangerous."

It is dangerous. It's too dangerous. "Jonah, I'm sorry, but I think I need to be alone."

He hesitates for a moment, then says, "Don't make trouble where there is none, Ramona."

"I'm not. Can you just give me a little space?"

"Absolutely." He raises his hands in surrender. "Call me."

When he's gone, I carry the wine inside and up the steps. Katie has done all the dishes and left the house kitchen exquisitely tidy. Seeing it, the action she took before she found out her father had attempted to kill himself—kill himself!—makes me furious. If he was close, I would shake him.

But anger will not help any of this. Squaring my shoulders, I head up to the third floor, where it's stuffy enough that I go into Sofia's bedroom first and open the windows. A breeze wafts through immediately, blowing away the scent of disuse.

Katie's door is closed. I knock. "Katie? Can I come in?"

"No. I don't want to talk."

I let the words fade away completely before I say, "I need to talk to you."

"No!" she cries, but I open the door anyway. As I come in, she screams, "Get out!" and flings a pillow at me.

I grab it and stop where I am. In here, it's cooler, with the wind coming through the screened balcony. "I'm sorry I didn't tell you."

She rolls away, pulling the pillow over her head. "Go away."

Merlin is sitting by the bed, guarding her. He's panting softly, giving his face the appearance of a grin. I think about that day I had hysterics after my mother hauled me out of the record shop, remembered how exhausted and overwhelmed I felt, by the pregnancy, by hormones, by the whole wide unfairness of the world.

How much worse to be Katie right now!

"You don't have to say anything, Katie, but I want to talk. Take the pillow off your head, please."

She hauls it off, leaving her hair in a wild mess over her wet red face. I desperately want to put my hands on her, smooth away her suffering, but I dare not. Suddenly I am my mother, looking down at me in my misery, helpless to change anything, and it makes me ache. "I wish things were better for you, sweetie. I wish I could wave a magic wand. But I can't. Nobody can make your life happy for you except yourself."

She sits up, her arms behind her on the bed, and looks at me with utter disdain. Her eyes glow against the tears. "Really."

"Sorry, that was stupid."

She stares at me, then, with an old expression, she says, "I've already heard all that stuff. You can't find a way to say it new." Her voice goes singsong. "'Things work out for the best. God has a plan. Life is what you make it.'"

I want to say I understand how it is to be exiled, to be alone with people you like but don't feel entirely comfortable with, to face something that seems almost insurmountable. But—and this is the first time I have ever had this thought—I had advantages that have not been given to her.

Still, in the mothering arsenal, it's about all I've got for this child in this moment. "How about, you didn't do anything to make this happen? How about, your dad loves you, but he's afraid? How about, you have a home here and you're safe and I care about you?"

Her voice is absolutely calm when she says, "Whatever." Her eyes bore into me. "Can I be alone now?"

My mother and Poppy tucked me into bed and left me to grieve. I can do the same for her. "Okay. Good night, sweetie."

FIFTY

Katie

After Ramona leaves, Katie sits up against the wall and stares out the window while the fan moves air around. Pretty soon Ramona will go to bed.

All of a sudden it's like she can see again after months of being in a bubble—a pink bubble where everything was all sweet-smelling and full of flowers and good clothes and the smell of bread. But tonight the bubble broke, and she can see that she has been really stupid. She's gotten as soft as a cheerleader living in one of those big houses near downtown El Paso. *Houses like this,* she thinks.

No wonder.

Bad things happen when you let yourself get soft. Over and over Katie has had to learn that lesson, so many times you'd think she'd remember not to do it. Soft as a little girl in her happy family, before her dad went to Iraq. Then her mom deployed, too, and she had to live with her grandma. Then everybody was home again—a happy soft life, until her mom and dad started fighting all the time and they got divorced. That was when Katie had to really learn to fend for herself, because her mom started using for the first time. When she went to live with her dad and Sofia, right after they got married when her dad was at Fort Bliss, it was good. It took her a while to like Sofia, but

Sofia was a good cook and Katie was only nine then and really hungry, so she liked to eat.

Now she is soft again. And maybe her mom isn't the greatest mother in the world, but she has been teaching Katie how to be tough all of her life.

And, honestly, who else does she have? Her coward of a dad, who tried to kill himself? Again the thought fills her with such a huge prickling of red spikes that she almost can't catch her breath. How could he *do* that to her? Her emotions are making so much noise that she can hardly think straight, even after two hours of crying.

The one thing she keeps thinking is that she needs to see her mom. Just go see her at the rehab. She has been thinking about that for a while and has even looked up the cost of a bus ticket, which is sixty-three dollars.

She hears Ramona turn on the shower downstairs.

Katie begins to make a plan. Some parts of it she doesn't like, but life has taught her you have to do what you have to do. Right now she has to see her mother.

FIFTY-ONE

Sofia's Journal

It's almost my mom's birthday. I'll have to remind Katie. If my grandmother is here, there won't be anyone to celebrate my mom's day properly, and after all the black balloons last year, she deserves something this year.

I've slept for almost two days straight through, and it's amazing how much better things look this morning. Oscar tried to kill himself, but he was not successful. I'm furious with him, but he's just in pain and lost and can't hear me. I'm not going away. I'm not going to let him down.

I'm so pregnant now, though, that it's kind of crazy. They sent me again for an ultrasound to make sure it wasn't two babies, but just like last time, it was fine. I'm just super-big, super-pregnant. It's a big baby. I think, more and more, that it's a boy. A big, hearty boy with arms and legs he keeps stretching into the sides of my body. A rambunctious boy who dances around in there like he has his own private radio station. I can't wait to see him, but once he's here, the scary part starts. As long as he's curled up there under my ribs, he's pretty safe.

It hit me last night as I was walking down to dinner that every single one of these soldiers was once a baby swirling around inside his mother's tummy. Every single one of them was a baby with a diaper, learning how to make noises for the first time and to spit SpaghettiOs all over the place.

And not just these soldiers here in this hospital, but all the others out there in the fields, on our side and the other side. All those fierce, bearded extremists were babies, too. That freaks me out!

It's starting to sink in that my mom is really not going to be here for the baby's birth. I love my grandmother, but I wish my mom was here. I know she cannot be here for the delivery, but it would mean a lot to me if she was, since Oscar isn't going to be there, either, unless I get wheeled into his room to go through labor. Which they probably wouldn't do, considering all the risk of infection.

Amazing how much better I feel after getting some sleep!

Later

I just had what my grandma Adelaide would have called a come-to-Jesus talk with Oscar. He was conscious again, feeling pretty sick, which serves him right. I stomped right up to the side of his bed and said, "Listen to me, Oscar Wilson. You are going to live, do you hear me? I need you. I love you. I am not giving up, do you hear me?"

He looked at me, his eyes so sad. "I can't do it, Sofia."

"Yes, you can." I kissed his fingers where they stick out of the bandages. "Listen, your daughter sent an email."

He swiveled his eyes up to the ceiling.

"Are you listening, Oscar? This is from the daughter who was living with her mother the crackhead, until I managed to get her to safety with my mother. Remember all that?"

He looked at me but didn't say anything.

So I read him the letter from Katie, which I glued in right here:

Dear Dad,

    It's kind of a big day around here. I cut my hair, which everyone has been trying to get me to do for ages, and it looks good, I have to say, all these curls showing up.

My hobby this summer, as I keep telling you, is flowers. I've planted so many it's crazy—geraniums and dahlias are summer flowers, and I love them. I also like the spring flowers that were blooming when I first got here (which is starting to feel like a different life to me!), which this old lady who visits says are lilacs. She's a big gardener, and Merlin, my dog, likes her a lot. He acts like a puppy when she's around. Sometimes I think she's kind of touched in the head, because the only time she talks to me is when she's in the garden, and she seems to forget things I've told her. But it's not touched in a bad way, just kind of like being old, you know? She knows everything about flowers, though, that's for sure.

Ramona got me a library card, so I'm reading a lot. I read seventeen books in June! That's a lot, even for me.

I wish you would write to me. I miss you and I love you. GET WELL SOON! Love (x10!), Katie

I folded the letter up and looked at him, and there were tears running out of his eyes. Which I took as a good sign.

"Next time somebody brings you some pills, you think about that daughter of yours when she hears the news."

He didn't say anything, but he didn't have to. I know the words went home.

My grandmother is coming to take me to dinner, so I'd better get ready.

Today is better. I don't know if he'll choose to live, but at least I'm back in the right place.

FIFTY-TWO

Ramona

My apprentices and I are awake and working by two this morning, just to have that extra bit of time. It's such a relief to be back at work, to have some way of forgetting about all the trouble in my daughter's and Katie's lives. Bread has always given me this, an escape. This morning, the rye starter is as dark and rich as the heart of a wild animal, and the smell of it is like earth and time and desire.

It is going to be a powerful bread, too powerful to be shaped into big loaves. I'm going to make small loaves studded with blue cheese, an old-world recipe that will please a certain contingent very much.

As I open the shutters and write the specials in neon, and the sun starts to tip above the edge of the earth, I feel a sense of possibility. Katie's flowers are blooming in profusion—exactly the same flowers, I suddenly realize, that my grandmother Adelaide had in this spot.

How extraordinary!

The sight of them draws me. Attired still in my chef's coat and tight braid, I walk down the sidewalk to admire the mix of daisies and blue bachelor's buttons she's planted along the wrought-iron fence.

"Ramona!"

I turn, thinking that the voice sounds very like my grandmother's, but no one is there. Looking up to the third-floor windows, I see movement, a head or body moving away. Katie must be up. Cheered, I head inside and up the stairs.

There is no one in the kitchen. Merlin is whining upstairs, and with an overwhelming sense of worry, I run up the last steps, panting by the time I reach the landing. Katie's door is closed, and for a single, searing second, my hand hovers over the doorknob. I'm afraid of what I might find.

Merlin, hearing me, barks sharply, and I open the door. Katie's bed is empty. Merlin is shut on the balcony, and I head across the room to let him in. He leaps through, whining anxiously, licking my hand, leaping toward the door. On the bed is a note. "Wait, Merlin."

He makes a noise of urgency. "Okay, okay." I snatch the note up as I rush toward the door.

Don't worry, it says. *I have something to do, but I will be fine.*

Oh, my God. What does that mean? Where has she gone?

Merlin is already at the foot of the stairs, waiting for me, and instead of going toward the backyard, he is most insistent that we go toward the front. After Katie, I suppose.

"I don't know where she went, Merlin. Wait."

He makes a pained, yipping noise and comes to take my hand, putting his teeth around my palm and then leaping backward. What can I do but find a leash and let him lead?

And I do follow, for about two blocks—when it becomes plain he will walk to wherever she is, and that's not possible. "Wait." I pull up on the leash, check the time, and tug him back around. He plants his feet and gives me a grave look. Not moving.

I think about all the child pornographers and kidnappers and rapists in the world, the sexual predators who would slurp her up without hesitation. Maybe Merlin knows something I don't. But when I let him lead again, he drags me toward

Colorado Avenue. There he stops, looking in both directions, a soft pitiful whine in his throat. He looks hard, as if he is listening, takes a step, stops. Looks up at me.

In my clogs and coat, I bend down and hug him. "It's okay." I pull back. "I promise we'll find her. Okay?"

His whiskey-brown eyes are grave. He almost nods.

We return to the bakery, and there are customers going up the walk, coming out. It shocks me a little to see business as usual. Leading Merlin around the side of the house, I let him free in the backyard, where he heads for the bench and sits down, making complaining noises to the invisible air.

Inside, I call Jimmy into my office. "I have a big problem. Katie seems to have run away, and I'm going to have to find her. If we don't stay open, the bakery will die. Can you cover it?"

"Yeah." She shrugs, pats a hand over her belly. "If I get in any trouble, I'll call Cat, right?"

"Actually, no. I'm going to make other arrangements. But thank you. I'll give you a raise. Someday."

She gives me a thumbs-up. "Get your girl."

I have no idea where to start, where she might be. Would she try to run all the way to her father? Go back to El Paso? The first person to call is Sofia, but I'm absolutely loath to add even a single minute of extra worry to her plate. The baby is due any day.

First I'll try some other things. In Katie's room, I look for the notebook she keeps, but it's gone—obviously with her. There's nothing else, really, except a letter from her friend Madison. It's written on pink paper and talks about a boy at the mall and getting a bra and nothing else. Still, it has a return address and a name I might be able to reach if I have to.

The next step is to try to open her email. It has a password, of course. I wonder if I can figure it out. The first thing I try is Merlin.

The account opens.

And there are the emails from her mother, manipulative and self-centered and begging Katie to come visit.

El Paso, then.

A half hour later, I'm at Jonah's door. He answers wearing only jeans, his hair tousled, and I realize it's not quite seven a.m. "Ramona, what's wrong?"

"Katie," I say, and tell him what I know. "I'm going down there to see if I can find her. I just wanted to let you know."

He runs a hand through his hair. "Give me ten minutes."

"You don't have to go."

He shakes his head, pushes open the screen door. "You aren't doing this alone. Come in and wait while I brush my teeth."

FIFTY-THREE

Katie

When the bus stops in Albuquerque, there's a layover.
Katie puts her sweater on her seat and asks if the
lady across the aisle will keep an eye on it for her. The woman
nods without smiling, and Katie heads for the bathroom to
brush her teeth and wash her face.

She got on the bus at one a.m., along with a guy who looked
like he might be a soldier, with that shaved-across-the-back-of-
the-head look, and two women who spoke only Spanish and
carried a baby. The people already on the bus were asleep. She
found an empty row and took the window seat.

It had not been that easy to get to the bus station at night, especially because she was worried about spending too much
money. Although she wasn't proud of it, she'd stolen money
from the bakery office, right out of the safe that Ramona never
locked. She took two hundred dollars in twenties, tucking them
into her bra, like her mom showed her, and feeling guilty because she knew very well that the bakery was hurting.

But so was her mother. So was Katie. She would pay it all
back.

In the end, she had to walk down Colorado Avenue, which
was a kind of busy street, to an all-night 7-Eleven. A guy with a

gold tooth was behind the counter, and he called her a cab without asking any questions. He probably thought she was older.

The cabdriver, though, wanted to ask a million questions and kept looking at her in the rearview mirror, which made her really nervous. Was he gonna call the cops on her? She said finally, "I live in a foster home, and I'm going to see my mom, who is in the hospital in El Paso."

"Wouldn't it have been better to do it in the daytime?"

Katie shook her head. "Nobody was gonna let me go." She looked at him in the mirror. "What would you do if it was your mom?"

He just nodded. When he dropped her off, he said, "Careful now, sweetie. The world isn't a very nice place."

"Believe me," she said. "I know that."

"Somehow I think you do."

It was also tricky to get a bus ticket, since the woman behind the counter said she needed an adult to buy it for her. Katie thought of her mom joking with some dealer, and said, "My mom's a meth addict. I don't think she cares if I take a bus to see my dad at Fort Bliss."

Her eyes softened. "He's a soldier, huh?"

Katie nodded. "He's been in Iraq, but he's out now."

The woman sold her a ticket for sixty-three dollars. When Katie settled into the seat by the window, she felt like crying and didn't know why. The bus was quiet and the baby fussed a little bit, and it seemed like the loneliest place in the world. If her head had been too noisy before, the silence seemed to echo now, and she didn't know what to do with it. She wished for Merlin. She wished for the smell of bread.

Get off the bus and go home, said a voice in her head.

And then she thought of her dad trying to kill himself, leaving her behind like she was some empty cup he was going to throw away, and she stayed where she was. Using her sweater as a blanket and her backpack as a pillow, she fell asleep and didn't wake up until they were outside Albuquerque.

In Albuquerque, it's pretty early and there aren't that many people around. A homeless guy with about twenty-seven years of grime on his neck and cuticles says, "Hey, girlie, you got some change for an old man?"

She shakes her head and pulls her pack closer to her. He calls out behind her, "Hope you're never hungry and homeless!" and for some reason it makes her mad. She turns around and glares at him. "I have been, thanks."

He looks sad, but Katie just stomps into the bathroom. She pees and washes her hands, carefully not touching anything without a paper towel. Looking at herself in the mirror, she sees that her face is greasy and there are bags under her eyes—eyes that look so mad bright that she wonders, with a fluttering in her chest, just what the heck she's doing here.

It passes. In the station, she finds a fake Egg McMuffin and a glass of orange juice. She buys a bag of Skittles from a machine and tucks those into her pocket, then she heads back to the bus.

It's still quiet. Other people are eating, too, and she can smell coffee. Unwrapping the sandwich, she stares out the window and waits for the bus to go, willing the seat beside her to stay empty.

In a few hours, she'll see her mom. Who has now been clean for two months, so she'll be in good shape. Once she sees her, talks to her, Katie thinks, she'll know what to do.

FIFTY-FOUR

Ramona

E l Paso is a ten-hour drive, straight down I-25 through New Mexico. Because I've been awake since two, I drink coffee and take the first shift. Merlin is in the backseat, his nose lifted to the two-inch crack at the window, but after a while he curls up on the blanket I put down for him and tucks his nose under his tail.

Jonah mans the CD player and eats a bagel and cream cheese we picked up at Starbucks. "Woman runs a bakery and I have to eat store-bought bagels," he says, lifting his eyebrow.

"I didn't know—"

"Joke!" he says, holding up a hand. The scent of his chai is exotic and pleasing, and I think that I don't know him well enough to be in love like this. He's essentially a stranger, someone I didn't even know existed a few months ago. It scares me, another layer of terror to add to the rest. I'm struggling to keep all my defenses in place. I've had a headache for two days, and that sense of threat that's been my ever-present companion has intensified times twelve.

If I hadn't become involved with him, would I have been a better guide to Katie? Would I have noticed more?

I'm grateful that he doesn't talk a lot. The music he plays is all upbeat and cheery, and I find myself letting go of the furious worry and anxiousness about everything and begin to see what's around us. Mountains; a sky so clear and blue it seems impossible that it isn't solid; fields of pale-green yucca and prickly walking-stick cactus. Jonah points to a herd of antelope, delicate and long-legged, springing across the landscape.

Driving becomes almost a meditation. There's something relaxing about the straight, clean, sunny highway rolling ahead of the windshield. I find myself letting go of a breath I've been holding since I found her note this morning.

"That's better," Jonah says.

"I'm still in shock that she did this, honestly. Stole money from me? Ran away in the middle of the night? She's been thriving here."

"She hasn't had an easy life."

"That's true. My mistake has been in forgetting that." I think about last night, standing by her bed, all the things I wanted to say and couldn't. "If Sofia had done something like this, it would have been dramatically awful. With Katie, I'm less worried because she's so street-smart, you know?"

He nods.

"I worry that she thinks she's savvier than she is, though. I mean, all it takes is one wrong move, and there you are with some bad man somewhere."

His finger moves on my arm. I move it away.

He says, "You or her?"

I glance at him. "I know, it's all mixed up together. The exile, the drama. But my parents, for all the mistakes they made, were always behind me. In my corner. What must it be like to have your parents really abandon you?"

"She's a strong kid. I've watched her. She's smart and astute and really good at getting her needs met. We'll find her, bring her back. She's going to be okay."

"It was a dozen little missteps, you know? She felt betrayed by my mother going to San Antonio, then I let her down over the flower show, and then I didn't tell her the truth when I should have." I look at him. "You know, no matter how hard you try, it's hard to be a good parent. You always drop the ball somewhere."

His eyes cloud. "Ethan was always so sick."

"I'm sorry. That was thoughtless."

"No, it wasn't. I hate when people tiptoe around it. It was hard to be a good parent to him, too. Hard to discipline him, and Claire, my ex, wouldn't."

"That is hard."

After a minute he says, "You know I'm not the enemy, right?"

I look at him. "Yes. That doesn't mean I think this is a good idea or that it's working out or—"

His chuckle surprises me. "It doesn't have to be decided today."

My phone rings. "Answer that, will you?"

"Hello," he says, "this is Ramona's phone. She's driving. Can I help you?" He listens for a minute, but I hear Sofia's voice, anxious and loud. Signaling, I head for the side of the road. "Hold on," Jonah says. "She's pulling over."

When I'm stopped, he hands me the phone. "Hi, Sofia. What's going on?"

"Where the hell is Katie? I had the weirdest email from her, and it sounds dire. I thought you weren't going to tell her about Oscar?"

"Her mother told her."

"How did her mother find out?"

"Through the grapevine somehow. I don't know. And because I didn't tell her, she has taken off, probably to go see her loser mother."

"She ran *away*, Mom? How could you let that happen?"

"I didn't *let* it happen. She's thirteen. Her mother is a crack-head and her dad is grievously injured and she feels betrayed on about a thousand fronts."

"But you were in charge of her!"

"Sofia! I'll thank you to lose that tone. I'm in the car, I'm on my way to El Paso, and I'm doing the best I can with a lousy situation."

"Sorry, but I am nine months pregnant and my life isn't the greatest, either, okay?"

"I don't want to have a fight."

"No, I know. Sorry." She sounds exhausted. "Why do you think she's going to El Paso?"

"I found some emails from her mom, trying to get her to go down there. I need addresses, phone numbers, anything you can give me. Do you know where her mom is in rehab?"

"I can get all of that. Damn it, I'm so mad at Oscar for this!"

The car is running under my feet. I turn it off to save gas. Lifting my hand to the back of my neck, I move my head back and forth to loosen it. "Me, too. But that won't help, either. I have to find her, and that means I can't be on the phone with you."

"Wait. Who's with you?"

I look at him flipping through a heavy CD case. "My friend Jonah."

"The sweater guy?"

He looks up and I realize he can hear her. "Yes," I say, meeting his eyes. "The sweater guy."

He smiles, and it hits me in the solar plexus. I want to cry and make love and hit him and scream and about a hundred other things. I bow my head, breaking away from his gaze. "Sofia, I have to go now. Get all those addresses and numbers together and then call me back."

"I will."

When I hang up, Jonah says, "The sweater guy?"

"I kept your sweater. It was with a bunch of stuff she used to like to go through."

"I don't remember a sweater."

"It doesn't matter."

He takes my hand. "Tell me."

"I wasn't planning to go to the shop, but I got stuck in a rainstorm. I was soaked when I came in, and you loaned me your sweater." I bend my head, feeling shy and silly. "It was—"

"I remember."

From here, those days seem so innocent. So much easier than this. I don't laugh. I can't look at him.

"Maybe I should drive for a while."

"Done. Merlin probably wants a potty break, too." I get out of the car and leash him, then walk him into the wide field beneath the bowl of New Mexico sky. Happy and sad, lost and found.

Let me find her, I think. *Keep her safe until I do.*

FIFTY-FIVE

Katie

When the bus pulls into El Paso, the sun is overhead and it's hot outside. Katie washes her face, changes into a pair of shorts, and heads for the city bus terminal.

She's tired in a way she'd forgotten about. Her shoulders ache, her eyes are grainy and dry from so much crying yesterday, and she's really hungry but not for junk food. Looking around, she sees a sandwich shop, which isn't open, and a diner and a convenience store. She ducks into the store and finds an apple and a banana and some pretzels. Later she'll eat with her mom, maybe. At a Village Inn or someplace like that, where they can have eggs and pancakes for lunch, the way they used to.

The bus maps here are familiar to her, and she's visited her mom at this rehab before, so she finds the right bus, pays the fare, and sits down. The city looks worn out, something she never noticed before. It's dusty and colorless and crowded, and it makes her feel lonely.

Why did she do this? What was she thinking? She doesn't want to see her mother. She doesn't want to live in El Paso anymore. She's mad, sure, but not mad enough that she wants to get swept into the foster-care system and lose everything she had.

Merlin! Her stomach sinks as she thinks of him. Her own special dog. Her *dog*. How could she have left him?

Tears choke her as a picture of his face moves over her imagination. She presses her fist really hard against the bottom of her jaw to keep from crying.

And then there is the bus stop. The one she remembers from before. She sits there for a minute, but when the bus starts to move again, she leaps up. "Wait! This is my stop! Sorry."

She's come this far. She might as well see it through.

FIFTY-SIX

Sofia's Journal

It's hot. My back is killing me. I'm thinking about Katie, wondering where the heck she might be. My grandmother went to the hospital chapel and lit a bunch of candles.

I marched into Oscar's room and told him that Katie had run away, that she found out that he had tried to kill himself. He looked shocked. "She ran away? Where is she?"

"They don't know." I had to sit down, because my belly makes my back sway so much it's hard to stand straight. "Probably to see her crazy mother."

"Jesus," he said, and it was the first time I've heard anything real out of him since he woke up. "I fucked up."

"Yeah." I was sitting there, rubbing my lower back with a fist, trying to get the knots out, and the baby was making a slow, hard turn that felt like a giant drum moving inside me.

"Sofia," he said, "I can't see you when you're sitting down."

"Yeah, well, my back hurts. You have to talk without seeing me."

"Baby." He held up one arm. "Please."

So I stood up, because that's me, Ms. Nice Guy, and Oscar, my big strong husband, had tears in his eyes. I put my hand in his and he said, finally, "I'm sorry." He brought my hand to his mouth. "I'm so, so sorry."

I kissed his fingers back. "We'll get through all of it, Oscar. Together. Okay?"

He nodded, and then I had to sit back down because my back was killing me. And now I've got to go find somebody, because it's hurting in a way I don't think I can handle for very much longer. Maybe there's some drug they can give me.

Ow!

FIFTY-SEVEN

Katie

There's some paperwork to get through, but Katie doesn't care. She's really sick to her stomach and knows this was the stupidest idea she's ever had, but her mom is right on the other side of that door and she has to see her now, doesn't she?

So she leans against her backpack, watching some Spanish soap opera. The door buzzes and then the room fills up with her mom. "Katie! Baby!" she yells, running forward.

Her voice is as loud as ever, but when Katie sees how much better her mom looks, her heart flips over and over, and she jumps up. "Mom!"

They hug, hard, hard, hard, right in the middle of the waiting room. Lacey smells like cigarettes and shampoo and a sweet, airy soapy smell that must be from the care package they sent her. Her arms are strong, and she's gained enough weight that she has a little bit of chest back. Katie is, however, a lot taller.

"Jeez, kid!" Lacey says, pulling back to look at her. "You've grown a half a foot since I saw you last!"

"Three and a half inches," Katie says, and laughs. "Can you believe it?"

"You look so beautiful! Look at your hair and your figure."

She steps back to look Katie up and down, holding on to her hand.

"So do you, Mom." And it's true. All the wounds and scabs are gone, and her hair is cut neatly at her shoulders. Katie can't remember the last time she saw it this short.

"You ready to go? We only have an hour. But we can go to the park up the way."

"Can we go get something to eat? I'm really hungry. I saw a Denny's up the street a few blocks."

"Oh, sweets, I'm sorry, but I can't be gone that long. Do you want to skip it, come back tomorrow?"

"No, it's all right. I can eat later."

"Good. Come on. There's a picnic table right by the river and it's real nice. You'll like it."

They walk across the street. Her mom has an ankle bracelet on, which is why they let her go, Katie guesses. The street is busy, but they cross at the light and walk six blocks up to a skanky-looking park with hardly any grass and a picnic table covered with gang graffiti. "This is it?" Katie asks.

"Oh, have you gone soft on me?" Lacey says. She takes a cigarette out and lights it, blowing smoke away from Katie but looking at her hard. "It looks worse than it is. I like to be by the river."

"Okay."

When they sit there, it isn't so bad. There's shade and the water sounds nice slushing by, though Katie suddenly remembers there are probably snakes in that water, not like in Colorado. Her mom asks, "How is your dad doing?"

Katie's heart goes hard. "I don't know. I'm not talking to him again."

"It'll be all right, kiddo." She smokes restlessly, her eyes moving all around them as if she's looking for someone. Katie feels a little uneasy and looks over her shoulder. No one is there.

"How much longer do you think you'll be in?"

"Damn, girl, forever. They want to keep me on this damned bracelet for two years, you believe that?" She puts out one cigarette after lighting another from the end of it. When she sees Katie watching, she says, "I know, I am working on it. There's just not much else to do but smoke in there."

"You're doing good. Maybe when they let you out, you could come to Colorado. It's beautiful there."

"Yeah? You like it, huh? All those rich bitches taking care of you, I guess you would. They sure must be feeding you, because I can see with the naked eye that you've gained weight."

Katie flushes. "I'm growing. I need to eat."

Lacey narrows her eyes. "My mama was as big as a cow. Long as you remember that, you'll be fine."

Katie realizes she should have gone to the bathroom inside the treatment center. It's been a long, long time, and she suddenly has to pee really bad. "Is there a bathroom in this park?"

"Yeah, baby. It's right over there, that white building."

"Is it safe?"

"Of course. And even if it wasn't, I'm right here. You'll be in my sight the whole time. Don't sit down."

Katie smiles. "No way." She slides the pack off her shoulders. "I'll be back."

Lacey taps the ash off her cigarette. "I'll be waiting."

Inside, it isn't as bad as it could be, just a normal park kind of bathroom. There are even paper towels, and Katie uses them to cover anything she has to touch, then comes out and washes her hands. Her face in the grimy, spotted mirror looks bad—circles under her eyes and her mouth all sad.

It suddenly hits her that this is how she used to look all the time.

Why in the world would she want to go back to this?

Splashing cold water on her face, she thinks about Ramona and how worried she must be. She thinks about her bedroom and her flowers and *pain au chocolat,* with all the layers of pastry, crisp and buttery, falling to pieces on her plate. *I want to go back.*

She'll be in major, major trouble.

But it won't be as bad as this. Taking a deep breath, she dries her hands and face and decides to endure the hour with her mother, then she'll ask the desk clerk to call Ramona.

When she steps back outside, the sun is in her eyes and she doesn't understand what she's seeing right away.

Her mother is gone.

And so is the backpack with her clothes and all the money.

FIFTY-EIGHT

Ramona

We get to El Paso at about six p.m. Jonah drove the last three hours, so I slept, and I'm anxious but not exhausted when we arrive. "What first?" he asks.

Sofia emailed directions to the rehab facility, and we head there first. My heart stops when I see a cop car in front and two officers interviewing people in the main room as we go in.

"Excuse me," I say to the woman behind the counter. "I'm looking for Lacey Wilson."

"You and everybody else." She jerks a thumb toward the cops. "She left on a pass with her daughter at about two, and we haven't seen her since."

"Her daughter was with her?"

A nod.

"Do you know where they went, where they might have—"

"Lady, if I did, the cops wouldn't be here now, and my job is in serious trouble thanks to that crackhead, so if you don't mind, I'm going to shut you off now, all right?"

Jonah leans in and uses his magic voice. "Where do people usually go when they get visitors?"

"Across the street, to a park by the river."

We start there, and when we find nothing, we head to the Petroskys' house. There is no one home.

"Why didn't I ever buy her a cell phone?" I say without expecting an answer. I know the reason is that I didn't think I could afford it, but I'd planned to see that she had one for the fall when she started school.

Jonah stands with me, not speaking. Merlin is hanging his head out the window, whining, and I let him out of the car to do his business. We wait there for a long five minutes, and I finally admit, "I have no idea what to do next."

"Maybe we should have something to eat, find a room for the night, and brainstorm."

I feel sick to my stomach. "Where could she be? Why would she go with her mom anywhere?"

Jonah just shakes his head. Then he says, "Her mom's an addict, right? So why would she run unless she wanted to use?"

"Ah, right."

"Do you know where Katie was living before she came to you?"

"No." Merlin leans on my leg, and I remember that Katie said she found him near the railroad tracks. "In a house by the tracks somewhere. I got the impression it was sort of homeless territory."

"We could drive around, see if we can find something like that if you want to."

Merlin climbs into the backseat. Maybe he'll help us. "Yeah. If we don't find any leads by nine, we'll eat and go to bed."

"Deal."

But we don't find anything. Exhausted, we head for a Village Inn, and my cell phone buzzes with a text from an unfamiliar number.

Help. I'm at a coffee shop in El Paso. So, so, so sorry about everything. Can you help me? Katie.

I text back:

Address?

She gives it to me.

STAY RIGHT THERE!

I ask the waitress for directions, and she sends us barely two miles down the road. When we pull up in front, Merlin goes insane barking and flinging his body around the backseat, and I have a hard time even getting him on his leash. When he leaps out, I see Katie, too: She's looking forlorn, in a booth with a glass of water and nothing else, staring out the window into the darkness.

The moment she sees us, she's on her feet and running, out the door before we reach it. She launches herself into my arms, full body weight, and I catch her close to me, hugging her, and both of us are crying. "I'm so stupid, Ramona. I'm so sorry. My mother stole everything from me, all my clothes—my new clothes!—and the money I took."

Merlin is wiggling, whining, and shoving himself between our shins, but still Katie clings to me.

I hold her as tightly as I can, so enormously relieved that my legs are shaking. "It doesn't matter. I'm so glad you're safe. So glad." I kiss her curly hair and breathe in the slightly sweaty teenager smell of her neck. Love sloshes through me like the ocean, changing me forever and ever, giving me yet another hostage to fortune. "Let's go."

"Can we eat? I am so, so, so hungry."

"Of course." I look at Jonah over her head, and he nods.

Katie, Merlin, and I take one room and Jonah takes the room next door. Katie calls Sofia from my phone and talks to Lily, too, then we all crash like the dead.

Naturally, I awaken long before anyone else. Leashing Merlin, I walk for a couple of miles in the cool morning air, mulling things over. The long, quiet drive had given me plenty of time to think, and I've come to some decisions about the bakery, and Katie, and my life.

I can't continue to live so precariously, with the bakery so close to the edge. I'm exhausted, and it isn't fair to my employees or my customers to teeter on the brink of disaster all the damned time. I don't want to lose it, but I am also really tired of working so many hours with no time for a life. I need balance, which I haven't had since starting to build the bakery.

It's time to make a decision. If I sell the business to the Gallagher Group, I'll lose some autonomy, but I'll gain some freedom and peace of mind. It might ease things with my family, as well.

I also have been thinking of Katie's presence as a temporary thing, but she's with us now for good. Me, or Sofia and Oscar and the new baby, or whatever arrangement we make. Sofia will need me, that much is clear—she'll need all of us. *Oscar* will need all of us—his wife and his children, his mother-in-law and all the rest of my clan, annoying as they can be.

And Katie needs us all, too. My mistake has been in thinking that she could heal from all her wounds if I simply fed her well and helped her find some hobbies and loved her. In time, all those things will help, but she also needs some therapy, some professional help, to allow her to express whatever she's feeling, to work through the shit that's been piled on her poor young head.

Finally, I think about Jonah. As I walk along the road, just the thought of him makes my throat hurt. I am in love. I don't know what to do with that.

I've had three cups of coffee in the attached restaurant before the other two awaken. They come into the restaurant looking sleepy and tousled. Jonah's eyes are a little swollen, and he has a slight cowlick in the back of his hair. His jaw is bristly, and he rubs it apologetically. "I didn't bring a razor."

"Looks sexy. Very 1985."

His eyes crinkle at the corners. "A very good year."

The waitress brings water and menus. Jonah asks for hot tea. "And will you do me a favor and make sure the water is very hot?"

Katie asks, "Can I have coffee?"

I shrug. "Sure." Then, "Tomorrow is my birthday," I announce. "And I was wondering, Jonah, if you have a couple of days to spare."

"Yes!" He takes my hand. The hope in his face makes me feel slightly ashamed of myself for making him suffer when he's been so . . . steadfast.

Yes. Steadfast.

"Wish I'd known sooner," he says.

"When is yours?"

"November twenty-ninth."

"Katie?"

"February second."

"Good." I take a sip of coffee and lean forward. "I believe in birthdays. I think they're important, and I like celebrating my own just as much as everybody else's. So what I was thinking is that I want to drive to San Antonio."

They both look at me blankly for a minute. "It's about a twelve-hour drive," Jonah says.

"Like today?" Katie asks.

"Yes. And yes. I'd like to see Sofia and Oscar, and I think you, Katie, need to see your dad. It'll be good for both of you."

She looks down. Her mouth gives away her fear. I reach out and take her hand. "Look at me, honey."

There's a sheen over her pale-green eyes when she does.

"When I was young," I say, "I never liked babies. They seemed really boring and loud and I didn't get why everybody thought they were so cute."

She looks perplexed. "Yeah?"

"To be honest, I still don't get terribly excited about most babies. But when Sofia was born and they put her in my arms, she was the most beautiful thing I'd ever seen. I couldn't believe how much love there was inside me, how big my heart got." I pause. "That man who used to frighten you was just a random man. When you see your father, you will see your father."

The glycerin swell of tears spills over. "What if I don't?"

I consider for a moment. "You can decide then what you want to do, how to proceed."

She nods. I let her go. "It's nonnegotiable, anyway. You're going with me."

A scowl wrinkles her forehead. "You're bossy."

"Yes, I am, because I am your guardian and I've been tiptoeing too much. Things are going to change a little. You are going to have to make restitution, and you will have to do some things when we get home if you want to live with me—"

"Like what?"

"We'll talk about that later. I do want you to know that you don't have to lug around a big bag of guilt over all this. I know you're upset. I know you're hurting, and that is going to take some time to get better, all right?"

She bows her head. "Thank you."

"In the meantime, I want to go to San Antonio. We'll have a real live road trip. Eat at greasy diners and listen to bad radio and whatever else goes along with that."

"Candy," Jonah says. "You have to have some candy in the car. Pixy Stix and sour cherries."

"Oh, yeah," Katie chimes in. "And those teeny chocolate balls. What are they called?"

"Sixlets," Jonah says, and holds up his hand for a high five.

"Dude," she says, "you do it like this." She punches forward, and he meets it.

"So we're in?"

"I am," Jonah says.

"I am," Katie echoes.

"Let's do it, then!"

FIFTY-NINE

Sofia's Journal

I am so tired of this heat and this eternal backache, I could scream. I want to go home and eat something I cooked, sitting at my table on a chair, not on a bench with twenty other people. I want to take a bath and read. I want to have this baby. When I walk in the hallway, I feel like some big ship sailing over the ocean. All I am now is pregnant, an oven with a giant bun risen to bursting. I'm not a woman or a friend or a granddaughter or a wife. I feel like I'm swimming through something thick and clear that muffles everything. I can hear people talking to me, but nothing much reaches me. Not that they know. I can fake it. My grandmother has been wonderful, picking up the things I can't figure out anymore, bullying orderlies to take care of Oscar first, bringing magazines and sandwiches and fruit. She's such a general.

Katie is safe, and that's important. My mother found her, as I guess I knew she would. She's pretty mighty, my mother. In all of this, I keep wanting her, like she's my handmaiden or something—Mommy, Mommy, come take care of me—and yet there's her life going on, taking some new turns, and I would love to hear about them, but maybe another day when I'll actually remember.

I am going to be pregnant forever.

SIXTY

Ramona

We pile into the car—Katie with a big paperback she bought at the drugstore, Merlin with a shiny new harness around his chest to make it easier to let him out to exercise, and Jonah with a bag of candies. The one fly in the whole thing is that my phone is dead, and in all the confusion I forgot to bring my charger. I looked for one in the small town we passed right after I realized it was completely out of power, but no luck. It's weirdly unsettling to be out of touch. Jonah has his, in case of emergencies, but I don't have access to the numbers on my phone.

It occurs to me that only a person middle-aged or older would make this mistake. Anyone younger is so attached to her phone she'd probably have spare chargers everywhere—purse, car, whatever.

Anyway, we're going to surprise Sofia, so it doesn't matter. I keep imagining her face when she sees us.

We take turns with the radio, Top 40 for Katie, classical for me, some jazz for Jonah. When the radio loses reception, we play CDs from the little suitcase Jonah has brought along.

We sing. We talk, all of us shifting the positions of the passengers and the driver: me and Jonah in front, then Jonah and me, then Katie and me, then Katie and Jonah. The person in the back sleeps with the dog or reads. It is not the most inspiring landscape, largely empty and windblown, as you might expect of West Texas, but I am still cheered by the simple act of travel.

We arrive in San Antonio at eight p.m. I'm not sure exactly where the hospital is, but Jonah finds that information on his phone, and we all agree that it's not so late we shouldn't give it a try.

As we enter the hospital, I'm nervous. I take Jonah's hand. Katie, uncharacteristically, takes my other hand. A volunteer at the visitors' desk tells us it's almost too late, but we have fifteen minutes. That's long enough.

In the elevator, we are quiet. The hospital is settling in for the night, with nurses talking quietly at the station and visitors saying their goodbyes. Most of the doors are propped open to show burn patients in various states of wrapping. They watch television, sit with friends or parents. A pair of toddlers play hide-and-seek in the waiting area, a mother bent into a phone nearby. She looks exhausted.

Katie stops as we near Oscar's room. Her hand is on her belly, and she's panting softly. "I don't know if I can do this."

"You don't have to." I don't let go of her hand. "If you aren't ready—"

A woman comes out of a room just ahead of us with a bundle in her arms, and even though I can't see her face, I recognize my mother's style at a hundred paces. A crisp sleeveless blouse, white trimmed with peach accents, and peach capris, and—

She's carrying a *baby*. "Mom!" I cry out without thinking, dropping both Katie's and Jonah's hands.

Lily turns, her mouth falling open for a second before she gets the biggest smile on her face. "Well, look who's here," she says in a mom-to-baby voice. "It's your grandma."

She brings the baby over, and it's plain he's a boy—a big, hearty creature, with giant hands and a headful of black hair. "Oh!" is all I can manage as she nestles him into my arms. His face is bruised and a little swollen from the trauma of birth, but his eyes are distinctly, clearly the same color as Katie's and Oscar's. He yawns and then looks at me, calmly and easily, and in that very second I am smitten. Falling down the rabbit hole of love all over again. It makes me dizzy, and, helplessly, I look up to find Jonah's face. He smiles broadly.

Breathless, I bend back over the baby, kiss his forehead. "Hello, little man. What is your name?"

"Marcus Gallagher Wilson," my mother says. "He was nine pounds, fourteen ounces."

I blink at her. "What? How is my daughter?"

"Fine. That child was born to have babies, Ramona. We'll go see her in a minute." She lifts a hand, scoops Katie into our circle. "Come see your brother."

She edges closer, all limbs and bristling joy and fear and anticipation as she bends in to look at him. "Oh," she cries. "He's beautiful!" At the sound of her voice, his head whips around. Babies are not supposed to be able to track, but this one knows that this voice matters.

"He knows his sister is here."

"Look at his fingernails! Oh, and look at his palm!" She touches him reverently.

"He needs to go back to his mommy right now," Lily says, and gives us directions to the maternity ward. "Come find us when you're done."

"Is Oscar awake?"

"Yes. Only one at a time."

"Okay."

Katie looks at the door.

"You're his blood," I say. "His only daughter. You go."

She swallows, smooths her hair. And opens the door.

SIXTY-ONE

Katie

It's kind of dim in the hospital room, only the light from the television flickering. Katie's heart is pounding really hard, so hard that it's making her hands shake, and she feels like she might cry.

In the bed is a person under the blankets. There are a lot of bandages, around arms and a head. His head turns and he sees her. "Katydid!" His voice is just the same. He sounds shocked.

She stands by the door, not sure what to do exactly. It's been more than a year since she's seen him, anyway, since before his last deployment. "Hi, Dad."

"How did you get here?"

"Ramona."

He is in the shadows. Katie can't see much, really. She feels frozen where she is. "Did you see your brother?"

"Yeah, he's really cute."

"He looks *just* like you. Except you were always more of a girly-looking thing than that. He's a bruiser."

He sounds exactly the same. Exactly, exactly the same. Without knowing that she would, she says, "I'm mad at you, Dad. I'm really mad that you tried to kill yourself."

"Baby, come here." His tone is the one you don't disobey, and it pulls her across the room to his side. "Give me your hand."

She raises it and he takes it in his left. His right is bandaged, and it is the right leg that's missing beneath the blanket. His forehead is not messed up and his eyebrows are growing back in, like they were singed off. She can't see his nose, but all of a sudden she's not afraid anymore. It's like Ramona said. Somebody else all burned and scarred would freak her out, but this person in this bed is looking at her with her dad's eyes and talking to her with her dad's voice.

"I was wrong," he says. "I was being a coward. I'm sorry."

And at that, Katie splits open like an overripe watermelon. "I went to see Mom, and she stole all my stuff and left me in this creepy park, and I didn't know where to go or what to do." She's crying now, and her dad is holding her hand really tight. "And she's not ever going to be well, even though I wanted her to be, and I need you to be alive, or I won't have any parents at all."

There are tears in her dad's eyes. "I promise you, Katie, that I am not going anywhere. And if I look as if I'm going to, you just take my leg off and hit me with it, all right?"

She laughs and has to cover her face, because her nose is getting all snotty.

"Give me a hug, Katydid, and then I gotta get some sleep."

She sniffs hard, then gingerly presses her cheek into his shoulder. But he lifts his left arm and grabs her tight. "I love you."

"I love you, too, Dad."

SIXTY-TWO

Sofia's Journal

JULY 15, 20—

I am a mother!!!!! That backache turned out to be labor, and by the time I got to the delivery room, I was in transition, so he was born two hours later. Big baby! They got him cleaned up and weighed and all that, got me all cleaned up and stitched (ow, it hurts to pee!!!!!!!!), and then they brought him back to me, all wrapped in a little white blanket. His poor face is smushed and his ears are all battered, but they said he'll be fine in a day or two. I nursed him and nursed him and nursed him, and he took to it like a champ, no problem at all. But then, I would guess he had to be pretty hungry. Nearly ten pounds! Holy cow.

He's fussing again. Gotta go.

SIXTY-THREE

Ramona

I spend the morning of my birthday with Sofia and Marcus. My daughter is beaming, awash in hormones and love and the possibility that life might work out all right. Nursing her son, her hair tied back in a ponytail, she says, "I had no idea you could feel love like this. I mean, I love Oscar, and you, and drinking margaritas, and all kinds of other things, but..." She shakes her head. "Nothing ever felt like it was going to swallow me whole."

"I know."

She looks at me. "It must have been so hard for you, Mom. You were so young."

"No. There was a day, when I first met Jonah, that I was in the record store and he played a record of Spanish guitar. You started to dance in my belly, and that was it. When I saw your face, it was like I already knew you, that you'd been in my world forever."

She nods, cupping the baby's head with her hand, ruffling his hair. He makes snorting sounds as he gulps milk. "Yes. Exactly." Leaning back on the pillows, she says, "I love the way Jonah looks at you."

She met him this morning, before he went out to do mysterious things, as my mother and Katie had done. He took her hand and gave her his gentle smile and said, "At last we meet," which made her laugh.

"How does he look at me?"

"What, are you kidding? You haven't seen it?"

"I don't know."

"Well, I wouldn't want to spoil it for you. Maybe you should notice." She strokes the baby's cheek. "Even better is how you look at him." She smiles her old-soul smile. "Like he's the morning."

I cover my face. "How embarrassing."

"No. It's great. He's the one, you know."

"The one?"

"Yeah. The. One. The one you've been waiting for. The one you want. The one from every song ever sung about love."

"We'll see."

She nods. "*You'll* see. I *know.*"

My mother, whose hotel room has a kitchenette, went shopping with Katie in the afternoon, and the pair of them have prepared a feast to serve in the courtyard of her hotel, not far away from the hospital. The air is soft and warm as we arrive, the night filled with crickets and, far away, the sound of music. There are tacos and strawberry shortcake and candles all in pink and white and red.

My mother comes forward, crisp and pressed. "Jonah," she says, holding out her hand. "We didn't have a chance to talk last night. How extraordinary that you are here."

He nods, grasps her hand, covers it with his own. "I am glad to see you again after so long. You look just the same."

"No, I don't, and neither do you, but I would have known you anywhere." For a minute she peers at him, then, finding whatever she was looking for, gestures for him to sit down. Merlin sidles up to him and flops down happily.

"Happy birthday, sweetheart," Lily says to me, kissing my cheek.

We settle in for serious feasting, talking about Marcus and Oscar, who has been cheerful if easily wearied today. Then my mother tells us the story of Sofia going into labor without knowing it. "That isn't how it happened with me," Lily says.

"What was it like, Lily," Jonah asks, "the day Ramona was born?"

She smiles and looks at me. "It was hot. Really hot. I was tired of being pregnant, and grumpy, and there was a thunderstorm every afternoon. Her dad was working twenty hours a day at the Erin, and he wasn't around. I was mad at him, too.

"When the lightning started, I knew the baby was coming, so I called my mother and she went with me to the hospital. Complaining all the way, of course, that my husband should be there, that men should take more responsibility."

I laugh. To Jonah and Katie, I say, "Let's just say she didn't have a lot of faith in the male of the species."

"Right." Lily brushes crumbs off the table. "So we got to the hospital and they whisked me away and it took about seven hours, but Ramona finally ambled into the world. And my mother"—she shakes her head—"who was not the best of mothers by anyone's measure, that woman took one look at Ramona and her red hair and fell head over heels in love. Right there, that minute. I think you changed your grandmother," she says.

There's such a wistful note in her voice that even Katie notices. She puts a comforting hand on my mother's arm. "She didn't mean to hurt you, your mom. Adelaide told me she always felt bad about it."

For a long, utterly quiet second, the air is charged. Finally my mother says, "What?"

"Adelaide told me, that lady who comes to pick the flowers."

A shiver runs down my spine. "Are you sure it was Adelaide?"

"Yeah. She's the one who taught me that rhyme:

> *One for the cutworm*
> *One for the crow*
> *One to rot and one to grow.*"

I think of the flowers in the front of the house, the bachelor's buttons and daisies. "Did she tell you how to plant the front yard?"

"Yeah, and she was right. It looks good." Katie glances between my mother and me. "She told me it was okay, that Ramona said it was all right."

"Honey, are you *sure* her name was Adelaide?" Lily asks.

The mood is so odd, Jonah takes my hand.

"Well, it's not exactly a name I'd make up. She's always forgetting to put her tooth in."

"Her bridge?" I ask.

"Yeah." She picks up a tortilla and rolls it into a tube. "She's the one who told me about your mom beating you when you were fifteen and that you felt bad the summer Ramona got pregnant and—"

"Stop," my mother says, and stands up. Her face is pure white. "This is a terrible joke."

"Mom," I say, and take her hand. "Sit down."

Katie looks stricken. "What did I do?"

"Nothing," I say. "Everything Adelaide told you is true." I keep a hand on my mother's shoulder, not letting her fly away.

"Well, I think I should say the last thing," Katie says, "which is that she said that your mom was always sorry and never found a way to make it better."

My mother's hand is visibly shaking as she reaches for Katie.

In a voice that I know means she is struggling for control, she says only, "Well, the next time you see her, you tell her that I forgave my mother a long time ago."

Katie frowns. "What is wrong with you guys?"

"Nothing, sweetie. Thanks for the report." I rub my hands together. "Now, isn't it time for presents?"

Jonah stands. "I'll be right back."

When he heads for the car, my mother leans in. "He really grew into his looks, didn't he? But such a shame about that hand."

"Mom!"

She straightens. "It's true."

When he returns, Jonah is carrying a guitar. As he lopes across the grass, I am fifteen again, and he is a little too old for me, his long brown hair loose on his shoulders and my young heart full to overflowing. The two Jonahs meld as he sits down in front of me and meets my gaze. "I wrote this in the summer of 1985," he says, "and it's called 'Ramona.'"

He begins to play. It is Spanish guitar, mournful and joyful all at once, full of the contradictions of life, of love. I see the colors of that summer winding around the notes, the gray of the clouds, the promise of our connection, and I smell bread.

And whatever else happens, whatever else I might know later, I know that even if soul mates don't exist, this one time the heavens or the Fates or whoever is in charge has made an exception.

When he stops playing and raises his head, vulnerable and shy and waiting, I stand up and kiss him with all of that on my mouth. What's one more hostage to fortune, after all? "I love you," I whisper so quietly only he can hear. He hugs me so hard I think it might break my ribs.

"I love you, too."

Behind us, Katie cheers and claps, and my mother, who I suspect is wiping away tears, joins her a split second later.

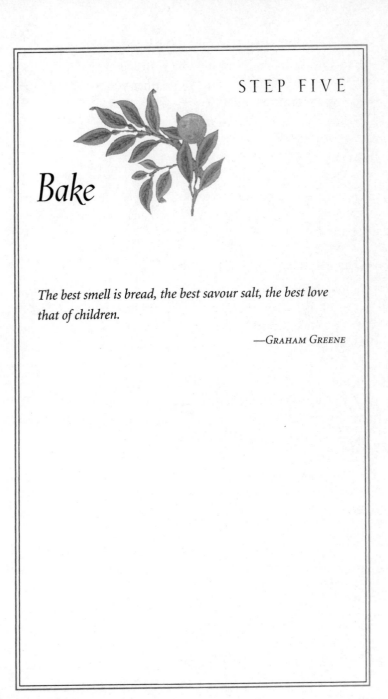

Bake

The best smell is bread, the best savour salt, the best love that of children.

—GRAHAM GREENE

SIXTY-FOUR

Katie

She's wearing a dress for maybe the third time in her entire life. She likes the way it swings around her legs as she cuts dahlias from the garden. Her father is coming home today, and Katie is moving in with him, Sofia, and her little brother, Marcus, who is the cutest baby she's ever, ever seen. Katie is glad, but she's also going to miss living here over the bakery, with all the smells of bread, and the garden, and her bedroom overlooking the back and the mountains. Ramona says the room is hers forever now, and she can come stay whenever she wants. Katie can tell Ramona is emotional about her moving. She keeps hugging her at odd times.

Which is why she's collecting the flowers, finding the very best ones from the entire garden. The kenora majestic is blooming, as big as Katie's head, and three of them fill a vase. She tucks in some asters, a soft bluish purple, and stands back to admire it. Behind the vase rises the house, and high up in the trees is her bedroom.

Ramona sold the bakery to the family corporation last month, and ever since, Lily and James have been over a lot. Ramona still runs the place, but her family—as she says herself—likes to be in the middle of things. This way she has the business and her grandmother's house, and she has access to the accountants and businesspeople in the corporation. She also has backup if she wants to travel, which she does, with Jonah, maybe next summer when everything is more settled.

A breeze rustles through the trees, and Merlin leaps up, rushing toward the back of the garden with a little yip. Katie freezes.

Because it turns out that the name *Adelaide* is the name of Ramona's grandmother. Which means that maybe the old lady who talks to her is a ghost.

She's afraid to turn around, and then she does.

No one's there. Only Merlin, acting silly, as if someone is there. When Milo comes sauntering out of the corn, Katie lets go of a breath and shakes her head at herself. Imagining things.

She picks up the vase of flowers and carries it inside, leaving it on the table for Ramona to find later. She bought a card with a picture of a woman and a little girl dancing. For a long time, she struggles with what to say exactly, and then it comes to her.

Dear Ramona,
I love you. Thanks for everything.

Katie

ABOUT THE AUTHOR

Barbara O'Neal fell in love with food and restaurants at the age of fifteen, when she landed a job in a Greek café and served baklava for the first time. She sold her first novel in her twenties, and has since won a plethora of awards, including two Colorado Book Awards and *six* prestigious RITAs, including one for *The Lost Recipe for Happiness*. Her novels have been widely published in Europe and Australia, and she travels all over the world, presenting workshops, hiking hundreds of miles, and, of course, eating. She lives with her partner, a British endurance athlete, and their collection of cats and dogs, in Colorado Springs.

ABOUT THE TYPE

This book was set in Minion, a 1990 Adobe Originals typeface by Robert Slimbach. Minion is inspired by classical, old-style typefaces of the late Renaissance, a period of elegant, beautiful, and highly readable type designs. Created primarily for text setting, Minion combines the aesthetic and functional qualities that make text type highly readable with the versatility of digital technology.